The Princess and The Stag

the lost princess series, book 2

jp roth

ISBN: 978-1-953735-94-2

Published by Satin Romance
An Imprint of Melange Books, LLC
White Bear Lake, MN 55110
www.satinromance.com

Published in the United States of America.

Cover Design by Ashley Redbird Designs

This book is dedicated to my sister Clare, who has never stopped believing in me, and tirelessly listened to all the stories in my mind, years before I decided to write some of them down. She has always been my sister, but I would like to believe that at least in one of our lives we were goddesses, maybe even pirate queens. To you I say:

May our men be brave, may our drink be strong, and may our souls' beauty glow brighter than the stars.

I might have more dedications as of course I want to thank everyone who worked on the book.

The Madness of a King
November 1, 1800

The room was dark and stuffy as a tomb. Thick velvet drapes pulled tight over the bolted windows. The little sunlight that managed to filter through the curtains cast mottled purple shadows over the gilded, golden walls. Peach and pomegranate paneling interlaced the glittering red threads that papered them. Creamy cherubs, fat and rouged to perfection, frolicked on the arched ceilings, pointing their arrows down at the King. Their reflections twinkled in the diamonds stringing a grand chandelier and swinging in a cloud of noxious vapors.

King George III, sprawled on his wide bed, surrounded by a grouping of Canaletto paintings, and flanked by a tall chest of silver polished drawers that previously graced the boudoir of Louis XVI. The high canopy of green and scarlet velvet overshadowing the bed fought off any weak, encroaching light, causing deeper shadows to fall on the vibrant blue Savonnerie rug. Aged, rancid incense bellowed white tufts of smoke and the smell of laudanum saturated everything.

William Pitt, a Tory statesman and eager politician was a tall, wiry man, sporting a limp in his gait and a small hunch on the left side of his back. His arms hung clear past their intended mark and the obvious bow in his knees offered him the overall look of a misshapen coat rack. He shuffled his feet near the head of the luxurious bed, his thin fingers rifling through a stack of papers balanced haphazardly in his arms. Abruptly, his blanched pupils flexed, and a choked cough escaped him. Flailing like tumbleweeds his slender hands made jerky, grabbing motions for the stack of papers intent on leaping from his tenuous grip.

The king woke from his shifty slumber with a start. He sat up, grunting, and snorting into his hands. "Christ, who...oh! You're tall Pitt, did you know that?"

Pitt gave an exaggerated bow, then bent down to pick up his fallen notes. "Yes, Your Majesty."

"Pah! What, what. You're tall and your breath reeks like rotting frogs."

"Forgive me, Your Majesty," Pitt said, sounding more exhausted than abashed.

King George leveled a cold stare at the top of Pitt's bobbing head. "So? What the devil are you doing in here, flapping your scarecrow limbs and breathing your frog breath?"

"I have news, Your Majesty," came Pitt's staunch reply.

King George perked up at this and tried to focus his watery eyes. Moisture dripped onto his veiny cheeks making little puddles in the divots of fat cluttering his rotund, double chin. "Eh? What news? Is it the French? Are they here?" King George made to leap from the bed, but his swollen feet got tangled in the plush, cream-silk covers, and his desperate efforts were quickly confounded. The king conceded with a belch and threw himself back against the pillows.

"They are coming, what, what? You know what they want... what they have always wanted. Godless demons, skin walkers, murders! Peace with France is not real, just a fantasy. One of the crying shadows in our brain. Napoleon will bring his ships with his rightful heir at the helm. It is true...we will not sign. NO TREATY! NEVER!"

"They are not here, per say," Pitt said, straightening the final papers and standing up with obvious difficulty. A hand flew to his lower back and he winced. "Unfortunately, it appears the rumors are in fact true, the heirs still live—the girl for certain, I have been informed that she has been taken into custody and is even now being held in the Tower. Prior to her alleged arrest there were dozens of sightings, most accompanied by strange and incredible stories. I will go to see for myself if it is in fact her, as I had the pleasure to meet her mother on two occasions, and they say her daughter is a spitting image. I feel events begin to spiral out of control." Pitt murmured that last part beneath his breath and the King leaned in to hear it.

"What's that you say? Here, here? This is your fault you sniveling coward! You and your damned treaty!" King George started to pant; his cheeks heated, going purple as a ripe grape. "We are here in daily expectation that Bonaparte will attempt his threatened invasion. Should his troops effect a landing, we shall certainly put ourselves at the head of ours, and our other armed subjects, to repel them. In fact, we shall do it now." King George ran a trembling hand through his clipped gray hair making the sparse strands stand up like pins in a cushion. "What's wrong with the princess we have, eh? Calm, stupid girl that she is."

"She is an imposter, sir."

"Don't speak to us as if we were a child, damn you! Who among us isn't? Surely not you, sir? Pah! You with your insane ramblings and useless ideas of peace, what, what? It's of no importance, Lord Clare will not fail us. Henry swore he would take her life. A true, gifted killer that one, a man of rare worth, certainly better than you, Pitt, what, what?" The king closed his eyes, his loose jowls flapped back against the pillows and his stomach rumbled like a slumbering monster. He was sleeping in seconds.

Pitt threw his monarch a disgusted look and straightened his limp cravat. He left the royal chambers without a backward look and closed the door firmly behind him. Two guards regaled in scarlet tunics with blue collars that carried the blazed insignia of a cross, stood immovable as stone statues on either side of the king's garish, golden door, their eyes fixed on a distant mark. They held a polished set of bayonets in front of them and Pitt wondered, like he always did—how their arms did not just fall off with exhaustion.

Without proper warning, a stinging pain took Pitt in the chest, and he gasped as his heart stopped for one complete second. Pitt grabbed at a silk panel near the right guard's head. His palm hit the wall and made a sharp smacking sound, the guard did not flinch. Pitt had no time to wonder at the Olympian feat, acid filled his gut, and his kneecaps speedily deteriorated into mush.

It was just fear, he told himself, not a heart attack, just terror. The road he took to reach his status in life had been too long, the struggle too real, he could not, would not risk it for the life of some nameless princess, who, by all rights should have done the world a favor and died years ago. His insane monarch was correct in one thing, the girl must die or everything he had worked for, these long painful years, would be for naught.

"That," Pitt assured the stoic guard with a gasping snarl, regaining his balance and straightening his cravat— "is simply unacceptable."

1

CAUGHT RED-HANDED

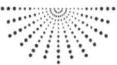

On this day we burry you in the ground, on this day we live with sight and no sound.

November 3, 1800

*D*ove grey morning light touched the empty fields in silver. Six men loitered in two groups of three, friends facing each other like enemies. Henry stood, the rising sun at his back and took in the sad sight of his sorry group of friends.

"This is your fault, Charles," Henry said. "I should be knocking you senseless for what you did to Nora, not standing as your second while you disgrace yourself in yet another duel."

Charles tossed his blonde locks from his blue eyes. "As I told Lord Dustin, it was his honorable lady wife who set her cap for me," said Charles, throwing up his gloved hands, "a piece of real truth, I vow. I don't deserve this, but us Newcastle men never run from a fight. A pastime we have kept till death."

"This is not a laughing matter," Henry barked. "Lord Dustin is one of the finest shots in the country. You were friends at Eton. I have vivid memories of you drinking, wenching, and dicing together, so do you really want him to be the one who kills you?"

Charles sniffed at the air, prissily he brushed imaginary dirt off his perfectly tailored cuff. "All this fuss over women and their virtue has my blood up. A good fight right now, is what I need."

"Because of Nora?" Henry asked.

"Because of all of them," Charles responded flippantly.

"Nora isn't like 'all of them'. She's a sister to us."

Charles dragged his sword from its sheath, inspected the blade, then threw his brother a meaningful look. "A sister to you, maybe. Always something else to me."

"Don't you care about the fate of your own child?" Henry roared, causing a few of the surrounding men to glance in their direction.

"Did you know her father is the king?" asked Charles, deftly ignoring his brother's outburst. "Old Georgie and his bastards." He sighed, shaking his golden head.

"Everyone knows that, Charles. Christ, you're almost too dense to be infuriating."

"Better an imbecile, than a traitor," chortled Charles. "For once, you are the wretched brother and I the supreme, even standing here on this field at dawn, to do what I mean to do." Charles tapped the tip of his rapier against the heel of his boot. Mud sprinkled to the earth. "Defying the order of the King," Charles said and sucked in a sharp breath through his teeth. "Never thought you had it in you man."

"I am not a traitor," Henry said. "I was under her spell. The French princess is powerful and beautiful. Cardinal Exeter tells me her mother slept with the devil, and she is the product of their union. He says King Louis was impotent."

"Don't tell me you believe that dribble."

"I don't know what I believe," Henry confessed. "I have spent the last three days, in prayer and fasting, still I feel her dark hands touching my soul." Unconsciously he ran his fingers through his hair, tussling it mercilessly. "She's the only thought in my mind. And every image of her is wrapped in my own guilt."

"Ah, the one emotion I was not blessed with," Charles said as he tapped his sword again and his voice turned serious. "You did nothing wrong. You were right to capture her. You are a loyal subject of King Georgie, a lord, and a captain in his army. You have no business running with pirates and gypsies."

Velvet was neither, but Henry chose not to correct his brother. Rather, he stared into the first light of the rising sun shielding his eyes with his right hand. "What if it's all a lie?" he said, his voice so low, Henry wondered if Charles heard his words. "What if she really is innocent of it all, falsely accused, fighting for her life. What if there is no Devil, no witches or magic, what if it is all an allusion of our times. They say our mother was a witch, but she was the best person I have ever met. Desperation and survival do not make the best decisions. What if Velvet just did what she thought she had to do, to keep herself and her brother alive? I swore to keep her safe, and I betrayed her."

"You obeyed your king," said Charles, placing his gloved hand on his brother's shoulder. "There is no shame in what you did. The shame would lie in betraying your king for a pretty face, regardless of what magic she cast, real or imagined." Charles gave Henry's shoulder a squeeze. "For what it's worth, I'm proud of you."

"Under the harsh light of your current actions, it's not worth much," Henry snapped.

Charles shrugged, stung. Pointedly he removed his hand.

"I'm sorry, Charles, I'm being a complete fool. Who am I to cast judgement? I've been chasing dreams and visions for a fortnight."

"To your positions, gentlemen," called Sir James, Viscount of Charrington. "This duel for lady Dustin's honor will conclude at first blood. Satisfaction will be had, my lords, but not at the risk of incarceration. Lord Newcastle, as the one who accepted the challenge, the choice of weapons is yours."

"Rapier," Charles called, skillfully brandishing his blade, the steel drank the weak morning light and glowed.

"Lord Dustin, do you accept this choice of weapons?" demanded Sir James, his voice pitched to carry across the whispering field, and early morning sounds.

"I do," said Dustin, and drew his thin blade.

"You wear your heart on your face, brother. It betrays you." Charles yawned and raised his sword arm in a lengthy stretch above his head, loudly cracking his neck, pulling the silk of his tailored coat tight across his broad shoulders. The sun had recently brightened his hair, and Henry thought it gave his brother the look of a fading specter. It whitened his skin, enhancing the paleness of his lips, and lashes. Under the dawn light, Charles was the spitting image of their father. At times, Henry wondered if that similarity in them tainted the brotherly love he was meant to feel.

"There is nothing on my face except old bruises and fresh exhaustion," Henry said.

"Both courtesy of our dead princess."

"Not dead yet," Henry said. Though he should not have, the words gave him hope. Hope of what? A happily ever after, running for his life with the woman of his dreams?

Sir James blew on a small, rectangular device that whistled like birdsong.

"You can still back out of this, Charles," Henry said, as his brother moved to take position.

Charles looked at Henry, his jaw fixed, his eyes flashing excitement. "If you can say such a thing brother, then you truly don't know me a' tall."

Henry threw a meaningful look at the men gathered round. "I know you, Charles, *this* is you!"

"Lord Newcastle."

Henry spun to the sound of his name. Paul Beauchamp stood to the right of Charles, hands folded behind his back. Kohl lined his large, blue eyes, and pink rouge blushed cheeks that were white and soft as a woman. Beneath a dark cap stuck with a painted pigeon feather, he wore a fashionably powdered wig, curled to perfection. A large mole decorated the left side of his upper lip, the painted dot added an exotic flare to an otherwise fashionably standard garb.

"Bonjour, Monsieur," Paul said, affecting a slight bow. "If your brother backs out before satisfaction is had, it is I who will test your metal."

"Good morning to you, sir. I hope it does not come to that," Henry said sincerely. Paul may be beautiful, and feminine enough to confound his sex, but Henry knew he was arguably one of the best swordsmen in Paris and had no desire to test the validity of gossips, on this day of all days. "I've heard great stories about you."

"Ha! Mon Die, but people like to talk, eh? I've heard some stories too, my lord. About you and the lost princess? They say you found Marie Therese, then delivered her to die?"

Wads of lace tumbling from the tailored cuff of Paul's riding jacket, fell over his thin fingers. Paul flipped the material back with a flourish. The motion was confusing as the rest of him. Despite its softness there was a deep warning in the speed of the movement, and the fineness in which he drew his blade. "Marie Therese of France, princess of Normandy is my niece," Paul said.

Henry felt the words lie heavy in his gut. "She is a traitor, a killer and a prisoner of the British crown."

"She is a frightened child, and you, monsieur, are a dead man. How could you?" Paul spat. "If she is anything like her mother, how could you? You are a lord serving a mad king and she is a princess of France! I heard you were just. I was grateful when they told me she had fallen under your protection. I was riding to rescue her when they told me you had delivered her to die."

"She is a witch," Henry said, even to himself the tone of his words was made of lies.

"You imbécile!" said Paul, "all women are witches, do you know nothing?"

"She bewitched me!" Henry insisted. "She took my sanity, my will."

"Mais oui? That is the power of woman, no? Are you angry because you wanted her? Is she as beautiful as they say?"

Yes. He had been incredibly angry. Because he wanted her always, and she made him act on it. She made him lose control, turned him into a senseless statue. Not senseless, his mind corrected. One sense had been very present and was enslaved.

Charles yawned long and loudly. "Leave it to you, brother, to upstage my duel. May my Lord Dustin and I get on with it? Or would you prefer to bandy about, throwing insults and playing with swords until the constable arrives?"

"Watch your back, my lord," Paul said, strolling away to take his place at lord Dustin's right-hand side. His last words were thrown over his shoulder like a curse. "You may find my knife in it."

Henry took his place beside Charles who clapped him on the back and gave him a friendly nudge in the ribs. "Turning out to be quite the exciting day, eh old chap?"

"I fear it won't improve for you. We will speak about Nora when this stupidity is concluded," Henry said.

Charles spat on the ground and wiped his mouth on the back of his hand. "What do you want me to do? Raise a bastard?"

"Marry her, give the child your protection and your name."

"You're out of your mind," said Charles. Henry reached out to touch his brother's shoulder. Peevishly, Charles slapped his hand away. "Nora and I are fine. You're the one walking like a dead man. See to your own guilt brother, kindly leave me to mine."

Rain poured in sheets from the fog-soaked sky, large, cold drops that splashed on the bowed heads of those gathered around the freshly dug hole in the muddy ground. A murder of crows screamed from the surrounding tree branches and flew in dizzying circles over the likely clad mourners.

"Today we say goodbye to Katie Miller, a child of Christ, a sister and a friend."

Nora stared at the casket being lowered into the ground in horror. The Parson, hands folded over a withered bible continued speaking in a low monotone voice. Nora ignored him. There was nothing particularly wrong with what he was saying, point of fact: it was quite beautiful; however, he did not know Katie, his words were only perfunctory, something real should be said, she knew it. But she felt too miserable to speak right now. It would not do; she knew that too. She was made of sterner stuff. Close your eyes and feel inside. Henry's mother spoke those words to

Nora a long time ago, but she held onto them now. *Close your eyes and feel inside. She told herself. Don't let them see you break. Don't let them know. You are a lady and a princess. You are made of stone. Your eyes, your ears, your heart—all stone. Stone doesn't cry.* The more she tried to compose herself, the more breathless and tearful she felt.

The ropes holding Katie's casket creaked loudly, Nora heard Katie's small body shift slightly inside her polished oak box. Nora wished there had been time to find a smaller casket and a better priest, but after what Henry had done, they were all in constant danger of arrest. So, Nora had found the most beautiful casket money could buy, on short notice, knowing it would dwarf Katie, and hoping that would be alright. It was, except for the thumping.

Rest in peace, Katie, Nora thought. *Would that I could have saved you, my dearest friend. Rest in peace, love.* Such thoughts did not help her resolution to be made of stone, Nora reflected, and decided to save her own mental eulogies until she was alone, then she would let go, alone she could cry out all the broken pieces of her heart. The casket thumped when it met earth, Katie's body rattled, the ropes sighed and released their hold as the coffin slid in place. It was done. Katie was really gone.

Nora took a step back, she wanted to move to the edge of the crowd unseen and slip away before the hymn singing began. Devon squeezed her hand. His was so warm and comforting, she felt her resolve to be a stone slip a little more, quietly she lay her head on his shoulder, sighing when he tucked a wandering curl behind her ear.

"It was a beautiful service," Nora said. "Simple and Catholic. Katie would have loved it."

Devon nodded, gazing at the men detaching the ropes from the coffin, now dusting their hands, and picking up their shovels. "Katie was always there," he said. "My first memory of you, at your come-out ball, Katie was at your side. I never once saw you without her."

"I know," Nora whispered. "To be honest, it still doesn't feel like she is gone. Do you think a dead friend can be like a phantom limb? In that you still feel it, long after it's been cut off?"

Devon made a low sound of agreement in his chest. "I think so. Our memories keep them alive."

"She wasn't supposed to die." Nora blinked her eyelids so that her tears might not fall. It worked, she swallowed them back. Somewhere above them a crow screamed, slowly it circled the giant elm bracing their sad, black garbed party.

Devon stepped back, Nora saw that beneath the many raindrops his face was pale, his bloodshot eyes rimmed in red. "I truly despise death," he muttered. "Today only firms my resolution to fight it until the end."

Nora almost smiled. The crow screamed again. It landed on a leafy branch overhanging the grave. Disturbed leaves fluttered to the ground and Nora followed their dizzy path until her eyes came to rest on a dark shadow standing just beyond the elm. Nora instantly recognized the face—it was not difficult—she had known the face since her sixth birthday. Nora coughed out a shredded gasp as her senses promptly deserted her. Uttering a broken growl, she shook off Devon's hand fervently enough to make him stumble. A few people blocked her path, people who had loved Katie, even one of her brothers—Nora did not see them. She saw only Henry, bathed in a red glow, a glow which she felt herself exuding in hot, rage filled waves from her eyes.

Henry saw her charging at him. His hands went up in surrender. Nora picked up her skirt and ran. Yelling something at him that sounded like traitor, or liar? She did not know, maybe a jumbled combination of both.

"Nora," Henry shouted, alarmed.

Nora's fist flashed out; Henry ducked his head seconds before her knuckles clipped his cheek. "Nora, for god's sake!" he roared. Nora let the other fist fly. It struck his chest with a solid thump. Her thumb nail clipped the golden buckle on the collar of his redcoat, but she hardly felt the small pain.

"You…! Lying…! Betrayer!" Nora could not find her words, so instead she kicked his shin with all her strength. Henry yelped, hopping backward.

"You didn't think to dive in after me? To wonder where I was. *Noooo*! You stood there and lost your mind. After, I managed to survive—no thanks to you, I return to find you arrested the girl I almost died for. More than once!" Nora swung again, both fists lashing out blindly. Henry caught her hands; his own grip was incredibly strong. The bastard!

Using his hold on her wrists, Henry spun her around, pulling her against him, firmly locking both her hands on either side of her waist. His heart thumped against the base of her neck, as he gulped in a deep breath, she felt his chin come to rest on the top of her head.

"Goddamn it, Nora," he growled. "Will you let me explain."

"Explain!" she screamed. "You lied to her, Henry, you lied to me. If they kill her, I will never forgive you." Nora struggled wildly for a useless moment, then went limp, Henry made a tisking sound and relaxed his hold. Nora threw her foot back and kicked him again. He stumbled, nearly falling. Nora broke free and spun away, then rounded on him. "You swore!" She railed and lifted her fists to pound on him again. Devon caught her around the waist and swung her away from temptation.

"Nora," Devon said, obviously striving for soothing tones. "Not now. Let it go. Let's get out of here."

"Are you...are you laughing?" Nora asked him, completely aghast.

"No," Devon said, cleanly wiping the smile off his face. "It's just..." His shoulders shook. "I've never seen you in hysterics. It's not something I'll forget."

"I am not hysterical! I am furious. There is a vast, marked difference."

"Devon," said Henry, winded and gasping. "Get her away from this place. Make sure she's safe."

Devon nodded, but said nothing. Nora saw his eyes, and noted the look he cast at Henry, angry and confused as her own, as though trying, yet failing to fully understand his friend's motives. Nora turned to face Devon and froze. Everything forgotten, mortality challenged.

Louis stood in a shaft of sunlight, pawing the ground, and watching her. She felt a second of shame at what he had most likely seen; ladies who were made of stone did not attack gentlemen moments after a funeral. She almost dropped her eyes, but he caught her gaze and held it.

"It's okay," said Louis, in that intoxicating mind voice. Last night it had seemed unreal, today, in broad daylight she felt paralyzed by the wonder of it.

"Let's get out of here," Devon said, his voice seeming to come to her from far away. "I'll take you to court…it's going to be…"

When Devon saw he had none of her attention, his words trailed off. Nora tapped his hand still locked around her waist; he released her muttering an apology. She took a step toward Louis, battling the silly urge to pinch herself. She had never seen him in daylight before, something about the way the sun merged in his golden glow made it all so beautifully, impossibly true. It assured her that the night he saved her, had not been a fevered dream.

"Good day, my lady," said Louis and his words roved through her mind. She lifted her hands, touching her temples, meaning to keep them there.

"Why did you stop me?" she said aloud, not giving two hoots who saw her chatting up the thin air. "He," she pointed an outraged finger in Henry's general direction, possibly implicating Devon in the process. "He is responsible for your sister's current predicament. He…" Her finger shook. "He…my once 'brother,' he…"

"Allow me to speak from experience," Louis told her, waiting politely for her to regain a modicum of composure. "Men don't usually like being enslaved to a spell, no matter how well meaning."

Devon came to stand beside her and cleared his throat. "Should I be concerned that this is the second time you have spoken to thin air in a matter of days?"

"Do hush!" Nora pleaded. "I've already explained it to you once. Don't ask me to do it again right now, I can barely form a complete thought."

"I'll just wait over here," said Devon, clearing his throat and pointing to a patch of sun falling on the close cobblestones lining lower Sunbury road.

Nora turned toward where he was pointing just in time to see

Henry walk away. "The pox take him," she muttered, and Louis's peal of rich laughter echoed in her mind.

"You have a beautiful laugh," Nora said.

"Thank you. That's truly kind." Devon bowed.

Nora ignored him.

2

A HEAD FOR A BED

November 5, 1800

ecapitation. They were going to cut off her head. Velvet thought of her sentence as sad poetry, much like her life. She knew she was feeling sorry for herself—an emotion Queenie had cautioned her never to feel—but Velvet decided it could not be helped. The hag, with stringy grey hair and warts on her hands and nose who had shown her to her cell, gave her a red dress to wear. Said the color would keep her appraised of the hellfire that awaited her. The cloth was old and badly over starched, but it was clean, and that was enough.

Idly, Velvet straightened the wrinkles in her skirt and sat down on her lumpy bed. On the mad dash away from Nora's smoldering town home, the dark specter of the London Tower had scared her. Now, sitting in her tiny cell, she knew why. The building itself was so large it appeared to scrape the sky, yet the cells were small enough to suffocate, making a person feel lost and trapped at the same time.

She should not be shocked by what was most certainly an imminent sentence, Velvet told herself. Losing one's head appeared to be a hereditary problem of her bloodline.

"I won't be afraid," Velvet said aloud, running her hands up and down her arms to stop the incessant chills. Her statement was a bold lie, and she knew it. "I will not show them my fear," she corrected. "I will not let them see it." She spoke to the small room like it could offer some council or comfort when she knew it could do neither.

It was her fault she was in this cell, her doing alone. Sure, she had not meant to bewitch Henry, had not planned on ending the night in his arms, but the fault for the carnage her dance wrought was on her head, Katie's blood on her hands. Velvet felt a stab of fresh pain and rubbed at a spot just above her heart. She had not taken a moment to imagine the possibility of failure, because she had so deeply wanted to succeed. She truly feared some large part of her actually wanted to use her magic on the men who had hurt her, who meant to kill her. That terrible part of her had needed to see them fall under her spell, to hear the thump of their knees as they hit the deck of the Bacchus in servitude.

Velvet heard a small sound issue out of her throat, her nails dug in the soft flesh of her palms until it hurt. That is what she had wanted then. It was not what she wanted now. Now she wanted to hear Katie's soft voice telling Nora she was her lady, she wanted to see Nora's brilliant smile, a smile Velvet feared her friend would never wear again. She wanted to see Louis and sleep, really sleep, without the torment of dreams. Sleep refused to come. Every time she closed her eyes, she saw Katie's vacant expression and her cheek resting in that ever-expanding pool of blood. How was there so much blood? Why did it not stop flowing? How long did it take her to really die? Velvet put her hands over her eyes. On top of everything, for some unfathomable reason, she missed her mother.

Velvet threw her body down on the small cot where it bounced unevenly and something sharp jabbed in her ribs. She left it there, too numb to really care. Last night she dreamed of a large castle that had wide stone windows draped in pink silk. Rose petals floated in a tub that sat in the corner of gold tiled bathroom on embellished claws. Blood red petals swirled crazily down a marble drain. There were long halls with chandeliers that sparkled like raindrops in sunlight. Beautiful passageways, their polished golden floors enhancing the echo of a woman's heartbreaking screams.

Velvet's eyes watered, but no tears came. She had been crying for three days, ever since the redcoat soldiers threw her in this dark, timeless room. She wondered if a human had only so many tears, perhaps one could judge the depths of a tragedy by how fast they ran out.

Velvet did not remember how she got here, her feet moved to the soldier's commands, but her mind was stuck on the Bacchus, watching Nora's red hair shine against the night sky, flashing brilliantly for mere seconds before the Thames swallowed it in darkness. How had it come to this? How had she been so stupid and blind?

Footsteps sounded in the hall, shattering her miserable thoughts, Velvet sat up. She did not bother to straighten her hair or dress, let them see her as she was. Let them see the real her, not just her famous face. She had less than a second to lift her chin before the splintered wooden door—firmly preventing her freedom—shook and swung open. A tall man with long arms and a hollow face stepped in her stuffy cell. The light spilling from the small arrow slits in the tower wall at his back cast his eyes and hands in silhouette.

"The princess Marie of France," he said. His voice reverent and strangely deep. "My name is William Pitt." His right hand flipped through the air before he dropped in a low bow. Something about the way he addressed her sparked a hidden memory of another place and a brighter time. Where thousands bowed to her, threw flowers at her feet, and called her princess.

"You are every bit your mother," the thin man continued. "That arrogant tilt to the head, that look in the eyes, somehow fueled by equal parts of wisdom and innocence." He reached out a finger toward her face, then retracted his hand before he touched her cheek. "You're probably wondering how you came to be locked in here?"

"No," Velvet said. "Seems fitting, I hurt everyone I come in contact with." She gave the room a sweeping glance. "This is as good a place for me as any. I'm a princess in a tower. It's where I belong."

"Hum, quite right, dear," said Pitt. "Good to see you understand the full situation. It's not your fault really." Pitt pulled a small silver box from the front pocket of his great coat. "You, princess, were born in a tempestuous time. I honestly believe your mother had a kind heart, a soul who gave the devil no place. She was, as so many of the great ones are, a victim of cruel gossip. The writers of those rags painted her as a monster, and the common folk ate it up, they believe the gossip columns like scripture."

Velvet watched Pitt used the pad of his right thumb to flick open the lid of the box. He took a pinch of the white powder resting inside the box and slowly placed it on the back of his left hand. It made a little white mountain in the dip between his forefinger and thumb. For a dull second, he eyed the powder with a cringe of disgust. He seemed to steel himself like one preparing to single handedly take on a battalion charge, while his nostrils expanded to their capacity. Then, he tilted his head and snorted the mountain of white powder up his nose, first the right nostril then the left. His body shook for a violent second while he snapped the silver lid of the box shut. It clicked loudly in the silence. Slowly, he lifted a finger to touch his offended nostrils, before pocketing the box.

"What was I saying? Oh yes!" Pitt cleared his throat, shuddering excessively and pulling another face. "Of course, your mother, a real queen and a true unfortunate." His hand twitched toward the pocket holding the silver box.

"Did you come here to talk about my mother?" Velvet asked, wanting to ask him a million questions, wanting to be left alone.

"No. I did not," he said and took the box out of his pocket again. "I came here to decide if you should live or die."

"I see," Velvet said. Though she truly did not. "And this, my life—it's up to you?"

"Yes. In a way it is. Coming in here, I thought I knew my mind on the subject," Pitt lifted his gaze to hers. "It appears I did not." His dark eyes roved over her, taking it all in. "The face you wear, it fogs my resolution."

"Well." Velvet listened to her own exhausted sigh. "Then at least it's good for something. This cursed face of mine."

Pitt's gaze weaseled its way through her senses to cast a spotlight on her soul. Under the piercing look, Velvet visibly bristled. She wanted her stones, needed in that moment to feel their warmth in her hands, and hated herself for that need. The stones were evil, or she was—either way they did not belong in her hands. She knew that now.

"Queenie told me a story once, of a girl so beautiful it started a war that launched a thousand ships," Velvet said, absently picking at a loose string on her dress.

Pitt moved closer; Velvet retreated until the edge of the cot crashed into the backs of her calves. "Are you thinking of doing the same?" he asked.

"Could I do the same? I thought the plan was to take my head?" Velvet replied. Pitt took another step, their shadows touched and merged. "Would I even want to? When Queenie told me the story of the beautiful girl they called Helen of Troy, all I could think about was how terribly lonely her life must have been. Lonely, heartbroken, scared and eventually dead. So much for her armies, and her historic war, so much for her pretty face. No, I don't want the throne of France or England, or any other chair."

Pitt touched a lock of her golden hair, Velvet shied away. "You wouldn't lie to me, would you?" he asked. "Here on the eve of your death?"

"I might," Velvet told him honestly, "if I thought it would help, but I'm not lying. I don't remember having a throne, so why would I want to reclaim it? Why would I want to rule over a people who want me dead? No. I'm not lying. I've never wanted the throne. It belongs to Louis the seventeenth, my brother, it always has, and he is dead," she added. This was a lie, a good one though, she told herself. An exceptionally good one.

"Informative," said Pitt. Touching his nose and dabbing gently at his watering eyes. "Your accommodations are quite—" he cast his eyes around the cell searching for a word, "misty," he finally said. "You're like a flower here, wilting in the dark." He reached for her again. The light spilling in from the open door fell on his hand, making the skin look sallow, the prominent bones skeletal and terrifying. His hand reached for her face; Velvet felt herself dodge reflexively. Pitt saw the tiny movement and froze, then his hand went for the silver box again.

"I have a home, here in London," he told her, "I could postpone your trial, a fortnight, perhaps a month? I would offer you sanctuary, clothe you in something finer than those rags you wear. You would sleep on silk sheets, and…" his finger ran down the length of her arm, "oils for your face and hair, do you remember what that felt like? To be wrapped in luxury, your every need attended?" His voice dropped; his next words were nearly inaudible. "Do you recall the touch of silk sliding against your skin?"

Velvet grabbed his wandering hand. Though Pitt jumped at her touch, he did not pull away.

"No. I don't!" Velvet said, her words screeched behind her clenched teeth. She let go of his hand like it was something venomous. "I thank you for your kind offer, sir, but I fear I must decline. I've grown fond of my tower room."

A cold light sparked in Pitt's dark eyes. Dangerous and feral. "It would not be wise to refuse my kindness," he told her, taking a step back and another pinch of powder up his nose. He sniffed loudly. "You may not have many other offers forthcoming."

Suddenly, Katie's blood dripped down Velvet's vision and she wiped her eyes, half afraid she would feel the warm, sticky liquid on her hands. "No, I don't suspect I will," she said finally.

"I won't make this offer again," promised Pitt.

"I pray not," Velvet said sincerely.

Pitt threw her a tempestuous look over another snort of powder. Velvet watched his pupils expand, nearly overtake the whites of his eyes. "I am your life and death," he told her, stepping back, and straightening a wrinkle in his cream-colored cravat. "If you refuse me, I fear there is nothing more I can do for you, save bid you farewell for now."

"For now?" Velvet echoed, wholeheartedly fearing his answer.

"The trial my dear," he said in patronizing tones. "I was unable to attend your mother's, I wouldn't miss yours for the world. God knows I want a second look at that pretty head before the executioner cuts it off."

He left her small cell, slamming the door and taking the last word with him.

3

PIRATE QUEEN

*N*ora lay on her side, knees drawn up to her chest, and folded hands resting under her teary cheek. She could feel her eyes swimming in their sockets, so many tears, and none of them had the bravery to escape the barrier of her lashes. She was still and silent as the stone she had tried and failed to be on the day they buried Katie. It was an hour past since evening fell, and for all of it Devon prowled the captain's cabin, holding a crystal decanter of scarlet wine in his hand, and wearing the stain of it on his lips.

Broken crystal decorated the Persian rug rolled out across the spherical room. A colorful assortment of foods and fruits sweated on the round dining table situated near the door, forgotten, and collecting flies. The glass filling the oval port window carried the steam of their breaths mixed in sticky London fog. Iron chests, spilling gold were stacked near the foot of the bed, nearly buried under endless rolls of Chinese silk and Indian satin. Sweet scents of myrrh twined in the oil of chrysanthemum drenched the stale air, nauseating Nora in the extreme. She had vomited all morning and the taste of it was a sour pall in her mouth, vomited until there was nothing left to purge, vomited until she feared the baby in her womb intended her death.

Devon kicked a fallen chair, lying tiredly in his path. It skittered across the room to shatter against the wall. The ear-splitting crash of it breaking in pieces was made louder by the silence. Devon walked to the broken chair and kicked it again, for what she assumed was good measure.

Nora squeezed her eyes shut and took a trembling breath. "Just go, Devon. Get out of here." Nora's voice, scratchy from lack of use sounded deflated as her heart felt. "Go to court, find out what in blazes is going on, so at least one of us will have some surcease from all this nervous wondering."

Devon stopped pacing and his hand jolted, sloshing a bit of wine on the floor. "Leave you here? With all these men, alone? Unprotected? If that's a jest— it's not funny," he said distinctly. "Henry would kill me out of hand."

"I'm going to kill him, by my hand!" Nora promised peevishly. Sluggish and exhausted by grief, she sat up, rolled haphazardly off the bed, and staggered to the washstand situated near the large port window. She filled the bowl from the jug of water resting beside it and splashed her face. It felt good, so she did it again, then rinsed her mouth and ran her wet hands through her wild, unbound hair.

"Henry hates being out of control. He didn't help his mother, couldn't run fast enough when his father turned the evil eye on him," she said.

"Tell me a thing I don't know," muttered Devon.

Nora nodded. "I suspect being under Velvet's spell brought up old pain and a number of unresolved issues. Which, gah! I guess it is understandable, for he really was the sweetest, saddest little boy in the world. Breaks my heart to think about someone hurting that little darling, dirt on his face and a stolen sweet from the kitchen, in his hand. But It wasn't Velvet's fault!" Nora shook the water from her hands. "It was a good plan. It really was. I'd seen the stones work before. I knew—a least a little—what they were capable of. I could have stopped her. I chose not to. Katie said they were dangerous, she warned me. I didn't care. I wanted to see the magic." Nora bit her lower lip until it hurt. "It seems so insane now, all of it! Ropes changing into snakes, dancing men, mindless love." Nora sighed, she looked out the dusky window and stared deep in the eyes of her own reflection. "I know it's cliché to say, but it's the stuff of dreams and fairytales. None of this really seems real! Every time I close my eyes, some part of me thinks I will wake up in my own bed with Katie's chatter in my ears and a steaming cup of tea in my hands. Then, of course, I realize it's not a dream, it's very real and I'm living it."

"I want to argue with you," Devon said, knocking back another gulp of wine. "I want to tell you how crazy you sound."

"But you won't," Nora stated. "Because, like me, you saw it with your own eyes." Nora shuddered. "Hell fire! I even felt a little of it, the same way I felt it during the impromptu dance party at the Blind Pig." The water on her face started to dry in sticky patterns, so she bent down and splashed it again, then shook her hands dry. "The way Henry looked at her, he was there, but not there." Nora shook her head, she walked back to the bed and sat down, sighing. "It's all real. Spells, witchcraft, enchantments…that beautiful, glimmering ruby." She met Devon's bloodshot eyes. "It stole his soul."

"Maybe Henry was right to have her arrested then," Devon said, looking sickened by the taste of his words. "Witchcraft is a death sentence, perhaps it is evil as they say."

"Hum," Nora tapped the nail of her forefinger on her bottom lip, "an axe can build a house, or take a life."

Devon resumed pacing. "What's your point?"

"Only that magic, like anything else, is simply a tool. It's the user who defines its actions. The user who is good or evil. Velvet is good, she has a pure heart."

"Stubborn to the core," Devon muttered.

"Yes. She is. But so am I. I don't understand all her choices, she just did what she thought she had to do, and that's something. If Henry, or you, even Charles was hurt or in trouble, I would move heaven and earth. I want to say I would care who got hurt in the process, but…it's terrible to even think…"

"You would do whatever it took," Devon finished.

"I would do whatever it took," Nora confirmed.

Devon altered his swerving course, he sat down beside Nora. She took the crystal decanter from his hand, steeled herself, then gulped a hearty swallow. Warm fire rushed down her throat, it settled snugly in her empty stomach. It was good, Nora reflected, sweet, with hints of cinnamon brushed with blackberry. Expensive, tasteful, like many elements in this opulent cabin. Life was a crazy thing, one moment she was sitting in her drawing room trying to choose which party would be the lesser of the evils, the next—due to Velvet's brother, and a rather daring dive—she was queen of Pirate ship. This afforded her a certain satisfaction, for so long she had been beholden to the crown for her wellbeing, now, she had more riches than she knew what to do with, she had a ship and a crew.

The idea of the open seas stretched in her mind like a metaphor for all the new possibilities in her story. Katie's death, however, did darken the horizon, she felt it in her gut, a ball of agony hovering over the little ball of life struggling in her stomach— and that was something too. "I don't blame Velvet for what happened, she loves her brother." A golden vision of Louis flashed in Nora's mind, she shuddered deeply over another gulp of wine. "I don't blame her, Katie wouldn't either."

"Prince Louis?" Devon asked, meeting Nora's teary gaze with unaccustomed seriousness, "I know what you've said, and I still have to ask one more time. Is he really an invisible golden stag?" Devon made a rough motion with both hands over his head. "Antlers and everything? I know you, if you say yes, I swear I'll believe you—god knows how."

"Yes. He is, and he does. I told you, he skewered Captain Chance with them."

"Of course," Devon groaned. "Forgive me for forgetting that tiny detail hidden in the most ridiculous story I've ever heard."

"I've heard worse. Read worse," Nora said. "I just didn't believe it. I mean, I wanted to, but it just isn't done, believing in fairies, mermaids, and the like, very unfashionable, you know? My father would have locked me in Bedlam for even whispering about the things I've seen."

"Go to the king, Nora. Don't tell him about the antlers for god's sake but go to him. He loves you. He'll help."

"Maybe." Nora took another sip of wine, then another. "Maybe he loves me, it depends on what mood he's in." She waved her hand in front of her face, dismissing dark thoughts. "No, I can't. Not right now. It's too risky, not only for me. For Velvet, too."

"Nora." Devon grabbed her flailing hand. "We have to do something. It's been three days since we buried Katie. Four night's since you've stepped off this cursed ship."

"My cursed ship," Nora corrected.

"Your ship," Devon agreed. "Though," Devon reclaimed the decanter. "Technically, it belongs to the current king of France, even though he does find himself the unfortunate victim of a well-meant gypsy spell. You said it was him who did the killing, right? You only decapitated the chap?"

"That's the detail you remembered?"

"It's a bigger detail."

"Subjective supposition," Nora shot back, then heaved a restless sigh. "You might be right, it was extremely difficult to do, and I violently hated each second of it."

"I don't doubt it, my dear," Devon soothed. "It gets easier with time."

"Christ! Once is quite enough for me, thank you! It was terrible! If Louis had not killed him already, I never could've done it." Nora ran her hands over the velvet bedspread, momentarily admiring the careful embroidery hidden in the soft cloth. "I miss her, Devon. I miss both. I know Henry is angry with her, in a way, I understand him. I do. But it doesn't change the fact that I want her back."

"I do, too," Devon said, sounding tired and honest. "Velvet tried. I know she did. She would have given her life for Katie in an instant. I saw the look in her eyes, the split second before Captain Chance..." His words dropped off, loudly, and he cleared his throat with a harsh cough. "I've seen that look before on the battlefield, in the eyes of a soldier about to die for king and country. I've seen that look too many times." Devon drank deep from the decanter until he finished it. "What's done is done," he said, wiping his mouth with the back of his hand.

"What are we going to do about Alfonso?" Nora asked.

"I don't know," Devon answered. "Velvet told me to keep him alive, she begged me, it was the last thing she said to me. Gods!" Devon roared; he pitched the empty decanter across the room. It hit the wall and shattered in a thousand pieces.

Nora jumped hard at the sound, feeling much like doing the same, yet she said nothing, only watched the few remaining drops slide down pretty, satin wallpaper.

Wine soaked the carpet, reinforcing the musty air in the room. Nora stood up, walked to the table and, ignoring the food, she reached for a fresh jug of wine. Drinking straight from the jug, she returned to Devon and sat down with a thump. A drop of wine splashed her knee, and absently she watched it expand into the fibers of her black dress. A few mouthfuls later, Nora handed Devon the jug, he took it with a grateful nod.

"If the revolution never occurred, if the Bastille had not fallen, her brother would be the king of France, or very nearly. You and I are trained to give our lives for kings and queens. That's all Velvet wanted to do, protect him. Give her life if need be." Devon chugged more wine. "It had to feel good though, for someone like her?"

Nora raised a judgmental brow. "What are you saying?"

Devon threw up one hand in defense, and with the other he took another drink. "Nothing, I'm not saying anything. Just—it must have—that's all. It had to feel good, to taste real power after so long. That girl has had queens and kings bow to her."

"Not for many years," Nora said, and took the crystal decanter from his shaking hand.

"Yeah," Devon agreed, "that's my point. That is not a thing a soul ever forgets. Memories may fade, but feelings?" Devon shook his head. "Feelings linger."

Nora took a sip and met Devon's eyes over the rim of the jug. "Alfonso. Where are we holding him?"

"He's in the brig with a half dozen of his men."

Nora set the wine on the floor, intentionally out of Devon's immediate reach. "Take me to him."

"Not a chance. I am going to take you to the Four Seasons, deposit you in a suite, then find Henry and shake some answers out of him. This was his quest, our quest… I just…everything is so blurry when I look back at it. Maybe I just don't understand all the pieces enough to put together a proper conclusion. I honestly don't know what happened. One moment Katie was on top of me, screaming in my ear and covering my eyes—in the next, she was dead. I know some time must have passed between those two events, but it's just so…"

"Blurry?" Nora offered.

Devon made a violent show of rolling his eyes.

"Regardless, Alfonso is an interesting player on the board. We traveled with him for days. He treated us abominably, of course, but not once did he even allude to knowing anything about Velvet or her life, save that she was the lost princess. I need to know what he does."

"Nora," Devon cautioned.

"Don't tell me what I can and can't do. This is my prisoner, and he is currently occupying my brig. If I wish to speak with him, I will. If I wish to make him my dancing concubine, then I'll do that too."

Devon shuddered. "Heaven forfend."

"You go talk to him, then. We have to know, if you won't let me interrogate him, then you must do it!"

"Must I though?" Devon asked, quickly reaching around her leg, and snagging the jug, then he drank until it gave up its last drop. "I care about you, Nora, I do. You have been the sunspot on the horizon of my life since I was a little boy. But I am embroiled in this incredible nonsense because of Henry, alone. I suspect Velvet is safely locked in the Tower by now, and Henry is back where he belongs, at court. Everything has returned to its version of normal, I guess my life should too."

"Normal!?" Nora screeched; she threw the empty decanter a scathing look. "Normal? I'm a pirate queen, I lost my house to gain a ship and a large portion of an island, apparently. Velvet's brother saved my life, and Katie gave hers. Spells are real, and gypsy magic is not just a story to scar children with. Nothing is ever going to be normal again." Nora slapped her hands on her knees and stood up. "You are your own man, Devon. Henry made his choice—it was the wrong one. What is yours to be?"

Devon shook his head, giving Nora a pleading look. "Nora, there aren't many choices for a soldier like me, the third son of a titled, penniless lord. My fate has ever been entwined with Henry's.

I am sworn to him. My word, my honor—It's all I have. That is of course, if we are discounting my good looks and unquenchable charm."

"Of course." Nora replied. "Well!" She clapped her hands and stood. "That's just about enough of this moping around." Almost tentatively, she moved to the corner of the room, reached down, and lifted the bag of jewels. Katie's blood stained the fabric. Little misshapen splotches, bright in the center, going brown around the edges. No time for tears. Not right now. No more. Nora decided to cry later, even set a time for it in her mind. There was too much to do right now. The last five seconds had packed her schedule. She would need to talk to Alfonso, maybe make some small protests as Devon hit him a little, then of course she would need to do the most important thing—obviously, it was time to break Velvet out of her tower.

"No, Nora," said Devon. Watching her actions and reading her mind. "Don't do anything rash. Take it from me, grief changes you."

Nora tucked the bag of gems in the front pocket of her black mourning gown. "Incorrect," she said and took a heavy cloak—colored like a rainy English forest—and threw it over her shoulders. One hand touching the gems in her pocket, she drew up the hood with the other. "Grief doesn't change you, Devon, not really—it reveals you." Nora threw the door open, lifting her small chin she stepped in the cramped hall. "I have been revealed, and I wonder what I shall find."

～

November 6, 1800

They say you are a witch, that you see with black eyes.
Still—you sold me to the flames. In you my love does die.

Torches illuminated a small portion of the fallen night; light followed the edges of a dirt path leading to a small white chapel situated on the fringes of William Pitt's London townhome. Spider webs clung to the small windows, through them moved too many silhouettes for so cramped a space. The door swung inward, two men entered, ducking their heads to avoid the low beams bracing the crumbling frame. The two men took their seats beside a dozen others, hat brims pulled over their eyes, arms folded. The gaze of every man in the room was focused on the small girl in a red slip— red gold hair that fell past her hips—standing barefoot in a half-moon formation of flickering candles.

Velvet felt her chest move as she took a cleansing breath, trying not to feel their eyes boring holes in her skin. In front of her, three men sat behind a squat oak table, Pitt was the man in the center, the faces of two men on either side of him were unfamiliar— though they reminded Velvet of vultures hovering over a fresh carcass. Velvet wondered how long it would take them to pick her bones clean.

A gavel hit the oak table; a stunning THUD rang loudly in the small space. The gavel wielder had a beak nose hanging over frowning lips. Above the nose, his beady eyes simmered.

Tiny flames touched the hem of her filthy red dress, the torn gown sashayed around her bare feet, moving the candle smoke like a wand in a cauldron—the swirls of smoke from the candles that spiraled up, truly painted her the witch they all believed she was. Though they stared at her with hungry, expectant eyes, Velvet knew there was no point in saying anything; she had been damned long before this counsel forced her to stand in front of them, humbling herself for their holy judgement.

Velvet remained silent, her halo of candles plus the few stubs cluttering the space between Pitt and his gavel, were the only shining lights in the small room. Porous bees wax dripped from the dais, falling in puddles at the feet of the men who sat huddled before her, waiting—like her—to hear her sentence, and her doom.

Before her, twelve chairs sat on a raised dais, surrounding the podium where her next accuser would stand.

William Pitt loudly cleared his throat, and rose, moving slowly for one so young of years. "Honored gentlemen," he began, "I have asked you attended this gathering tonight, so you may listen to all charges laid against this woman." He pointed a finger at her, the nail was blackened from ink. "An orphan raised by gypsies, a girl with no family name, who simply calls herself Velvet. Darker whispers name her Marie Thérèse Antoinette, Joanna von Österreich-Lothringen, grand Duchess of Vienna, lost princess of France, and if her brother is dead, heir to the throne of France. Yet these are not all the titles bequeathed her—she has been given the name of sorcerer, from one of our own, an esteemed member of this holy council."

Velvet's eyes flew up at that, as a painful, foreign thing squeezed at her heart—it could not be true! *Please god, let it not be true.*

William Pitt, continued in the steady baritone, which it in its own, stole Velvet's very will to live. "My Lord, the Duke of Newcastle—Your Grace, this body calls on you to give us an accounting of events witnessed with your own eyes."

Velvet's hands and feet went terribly cold, a dark chasm was opening beneath her, filled with screams of betrayal. Her heart thundered in her ears as the weak legs of a wooden chair scraped over the floor, screaming across her nerves like long nails dragged down a wall of chalk. The ratty floorboards yelled as he stood; candlelight wavered under a small breath of rushing air.

Velvet dropped her eyes. If she looked at him, saw him, god forbid met his devastating gaze, Velvet knew her soul would turn to glass, frozen tears would fall, then she would shatter to slivers and dust. Her gaze fell to the small puddles of wax dripping from her halo of candles; they ran together like so many drops of rain, found divots between panels to make a collection of tiny, boiling rivers.

"Good evening, my lords," Henry said.

Velvet made a screeching noise in her throat; her hand flew to cover her lips and staunch further sound.

"You Grace," said a man in a slimy voice. A wretch in a powdered wig, the bags beneath his eyes rippling like shark skin. "Please tell us what you witnessed this woman perform on October twenty third, in the year of our Lord, eighteen hundred. The night Miss Miller, a treasured citizen of the crown brutally lost her life. We all know you to be a devout man, Your Grace, and one of great honor. This court wishes to hear all events spoken in your own words."

Velvet could feel Henry's eyes on her. She kept her head bowed. His voice was deep when he finally spoke, each word, when it came, was a serrated knife cutting deep. "I cannot speak to it all, much of it is still a blur in my mind," said Henry.

William Pitt placed his hands on the table and leaned forward; under the dim light he was a scarecrow with a twisted smile. "Your Grace, did this girl—in all her unholy beauty—commune with Satan on the night to which referred? Did she knowingly and with a black heart, cast a spell on your person?"

"I cannot speak on Satan's location nor the color of her heart, yet I must answer, yes. That night a spell was cast," said Henry, his voice low and strong.

"Were you a victim of this woman? Did you lay eyes on the familiar she calls Cerberus?" William Pitt pressed ferociously.

"I was," Henry said. Never did Velvet know two simple words could so thoroughly break a heart. "Though," he added, "Cerberus is no familiar, just an overgrown mongrel posing as a dog."

At that last, Velvet finally lifted her eyes to meet his blistering gaze. Stormy, wild as a siren filled sea. They traced her face, open and almost tender before he had time to drop his shield.

Velvet wanted to be fearless, the way a true princess should be. She wanted to draw her head back and spit in the Devil's eyes, as it were. Instead, tears gathered in her throat, sticky misery that bound the words to her tongue. "Don't do this, Henry," she finally said. Desperation reducing her to a beggar, all her pride cast aside. She did not want to die, yet more than anything she did not want the death to come from him. "You promised to protect me," she breathed, and cringed at the misery in her voice—her words, that fell to the ground like empty air. She breathed deep, and watched his expression turn bleak as coal.

The counsel called more witnesses: Lord Melton, Byron, and others she had spelled at the Blind Pig, however, for Velvet it had been over the moment he said those two simple words. *I was.*

Words, that over time seemed to seal the crack in her heart with a chunky, throbbing scar, raised and purple as the lash of a whip. A scar formed to keep further pain away, a deep reminder to never let anyone touch her heart again. He was her champion, savior, obsession, accuser and now her enemy. Trust misplaced; Velvet knew she would never go looking for it.

She was glad for the scar, humans, unlike the populace of the animal kingdom she missed—needed all the protection they could get. Her eyes stayed on Henry's face as William Pitt banged the gavel and pronounced her sentence. It was to be off with her head then. Like mother like daughter—it was good to keep traditions alive.

~

November 7, 1800

The bowed hat was draped in silk, sporting the jauntiest blue feather, bright as a robin's egg. Nora had a rather challenging time choosing a suitable ornament for so daring a hat. After all, whatever part one was given—one must strive to play it their best. She was a bastard princess, pirate queen, with three score ruffians at her command. Fully emersed in the roll, Nora felt bold as the gentleman's outfit she wore. She checked the placement of the sword hanging from her belt, the thing she scarcely knew how to draw, much less use, then set about re-loading a brace of pistols, Nora would have traded the world and everything in it, just to have Katie at her side.

Since the night Katie was murdered, Nora felt some necessary part of herself had been cut away. Strange dreams had plagued her of late, maudlin tales of a spirt who wandered her ship. A frail whisp of a thing moving back and forth on the deck leaving bloody footprints, shiny as an oil spill, reflective as thick, black tar. Nora rarely had time to think on the dreams when she woke, in the cabin of the man she had decapitated. Her mornings were spent in a strict regime of sweating and vomiting, with little to no reprieve.

Even now the urge to hurl had not entirely passed. Alas, she was crouched atop the low wall which faced the Tower courtyard, beside Devon who lazily surveyed the scene, arms crossed over his chest, both swords drawn. The blood-stained block was set-in place, the hay spread at its base, all ready to catch Velvet's soon to be severed head. Nora stared at the splatters on the block, some fresh enough to shine crimson under the low afternoon light, and felt bile rise in her throat.

"Bloody hell," grumbled Darren, seeing her pallor, "now is not the time to toss your effects, my dear. If you haven't noticed we are in the middle of a daring rescue, stealth is all we must achieve. I doubt a viewing of your stomach's contents would do much to raise the men's morale."

"There's nothing left in my stomach," Nora said bitterly. "This child saps my very life-force."

Devon smiled, the flash of white teeth against the hot red bandana he had tied around his head was dramatic. Comical yet deadly. He brushed her clammy cheek with the back of his gloved knuckle. "Darling," he said softly, "I believe that's the nature of the thing."

Devon's jerkin was a pirate's castoff, and a size too small. The muscles of his bare arms bulged from the torn sleeves. As he was, swords drawn, committed to fighting for her, dying if necessary, Nora saw nothing of the boy she had once danced with in ballrooms washed in candlelight. Now he balanced sharp steel instead of champagne flutes in his capable hands. Nora was glad of him in every way. More at any rate, than that man she had once called brother—now villain turned traitor. Sweet Madonna! She could hardly think his name without her mind conjuring images of his decapitation, sending numerous, corresponding pictures she would rather not visualize.

"The men stand in place, Captain," said a deep commanding voice, as a shadow passed over the setting sun. Nora looked up into the face of a pirate—a prominent member of her rowdy brigade. Ajax, so called for the Greek warrior—and aptly named, was a bear of a man, with one eye, and only eight fingers. He wielded a two-sided axe, same as the legend of old, his lank, grey hair was tied back from his weathered forehead with a blackened rope, that looked as if it had been torn from the bottom of a ship, two hundred years marooned. "The execution is set to take place in less than two hours, we will be ready," he finished, his tone holding the appropriate amount of wicked bravado, and Nora felt for a wild moment like she had suddenly woken in the throes of a fever dream.

"Good, we must wait till the last, if we move too soon—" her voice trailed off. What did she know of battle strategies, or how to command a pirate hoard?

"Ash will not miss," said Ajax, as if the exploits of this Ash were a forgone fact—for the life of her, Nora could not remember who Ash was.

She shook her head. "That's good...I..."

Ajax misread her hesitation. He lifted his body higher up the wall, his knuckles going white under the strain of his hold, he puffed out his bare, inked chest. "We will not fail you, Captain," he said, flashing her a triumphant smile as if their battle was already won. "We only await your signal."

"My signal, right—" *Nora Hartington, pull your wits together!* her mind chided. "We must wait until the very last moment," she repeated, glancing back to the place where another Antoinette head would fall. "Her killers must think it's over. We won't strike until they truly believe they have won, and Ajax—no one touches the Duke of Newcastle. That one is mine to deal with in my own time."

Devon chuckled at that. "And what do you plan to do with our illustrious duke once you catch him?"

Nora smiled up at him, it was full to the brim of all the heartbreaking these last two months had brought. "I won't know that, until I have my hands around his throat. I cannot fathom what possessed him to testify against her, his words alone had the power to damn her. Bastard. For that action alone I can never forgive him."

Devon schooled his expression into one of thoughtful contemplation. "Not to offer excuses on his behalf, but technically Henry didn't lie. Velvet did cast a spell on him. On all of us".

Nora shook her head, making red hair fly. "Still, I've known Henry my whole life, I've never seen him look at anyone the way he looked at her. There was something more than passion. A reverence, tender sincerity, maybe even love. When you found us on the road, after our escape from Alfonso's camp—the way he touched her—his eyes—"

"I know. I saw," said Devon.

"Perhaps his mother, and sister received a look from him like that." Nora shrugged. "I would not know, I was never its recipient, and I believe he genuinely cares for me. The Henry I know is cold, calculated, even diabolical at times, but never tender. With her he was, I can't believe he actually went through with it, knowing the consequences."

Devon's face went soft. "Velvet seems to bring out the protective side in a man, even a monster like Alfonso."

"Really, Devon, not just a man!" Nora flung out a hand, to encompass the group of pirates hiding just within the Tower walls. "I have mobilized a small militia on her behalf."

Devon smiled gently at her. "Bless you, lady N. No one can say you won't make your own way in the world."

"No," Nora said, tilting her head to look up at the Tower rooms where a princess was locked away, "no, they can't, can they?"

CHAPTER FOUR

Away with you my love, away—you were the shadow
that dissolved in my hands, on this of all the days.

The Tower of London, November 7, 1800

She was there, brilliant in a crescent of candlelight, glowing more beautiful than any of the perfect, golden flames. Black shadows jumped in her crystal blue eyes, the look of pain she cast on him was a knife in his gut. In his dream he gasped at the agony of it.

The gavel banged; questions were asked. 'Did this girl cast a spell on you?"

Though he tried to call it back, his voice rushed forth strong and clear. 'A spell was cast'.

Then she was on her knees, hypocritical hands locked over her upper arms, dragged her away to the very mouth of death. Her hands were folded in prayer, on her head he could see a luminous halo, on her back, wings of the Seraphim. Cold as fallen snow. That was the base temperature of his stopped heart.

Her hair was bright white, and glowing, drenched in mystical dream light. It tumbled wildly around her, tipped in colors of sunset. Hands shoved her small shoulders, Velvet lurched forward, her head falling in place on the block, the last spot it would ever lie. Henry tried to move; his feet stayed anchored to the ground. The hooded executioner hovered over the bowed form of the princess like a dark storm cloud—the silver blade in his hand, the coming lightening. The sword was slim and sharp, glimmering like black glass.

Velvet lifted her head, for one precious moment, her wide eyes found his own. Strands of hair blew across her brave face, stuck to silver trails of tears falling down her cheeks. "You promised to die for me," she said.

Henry reached out his arms to save her, opened his mouth to call her name, he was mute and paralyzed—silent as the sound of the slender blade as it cut through the air, and landed against her precious neck. The sword sawed through bone, and he heard the screeching click of her spine as it snapped, her blood was a cerise fountain that dripped down his vision. More fanned the courtyard and the ghosts of London Tower cheered as another joined their ranks. Velvet's severed head rolled over the waiting straw, her eyes open and staring. Her lips parted, then the dead eyes blinked. "Traitor," her pale lips said, "traitor…traitor…traitor."

Henry woke up screaming like a child. His hands twisted in his bed sheets, his bare chest drenched and burning. He swung his legs over the side of his huge bed. His elbows went to his braced knees, as his head plummeted to his waiting hands. *"God in heaven, what have I done?"* he asked aloud. Behind his closed lids, he could see her dead eyes blinking up at him, and the blood, so much blood.

He stood and moved to his windows then threw them wide. Gold curtains blew, sucked outward by the wild wind. Staring at the night, his mind stumbled back to the night on the Bacchus, and the spell—he could feel her in his arms, soft and desperate under his hungry hands. Seven days ago, he would have readily died for her, last night he opened his mouth and delivered her to the wolves. He would never be free from the image of her standing in the half moon of candlelight, looking exactly as an angel should

—that quick flash of hope on her face, the way it vanished as he betrayed her.

Henry sunk his fist in the wall, the soft paper—so common at court—tore down an invisible seam as boards of wood turned to chips, he watched his knuckles split. He remembered riding with her across the Moors, the way she had shared his warmth, curled against his chest, pulling secrets from his past with her endless blue eyes. She had trusted him, more than that—she had hoped, hope differed was the worst pain of all.

Like a tormented sleepwalker, Henry moved through the room in a daze, flexing his bleeding hand. He found his discarded trousers on a nearby chair, and struggled to pull them on, nearly pitching forward when his foot momentarily tangled in the limp pant leg. Anger and guilt making his hands shake, he found a linen shirt, and dragged it over his head. Blindly he fitted on his boots, grabbed his cloak from the foot of the bed, and slammed his way free of the luscious suite. Life at Buckingham palace was a bit much, even on the best of days. The endless gold-soaked halls, the lavish, ostentatious clothing—peers of the realm done up like preening peacocks, or polished porcelain dolls on a shelf. All lost in the sickening, sweet smell pervading everything. Rose water, and human waste.

Henry stormed his way through the great hall, courtiers acted on instinct, spinning from his path, bowing low if they were beneath his rank. He gave them no notice; a singular purpose guided his feet. He had to see her. Had to know if it was all an enchantment. If anything had been real.

Her tower room was small, situated to the northeast of the chilling structure, just down the hall from where Anne Boleyn had waited to die. It was a quaint room, always in the grip of some windy gale. Henry locked his cloak around his shoulders and wondered if she was cold. A part of him wanted to kill the stoic, innocent guards standing before her door, lift her in his arms and spirit her away.

The guards looked him up and down when Henry came to a panting halt before them. Winded by desperation.

"Your Grace," one of them finally said, his pale, splotchy face flooding with recognition. Black plumed helmets tilted when both men performed a lithe bow. Henry wanted to simultaneously punch them in the face, for no other reason save they were in his way, blocking his only path to her.

"I must speak with the prisoner," he demanded, his voice hovering on the precipice of a shout.

Both men hesitated. Grinding his teeth, Henry reached in a pocket of his cloak and withdrew a heavy bag of gold. One of the soldiers instantly reached out his hand. Henry dropped the bag on his thirsty palm. The man hefted the weight and smiled. Almost gingerly he stepped aside, turning to speak to his companion in low tones. Henry opened the door and forgot them instantly.

Velvet stood gowned in gossamer white, framed by a small, ice encrusted window. Streamers of rainy, silver light cast squares of moving gold at her feet. Her hair was unbound, some maid of this wretched place had brushed the locks, so they glowed like sunlight. Her skin was clean and flushed, the bruises she had collected were fading.

Velvet looked up and saw him, the book she held, dropped as her eyes flew wide. Her hands fluttered for a second before she locked them in front of her, linking her fingers like braided ribbons. "Your Grace," she said, her voice flat as her eyes.

Henry would never know how he managed to stay in place. In his mind he ran to her, gathered her in his arms, kissed the frown from her pale lips. In reality, he watched her back stiffen, a glaze of sheer ice dropped over her expression, then she turned away. She faced the window, looked through the glass, her gaze traveled to the dais where she would spend her last moments.

"I can't for the life of me, imagine what you are doing here, my lord. Or what more we could possibly have to say to each other," she softly said, her last word breaking on a sigh.

A red desert seemed to have invaded Henry's mouth; his words were lost beneath the hot dunes.

"Did you mean to cast a spell on me?" he finally managed to rasp, and saw her slender shoulders sag a little.

"You know I did not. You know I had no idea you were there. I believed you were dead."

Henry stepped fully in the room and slammed the door behind him. Velvet flinched but made no sound. A long silence followed the crash.

"Are you a witch?" he demanded, his feet closing the distance between them. "Are you?" he nearly shouted. Her stormy silence began to cast a chill.

"I am a princess of France," she finally said, her body deathly still. "I grew up with the Romani people. I know how to fly better than I can walk, and I've been fighting for my life, and that of my brothers' for long as I remember."

"That doesn't answer my question," he said, close enough to reach out and touch her.

"Doesn't it?" she whispered; her voice sounded choked with tears. Her breath trembled out in a small gush. "I am not a minion of the Anti-Christ if that's what you're asking." She spun then, her heart in her luminous eyes. "Know this, I trusted you, Your Grace, I would have died before I hurt you. Yet I did what I did, and now I will die for it. What more do you want?"

He moved closer. "Not your life," he rasped, even to his own ears his voice sounded menacing.

"It is credit to your testimony that it is forfeit," she said. His hand smoothed a golden curl tumbling over her shoulder, and she recoiled. Whatever softness he had seen in her eyes was now gone. Strength and royalty embellished all her lines, heightened the color in her cheeks, the intoxicating flush in her lips. He reached out again, not thinking at all, only needing to touch her. His fingers folded over her arms, wanting to shake her until the past retreated, and ran from him. God! Would the magic of her never leave him?

Henry knew the answer to his inner cry was a resounding no. If he lost her now, the face filling his eyes would haunt him beyond the grave.

Velvet's trembling hands pressed against his chest, pausing a brief second as Henry caught his breath. She shoved him away, spinning out of his reach, then dropping in a small curtsey. He could see the shadows of her long legs beneath the glossy gown, her chin tilted up, revealing the graceful line of her neck. "I will never forget the way you stood against me, giving testimony with no proceeding facts. You should have killed me the day we met, Your Grace," she said.

Henry felt the words sear straight through his gut. "It would have been far kinder," she finished beneath her breath. In the soft words he could hear the wealth of rage and rebellious fire. She would remain proud and brave till the end. Just like her mother—a true queen. One last scathing look that had the power to strip skin from bone, and Velvet turned away. "Farewell, Your Grace," she said calmy, her voice drifting over her shoulder. "They mean to take my head in two hours' time, perhaps you will watch with the others? My guards say it will be quite the well-attended spectacle. The witch-princess vanquished, rather droll, don't you think?" she said sweetly.

Past her he could see the courtyard and the shadows it hosted; movement alerted his eyes. Rough men dressed as foot soldiers, lurking with excessive stealth, or crouched in corners still as the stone gargoyle on the mantel piece of his ancestral home. Henry suspected Nora's hand in these goings on—his eyes returned to Velvet. She was too well guarded, too fine a target, he feared any attempts at rescue would meet with disaster.

Her profile radiated the muted light of fading day. She was too beautiful like this—and regardless of what she said, he could feel her magic, the old Celtic blood in him sensed it. The very air around her felt charged. He stared at her for one long moment more, the last sight of her angel face filling his vision, and he knew he was the worst villain alive. His chest burned under the harsh rise and fall of his breath. Fury, and fear flashed hot and cold in his gut, fury at the spell she had cast on him, fear for himself, for he had wished so desperately for it all to be real.

∿

November 7, 1800
One hour until Velvet's execution.

You ran from me, but I will find you. Us two are joined by no mortal device. You lied to me, but I will own you—everything has a price.

King George III was in a rare temper when Henry strode in the anti-chamber of the monarch's lustrous boudoir. The old king sat heavy in an overstuffed chair, his bare, swollen feet were soaking in a wooden basin, filled to the slatted brim with steaming, jasmine scented water. It did little to expel the king's ever roving cloud of flatulence.

King George looked up sharply as Henry brushed past his valet and came to what could only be called a screeching halt, close as propriety to the sovereign would allow. "Newcastle, my good man," cried the king, nonplussed, "you look fresh drug through the garden, what, what? A man teetering on the edge of sanity! Here, here!" King George laughed loudly. "Trust me, my boy, I would know."

"Sire," Henry tried to breathe, tried to calm his racing heart. "You cannot kill her. I do not care what demons she may serve. I will not watch her die."

The king harumphed, and settled back in the chair, low noises emitted from the tormented cushions. "This again," he muttered, "the girl is a danger to the kingdom, and from all accounts, a danger to you. A witch, they say. Did she not cast her spell on your very own person? What? What?"

"She did," said Henry, the words coming no easier a second time. "Sire, nonetheless—"

"Nonetheless you are addicted, what? What?" King George laughed again, "got your breaches in a twist, eh? Give you the old lower itch?"

Henry began to pace in tight lines. "My breaches remain unaffected your majesty. It is only—" he ran his hands through his hair, tugging on the dark strands, and stopped walking, then spun to face the king. "Give her to me," he said suddenly.

The king made a broken, cawing sound, like a vulture struck down in its prime. "Famous. You want a princess, do you, what? What?"

"She can do no harm to the crown if I make her my wife. I will keep her from all sedition, and in doing so, spare your own hands from the stain of royal blood." Henry swallowed, fear of his actions nearly stealing his words. Velvet was dangerous, and lovely enough to steal his soul, majestic as some mythical creature. He would never be safe from her, but he could not watch her die.

The king considered his words, his thoughts making furrows deep as craters on his splotchy brow, and Henry stood in stilted silence. Finally, the king threw up his hands. "Oh, what do we say? She is a pretty thing, and we do loathe killing princesses, it sets a terrible precedent, what? What?"

"Then she is mine?" croaked Henry, already backing toward the door.

"You will marry her by proxy, as I doubt the chit will be willing, eh? I heard you testified in Pitt's trial—" the king shook his head—"that one is an anomaly on his own, Pitt, pah!" the king spit the word. "First rate brain combined with the breath of a deceased frog, what, what? Go to the palace chapel and see that it is done. We will demand this marriage be consummated," chortled the king. "We will need to know she is yours body and soul, only then will we rest." The king leaned back his head; his eyelids slid closed like globs of hot wax. "Yes, she is yours," the king said, "if you dare...the princess is yours. And Newcastle," cautioned the king when Henry was moments from making his exit. "Capture your flower's heart, we do need our rest, what? What?"

∽

Velvet's heart stopped dead when a knock sounded at her door. She swallowed a dry gulp of air that burned like fire as it went down. It was time. They were here to take her. Fingers strangely calm, lips silent, she gathered her hair in a sleek bundle, and began to braid it. No use taking the risk of it getting in the way of the blade, the cleaner the cut, the faster it would all be over.

Velvet turned away from the window—her body moving differently, now that it knew it lived in final moments—she called for her murders to enter in a voice perfectly crisp, and cool.

What was life without risk, bravery absent death? Many kings and queens, greater souls than her, had met this same fate. They say her mother died with honor, Henry had spoken to her of such things just a few days ago, days that now seemed to span generations.

As two guards dragged her down the hall, Velvet prayed to the holy Madonna, and the spirits who soared the sky; that something outside herself, something strong and bright, would give her the power to die with grace. Bare fingers slid up and down her arms; Velvet had to grit her teeth not to wrench away from the slimly grasping hands of the guards dragging her to her death. She wanted to scream and fight, perhaps she could disarm one of them, maybe even drag one with her to the grave, but overall, there was no point —because in the end, to the grave would she go.

Time moved slowly, the lingering scent of torches, the cling of her grave clothes, all played on her senses—little windows lined the damp halls, showing views others before her had seen on their last trip down this deadliest of walks.

There was so much she still wanted to do, there had been no time to be human, not really—only survival, no living. She wanted to see her brother one final time. Her collusion with the Duke had torn through her heart and left that chunky scar—Velvet was glad she said goodbye.

A flight of stairs, dripping wet and slippery, curved around a stout pillar, then ran into an archway that swept up in a delicate pinnacle, proudly displaying a stone-mason's life's work. Behind the cobbled archway, past a set of cathedral doors, Velvet could hear the low hum of a gathering crowd.

Hard hands at her back pushed her forward; Velvet let out a shaky breath, battling not to resist their prodding, struggling to obey. Bitter queasiness roiled in her stomach, cold sweat popped out on her brow, ran in bracing rivulets down her neck, between her tense shoulder blades, pooling at the base of her spine.

Two more guards stationed at the end of the hall, threw open the double doors, passing their spears before their face in salute. It took Velvet a moment to realize the salute was for her. A royal execution. Velvet had not lived much as a princess, it felt strange to die like one. Velvet squinted her eyes as clean night rushed through the dungeon hall, the pale light was blinding, and they watered profusely. *Shame*, she thought before the guards took hold of her arms, and again began to drag her along, *it would have been nice to be human for just a while longer, a girl, an animal, I wonder what I shall be like as a spirit?"*

Velvet decided it would have been easy to die, really—it was just all the sorrow. What you left behind, what you had yet to find. Henry had taken the trust she had given him—new and fragile—he had taken it, then destroyed it—that was her remorse. Broken promises, desire, and fear, that is all she would take with her to the grave, if only there had been more. If only. Two more simple words that said overly much.

The guards shoved her into the light, night wind washed her burning eyes—the crowed rumbled, it was a soothing sound, spliced with misplaced sighs. They pitied her, Velvet could see that some even reached for her hand, whispered her real name.

She blinked her eyes, looking to where she must go. Moonlight touched the block; it was the first thing she saw. The walk was slow, sometime in the middle of it she began to shake until her teeth clacked, and she called herself ten kinds of ninny. No one shouted, or threw things, called her names or epithets of any kind. They only watched her place one foot in front of the other, stared at the way she gasped in her breaths, how her dress moved between her thighs. A little girl with dirty cheeks, and broken shoeless feet, grabbed a handful of her hair and tugged. Velvet let her take the locks, what did she need with them anyway?

"You go to your mother!" a man called.

"God save you, princess," said another.

"Mercy," someone whispered.

"Mercy, mercy," many echoed.

Velvet began to climb the stairs, the old, worn boards creaked under her toes. Straw caught and tangled in the hem of her gown. She tried to shake the clingy stalks away, but that only made them cling harder. She shook again, her heart was pounding too hard, her blood rushing hot beneath her skin, filling her cheeks, drowning her.

Somewhere in the fire of fear, she thought, *die like a princess, like a princess.* Velvet dropped the gown and knelt before the block. She stayed there for a moment, on her knees, staring at sympathetic faces, strangers all. The moon painted more pale shadows on their bowed heads. Then the man standing beside her, wearing the Grim Reaper's very own robes, knelt and placed his gloved hand lightly atop her head.

"Forgive me, my lady, Je suis désolé ma dame," the executioner said.

"I do," Velvet breathed. "I wish I had gold to give you." She reached out to lightly touch his stubbled jaw, the only portion of his face showing beneath his tight black hood. "You are not like the others who sought my death, you only do as your king commands."

"Try to relax, my lady, do not tense your shoulders, I swear it will be over in a single stroke," he said. Velvet blanched. "You will not feel a thing, I swear it, Madonna—I do not wish to take your life."

"I know," Velvet said. Two guards cut her bonds, they gathered up the ropes as she clutched her wrists to her chest, then turned, and walked down the steps, leaving her to her fate. It was coming now. Velvet's deep breaths were making her feel dizzy, but she could not seem to calm them. "Should I lie down now?" she asked, "I don't…I'm not…"

"Yes," said the executioner. "Now you lie down, close your eyes and dream of heaven."

Velvet nodded her mouth too full of tears to speak one more word around them. She lay her head on the block and tried to picture her mother's face. It was hazy, like the reflection of a forgotten dream seen through smoke and mirrors.

In the distance she heard shouting, beneath her cheek, she felt the rumble of galloping horses. Velvet swallowed her tears and closed her eyes.

The executioner lifted his sword.

"Halt," someone cried.

The distinct hiss of an arrow whizzed over her head, Velvet's eyes flew open, so she was able to watch as the flying arrow struck her executioner directly in the center of his chest. The arrowhead was aflame. Sword still raised high, the executioner made no sound as he burst in noisy flames, his dark robes igniting like stalks of dry wheat. Then, the world exploded in chaos.

CHAPTER FIVE

No knight or manly champion, only a pirate queen.

*N*ora watched the arrow fly and knew why the other pirates called this one Ash. It was what his victims became. Seconds ago, Nora had seen Velvet lie her head on the block, badly stained from the blood of other fallen, sighing out what the girl probably thought was her last breath. The moment the man was about to cut off Velvet's head, he burst in righteous flames.

Nora's men catapulted from all the dark corners they occupied, more crouching in the crowds cast off their hoods, and drew their swords. Ajax rushed through the courtyard with a bellowing cry, swinging his axe at the first hapless soldier who stupidly got in his way. Steel crashed on steel, and for a time mayhem regained supreme. Shouts and shots, the twang of led balls finding their mark followed by screams of the damned.

Devon pulled up his bright red kerchief, so it covered his mouth, then dropped like an attacking feline from the wall and landed lightly on his feet, not breaking stride—he ran to Velvet, shoving faceless members of the crowd from his path. Twilight painted his blades, then blood as scores of guards moved to block him.

Watching him, Nora felt like she swallowed her heart—they were truly traitors now. Through the smoke she saw Henry, yelling at two guards, motioning wildly—Nora looked away from him, the monster! She turned to find the girl she had come to save.

The moment Velvet saw Nora through the melee, her blue eyes went wide, then flicked to the side, and Velvet screamed when they locked on Devon. She held her arms out to him, like a hungry child to a caring parent. A sort of mad scrambling haste made Velvet fall twice before she launched herself at him. Devon caught her shaking body and gathered her close. He sheathed one of his swords, placed a gentle arm beneath her knees and lifted her off the dais, away from the jaws of death. Velvet struggled in his hold, Nora could hear her begging for a sword, but Devon only ran, his single blade cutting through the jostling crowd like a host of boneless phantoms.

In what seemed a few seconds, Devon was standing in front of Nora, panting hard, laying a shocked Velvet at her feet. Velvet stood, swaying like a drunken sailor, then cast her arms around Nora's neck, and gave her a back breaking hug, Nora returned the gesture, gently patting the girl's trembling shoulder.

"There, there," Nora whispered, eyes trained on the crowd, "welcome to your daring rescue, dear."

Velvet looked up, and scrunched her nose, tilting her head a little. "You look like a pirate, my lady," she observed. Velvet put her head back on Nora's shoulder and continued hugging. Nora's hands fluttered in the air; hot tears burned her eyes as Velvet began to sob.

Nora took the girl's shoulders and set her back to give the disheveled French princess a once over. "You look terrible," Nora replied, and ran her knuckles over Velvet's cheekbone sporting a blotchy patch of fading bruises. "Let's go," Nora said, trying to breathe through her nose. "The smell of charring executioner is playing havoc with my constitution." She spared a brief glance for her men, listened to the cries as more place guards fell to pirate blades. "We will be safe on the Bacchus. The men I left behind have readied the ship, we set sail immediately. Devon, call them off."

"Anarchy unleashed is hard to recall," said Devon, looking on the sea of raging pirates, "yet, I shall try." He sighed and dropped a courtly bow, crossing his legs and holding his blades out on either side of him as he bent forward at the waist." His cherub face was harsh under the flickering glow of the chopping block now aflame. He righted himself with grace, turned and lifted his sword in the air. "Justice and freedom for innocence!" he yelled. Instantly the thirsty pirates stopped their play. Nora raised her eyes and met Henry's over the sea of stunned onlookers.

He stood just feet from the burning block, backlit by fading points of light in the darkening sky. He held a piece of parchment in his gloved hand and, even at this distance, Nora could see the signature of the king scrawled at the base of the document. As their eyes locked and held, she watched him shake his head, his lips mouthing a word she did not hear, and thank god for that!

Nora did not give a single fig for anything he might have to say. She tore her eyes away from him, hating him enough in that moment to wish him physical harm. In a vulgar display of pique—because she knew there was no way he could reach her before she turned the corner and disappeared in the night—Nora raised her middle finger; her lacy gloves made the gesture dramatic. She held it up in the air to prolong the moment of emphasis, then turned, placed her arm gently around Velvet's shoulder, and put a dagger in the girl's hand. She tugged Velvet to the hobbled horses which had carried them here. Velvet mounted without assistance, and Nora saw to her own seat, and gathered the reins in her hand.

"Yah! Yah!" Nora prodded, pressing her heels in the horse's side, the beast leapt into action, and bolted. Iron clacking against cobble stone, told her Velvet stayed on her heels.

They rode hard till they reached the docks. The moment they dismounted, both trembling and gulping at the air, winded from their race, men swarmed in from the surrounding ships, and closed a protective shield around them.

"You have a lot of men," Velvet said, blithely stating the obvious.

Nora laughed. "I do, don't I? All thanks to your brother."

"Louis? Why?"

Nora shook her head. "A terribly long story, darling, and one we don't at all have time for now." She winked at Velvet. "It is a juicy one though, and I do know how you cherish my stories."

"Only because I think most of them are made up," Velvet quipped back.

"It's called dramatic presentation, my dear. I have it in spades." Nora took an extended hand and vowed to start writing these men's names down, so she could thank them properly. Fully armed and silent as assassins, the pirates escorted them both to the black ship that was now her very own. "I have your stones as well," Nora said, as they began to climb the gangway.

Velvet's pale visage whitened. "No," she gasped, hand going to her heart. "Why? I thought they were forever lost," her voice fell, "it would have been fitting justice."

Nora's cheeks heated as her mind quickly drifted through a few unsavory memories. "There was good and bad that night, two opposing sides of the same coin. We can speak of all this later. What matters now is escaping Henry, for I fear he is already in hot pursuit. The villain!" she hissed.

Velvet's lips thinned to a slash of white when Nora mentioned his name. Her eyes fell closed, and Nora knew the girl struggled to control an internal, strangling pain. "He had his reason," she finally said.

Nora snorted loudly, making a few of the pirates look in her direction. "That's terribly gracious of you. I for one shall never speak to him again. The bastard! Lecherous rake! It would serve him right to spend the next few years consumed by misery and guilt over the undeniable fact that he has lost what he wanted most."

"What does he want most?" asked Velvet as they stepped on the main deck, and the smoky night moved around them like a settling cloak.

"You," said Nora, turning to take both of Velvet's freezing hands in her own. "More than anything in the world, Henry wanted you."

∽

It was what I expected, but nothing that could be done.

Velvet felt desperately ill when her feet touched the weathered planks of the Bacchus. Chattering like a blue-jay, Nora dragged her below stairs, and on down a titled pine-scented hall, to the Captain's staterooms.

Nora threw open the door and whirled into the cabin. The slatted ceiling hung low, but the room was long and lusciously appointed. In truth, Velvet could not remember having ever seen it's like. Last time her feet walked these decks, she had only seen the bathing rooms, and even those had been a spectacular thing to find on any ship.

"I know," Nora said, pausing to take in Velvet's expression, "it truly is ghastly, like a drunken sultan had a seizure."

"It is an awful lot of gold," whispered Velvet, glancing at the ribboned wallpaper, and bulbous, golden scones situated in each corner of the room.

"Isn't it though? Ostentatious hubris at its finest, but the bed is soft as thistle down. I washed the sheets myself with boiling water, uncut lye, and salt. Same mixture Jerry Littleton uses to swab the deck."

"Good enough for a girl who thought she would be dead right now," Velvet said, moving to sit gingerly on the edge of the wide, four-poster bed, all mahogany, affixed to the wall with black ropes. "It's quite strange actually—I don't think many people ever truly wish for life until the second they know it's over."

Nora sighed. "Profound, and rather sad if it's true. Never mind, it's over now. The men will be about the business of setting sail, which means we will have a moment to ourselves." A giant lurch of the vessel punctuated Nora's words.

Velvet grabbed the bed's swing rope for support. Unconsciously her free hand went to her throat, her fingers inspecting its smooth contours—it had been so remarkably close.

"Don't think about all that now, you are safe," Nora said.

"It's not that, it's just…I can't get his face out of my mind."

"Henry?"

"Of course, Henry." Velvet shook her head, her fingers falling to that place that ached in her heart. "The way he looked at me when he named me a witch." She dropped her eyes, the thought of that night making her suddenly sick. Her hands fisted in the soft white of her death-dress. "I want to rip this dress from my body and watch it burn. A statesman, William Pitt, brought it to me the day I was condemned to die. He smiled and told me the white would best display my spilling blood—a victory flag if you will."

Nora tossed her hand before her face, as if the very name William Pitt, brought with it a bad smell. "Rancid man," Nora shuddered, "you can tell just by looking at him, though I have been appraised of his more nefarious acts, that creatin is perpetually up to no good."

Velvet gnawed at her lower lip. "He said he would save my life if…he wanted me to…to…"

"You don't have to finish that sentence, Velvet dear. I know exactly what he wanted—lecherous goat." Nora stood up and moved to a chest at the foot of the bed, stuffed with a various assortment of gowns. Muttering beneath her breath of men and the ills they brought, Nora rifled through the bright material until her hands settled on a soft blue gown trimmed in watered silk.

"Put this on now, and try to sleep," Nora commanded. "I'd wager you haven't had a proper shut eye in days."

"Seems like forever," sighed Velvet, standing up to cast off the dress she loathed. It was a little petty, but she took a moment to stomp it under foot. Then, she stood beside the bed shivering, hands held across her breasts, goosebumps prickled her skin as the ship lurched again. Nora shook out the dress, saying, "Bother, but I do miss Katie so! Put your arms above your head," she directed, and Velvet obeyed.

That was exactly as Devon found them, Velvet all but naked,

hands high in the air, while Nora tried rather unsuccessfully to get her arms through the flowing sleeves. Devon froze with his hand on the metal knob of the door, his mouth dropped wide as a moat.

Nora tried to move quickly, her nervous fingers hustling to stuff Velvet's limbs through the cloth—it was to no avail. Her desperate efforts only further tangled the pair of ladies. Beneath mounds of silk, Devon could hear Velvet shrieking in embarrassment. "Will you kindly make your departure?" Lord Eden, "Nora asked in an overly sweet tone, her breath tearing between her teeth.

Devon blinked, then stepped inside, and closed the door quietly behind him. "We are free of the harbor," he said, politely adverting his eyes, "I have set a course for Madagascar."

"Why on earth would we go there?" Nora hissed, as the stubborn dress finally settled over Velvet's head. Velvet stuffed her arms fully through the sleeves, momentarily blinded by blue. The skirts slid down her legs, and she kicked them in place, then stumbled to the bed as Devon turned back to face them.

Velvet lay her head down on a fluffy pillow that smelled like sea water—it was peaceful, much better than the varied, appalling scents of the London tower.

Across the room Nora spoke to Devon in low tones, and she heard words like 'hot pursuit', 'marriage contract,' and 'special license'. At one point she thought they said Henry's name, but it was difficult to be sure.

Velvet loathed to fall asleep, knowing dark dreams would come, dreams of the sword falling—the sword which had been swinging at her neck since she was a child.

Somewhere in the sleepy chaos of her mind, Velvet felt Nora move softly across the room to lie a blanket over her still form— Velvet opened her lips to say thank you, then prayed the girl somehow heard her soundless words.

~

I wish to say goodbye to you and your siren's song—yet my heart tells me to do no such thing—I will catch you before long.

Shouting internally, Henry stood and watched the Bacchus sail away—the endless sea now carrying what he coveted. Henry had made his way to the chapel after Nora's rescue, meaning to fall to his tired knees, and beg an invisible deity for aid.

Guilt and grief had faded to a dull roar in the back of his mind. At least she lived. At least the fear of that had receded. He strode under the golden arches, halting before the melancholy Madonna, but today he could not pray. Not a hint of warmth roved the stale air of this cold room—and it felt empty and echoing like the halls of an abandoned palace. In that moment Henry knew he would find no help from this silent deity he had worshiped his lifelong. Standing in the middle of the place chapel, surrounded by varied hews of muted splendor, Henry felt something inside himself break. He betrayed her, for king and country, for a dead god that never speaks.

He had wanted to rescue her, wanted deeply to call her his own. It was a hideous lie to say he did not. Nora had beaten him to the punch—and it had hurt. Some small part of himself whispered to let her go, forget his obsession, and torment her no longer— while the other, more dominant part was bursting into action, racing through plans and contingencies. Henry stormed from the chapel to the Palace stables where he saddled his own horse, then set a crushing pace for the docks.

Henry wanted more than anything just to see her once more, what words of attrition he had would be hers. He should have lifted her from her Tower room and kept the promise he had made to her so many times. Yet, to do that, he had to catch her. He rode through rainy London town, like the devil himself nipped at his heels. His destination was the London docks, and the safety of his own ship. The Siren was always ready to sail.

Intensely wrapped up in his dark, turbulent thoughts, Henry turned to ask Devon where he thought the Bacchus would first make port—then realized he was alone, only cold thick clouds of brown smog and sheets of rain walked beside him as companions. This knowledge took Henry like a punch in the gut, his own pride, and fury had broken them all. *'You should have killed me when we met—it would have been kinder'.* Painful words she had spoken which he could not get out of his mind.

Now she was his by betrayal and the laws of the land—Henry knew he would sell his soul to keep it so.

CHAPTER SIX

It was okay, I got to feel free for a single day.

November 28, 1800

Velvet stood with her toes creeping over the Fo'c'sle's edge, her body was straight, her arms outspread she boldly faced the rushing wind. It was the closest she had come to flying in a long time. Salty air stung her eyes, as she watched a fluffy cloud drift alone in the sky. It seemed like ages since she had felt so free. The sun was a hot thing, squished between the break of earth and sky. The burning orb looked slashed somewhere at the base because it bled orange and scarlet into the waves. Wild waves that ever tossed and bumped the Bacchus between their rising, falling swells.

Velvet loved the ship's rolling, it felt so much like when she had done tumble-wheels in the sky. Oft as an owl, Velvet had ridden invisible on Queenie's shoulder while the old Romani woman clung bare-back to her galloping steed. The earth and sky rushing —her wings still. It was thrilling, exultation. Standing here, at the ship's edge it all came rushing back. Soaring, wind, and flying with no wings.

The last two weeks on the Bacchus had been the best of Velvet's life to date. Nights were starry, dreams were quiet, and Nora filled her days with laughter. In times of sunlight, it was between them, like nothing unthinkable had ever occurred, yet in the silence of the night, when they sat hand in hand—the wheel at their backs, watching the moon play on the waves—the ghost of Katie always between them.

"I do not fault you, dear," Nora had said, just two nights after they first set sail.

Velvet had said nothing for she knew the words were kind lies.

"I mean it!" Nora had insisted until Velvet shook her head.

"No, I'll never forgive myself and you shouldn't either. More than that—I feel justice is coming for me. The flames of retribution always burn hot."

"Will you never use the stones again?" Nora had asked.

Velvet had locked her arms around her legs, and rested her chin on her knees, then stared up at the face of the moon. "I fear I will. I am terrified what it will mean when I do, what they might take from me this time. Yet, I must use them at least once more, to change Louis back to the prince he was born to be."

"Then, we ride to France and reclaim his throne?" Nora had asked, not sounding at all like she was joking. Her eyes grew wistful, her fingers tenderly stroking the glimmering air.

"I don't know," Velvet said honestly, "if I were to make the choice this very instant, I would say never. I want to use what remains of Queenie's gold to acquire my own ship, and set sail, destination—oblivion."

Nora had laughed, sounding like a crystal bell. "If we managed to kiss this prince and turn him human, you can have this ship, and I will set sail right beside you."

A wave broke against the front rudder and sent up a spray of orange froth. Flying droplets of silverly gold splashed Velvet's face, soaking her hair, and snapping her back to the present.

Less than three days remained before they reached Madagascar —a place where no saint was ever found, to use a map no one alive knew how to read, to find a spell no one believed was real—all to help a prince no one could see. Her life's plot was stacked against her like a crooked house of cards, all set up to follow the path of a good Greek tragedy. A shadow fell over Velvet's legs and she glanced up. Nora stood above her, tense hands looking glued to her hips.

"You must come down this instant. Devon swears a storm is coming," Nora railed, rolling flashing blue eyes as she spoke. "He is in the Captain's cabin screaming about us lashing ourselves to the headboard—like such a thing is even feasible! It's a solid slat of wood, the rope would find no purchase on that polished surface, and we will be washed to sea despite our best efforts," Nora paused to gasp in a shuddering breath. "I've never been in a storm before, I think I'm rather afraid, Devon's right, it is exhilarating."

Velvet looked up. The sky was clear, endless, seeming to stretch far beyond human conception. "He might be right, I do smell a storm, I think. My nose isn't quite what it once was."

Nora gave her a disturbed look. "People don't smell storms, Velvet dear…Oh? Wait! Really?" Her blue eyes pulled together before they rolled again. "Never mind, your brother says they do—goes to show what I know," she sighed. "Well Devon is beside himself, perhaps the three of us should go below," she said, looking at the place where Louis always glowed beside her.

Velvet held onto the helm for a tense moment, loathe to leave the open air, then she turned and began her descent to the foredeck. Nora caught her freezing hands when Velvet reached her at last. "I had a dream about Katie," Nora said. "When I woke, I thought I heard her screaming. Strange, right? I have tried not to think about it all day." She shook her head and added, "A nearly impossible task." Her hands dropped to her stomach, now showing a slight curve. "Blast! I think I'm hungry again. I believe Abigail has laid out food in the cabin," she finished, sourly.

"She still won't take her freedom?"

Nora scowled darkly. "No! Obstinate girl! I gave her a queen's ransom in gold, told her this ship would take her anywhere in the world she wished to go."

"She won't hear of it, will she?" Velvet asked.

"No. She says this ship is her home, as I am her captain."

Velvet smiled. "She's part of the crew, and her choices are her own. I think she knows you would never intentionally take advantage of her, if she feels at home here, then she should be. For some of us, just being safe for a single moment is enough."

Nora tilted her head to catch Velvet's downcast gaze. "You will never forgive yourself, will you?" she asked sadly.

Velvet sniffed, and turning away she started for the cabin. Nora followed close, her clipped steps echoing. "Why should I? Guilt is the only thing keeping me from repeating my errors."

"You might not have a choice—to repeat those errors I mean," said Nora. Behind her, Velvet could hear the rustle of crinoline and pearls as Nora shook her head. "No!" she said, her voice abrupt and sharp. "That is not an option, Louis, bringing it up again will be the fastest way to make me very cross. That particular line of discussion is closed, now and forever!"

Velvet stopped walking and glanced over her shoulder. "Is he telling you to leave him a stag?" she asked, knowing her brother well.

Nora unleashed a great gust of air, that made her lips quiver. "He says everyone has a choice, and no one is taking his into consideration."

"Really, Louis?" Velvet called to the darkness, incensed. "If you remain as you are, I will never see you again. Nora was right. This line of discussion is indeed closed. Now and forever."

Nora continued shaking her head. "He says his life is not worth the cost of your soul—when Queenie changed you, dozens of people soon died—cause and effect. He says, what is best of you may not survive his changing." Nora's face fell, like Louis's words had suddenly made sense—and frightened her.

"Don't let him get in your head," said Velvet, "any more than he already is, I mean."

Nora chewed at a piece of skin dangling from her thumb and bleeding a little. "He does make some fair points," she admitted.

Velvet threw up her hands and turned away from the pair of them. "We are talking about the rightful king of France. He cannot remain an enchanted beast forever."

Nora shrugged before she pushed in front of Velvet, then threw open the cabin door. "I like him how he is."

Velvet stormed in the room, kicking off her shoes as she went. One flew atop the wide bed, the other skittered beneath it. "What about after you deliver the baby, when you become blind as me?" Velvet asked, throwing herself on the thick duvet.

Nora visibly paled. "We certainly can't have that," she said.

"Precisely." Velvet grabbed a fluffy pillow and cuddled it to her chest.

Nora placed her hand on the silver knob and looked pointedly through the door to the glimmering shadows that moved like spilling ink. "In or out," she said, then, "no I won't! Fine! Have it your way," she finished. Cheeks heating like blazing coal, she slammed the door shut.

The trail of Nora's silver cloak flew wide as she strode angrily to the fragrant trays of food set out neatly in the attaching stateroom, decorated between a set of flushed divans. She took a dainty seat on the gold-striped upholstery, her trousers pulling tight over her slender thighs. Velvet watched her lift various lids and press her nose close to the steaming plates. "Asparagus, in white wine and garlic sauce, your favorite," Nora called. Lifting a square of cornbread, she took a generous bite. The fluffy confection squished like a sponge and made Velvet's stomach roar.

"Ship ahoy! Ship Ahoy! Twelve knots east, coming up fast! Ship ahoy!" The call came from above deck, Nora gasped, her body flinching from the urgency of the sharp cry, then she stood, furiously chewing her bite of corn bread. Velvet launched herself from the bed, and began to search for her other shoe, at the same time, the door flew open, and slapped the wall; strained hinges screamed.

"The Siren," panted Devon, bent at the waist, hands on his knees.

"Bloody hell and bastards on a biscuit!" Nora raged.

"The Siren?" Velvet dared, fearing she already knew.

Devon gave her a measured look, as if he were deciding how much to tell her. Velvet made a frustrated sound and threw up her hands, he relented. "Henry," he said, then spun to Nora. "He'll be abreast of us in less than an hour. The Bacchus is fast, but she does not hold a candle to the Siren at full mast. She is a battleship, built for speed and ramming, this is a merchant's vessel."

"Henry would never," screeched Nora as one of her hands flared up. "Oh, the hell do I know what that man would do anymore?"

"We can fight him," said Devon, face grim, "though I wouldn't advise it."

"You would do that? Both of you? He is a brother to you, Nora," said Velvet, striving to be the voice of reason, even though she wanted with all her heart to punch the duke, squarely on his perfect jaw.

Nora momentarily spluttered over her answer. "He...he, he turned you in, let Lord Byron put his filth infested hands on you—"

"Not to mention the ultimate betrayal at your trial, these are not the actions of a brother," said Devon, raising his brows for emphasis. "There are many variables, but one thing is for certain, he is here for you, and I have no idea if he desires your life or death."

"Either way, if we want to keep her, we must fight," Nora said.

Velvet placed cold hands that held a sudden tremble over her eyes. "I have suffered much from that one, but I don't want anyone else dying for me. I have debts to pay, not the least of them to the both of you." She dropped her hands and looked deep in Nora's violet eyes. "Nothing more will happen to you, not because of me."

Nora gave Velvet an obstinate scowl. "I believe the duke will force my involvement when he presently attacks my ship."

Velvet gave a glad cry when she finally found her slipper, then sat down to put it on. "He will not need to attack, not if I willingly surrender, however," she grunted, struggling to get the edge of her lacy slipper over the arch in her heel. "If I must be dragged to perdition, I will not do so barefoot." She sighed, as the shoe finally slipped in place. "What about Alfonso?" she asked on a thought.

Devon's scowl turned thunderous. "The bastard continues to be more trouble than he's worth."

"Does he know who betrayed me to the English king? Does he

know about my map? The jewels? I would of course ask him all these things myself, if only you would agree to let me speak to him."

"I am trying to protect you," said Devon, "as many of my misbegotten quests, it remains a nearly impossible task, and no, he refuses to say anything, though I suspect he knows a great deal. He speaks to me at times of Queenie's exploits—I believe they were well acquainted—talks of ancient tribes of Romani who once roamed the moors, and the secrets they knew—though, unless it is complete tripe, he refuses to share." Devon pinched the bridge of his nose. "The man speaks incessantly of all the wrong things. I have not used any methods of real torture yet, just inflicted the filthy hold on him. I also have him on a strict diet of bread and water."

"It's not enough!" Nora said.

"Ugh!" Devon shuddered with a series of almost delicate twitches, "just the rats alone would be enough to send me running for confession."

Velvet could not help but smile at his consistent attention to drama. "What are we going to do?" she asked, catching Nora's gaze as it flicked to the velvet bag of stones lying atop the ornate vanity, standing near the tall dressing screen.

"No!" Velvet said instantly.

Nora had no response to the outburst. Her eyes stayed locked on the jewels as slowly she stood and walked across the room.

"No!" Velvet cried again, rushing forward, and reaching out to snatch the bag away. Nora was quicker, curling her fingers around the careful stitching, lifted it in her hand, tested the weight against her palm. "I am sure one of these in here could form some type of defense. Maybe a storm, or a blinding fog," she said, studiously ignoring Velvet's outbursts.

"Nora," interjected Devon, "having Henry on our tail is trouble enough, must you really invite minions of the devil to join the fray?"

"The devil my pretty left foot! This is earth magic," snapped Nora.

"It still demands a price," Velvet said, trying to keep her breathing calm, "one we have found to be dear!"

Nora paused, then set the bag down, precious stones clinked and chimed. "Just considering all our options."

Velvet threw the gems a venomous look. "Those stones are not one of them. I will surrender to Henry, then you and Devon will take Louis to St. Mary."

"I don't think we can do this without you," Nora said.

Velvet almost smiled. When Nora was stressed her pretty wash of freckles all looked like tiny strawberries. "You can, you have the stones, the map, and your first-rate brain, Spencer and your entire household, who wouldn't dream of being left behind, Devon, even Abigale."

Nora cast her eyes to the fireplace, and the hulking black monster sleeping before it. "Yes," said Velvet softly, "you'll have Cerberus, he will protect Louis with his life, you too, I think." Cerberus twitched his ears when he heard his name spoken, he looked up to assess the trouble with big, watery eyes and found nothing of interest. Licking his lips, he lay his head back down on his giant paws, looking bored.

"A sell sword, a lady, a dog, and a stolen woman." Devon shook his head. "Like a circus of errors. I won't say our chances of survival are strong because I do so hate to lie, yet, if we all go down in flames at least it will be a worthy adventure. You know how I crave those—it has always been my most fervent desire to go out in a blaze of glory."

"Then we fight," Nora said, "we arm ourselves and refuse to let him take her!"

Devon shrugged. "Not at all what I meant, but sure—we could die that way too, not so much a blaze of glory, that. More a blade to the chest from the hand of the friend," he finished with a bitter grimace, his expression crestfallen as Velvet had ever seen it.

"Oh, Devon!" Nora said, "maybe you can go to him, talk to him? Make the bastard see reason."

"Sadly, making the duke see reason has always stood beyond my scope of abilities. From what you both said, even a damn magic stone was unable to fully bend Henry to its power—I assure you; I will have no greater success. Besides, the urge to beat him senseless might obliterate rational on my part."

"Is there any way at all that we could win?" Nora asked, moving till she stood, looking up at Devon. "I have nearly fifty murderous pirates, and I have you." Her hands fluttered down to rest on his shoulders, his height and brawn dwarfing her. Devon's eyes went soft as he looked at her. "Nora, I don't want you to get hurt."

"Please, Devon, I want to fight."

Velvet felt her own cause failing wretchedly, and knew she had to make a last ditch try.

Devon spoke first. "Nora, love," he said gently, brushing the back of his gloved knuckles against her rosy cheek. "I've known you through ballrooms and battlefields. I am a member of your crew, you the pirate captain queen, my sword is yours if you demand it."

"For no good reason," snapped Velvet, angered at the touching scene, something about it seemed far too final for her liking. Her eyes flicked—against her will—to the bag of treacherous stones before she looked violently away.

With some aguish in her tone, Nora said. "I can't have come all this way just to lose her after all."

Devon stepped back and placed a kiss on her brow. "Very well then." He gave her a fine salute and said, "Aye, aye, Captain, your wish is my command."

"Only I know nothing of battle or the sea. Our continued life spans are all up to you now," sighed Nora.

"I will consider them my number one responsibility, and a feat for an angel." He cast Nora a smile chalk full of devastating charm. "Considering the bang-up job, I've done this far, I have great faith in my future efforts."

"Your sarcasm is neither appreciated nor desired," Nora said sweetly.

"*Ship ahoy! Ship ahoy!*" the topside voice called again. "*Five knots, moving full speed ahead.*"

Nora audibly caught her breath. "Moment of truth," she muttered, and Velvet felt the words like led stones in her gut.

"Stay down here, both of you!" said Devon, "lock the door, and don't open it for anyone but myself," he finished, then his head whipped about like he had been nipped by a bee. "Did you hear that?"

Nora cocked her head. "Hear what?"

"Amazing grace, I hear...notes," Devon said softly, then closed his eyes, and moved his fingers through the air like he stroked the keys of an invisible piano. Astonishment softened the contours of his boyishly handsome face.

Velvet listened for all she was worth—yet heard nothing but the endless crash of waves breaking against the hull.

Devon blinked. "I'm becoming maudlin in my old age," he observed, his eyes again searching the room, a wrinkle in his brow. "I'll be up on the deck if either of you have need of me, attempting to own the role of knight in shining armor. I know it goes against your very natures, but it would help if you both played the part of damsel in distress. In times like this a little screaming and hiding would not be amiss."

Nora snorted. "I would sooner surrender to my father's executioner, than behave like a ninny."

"Of course," said Devon solemnly, "I can't imagine at all what I was thinking." He sighed. "I must have momentarily allowed my mind to dream."

Nora snorted. "See that it doesn't happen again."

Head bowed and shoulders shaking, Devon turned and started for the door.

BROKEN GLASS

You are the thing I want the most—yet I know you will fight me to the bitter end. I ride with the angel's and all their hosts—just the touch of our bodies will trouble amend.

*H*enry stood at the helm. Stars at his back, night wind rushing through his hair—eyes trained on his target. The moon was bright, the waves moving, and he could smell a storm in the air, even hear it in the forewarning groans of the Siren's bones. Sixteen agonizing days of pursuit, he should have caught up long before now. It was the damnedest thing, the second his crew would spot the black sails of the Bacchus, flapping high on the horizon—was the very moment she would vanish in smoke, as if the world as flat after all, and in a strange link of repeating time, the Bacchus continually fell off its steepest edge. Like some ancient spell of invisibility fueled its boilers. His men were gathered on the forecastle, ready for battle in full crimson regalia, red-coats buttoned high, rope-gold trim on their fitted white breaches. Royal British Navy all.

Paul Ritchie, a man who had stood beside Devon and Henry during the Siege of Yorktown, when they were just boys of nine and eleven, riding with the duke's—his father's party, cleaning rifles and carting gunpowder. Paul had only been seventeen at the time, Henry made him first-mate nearly a decade ago and had not regretted his decision for a second. Weathered, and strong as the vessel under foot, the man was loyal and intelligent enough to trip-up a world class philosopher. He was standing a few feet in front of Henry, staring at him through hooded eyes, both dark as hammered iron. "The boats are ready, Captain, we are less than two knots out."

"Good, give the order to come about," said Henry.

"The Bacchus rides with twelve guns, and they dropped in position not fifteen minutes ago. I think they mean to fight," said Ritchie.

"Forget the guns, they have Lady N. I know they'll fight," said Henry, pushing his dark hat down on his head, and pulling his mask over his mouth and nose. He spoke through it. "I want minimal casualties—the first man who lays a finger on Lady N. or the princess, will be the first to die."

Ritchie glanced up at the cloudless sky, overrun with glittering stars. "Storms coming," he said, then, "what are your orders regarding Lord Eden?"

Henry grunted. "I believe Devon can take care of himself, don't you?"

"Believe it like gospel." Ritchie laughed. "The men say the two of you made a deal with Satan, while trapped in that Spanish hell you found yourselves in a few years back."

Henry gave the man a quelling look. "To what end?"

"Immortality," said Ritchie, like such things were normal.

"In exchange for?" demanded Henry.

"Your soul, of course," Ritchie said simply.

"Horseshit," said Henry.

Paul affected a pensive façade. "Well, I don't rightly know, your plans are diabolical at times, and despite your overbearing size, you remain a rather competent spy,"

"Thanks," Henry said pointedly.

"And you are incredibly difficult to kill. I know a fair few who have died trying—" continued Ritchie, like Henry had not spoken. "Stranger things have happened on a Tuesday," he finished.

"Too much rum and moonlight has made you lose your damn mind," said Henry.

"Not I, Captain," Ritchie exclaimed, the lines bracketing his eyes deepened with humor. "You are the one who plans to sneak on a pirate ship with only a handful of men, and a half-baked plan. Lets reserve judgement on mental competence, until we see how this scheme of yours plays out."

"It's the only way to take her without bloodshed," said Henry.

Ritchie's mouth curled up at one corner. "A mercenary with a conscience, how refreshing," he exclaimed.

"You're in rare form tonight," Henry observed darkly.

Ritchie shrugged, his striped shirt stretching tight over his slight paunch. "It's not every day one plots to steal a princess," he said, the tone of his voice borderline gleeful.

"She is my wife, you know we were married by proxy—if there was theft committed, it is already done."

Rhee, the deck swab, a skinny boy with red cheeks, and hair like a mudslide rushed up the quarterdeck stairs. "Less than a knot now, Captain," he panted, his little shoulders rising and falling in rapid, broken beats. "The boats have been lowered," he said, then smirked, and added, "fat Duval says you're up here losing your nerve sir, so Clattery punched him in the face—Duval's nose popped right good. Blood all over the oars—you better get down there, sir," he said.

Ritchie shook his head. "It begins," he muttered, then, "you know, they say it's bad luck to bring a woman abord a war vessel."

"Stupid superstition," snapped Henry, "at any rate, can't be any worse than the nasty brand of luck I bring all on my own. No," Henry held up a hand, stalling Ritchie's words, "do not say anything, I beg you. I have had my fill of your endless wisdom tonight, when we drop the plank, raise the parle flag. I will do the rest."

"I know, that's what I'm afraid of," sighed Ritchie, as Henry followed Rhee to the small boats bobbing in the dark water below.

"I heard that!" yelled Henry, suddenly needing to pitch his voice over the rising wind. Ritchie's ringing laugh echoed as Henry swung his legs over the rail—it followed him down to the deep.

~

"Parle?" screeched Nora, lowering her spyglass, and scowling ferociously. "I thought that word was only used in novels, honestly!" she huffed.

"I don't trust it," said Devon, taking the glass from Nora and putting it to his own eye before squinting the other.

"Knowing Henry, he probably has some ratchet trick up his sleeve," moaned Nora. "Do you even see Henry, I only saw his first mate, Paul is it? One can never be sure, the duke collects fighting men, like I collect shoes—always purchase the best, and buy in quantity."

"Parle?" Velvet wanted to know.

"A supposedly peaceful discussion between two captains, mainly they consist of harsh words, insults exchanged—"

"And normally preclude bloodshed," said Devon, cutting smoothly over Nora's words. "If the case is you and Henry in a room alone together—bloodshed will be a forgone conclusion."

"You say that, as if that's a bad thing," said Nora, lifting her prim nose. "And harsh if you mean it. I can be reasonable."

Devon's eyes narrowed. "Lord, Nora, even you can hardly say that with a straight face. Now, will you please go below? I expressly forbade you to come up here, did you listen, no! How can I fight if my only concern is you?" He turned to Velvet, his open expression pleading. "Please, in a few seconds it won't be safe for her and the babe, up here. No matter what Henry's intentions are, the good fellows of the Bacchus will want to fight."

"Want to?" shrieked Nora, "if they hesitate even for a second, I will command them to." Her hand disappeared into the front of her fur-lined blue cape; the hood embroidered in hot red flowers that matched her waving hair. From silky, pleated folds, she withdrew the heavy black bag Velvet knew so well. Unconsciously, Velvet stumbled, backing away like Nora presented the most noxious of all poisons. Nora held the bag out to Velvet.

She shook her head, backing further away, her hand flying up to her mouth, her teeth sinking in the skin over her knuckles till it bubbled.

"Take it," Nora said.

"No…I won't…I can't."

"You must," Nora demanded, then glanced to her right and sighed. "Do shut up, Louis." She put her fingers to her temples and pressed delicately. "I declare, your running commentary is not helping at all. I won't to be in a world where you disappear. There is no choice now, not for any of us, maybe there never has been."

"What is he saying?" Velvet whispered, taking another stilted step back, keeping a wary eye on the deadly bag, clasped in Nora's steady hand.

"He agrees with your unnecessary theatrics and says the stones are too dangerous," said Nora, not taking her eyes from Louis. His glow danced over her face, making her wide eyes luminous as the full moon.

"He's right," Velvet said.

Nora rolled her eyes heavenward. "Nonsense, where is the brave, daring woman who turned a room full of grown men into a pack of her very own dancing monkeys?"

"She killed her friend," said Velvet in a voice wretched and bitter.

"Take it," said Nora.

Velvet almost growled. "No!"

"Take it!"

"No!"

"Oh, for the love of God!" Devon exploded. He snatched the bag from Nora and upended it into his palm. Eight glimmering stones fell, ocean starlight washed through their prismed centers, and cast jagged beams of multi-colored light over his face. "Pretty," he said reverently, but quickly glanced away. "Your father has a thousand of these—I really don't see what all the fuss is about."

"Not exactly like those," Nora said slowly. "I think you should put those away, and better not to think of anything specific while you're doing so."

"Rather ordinary, boring things, I say. Except for the amethyst, why do I feel like it's looking at me?" Devon asked.

Velvet swallowed a gulp of air and felt like streamers of ice slid down her spine. "Because it probably is," she whispered.

Devon poured the stones back in their bag and, hardly giving the shiny rocks a second glance, with an impatient jerk, he shoved the gems in the stitched lining of his jerkin. To Nora he said, "I swear to give them over directly to Velvet's care if I feel all is lost." With those words, he turned away, and strode to the helm. "Raise the mainsail," he said, his voice swayed by the rising gale. "Drag anchor and prepare to be boarded." Devon spun on his heels, his eyes already flashing, his mind preparing for a fight. "Spencer," he called loudly now, for the wind was beginning to wail. "Please escort your lady below stairs—by force if necessary."

Spencer nodded, then moved cautiously, the right railing clutched in a white-knuckled hand—still garbed in his strict black and white livery, and well cropped silver hair, his face was a blend of shadows, shifting and jumping with his slightly uneven gait. "Come, my lady," he said calmly, his chocolate eyes kind. Nearly stumbling, he reached her, and took her freezing hands between his own.

Nora hesitated, loathe to disagree with Spencer. Velvet watched her throw Devon a filthy look—that if it could have killed would have reduced him to simmering ash, for turning her best man on her.

"Nora, I won't let a thing happen to Velvet, you know that. If necessary, we will fight," said Devon.

"Very well," Nora muttered, linking her fingers around Spencer's extended arm, she continued to hiss beneath her breath, as Spencer escorted her away.

Velvet remained, and caught Devon's raised, then wriggling brows. She shook her head. "No. If you want me to be cloistered somewhere safe you can bloody well drag me there yourself, I don't have any beloved butters who have been with me since birth who will calmly escort me away, I think they are all traitors, or dead."

Devon flashed her a toothy smile. "Never thought it for a moment, dear girl, you are after all the coveted prize—the beautiful bait extraordinaire." He unsheathed one of his swords and flipped it in his hand, so his nimble fingers caught the edge of the slender, shiny blade, then handed it to her, hilt first.

Velvet closed her fingers over the delicately twined metal. The weight of the sword felt good, as did the rocking deck beneath her feet. The sails snapped, flapping hard as they were pulled down and strapped to their posts, the anchor fell and the great ship shuddered, then did as commanded.

"Come about!" someone yelled. Devon tugged at the wheel, it spun and caught.

"Drop the plank," another cried.

A cloud slipped over the moon, and it dripped silver on the waves. The darkness thickened, so vivid it was almost intimate. Devon's hair, now grown to his shoulders, blew like angel feathers in the chill wind. "I don't want bloodshed," she said, squinting through the black to see his eyes. Her skin felt like it rippled. Animalistic senses her humanity had not fully been able to suppress, returned with a wash of chills. "I know Nora would fight to the death, but I..."

Devon released the wheel, and walked to her, caught her hands in his. "You are Marie Antoinette's daughter, and I fear bloodshed is your birthright." His tone was soft, then he cast her a rakish smile and winked. "You were born to rule, all good leaders eventually bathe their blades in blood, it's the dastardly way of our times. No matter, you and I shall meet it head on. Draw up your hood and stay hidden for now." Devon stepped back, his hand going to his chest. "God's blood, are these jewels of yours comprised of lead? Blast, the weight of them is messing with my balance. I fear I must ask..."

"No," Velvet said, "they are far safer with you than anyone—" she shrugged, "no darkness in your soul, none at all I'm afraid."

Devon snorted. "The little you know."

Velvet smiled at him, drawing up her hood. "I think you are more than strong enough to carry them. Why is Henry not with the men crossing?"

"I believe our crafty duke is currently scaling the stout frame of the Bacchus with a few of his best men—it's what I would do."

Velvet stepped back, her legs struck the uneven slats of a high wooden box, her feet got tangled in a length of hemp rope, all coiled up like a cobra. "Do you think he may already be aboard?"

Devon shrugged. "If not yet then nearly. Stay where you are, keep a wary eye, I'll see what the envoy has to say." Ajax moved to stand at Devon's back, his double-sided axe playing with fringes of moonlight.

A hush fell over the gathered men, as the taut plank suspended over black water, creaked. Not a soul moved when a dozen ducal soldiers marched across, all wearing the Newcastle crest.

Velvet could see the emblazoned coat of arms proudly displayed on the red lapels of that regiment standard coat she loathed. They marched in a singular formation. Rifles held high, bayonets stabbing the darkness. The man at the front of the line had hair like a silver fox, backswept and glimmering. His face was jowl free, and solemn, but his deep brown eyes looked kind.

"Lord Eden," he called amicably, jumping lithely from the bouncing plank, disturbing the precarious weight, making a few of the others behind him cast their arms out for balance.

"Ritchie, my good man!" Devon hailed. The men clasped hands for a long second before Ritchie stepped away and braced his arms behind his back.

"I see he sent his best weapon in first," laughed Devon. "Always the tactician, our Henry."

Ritchie nodded; his next words fell like dynamite on Velvet's ears. "I hate to be the bearer of this particular news, especially since I feel she is not far—but the Duke has married the princess by proxy, he's here to lay claim his bride."

"I heard rumors," said Devon. "I never believed, not really—Henry, married?"

Velvet sat down on the crate. Feeling shocked as Devon sounded. She had no idea what 'proxy' meant, but she knew the word 'married', knew—and revolted to it wholeheartedly. She bit down on the back of her hand to stifle all her sounds. Marry, Henry? The hand not being gnawed on went to her chest—her reality felt altered. Shock parched her throat. Marry, Henry. The man who had betrayed her, not once, but twice? Never! He would first need raise her bones to ash. Shaking in dark silence, Velvet scanned the lines of the Bacchus for sight of him, her eyes searching out familiar faces in the gathering crowd of brigands.

When her gaze returned to Devon, it was to see his arms crossed over his chest, and his head shaking out an adamant negative.

"Nora will never consent to that, and these rowdy men below take their marching orders from hers. Besides—what about Velvet, has she no say in this?"

Ritchie looked mildly distressed, his silver hair blowing about his clenched jaw. "No, she does not. It is the king's decree. The duke means to claim his prize at any cost."

"As we will furiously defend it," argued Devon.

Velvet slumped back, the shot of adrenaline the shock had brought faded to a bone deep exhaustion. She wiped a hand across her clammy brow. Would it never be over? More yelling, more fighting. It was up to her and her alone, to stave off more senseless loss by giving herself over like a lamb to the slaughter. Marry, Henry, Velvet shook her head. Spirits of earth and sky, she would not submit to this madness.

Taking care to make no sound, Velvet leaned down to tighten the laces on her brown leather boots, which ran all the way to her knees, beneath her layered white skirt, two daggers strapped her thighs. Two more hid in the sleeves of her fitted leather coat, pressing deep in the silk of her white blouse. She was ready to battle the devil. She would give herself to him—pretend submission, then fight on her own time—when other lives were not at stake. Ever was he after her, like a predator, a stalking panther.

Poised on the edge of decision, Velvet was unprepared for the loud crash, proceeded by a gunpower explosion that painted the air red. There was another, like crystal shattering on ice, sharp and ringing. More eruptions, one after another, thick, acrid smoke replaced the red.

She lifted the white scarf she had tied around her neck up to fully cover her mouth and moved to peer over the top rail. Shouts rang out against the enthusiastic crackle of fresh flames. Rum bottles stuffed with lit strips of cloth flew up and over the side of the Bacchus, smashed against the forecastle, rolled to detonate against the quarterdeck below.

Pirates scrambled from the path of the missiles, they spun,

confused—looking for an enemy to fight, while still others struggled to extinguish the flames.

To her left Devon was shouting, towering over Ritchie, shaking head and fists in the man's face. "I would fight you now if I didn't know for certain that you hated this plan at its inception!" he railed.

Ritchie said nothing. Shock tugged a downward trajectory on his wrinkles as he watched the orange flames eating at the main deck.

Velvet realized from the look in his eyes—the Siren's first mate had not known the full extent of the duke's plan. Additional men presently scaling the Bacchus's rough side, began to jump aboard, swords swinging, the red coats of their rank colored well to hide the blood they spilled. Pirates shouted loud cries—even their own names—and the battle dance began among the leaping flames.

The rail creaked under her white-knuckled hand, Velvet wanted to be down there, fighting alongside the ones who protected her without knowing her at all. Just as she was preparing herself to completely disobey Devon, feeling that forgiveness would be far easier to come by then permission—she felt him.

Chills raced over her skin, tickled the fine hairs at the base of her neck. There was a ringing in her ears that had nothing to do with the explosions or flames. All her senses hummed, like she was a golden harp, and someone had plucked her strings. Her eyes flew up. She saw him, dark as a slice of the night, his every motion the epitome of stealth. He swung his legs over the rail and was standing in the same motion. Black smoke surged beside him. A man with a bright crop of red hair—his broad face terrifying over the elaborate lace trim of his full, white-ruffed shirt—dove at Henry, a dagger in his raised hand. Henry nimbly stepped from the path of danger and thwacked the man on the back of his head with the hilt of his silver sword. The man crumbled like an old statue, instantly senseless he sprawled at Henry's feet.

"Henry! Enough! This is not a parle, this is an all-out attack, call your men off and I will do the same," yelled Devon, staring down at his one-time friend.

Velvet thought Devon cut a forlorn figure against the backdrop of recently gathered clouds, wearing his sorrow like a shroud. Regardless of what Nora had wanted, Velvet knew Devon had prayed it would not come to this.

"I think it's too late for that," Velvet heard Henry say, his deep voice beguiling as liquid silk.

Velvet could sit in the shadows no longer. She lifted her sword and shifted her mental direction to that of battle alone, shut out everything else, save what she was about to do. Wheeling around, Velvet charged for the twisted stairs to her right, leading down to the main deck—and found herself unexpectedly lost.

A white fog, thick and moving, wet as a wool blanket left out in the rain, fell atop her like an invisible avalanche—she could not speak, see, or move. Men cried out as they too were blinded. The wet cotton extended to Velvet's ears, stuffing them up like a dam. It was everywhere, sticky, grasping stuff that made simple movement nearly impossible.

There was magic in the air, of that Velvet was beyond certain—but not her magic. This was another thing entirely, something old and ghostly. In the depths of this fallen cloud, a voice rose—soft and lilting, making more cold chills run up and down Velvet's arms. The words were clear, Velvet had heard this song only once, beside Queenie's grave amidst the burnt bones of her family. *'I once was lost, but now am found, was blind, but now I see'*. Sang in the same voice she remembered well. Velvet held her breath until it burned, the haunting song continued, as the notes swept over the ship, cracking flames stopped their burning, the clash and slash of blades hushed.

"Devon," Velvet said, using her best imitation of Nora's whispered shout. "Devon, are you doing this?" Her voice rippled like she spoke beneath the dark waves. No human voice answered her question, only the high, ringing notes coming from the ghost who serenaded them all.

The song did not so much stop as drift away, like an eagle's cry on a windy mountaintop. For a time, as the thick white mists dissipated, and the last notes faded, all was deathly silent.

Velvet's vision cleared, she saw him again, in fact her eyes went nowhere else. He had moved to the helm, to yell a thing at Devon

—moonlight ran down his profile, reflecting in his stormy eyes, turning them black as his wild hair. Around her, Velvet could see the Siren's crew had their own at a disadvantage. Three of the pirates in particular, Philip the cook, Penny—an Ethiopian warrior, fierce as he was massive, and Ajax the strongest of them all, were on their knees. Ajax's axe was in the hand of a man who held a pistol at his face.

Some muddled sense of self-preservation had Velvet scooting back into the safety of her shadow, wanting to surrender, and so afraid to willingly give herself over to Henry's indomitable power.

"My lady Antoinette," shouted Henry, glancing way too near the spot where she huddled. "No one wants this, Velvet, you can put a stop to it, no one else need be hurt, all you have to do is leave with me."

The authoritarian command in his voice made Velvet want to roll her eyes the way Nora did when something was just too much to cope with. Velvet took a deep breath; afraid she may be, but she was no coward, and had vowed to herself no more would die.

She straightened her spine, glaring at his harsh profile, and stepped from her hiding place, taking care not to trip on the coiled rope. "I am here," she said, her voice clear and cold as an arctic gale. "Tell your men to stand down, I leave with you willingly."

Henry's head snapped in her direction; his eyes linked with hers. He looked furious, yet his lips were lifted at the corners in his wicked, slightly crooked smile. Not taking his gaze from her face, he dropped in a low bow.

"Like a martyr to her pyre," he said, and the ghastly man actually had the audacity to laugh.

Velvet could taste the hot blade of rage cutting through her chest. "Sheathe your sword, Henry, Devon has nothing to do with what's between us."

Her words made his eyes smolder. "In that we agree," he said. The way he looked at her seemed sinful, and she feared all men present knew the thoughts in his mind. Velvet could feel blood rising in her cheeks, but she refused to drop her eyes. She would not give him the satisfaction of knowing how much she feared him, would not let him see how the pain he had caused tore her apart. Point of fact, Velvet wanted to rush and slap the mocking smile off his handsome face with a good, open-handed hit.

Instead, she lifted her voice so all present would hear it. "Put your weapons down," she said, placing her own sword on the deck. She held up her hands. "I go willingly."

Ritchie lowered his sword, but Devon held his to the man's chest for a moment longer—both men were smiling. Velvet shook her head knowing she would never understand that gender. They were truly a species all on their own. Ritchie looked pointedly down the sword leveled at his heart, Devon shrugged, then sheathed it, and turned to her.

"It might be for the best, love," he said, moving to stand near her. Velvet reached for him, and he took her hand, squeezed it hard. "Henry won't hurt you, Velvet."

"He already has." She sighed, her mouth felt dry and hot. "What you mean to say is he will not hurt me again, and in that you are correct." She paused, fighting not to bite at her lip.

"Best go down to him now," said Devon, eyeing Henry. "Best make it quick, for I am not sure how much longer Spencer can sit on Nora, if she breaks free and makes it up here—we both know all hell will break loose."

"Indeed." Velvet sighed, her eyes returning to Henry and his villainous simile. He was in control, held all the winning cards and knew it. She sighed deeply. "To the devil I go."

"We will come for you, better time, better place," said Devon.

"No, take Louis to St. Mary, I don't matter, only him," Velvet said, then leaned in to place an impulsive kiss on Devon's cheek. "Take care of my stones for me, I'll find you soon and collect them," she whispered.

Devon touched her hand gently. "I pray that's a promise."

"My lady, we all breathlessly await your pleasure," said Henry.

Velvet wanted to bare her teeth at him. She took hold of her skirt's ruffled hem and began her descent that would take her to the man she dreamed of. Face hard as stone and only dark intention shining in his humorless eyes.

CHAPTER EIGHT

You rendered me to ash, and still, I crave your flame.
You crash into me and I die, once in a lifetime,
a comet in my sky.

*V*elvet huddled, sandwiched between half a dozen red coats, Henry sat opposite her, at the stern of the small boat he rowed. His arms moving in and out, so the paddles splashed and pulled at the moon-kissed waves. Dancing silver reflections crisscrossed his face, jumped in his eyes. Velvet could feel her fingertips biting into the top of her thighs as she bristled under his unwavering stare. It was a struggle to keep her composure.

"You're wearing this moment like a hair shirt, my love," said Henry, his smile was biting, "I know submission and surrender are not in your vocabulary much less your nature," he observed, and Velvet wanted to spit in his eye.

The man directly to her left, wiry body pressed up against her arm, lowered his head and cast her a wink. He was young and handsome, clearly of Spanish descent, but the red coat he wore did much to diminish his boyish charm. "Aye, Captain, 'tis a live keg of powder you've got your self here," he quipped.

The man on her right sat back and shoved his hands in his shallow pockets and laughed. "Yep, a veritable firecracker, sir," he said.

The moon bounced off the sailor's head making the clubbed back hair there gleam white as snow—the hot absence of color bolstered his cheery smile. "You'll be right comfortable on the Siren, Your Grace. She's one of the finest vessels to roam the British seas," he said.

Velvet saw he had a thin white scar that ran from the corner of his left eye down to the tip of his nose, and a perfect dimple in both cheeks, something about the boy reminded her of Devon.

"I am not concerned with my comfort, sir, I merely wish to conclude this unfortunate business with the duke and return to my people," she said, then watched the boy's face go strangely blank, the scar on his cheek turned beet-red, and his lips struggled not to quiver. He made a fist and punched his chest; then roughly cleared his throat and spoke like he could not help doing anything but. "What business is that, Your Grace?'

It was obvious the boy was fighting a smile; it was not obvious why. Velvet felt a stupid, burning blush rising to her own cheeks, and lifted her chin. "Whatever I must do so he will release me."

A couple snickers followed her words. The boy coughed again, his scar now pulsing, red as a ripe tomato.

"I'm sure whatever he has in mind will not take that long," she said, wondering what on earth they all found so amusing. Unconscious that she was delivering an insult of the highest order.

Henry grimaced. "Now you malign me, madam," he said, his hot eyes grazing over her face.

Good, Velvet thought, though she had no idea how or why.

"Do you know what this business is?" asked the boy to her left, not bothering at all to hide his smile.

"I cannot imagine, though I feel certain it will be something both of us will regret," she said primly.

One of the older men sitting near Henry, gave up the fight, threw back his bushy head, and laughed aloud. "Said many a bride to a groom, eh?" he chortled, elbowing Henry in the ribs. "They say...enjo...enjoyment grows over time, Your Grace," he said, guffawing like a fool.

The blood in Velvet cheeks was boiling. "I seriously doubt that will be the case...and why, why do you keep calling me that? I will never consent to marry your duke," she finished, looking at Henry as she said the words. He returned her stare, his eyes so intense, she was forced to drop her own.

The boy with the scar sobered and shook his head. "But you are, Your Grace. You are a duchess, married to the duke of Newcastle by proxy not a fortnight ago," he said. At her look of horrid distress, he rushed on, "Not to fear my lady, it is often done."

Henry's indigo eyes snapped. "Her grace is not afraid, she is bloody furious, isn't that right, Velvet?"

"You know me too well, Your Grace," she spat between her teeth. Henry flexed his massive arms and moved the oars, beneath his tailored black coat, the muscles tensed and flexed. Breathtaking and strong. Again, Velvet was reminded of a panther on the prowl, and felt herself shudder. The devil was purported to be beautiful and possessed of a heartbreaking charm that dragged Eve to disaster. Henry's charm, and tender smile had disarmed her once, and she vowed it would not do so again.

"I will never be your wife," she said calmly, making sure he saw the truth in her eyes.

The boy on her right leaned in again, so his raised scar nearly brushed her cheek. "You are wed in name only."

Velvet faced him, knowing her deep befuddlement was showing. "I beg your pardon?" she managed to gasp.

"You must consummate your vows before the church will recognized their validity," the boy said, the words like crashing symbols in her ears.

Velvet made a disgruntled sound, felt her raised brows reaching to touch her hairline, and the scared boy rolled his huge amber eyes. "If you do not wish for this marriage, you must keep yourself from his bed," he said, jerking a thumb in Henry's direction.

"Zoe," Henry called, giving the scared boy a level look. Zoe only smiled and gave Velvet another wink. "Just thought the lady should know all her options, Captain—it's the only way she can make a fair battle plan," he said, smiling at her with a kind smile. Unexpected from a red coat. Henry's expression darkened. Zoe shrugged and carried on speaking. "Seems fair, seeing we tied her hands and ferried her off against her will."

Henry said nothing, though his glare grew quite terrifying. Zoe did not seem phased by his captain's stormy mood in the slightest. He crossed his arms over his chest and settled deep into whatever warmth their closely pressed bodies would afford.

The wind increased her pace, reaching under Velvet's clothes to shake her very bones. She gathered her bound hands to her heart, tucked her chin to her knuckles, and tried to brace against the chill.

Soon, the waves bashing the tanned sides of their small vessel crew choppy and white-tipped. The rowing men began to pant, perspiration broke on their brows. Only Henry seemed to remain unaffected, he continued to row when the others paused to switch off, take a glug from the communal skin of wine, or rub their wrists.

The boat's endless rocking soothed Velvet, her eyelids fluttered...when next they opened, Henry was standing over her, hands on his narrow hips, like some ancient conqueror intent on claiming his virgin prize. The rocking boat and cold wind was gone, she was lying in a warm, soft bed atop a thick feather tick that smelled like roses. It was so comfortable, she wanted to snuggle down in the fluff and stay forever. She wiggled her toes, they were cold—her boots had been removed, which was odd, at least she could still feel the weight of the daggers strapped to her thighs.

Velvet came fully awake with a breathless jolt—like she always did—sitting up and scrambling back drawing her knees to her chest. Henry watched her useless retreat, his eyes missing nothing. He wore a white shirt, open at the throat, and black breaches. In the colors of dim lantern light, he looked more a pirate then any of those she had left behind on the Bacchus. She saw that dark smudges framed the base of his eyes. His cheeks were slightly wind chapped and tan, as if he had spent the last two weeks at the helm, staring out to the horizon, the chiseled bones cast shadows in the hollows beneath. They stared at each other till the air between them seemed to crackle as his eyes devoured her, and for a while there was no sound in the room besides their merging, rasping breaths.

Velvet's hand went to her throat, the last time she had stood this close to him, she had been about to die. Nothing much had seemed to matter then. It did now, all the unspoken words, hurting just as terribly as the ones already said.

He straightened and cordially inclined his head, casting his look briefly around the captain's rooms. "Welcome to the Siren, Your Grace," he said. His voice low and carrying, deceptively casual, yet Velvet was not fooled as she could see the wild thing stirring in his eyes, hear the underlining thread of steel in his tone.

She lifted her chin. "That title is not mine. I will never be your wife," she said.

"You have no choice in the matter, my love. The king has given you to me. It is done."

"He is not my king, and I am not your love!" she cried, coming to her knees, fists clenching over her racing heart. "What will you do, Henry? Rape me? Beat me? Drag me through the streets and take my head as they meant to do? What can you possibly do to me that has not been threatened, or done before?"

"This is your doing! You set us on this course with your use of magic, and now there is no retreat!" he yelled.

"My doing?!" she screamed, the nerves in her head grinding to an unbearable pitch. "Ever am I hunted, the taking of my head will a village hero make. I do what I must to survive!"

Henry said nothing for five beats of her pounding heart, a feral thing had taken over his expression at her words, his lips twisted in a terrifying snarl. "I came for you! Nearly died for you, and you cursed me!" His eyes narrowed as he strode forward and took her arms, her struggles mattered not at all as he dragged her hard against his chest. "Was it all a spell with us, from the very beginning?" he asked, his voice deep and grinding.

Velvet slammed her hands against his chest, tried to shove him away. "You wretch...you...jackanape...I have told you it was not," she shrieked, her voice now as high as any fish wife. "How can you even ask me such a thing after what has been between us...you were my protector...my," she gasped as hot tears burned the back of her throat. "I will say no more, I'm tired of constantly professing my innocence to you. Believe what cheers you, Henry." She dropped her eyes, unable to take the blaze of his stare, the world kept wanting to haze and spin out of focus. "What more can you want? You want revenge? Very well, you have commandeered me, now you say I am to be your prisoner for life, and it seems I have no say. Will it satisfy you, Henry?" she asked, trying again to wrench away. Every scalding moment that had been between them hung hot and heavy, encasing, looping, invisible waves that seemed to make this moment all their own.

"Where are your stones?" he asked, surprising her.

Velvet sniffed turning her head far away from his intoxicating person as her neck would allow. "Far from me now, I want nothing to do with them," she muttered.

Henry's hands were gentle, and he pushed her down, pillows squished behind her head as he moved over her, his legs crisscrossing her own. He leaned forward, his hair falling from its club, dark curls brushed her cheeks. "Look at me," he said.

Stubbornly Velvet squeezed her eyes shut, not putting it past him to pry them open.

Henry sighed. "The king would have killed you, Velvet. While I suspected Nora's plot, I did not trust that it would succeed. I went to the king to beg him to save your life. He would not. He wants peace—your life brings him none. Taking you as my wife was the only choice," he said, nudging her chin with the top of his head, he smelled like sandalwood and sea. "Look at me, Velvet," he said again, softer now, his words almost a request. Slowly Velvet opened her eyes and gazed up at him. "It was the only way to save your life, love."

"How noble, seeing that you were the one who put it in danger," she snapped.

Henry growled, showing teeth. "I was asked by my peers to speak in a trial, they all know me to be a devout Catholic—I could not lie, but I never would have let you die. A great many things confuse me about that night on the Bacchus—as has much, since I met you, but I know for certain, that night I was under your spell. Can you imagine what it felt like to be screaming inside my own head, unable to control my own body, how powerless—betrayed."

"Of course I can imagine. I was an owl for eight years! When the spell was first cast on me, my bones broke like I was on a rack. I screamed until my eyes bled, then changed—give over, Your Grace," she said, trying to roll out from beneath him—completely futile, obviously. She sighed so her whole body slumped. "It may content you to know, I spend my days and nights tortured by guilt, and I have abandoned magic of any kind. Find another way to take your revenge on me, Henry, in this there is nothing you could do or say for I will never be your wife. I will never belong to any man—certainly not a man who has professed to loathe me."

Henry smiled. "I've never said anything of the kind."

"It doesn't matter, none of it. I will never make the mistake of trusting you again," she said.

"Velvet," he started.

"No! You knew they meant to kill me, and still you looked at me like I was the evil in a room full of saints. You will never understand what drives me, and in the end will hate me for the chaos I mean to bring. Your pride takes precedence over your heart, Henry."

"You little fool!" he hissed. "Can't you see there is no choice? Without the protection of my name the king will hunt you down and kill you. Do you really want to keep running? With me you are safe."

"Safe from everyone in the world except for you. L'homme que je crains le plus—the man I fear the most. Perhaps it is with you where the greatest danger lies. N'est-ce pas? I was safe with Nora, Devon, Cerberus and Louis," she said, then watched his eyes widen, and knew an occupant of her guestlist had surprised him.

"You lie here professing your innocence, yet I know you mean to use your magic to save your brother," he said.

Velvet flinched away. "I told you once, Henry, I will always do what I must."

"No matter the cost?" he asked, his voice now tight with anger. "This time the cost may be your life, princess."

"You think that matters? I said goodbye to life at eleven years old. I would gladly die for my brother. Besides, I am stronger than you think," she said, moving, shifting, squirming under him like worm on a hook, desperate to get away—anything to keep her gaze from locking with his.

"Doubtful," Henry grunted. "In my eyes you are too strong for your own good, yet even mountains fall to time," he said softly, his hand stroking down her cheek, she shivered under the touch. "Take my name, Velvet, let me offer what atonement I can."

Velvet inhaled on a sudden gasp. Her eyes flew to his. "Atone? You mean to say you are sorry for betraying me, breaking your word, and condemning me to die? You actually think that will change anything?"

"I told you. I would never have let you die, and no I don't think it will change anything, but it deserves to be said," he breathed, staring at her face in that unnerving, burning way, and she was made breathless by his nearness. There was a curious, hot tremor rushing through her body. He seemed hard and unbroken as the waves around them, and she felt afraid beneath him, powerless between his strong hands in a way she had not before. She was afraid of herself, and all the confusing things he made her feel. She would not admit it in a thousand years, but Velvet also feared she would not have traded this moment for anything. She had missed him so terribly—the persistent curls that always fell across his brow. Sharp strong features ever imprinted like a tattoo on her mind, the sound of his heartbeat, his sinful smile and intoxicating smell. Less than two months since he stormed in her life, yet Velvet already felt like he had become an irreplaceable part of her.

He moved fully over her body, his legs stretching out alongside hers. The hands on her were gentle as the kiss of steel. His head lowered, his eyes like twin bonfires. "We are already wed," he breathed, "the king has commanded it."

"I will never submit to such an edict."

"You will," he said huskily. "I demand it."

"Never," she breathed.

"Humility is a virtue, my love. A touch of it might do wonders for your survival," he said.

Velvet's hackles rose. "You, ugh! I have no desire to survive if I must be locked to you." She bucked, arched, and squirmed, trying to break free of his touch, for she feared it would diffuse her anger, bind her to him in some terrifying way. "If you would just listen—I—"

"No, my lady, you listen," he snapped, shaking her still. Outside a peal of thunder rolled over the waves, and the ship rocked wildly. "You were not my choice either, I too swore never to marry—the whole institution is a chilling concept at best, but it is done. You are mine."

Velvet felt like melting. "Your prisoner," she snapped, struggling to keep her fury alive.

"If that is your desire, would you prefer I tie you to this bed, or perhaps the foremast?"

"Whatever you wish, Your Grace," she snarled.

"Hellfire! None of this is what I wished. I meant to save you, take you away, you fought me, ran from me, bewitched my soul. Like I said, we are here my dangerous bride, and it is your doing."

"You are crushing me, Your Grace," she said, stung, then commanded definitely, "if you do not mean to have me now, soaking in sea water and shivering, then I beg you, release me so I am not suffocated by your overbearing person."

"If only I could," he said, and then his hands were in her hair, his fingers caressing the locks. He was watching her face with pensive, feline concentration. "If only I could, but your hair burns like firelight, shiny as spun gold, your eyes are so luminously beautiful when you try to hold back tears, like you're doing right now." His knuckles traced a line of shivers across her cheek, then smoothed a wild lock from her face.

"Henry," she breathed, not knowing what she wished. Her chest was rising and falling, crashing into his own. She could feel his heartbeat reverberating through her body, and Velvet had that strange instinct she was flowing into him again. How, oh how could you fight an enemy when you became a part of them? He was steel and fire, deadly as the sharpest blade, and he would only ever hurt her. Yet when he lowered his head until their lips brushed, Velvet could not find it in herself to pull away.

"I dreamed of you," he said, his breath washing over her mouth. "You haunted me, baited, accused, tormented, and still I wanted this." His voice was low and hot, his thumb touched her lower lip, traced where he wanted to kiss, her whole body shivered as her thoughts scattered. Her hands fluttered to his shoulders, felt the muscles flex under her fingertips as he pressed her deeper in the pillows, and his mouth finally covered hers.

Velvet's eyes crashed closed; her hands crept around his neck. His kiss was slow, drugging, perilous enough to bind her to him for always. On a surrendering sigh, she parted her lips, let him ravage as he will. The wait for this moment had seemed interminable, but she had dreamed of him too, long before the misplaced spell threw them together, and gods above and below—how she wanted him.

He locked his hands in her hair, tilted her head, stole her breath, her will. Velvet knew if she died in this instant, she, would taste him forever. It was so much better than the last time, no confusion or sickening magic grifted her strength. Her limbs felt disillusioned, and she was glad of his hands on her body somehow mooring her to the earth. She gasped and the kiss became more— elemental, necessary to her very survival. He rolled fully atop her, his hips settling perfectly between her legs. Power radiated in his every movement; she could feel it roaring beneath his skin like leashed lightening. A fever burned in her chest, heated her breath, she made a desperate, wild sound, and tore her mouth away, turned her head to the side and tried to control her trembling. "Madness," she breathed, not daring to look at hm, "we cannot do this."

His hot lips traced the taut line of her throat. "We must," he said, and Velvet wanted to scream at the twisting urgency tensing her limbs, making her writhe, wanting a thing she could not name. Through the ship's pine walls she could hear more thunder breaking in the distance, hear the rise and crash of waves.

"No, I want no part of you," she lied, "I am not your wife until you take me, and if that is your wish, you must take me by force."

Henry smiled, black lashes lowering over his crystal gaze. She shook when their eyes locked, wanting him, despising him. Hard fingers fell to her jaw raising her face to his. Velvet could not breathe, she could not move, only feel him. "You are my wife, and I suppose it would be ungentlemanly to denounce you as a complete liar," he whispered. "I could take your innocence now, do all the things I want, and you would only beg me for more."

"All that would prove is the willfulness of my body, but the decision of my heart and mind remain the same," she said.

His lips brushed hers. "It's not the same though, is it? I thought the madness between us stemmed from the spells you cast." His thumb touched the moisture on her lips. "But it was more just now, it was—" He broke off, and kissed her again, like he was a drowning man, and she alone, his only chance for air. His mouth was sizzling and carnal, his tongue locked with hers, and Velvet was spinning once more, pinwheeling through an open sky. Human girls did not need wings to fly, she realized, just a man with a kiss wicked as Satan, and hands that burned hotter than the sun.

Breaths tangled as they rose to their knees, something primal and screaming forced her to straddle his lap, his hands fell to her waist, he crushed their hips together, and made a deep, hungry sound in his throat. Velvet knew she was fast passing the moment of no return. If she did this—she would be his forever. The thought brought terror, but her traitor body whispered, let him come.

The ship swayed and more thunder cracked. The surging waves crushed her tighter to him. He leaned back to look at her, his hands skated up her ribs, the hollow of her throat. "You are so beautiful. It feels like I can't remember a time when I didn't want you," he said.

Princess, owl, human, slave, Velvet did not know which version of her he wanted, but knew she was on the verge of giving them all to him. Lucifer in the garden could have been no more inciting, Henry moved with the rolling motion of the ship, like he was god of the deep, commanding the restless waves. Then, his wandering hands cupped her breasts and Velvet shook like he flayed her. She arched against his palms, her head falling back of its own accord. He pushed the leather jacket from her shoulders, his hands fell to the high row of buttons running down the front of her blouse. Buttons slid rapidly through eyelet slits, and Velvet dared to meet his blistering stare.

Stop me if you can, his eyes taunted, and his wicked smile existed because they both knew she could not. His lips came back to hers.

A fist rapped at the door. Henry made a sound of dismissal, he locked his arms around her waist, and tumbled them to the twisted sheets. The knock came again, louder. Velvet gasped. "Henry?" she nearly moaned. Henry's hand came up to cradle her neck, then he rested his forehead against her own, and took a deep breath that shook him as it went down. "I will kill whoever opens that door," he said through his teeth, no jest in the words.

"Captain, I must speak with you, sir." It was Paul Ritchie's voice; Velvet instantly recognized the man's sophisticated, clipped tones.

"I believe I was very clear on what constituted as a viable excuse for disturbing me," Henry said.

"Yes, sir," called Ritchie, his voice muffled by the closed door, and rumbling thunder. "A French invasion, or a threat of mass extinction."

"Are either of those events currently taking place?" asked Henry, each word a growl.

"We've lost the main mast, snapped somewhere near the middle," Ritchie called, "the hull is shattered, and we're taking in water on the main deck."

"It will pass," Henry nearly shouted.

"It's a ragger, Captain," Ritchie persisted.

"I would have known, we would have felt something," said Henry.

"Are you sure, sir?" asked Ritchie, Velvet thought he might be laughing—and she was not sure at all. They had been too lost in the storm of their own creation to give any credence to the one attacking without.

Henry sat up and jerked his jacket in place, ran his hands through his hair, then pointed his finger directly at her flushed face, and said, "Stay!" as if he spoke to a willful stray.

"I will not!" she said, struggling to free her legs from the tangle of her gown, and rise. The ship rolled precariously. Without the strong bands of his iron arms holding her steady, Velvet lost her balance, and swayed dangerously, the next wave deposited her painfully on the floor. The harsh landing knocked the breath from her lungs as she tried to rise, choking in wheezing gasps.

Henry was on his knees beside her, a similar victim of gravity. Velvet's stomach felt like it hit her toes as the next wave came, and the ship went up, up, up. What goes up must come down, Velvet thought, and reached for Henry's hand. Their fingers locked, twisted, and the ship plummeted. The tilted hull struck the water with an unholy crash.

Above deck, Velvet could hear more men shouting as thunder broke like a drumroll. The paneling of the cabin's papered walls trembled, shivered, and creaked, then screamed as the sturdy boards split under the pressure of the waves. Thin streams of water trickled through the cracks. Velvet looked up in dismay. "I spent most my life in the sky, I'm unfamiliar with the ways of the sea, but that's not good is it?"

"No, love," said Henry, voice grim, "it is most definitely not good."

"Captain!" Ritchie yelled again. Henry was instantly on his feet as he met her wide eyes.

"No," Velvet said, strongly objecting to what she saw in them. "If you tell me to stay here and stay safe—" she started angrily, but her words were squelched as he reached for her, locked his hands around her waist, swept her off the floor and tosssed her over his shoulder. Before she had time to shriek her indignation, he threw her down on the bed. It bowed in the middle as Velvet's hands and feet flew above her head.

"My lady, you will stay put! If I see you on deck, I will strap you to the mast and thrash you myself."

"Brute!" railed Velvet scrambling to her knees. Gasping, and sweeping long skeins of hair from her eyes. "Brigand, piquer, fiend! I hate you, loathe you!"

Henry put a hand to his heart feigning sincerity. "Such words of love will bring me the greatest comfort when our bodies rot beneath the waves. I am warning you, Velvet. Two weeks at sea does not a sailor make. You would be kindling for the storm. I cannot worry about you and my ship."

The next wave pitched them violently. Henry fell against the wall, and Velvet's body slammed the bed's base, her head making a hollow, *thunking* sound as it struck the dense mahogany wood. "Stay!" Henry repeated, then half crawled, half stumbled to the door. He threw it wide. More than a foot of water came rushing in.

"Satan's balls, that's cold," hissed Henry, stamping toward the worst of it. The ship rocked again; Velvet struggled against the force. Henry stopped and looked over his shoulder at her, fire spilling somewhere in the ship ignited the ice in his eyes turning them to pinpoints of light that burned hot crimson.

Velvet gasped, her fingers crushing handfuls of the bedsheets. "Henry," she said, reaching for him, more afraid than angry now. "Don't leave me here, I can't stay in this room alone, and I'm not sure if I can swim." He moved further away, backing up like it was hard to walk away from her. "Please, I hate being locked in the dark, I can't breathe, Henry—"

The light changed turning his eyes dark blue and turbulent as the attacking sea. Not breaking the simmering contact between them, or giving one ounce of credence to her pleas, Henry reached out a hand, and slammed the door shut. The sharp bang seemed very final.

~

"Storm's here," said Alfonso, leaning back to eat the lice he plucked from his beard. The fat, snot colored body popped between his teeth, crunching as it went down.

Devon shuddered. He braced his arms against the wall across from Alfonso's cell, as the Bacchus rocked like a cork caught in a tidal wave. "Sage observation, was it the hail crashing above deck that tipped you off?"

"That, and the pallor of your pasty face," Alfonso laughed.

"You best pray fortune favors us this night, heavy as it would make my heart, I would wager you sink first," said Devon.

"You would never allow me to perish," said Alfonso, puffing out his chest, the hard line of his currently sparse ribs showed vividly under his filthy linen shirt. "The hole I would leave in your life would be fist sized."

Devon smiled warily. "You'll never hear me admit to such a horrid thing."

"Pah! Everyone who has met the great Alfonso, has loved the great Alfonso—two weeks as your guest is all the time I needed to crawl under your skin, the way these little worms have burrowed in mine." Alfonso tossed another chubby louse in his mouth, after which, he held up his giant paw of a hand and studied the thick layer of dirt beneath his nails, then sighed. "The great Alfonso does not enjoy being filthy. I hope I do get a good toss in the ocean." He closed his eyes in wistful, imagined bliss. "Just the thought of all that salty water, my lice would run for their lives—better not then," he plucked another from behind his ear, stared at it for a second, then ate it. "The great Alfonso also hates being hungry."

Devon lifted the narrow sack lying beside his feet and tossed it through the iron bars of the Bacchus's largest cell. "There's bread and cheese in there, your current diet is making me sicker than the storm. I've already given rations to your men."

Alfonso fished inside the bag, saluted Devon with the loaf of bread he withdrew, then tore into it ravenously while more thunder trembled the timbers. The Bacchus heaved forward to smash its figurehead against the next, white-tipped swell. The metal bars of Alfonso's cell groaned against the increased pressure, as they took on water above.

Devon's face went a mottled shade of green, he pitched from right to left, his hand went to his mouth, he gagged behind the constriction. "God," he breathed through his nose, "hell and blazes! I hate sailing—always have."

Alfonso chuckled, chewing loudly, smacking his lips sporadically. "The great Alfonso has learned ships are a necessary evil, when one has chosen to search the world for the ultimate lost treasure in existence." He jabbed a large thumb at his chest, spewing a few bits of masticated bread from his mouth. "And where do I find this treasure at last? On the person of a strutting prick, an imbecilic twerp who doesn't even know what he has."

Devon's hand went to the double silk panel stitched in his cloak, touching the place where the stones burned. Every pulse they emanated seemed to whisper strange secrets to him in a language no living person could ever translate, or even hope to understand. "I assume you are speaking of me," said Devon. "I'll take imbecilic and strutting prick, but I draw the line at twerp." His fingers closed tightly around the velvet bag, pins and needles rushed up his arms.

"Give me a clean shirt, and a bucket of water to bathe, and I will tell you a secret you dearly wish to know," said Alfonso, his taunting voice carried a clear challenge.

"What secret?" Devon asked absently, lost in the heat coursing through his fingertips, shivering up his arm.

Alfonso lifted his mouth to reply, then shrugged.

"You can go straight to hell," snorted Devon, trying to find equilibrium and purchase on the slippery walls as he began to turn away.

"It's regarding a dead girl, and an amethyst stone," said Alfonso, and Devon froze. It felt like his heart stopped for a second too long.

"Her spirit remains," continued Alfonso, "unshriven and wandering. The amethyst lets you see what is trapped in between." Alfonso took another bite of bread and spoke over it. "She haunts you, does she not? I hear singing when I sleep, Amazing Grace…" Alfonso sighed. "What a lovely voice Katie had, or has…I suppose that decision lies in your hands."

Devon spun looking deep in Alfonso's eyes. Like twin black holes, fathomless and empty.

"You dream of her, I think," said Alfonso, his voice low and leading, reminding Devon of those fortune tellers who truly communed with those they should not. "Because you loved her in life, it is you she has chosen to revisit. She knows the contents of the bag you now carry. I believe she may have had much to do with why you find your humble self in possession of artifacts made for the old gods, and since abused by human kings and queens of empires fallen."

Devon stripped off his cloak and shirt, then tossed the latter through the bars. "How do you know these things?" he asked, afraid of the answer the old gypsy would give.

Alfonso closed his eyes, as if he felt the weight of the world and was exhausted by it. "Because you simple man, she is ghost, and I have dreamed of her too."

"Velvet said I should dispose of the stones, let them sink to the bottom of the sea," said Devon.

"Do that, and I vow mine will be the last face you see," Alfonso said, lifting the shirt from the floor and holding it up to his broad chest. "Besides, if you rid yourself of them, you will truly lose her forever."

Devon shook his head, bracing his feet to stay standing, and again throwing his dark cloak over his now bare shoulders. "I will keep them safe for the moment, you have my word—just based on our brief acquaintance, I believe it is worth far more value than yours. Besides, the idea that I will take visions of your ugly mug with me to the grave, is more dire a threat than I have ever received."

"Hold the stone, and follow the music," said Alfonso, settling deeper into the piss-soaked straw, and crossing his legs, letting himself rock to the rhythm of the waves. "When it comes to ghosts, especially of the female variety, always follow the singing."

Devon's eyes narrowed. "Do you expect me to decipher such a stream of nonsense as you spout?"

Alfonso had no response, he continued to rock, his fat lips closed tight as a tomb.

CHAPTER NINE

Swimming in the dark.
You are made of moonlight—of silence and storm.

 elvet screamed as she slid across the room on her stomach, her arms stretched above her head like some invisible force dragged her forward by the wrists. Her body hovered roughly a foot above ground, parallel to the teetering floor. A flying table leg crashed against her skull—the pain was sharp and brought a flash of temporary blindness. She tried to use her hands to shelter her head from any further assault, but the wild tossing of the waves made intentional movement nearly impossible.

The might of the sea had turned her into a rag doll, tossing her about like her limbs were made of cloth and string. Gritting her teeth, soaked with seawater and perspiration, Velvet dug her fingers in the carpet, and found purchase for her left foot on the rung of a chair toppled on its side. She tried to curl her toes around the slender wooden cane, but her satin shoe slipped against the varnish and flew forward, her shin smacked against the rung. She screamed. Groaning, and running through the repertoire of every curse word she knew—Velvet tried again, kicked off her shoe, and attempted to grab hold, instead her big toe knocked the leg, and the chair skittered away. Velvet rolled across the room, losing all the ground she had gained in her quest to reach the door.

She clawed her fingers, dug her nails deep in the jagged floorboards and began her trek again. The ship vibrated as another wave came, her hands slipped a little, and she held on till her nails tore and bled. The ship jackknifed through the waves, her hold on the carpet was the only thing keeping her from flying into the back wall and splattering against the slats like an uncooked pancake. Despite the icy November chill, sweat trickled down the back of her neck as she continued to drag herself forward, one inch at a time.

Every crack of thunder that shook her world—seemed to bring a new crash above, like the storm tore the ship apart at the very seams. For the first hour of her confinement in this wretched room, Velvet had struggled to stay atop the bed, holding onto the binding ropes until they burnt her hands, while the Siren rolled, and rolled.

At first, she suspected Henry simply meant to leave her in here while the angry waves made short work of swallowing the ship—then, when the inertia threw her to the floor with enough force to break bone, Velvet had truly begun to believe she would die in this room. Surely no one could survive such a torrential gale. In the beginning, the bight flashes of lighting were followed by shouts, and garbled commands. Now, there was only the occasional wailing crash, and endless, screaming wind.

Well, enough had finally been enough—Velvet refused to be smashed to bits or drown in a cramped cabin. Spirits! The block would have been preferable. If Davy Jones were indeed to be her companion this night, she would meet him head on.

Velvet screamed behind her teeth as she hauled herself up another foot, then another. She almost burst into noisy tears when her knuckles struck the base of the door. She arched her body at an unnatural angle, till she thought her back might snap, then reached up for the doorknob. "Merde!" she gasped, clinging to it with all the strength in her tired arms.

Thunder shouted as she twisted the bulbous metal handle, yanked the door open and more water rushed in. Velvet barely held her breath in time before a great, slurping swell gushed over her head. Icy water, cold enough to stop a heart. She came up spluttering a few seconds later when the Siren temporarily righted, hauled herself to her feet, and ran down the hall.

The stairs to the main deck were a waterfall—torrents of black waves that flowed from the flooded deck, gushed in from the splintered keel.

A coil of hemp rope was tied off tight at its end to the metal rail edging the length of the vanished stairs. Velvet grabbed it like a lifeline. When the Siren rolled again her legs practically flew above her head, but she wrapped the rope around her palms, and held fast.

Giant waves receded, gathered, rose high. The Siren tilted, forced to scale the swell. The ship climbed nearly thirty feet straight up, before it came to a teetering pause on the precipice of a steep drop. The figurehead speared down, the Siren swayed back and forth like a child's see-saw while the wind screamed and screamed, then they fell.

Velvet's whole body went weightless, her feet cleared the ground and her body dangled, suspended by the earth's pause—her tenuous hold on the rope all that kept her from sailing off into oblivion.

A body tumbled down the stairs, wrapped in swirls of white-capped waves. Velvet and the body stayed levitated as the ship made a daring dive for Davy Jones and his ghost infested locker. The Siren finally hit the waves with a mighty jolt that threw Velvet hard against the soggy boards underfoot, the body landed against the far wall—something in it snapping loudly, the water surrounding them both ran pink. Planks groaned, the bowsprit snapped, grinding chains protested as the ship fishtailed, and the rudders beat uselessly at the rainy air. This was briefly followed by the loudest crash of all as the hull scraped the choppy waves, and finally shattered in a thousand, expensive splinters.

Velvet dragged herself toward the fallen man, using the rope for leverage, heaving until she reached the body, and leaned down to lift the limp head clear of the water. It was the young boy who had sat to her right in the small dingy and called her a firecracker. His mouth was slack, his eyes open, staring at everything and nothing. Gently she lay him back down, and he floated beneath the waves, there was nothing to be done for it, he was dead. She reached beneath the water to close his eyes, the sea was now his forever home, and tonight, the god of it—had taken yet another.

Slowly she turned back and began to painstakingly make her way up the submerged stairs. Lightning whipped the sky, sharp lashes that tore into the black and made it bleed white.

Again, waves surged, and the thunder barked. More bursts of serrated light taunted the cracked foremast, striking the crow's nest with unerring accuracy and persistence. In effort to keep the ground she had gained, Velvet's fingers clawed the crumbling stairs, sharp splinters stabbed the soft skin beneath her nails. When at last she reached the landing, Velvet sat on the top stair in the knee deep, icy water, then wrapped the length of the rope around her waist and tied it off—not a second too soon. The next wave saw her airborne, meaning to wash her over the side rail. Velvet grabbed the raised lip of the top stair and held on, screaming for all she was worth. The wave that slapped her in the face absorbed the sound, so she screamed in watery silence as the Siren plateaued atop another wave, then dove through the center of the next rising tidal.

The water receded, sucking Velvet away from the rail to send her flying portside. In the last second the rope yanked her away from the edge, burning her skin as it tightened around her waist. The Siren tilted again, and her aching body rolled across the main deck. She flew against a net of fallen shrouds, and found her limbs tangled in the mesh. Kicking and shrieking, more frightened than hurt, Velvet opened her eyes, wiped water from her face, and peered through her trembling fingers—she saw him.

Henry stood before the broken mast, Ritchie and Zoe worked beside him, all fighting with the garble of knotted ropes preventing the main sail from lowering fully—it still flapped at half mast, giving the rampant gust more elements to heave and drag. Wind squealed like a woman, the thunder shouted out a series of angry responses, then the lightning came again, scattering coherent visual, transforming the world to black and white. Henry's skin and hair turned dark as polished ebony, and his eyes to blue crystals seething behind their own filter of storm. She saw that his linen shirt had been all but torn from his back, and lived red welts showed in harsh relief across his straining shoulders. He was slick with rain, glistening, reels of steam rose off his chest twirling in the droplets running down his chiseled stomach.

So transfixed was she, Velvet momentarily forgot about the next wave, soon incoming. She tripped over her own feet trying to run to him, hating him, and wanting badly to be in his arms. She must have made some sound—though Velvet could not imagine any human sound capable of competing with the storm—because Henry looked up, and their eyes met through the rain. During the first three beats of her heart, he simply looked terrified, then his eyes turned brittle, now fury burned there too. Appearing to struggle with some powerful emotion, Henry parted his lips shouting something, then dropped his handful of rope and reached for her.

Velvet never did hear what he said, the new wave chose that moment to hit. It curled around the Siren like a watery fist—Poseidon's death grip, she thought. The wind screamed some more, Velvet screamed with it. Water surged down her throat, it burned in her ears like sparking gunpowder—and beneath the waves she coughed and spluttered in breathless darkness.

Something snapped. Velvet felt a strong tug and release. The rope skimmed her waist, and for seconds she was purely weightless. *The railing, the wave has torn the railing from the wall,* she realized.

Well, that is not good at all, she thought, and would have laughed if she could. The wave retreated with lazy gusto, this time it dragged her straight over the side of the sinking ship.

Velvet gazed at the stars as she fell, they seemed strangely close, either that or this wave was remarkably high. Her arms snapped out, flung behind her by the force of the pull. The rope trailed her plummeting body, floating through the heavy rain like a drunken snake with a severed head. Then, she saw Henry and the others, saw him reach for the metal railing attached to her rope—and fail.

The base of Velvet's head hit the surface of the water; it was hard as ice. Henry's face disappeared in a flash of white. Velvet's eyes tumbled closed as the furious sea pulled her down.

~

I could not save you, only want you—I pray they are one and the same.

Henry watched Velvet go over the side of his ship—he felt his body go into cold shock as his mind stumbled over the truth of the moment's reality. A surge of adrenaline spiked in his brain, shortened his ragged breath—he was running before her dainty feet—clad only in a single satin slipper—flipped over the edge. The stubborn chit had tied a rope around her waist, now it shot across the deck, slave to the power of gravity. He fell to his knees, dove to catch it, another wave washed his chances away.

Endless seconds passed when Henry did not think of his sinking ship, or the men his actions would blindly relegate to the deep—there was only her, and that last look in her eyes. No fear at all, not his princess, only sadness, and on her lips had played the barest hint of a smile—like some part of her was glad it was finally over. Henry did not think. He jumped.

The bones in his legs felt like they both snapped on contact with the choppy waves. His body shot downward like an arrow. The water was cold, deep, dark, and wild. Henry was a seasoned sailor and a strong swimmer—Velvet was neither, not to mention the bar of iron the silly girl had tied to herself, now weighing her down like an anchor.

Henry threw his head above the waves, around him, the ocean groaned and heaved, he battled it with all his strength, not fighting for his life, but hers. Debris falling off the Siren's breaking bones hit the water all around him. Planks and beams, deadly, flaming missiles that missed him by inches, twice, Henry was forced to dive deep to avoid an exploding barrel.

Hair stuck to his eyes, rain and salt ran down his face. He filled his lungs with a desperate wash of wet air, took another then arched, and dove under the next crashing swell. Beneath the water his eyes burned, but he held them open, looking for her, he saw her almost instantly, a vanishing speck receding into the darkness. Henry shook his head to clear his mind of the sick fear that slowed his limbs. He kicked his legs and swam toward her. Catching the rope trailing away from her, he lopped it around his hand, pulled till she was in his arms.

Her beautiful face was tinged blue, golden skeins of hair twisted her limp limbs. She was submissive as a feather in his hold. No bubbles escaped her parted lips, he pressed them to his own, tilted her head, and gave her what was left of his air. Henry kept his mouth locked to hers as he untied the rope from around her tiny waist, then let it go to sink into obscurity.

He said they had come to this place because of her, but he had lied. This was his doing, all of it. *Let her live,* Henry prayed, *let her live, and if she truly wishes it, I will let her go.* Even thinking the words felt like sacrilege, with her, like this, in his arms, Henry thought he would fight the world to keep her—yet he would not recant—today he would trade his soul to see her safe.

Cradling her close, Henry kicked his legs, his lungs were screaming by the time their heads broke the surface. "Breathe, Velvet," he begged, wiping water from her face, cupping her cheek in his hand, he tipped her head over his arm and gave her more air, forced it into her lungs until she was coughing, spitting, and shuddering against him. His hand moved to cradle her skull as the plank his men had used to board the Bacchus slapped the water, close enough to send a small wave crashing over them. Henry struck out for it, treading water hard to keep her head above the waves. She was still coughing, and her arms had a death grip around his neck when he lifted her. "Grab the edge, love, can you pull yourself up? Or do you need—"

"I can do it," she gasped. Her pale fingers found the edge of the plank, and she held on with more determination than strength. He saw that her nails were bleeding, and badly broken—the sight made him physically ill.

"I'm going to let go of you, now Velvet," he told her, and for the briefest of seconds rested his forehead against the base of her spine. "I must swim to the other side, so we can use our weight to level the plank," he said, shouting over the wind. Her white lips thinned, but she nodded. It was nearly impossible to let her go, but he did, and dove beneath the crashing waves once again.

They were both breathing heavy by the time they managed to situate themselves on the plank, it was in perfect time to witness the Siren's final demise. It should have hurt, Henry thought, to see the ship he loved murdered by one of nature's fiercest blades—yet all he could feel was glad of her—beside him, breathing, alive. Then, he looked at her pale, bruised face peeking through the slender fingers of her bleedings hands and felt only rage.

"I'm sorry about your ship," she said softly, her wide, violet eyes reflecting the flaming wreck—black oil igniting—gunpowder exploding.

"Did you do it?" he asked roughly, and instantly wished to withdraw the words, but his adrenaline, his terror—his need to kiss her until he erased from his mind the image of her fading away, disappearing in the dark—all blended, morphed to scalding, crimson rage.

Velvet cast him a filthy look, marred by a touch of bewildered annoyance. "But of course, while I was struggling in your cabin for my life, I took the time to whip up an enchantment, and start a storm."

Henry smiled at her; it felt cold on his lips. "Would seem a fitting vengeance on those who captured you—a way to escape my possession."

"Your possession?" she gasped; he saw her fingers twitch like she wanted to slap him. "Yes," she continued wrathfully, motioning to the roiling sky. "Yes, this entire affair was all my doing. My grandmaster plan was to end the night carried away by a wave—an activity I would probably find preferable to the one you had planned for me."

"A choice between myself, and the monsters of the deep," he sneered, "how very brave you are to face the waves."

Velvet shrugged. "At least the waves have not demanded my virginity."

"No—just your life!" he growled.

Velvet sniffed, and directly met his eyes. "Yes, like I said. Preferable."

Henry growled low in his throat, and reached for her, his fingers bit into the flare of her waist, she kept her glare pinned to his, peering up at him with defiance snapping in her eyes. Henry leaned close, so Velvet was forced to fall back on her elbows, exhausted, battered, breathless. His lips stroked her jaw, kissed the incensed wrinkle in her brow.

"Velvet, my love, I swear you would find it no hardship to lie beneath me," he said, and had the brief satisfaction of seeing those bewitching, violet eyes go wide, and her mouth drop in a fetching little O. He rubbed his hand down her back, touched her cheek. "Long as I live, I will never let you go to another man, the king has decreed you marry or die, so why not have me?"

Her pert chin twitched stubbornly. "I will never lie with a man who hates me, that's just bad form."

"I could not hate you," he breathed.

"Only judge me?" she asked, "I am sorry, Your Grace, it's one and the same."

Henry stared at her lips, here, in the middle of a storm, playing a game with the waves, the rules, chance alone—the penalty, death —he wanted this small, pale girl, more than he could ever remember wanting anything. Another wave came and lifted them high, he saw her bite down on her lip so she would not scream when they fell.

Velvet watched Henry's face as he tried to hold onto her using every ounce of his considerable might. The wave was high as a mountain, strong as an avalanche dragging, and tugging no matter how they fought back. He locked his teeth, and clutched at her, first her arms, then her wrist, now it was only her hand. She saw his lips move over her name, the moment before the wave ripped them apart. Hand still outstretched, still reaching for his, Velvet slid down the side of the swell, her limp body rolling like she merely tumbled through a hill of moonlit flowers.

～

Devon sat on the floor, his back resting against the bed, his arm slouched over his drawn-up knee. Nora lay on the bed, hanging her own arm over the high side of it, and holding his hand. Absently Devon stroked her fingers with his thumb. She was humming something soft which Devon found both depressing and rather soothing. The storm had begun to quiet; the Bacchus would do little more than limp into the port of Toamasina—but she would survive, they all would. Waves still sporadically tossed them about, yet their tone was calmer now, virtually hypnotic with their ceaseless surge and retreat.

Beneath them the planks of the Bacchus creaked, groaning loudly about the injustices of the day; they sounded like a tone-deaf soprano composing a ballad. Devon leaned his head back while Nora twirled her fingers through the hair curling at his temple, drying in irreparable kinks, and smelling of salt. He knew Nora finally submitted to sleep when the twirling stopped.

He smiled and closed his eyes, listened to her soft breaths become lady-like snores. He wanted to move, get to his feet, and help the struggling crew, grab a bucket, and start scooping water.

His seasickness was gone for the most part—he felt well overall, if a little tired from his brief battle with the mainsail after leaving Alfonso's depressing cell, yet throughout the long storm Devon had not been able to get the gypsy's words from his mind. 'Hold it in your hand and think of the thing you desire'.

Katie had always been his deepest and most secret desire. He had wanted the darling girl since the first moment he had clapped eyes on her, nearly eight years ago, standing like a fading shadow beside Nora, gowned in a soft grey dress wearing the saddest smile he had ever seen. Small and brave, a better version of human than any of the glittering shells around her. He had almost told her so many times, would have asked her to marry him if he had anything at all to offer her besides his heart. A thing worth little to no momentary value. It is possible Katie would not have cared, would have loved, and wanted him no matter what—possible but not probable. Still, Devon wished he had taken a chance on her—on them. He would carry the regret of not doing so to his grave.

Nora's fingers, still twisted his hair, went limp as she began to dream. Devon turned his head and lightly kissed her knuckles, his touch gentle as a falling snowflake when he untangled her digits from his hair without ripping it clean from the roots. When it was done, he stood slowly and placed her hand carefully on her chest. Nora mumbled, and smiled at a thing only she could see.

Devon had oft thought death would eventually find him on a nameless battlefield beside Henry, fighting for some rich lord's cause. If Katie had lived, Devon would probably be standing beside Henry on the Siren's deck right now—he had always been content to love Katie from afar—watching at a distance, resigned, if not content to let her find her own happiness with some man far better than him—a man who had something to give a girl besides bloodshed and death. Yet since Katie's death he had not been capable of leaving her lady. Katie would have wanted him to stay and protect Nora, it would be her most fervent wish he ensured the girl she loved most in the world would be alright—so he had remained, stood alone at night, and cried in the spot where she had died. Collapsed on his knees to rest his cheek against the blood stain they had not quite managed to scrub off the deck.

Rubbing his salty, wind burned eyes, Devon moved to the corner of the room. Unclasped his weapons belt and set it silently on the floor, then stretched out on a red-satin chase lounge, which was overly lumpy and smelled like a dead sailor's old boot—still, the most comfortable thing Devon had lain on in days.

He crossed his arm behind his head and stared up at the cabin's leaky roof. He had no real hope of anything now—except to find a way to die with a touch of honor. He was a near penniless lord, and a solider turned traitor—he could not go home, nor could he leave the last place where she was. He was unmoored in his life, drifting, wanting to wander to a place where he could change his name, yet ever tethered to the ghost of her.

Almost unconsciously, Devon's free hand went to the velvet bag hidden in his cape lining, which had been weighing him down all day. The bag was warm, heavy enough to defy nature's most basic of laws. His ears started to ring when he sat up, set it on the gaudy cushion near his feet, then undid the tiny golden string tying the top closed. The seams of the bag crumpled apart, as if it too felt the weight of the stones it carried. A warm, peachy glow instantly spread through the cabin, long spears of light shot from the stones, spun like prismed chimes on a windy day. Devon leaned down, resting his weight on his elbows. The light drew him in. The radiance was warm, enchanting, spellbinding. There was a blank yearning in his soul that scattered his logical thoughts, the sounds in his ears shouted all the words he had not said, told him stories that lasted for days and were over in seconds—stories of all the lives he wished he had lived with her.

In a kind of trance, Devon reached one hand inside the bag, half expecting something to jump up and bite the limb off.

He tried to steady his shaking fingers, guzzled a giant draft of shimmering air, and closed his hand around a stone. Agility stuttered as he removed his hand from the bag, clutched tight around the prize he had chosen, not taking his eyes off the twisting, spinning, brilliant beams, like hundreds of colorful, burning candles tossed down a dark well.

Devon unfurled his fingers to see he had chosen the amethyst without looking for it at all. It was bright purple, pulsing like a fresh bruise on an angel. Light filtered through the tiny cracks that ran through its hot center, spilled on his hand, impossibly warm liquid, the color of gold and blood.

The amethyst quivered, the thousands of voices in his ears began to shout. Devon's spine jerked, his free hand went to his heart, as he continued to stare deep into the amethyst's boiling center. A soft shimmer flowed down his arm, rippled over the stone, and dripped off his fingers until Devon sat in a burning, revolving pool of violet light.

A whoosh of icy air rushed past, blowing his hair, leaving a chill coursing down his neck. The shutters covering the cabin's windows—which had been bolted against the storm—crashed open, slammed closed, then flew open again in a discordant rhythm. Like invisible hands moved them, and not the dying wind.

Nora stirred, called out and punched a pillow. Devon's heart stopped completely, before it began to race. A metallic liquid, a combination of mercury and starlight climbed up his arm, split off into curling branches that reached his neck. It was insane, yet Devon could have sworn the stone was breathing.

A sharp sound of a creaking board made Devon glance up,

fearing Nora had woken for good, just in time to witness his mischief. He swallowed hard, feeling guilty as a child standing before a shattered vase. His gaze shot toward the bed. Nora was still, one hand cradled her cheek, the other was thrown wide. The amethyst's glow touched all the dark places, casting lights and strange shapes across the roof and floor, yet for a moment Devon hardly saw it, his eyes locked on a thing in the room that made no sense to his logical mind. If he had not been sitting, Devon knew he would have fallen to his knees. His wide, unbelieving stare crashed into a pair of tilted brown, beautiful eyes he had thought never to see again. Devon cried out, jumping so hard it jerked a muscle in his shoulder.

"Sweet Madonna! I had a bet going with myself on how long it would take you to notice me," Katie said, in a heartbreakingly familiar voice that singed the drums of his ears. She was standing, not three feet in front of him—transparent as lingerie, a bleeding wound slashed across her slender throat.

Devon made a strangled sound; the stone fell from his numb hand. Katie instantly vanished. Devon did a thing then, a thing which he had never done before—he put a hand to his mouth to mute his scream, and promptly fainted.

LOST IN PARADISE.

They say you were my lover—yet I can't recall your taste.
You say it is you and no other—yet if I run, will you only give chase?

November 29, 1800

and, white as shredded diamonds, stretching far as the eye could see—sand and endless, surging waves. White froth rushing over her body, leaving trails of seaweed in her hair. The tide receded, Velvet opened her eyes, gasped in a broken breath, and lifted her head. She could feel a thick coating of sand on her cheek, it ran down her neck, then fell to the shreds of her nearly disintegrated bodice. The surf surged; water covered her like a blanket from neck to toe for just a moment before it rushed away once more.

Velvet rolled on her back and began to cough out what felt like half the ocean. Hacking for all she was worth, she dragged her battered body to her knees, scooping handfuls of yet more sand from her mouth and ears. She coughed until her back arched, her chest heaved, and she thought her ribs would snap from strain.

When the fit was finally past, and her lungs were grabbing tentatively at the air without the coughing starting all over again.

Velvet wiped salty tears from her eyes, lifted her hand to shade her face from the blaze of the high sun, and searched the endless beach for sign of Henry, bits of the Siren, or sailors who had been washed ashore. Her hand went to her blazing temples, she could hardly remember what happened, everything buzzed in and out as her eyes flicked over the endless expanse of blue sea. There was no one, only a few lonely bits wood which the surf dragged back and forth, the white waves turning their focus to the sparse wreckage, now that they no longer had her body to play with.

The simmering sun bounced off the vast expanse of white sand, throwing around brilliant rays of blinding light. Velvet dropped her hands and looked at them, the nails were traumatic, smashed and bleeding. *Where am I?* she thought wildly, then closed her eyes and tried to search her foggy mind. "He was holding my hand," she breathed, then, "Henry...he was holding my hand."

Absently she rubbed her wrist while it all came rushing back. The Siren, the terrible storm. Henry fighting with the mainsail, that huge wave that washed up to rip her over the side, the rope she had tied to save her life, the very instrument dragging her down to the darkness. Henry, with her beneath the waves. His lips on hers, his air in her lungs. The look in his eyes when he had begged her to live, to breathe, then his hand desperately trying to hold onto hers as the final wave tore them apart.

Velvet stood and turned to gaze out on a sea of pure crystal. She was on an island, this much was simple to ascertain, she could clearly see both sides of it from where she stood. Not a ship in sight rode the peaceful, gleaming waves.

Henry was out there somewhere, hurt, maybe even dead. For a brief, terrible second, Velvet realized that if the sea had indeed swallowed him—she would be free. The second the wretched thought tore through her mind; Velvet knew it was the last thing it the world she wanted. In fact, if such a thing were true, it may cost her very soul.

Again, Velvet lifted her hands to shade her eyes against the blaze, her new world was white, blue, and emerald, green. Just feet from where she stood, the pearly sand rushed into tufts of springy green grass, where flocks of birds drenched in colorful plumes frolicked. Palm trees heavy with coconuts were clustered by bushes covered in pink and yellow pansies. She could see unruly clumps of banana trees peopled in ripe yellow fruit. Velvet was already running before her stomach finished growling. Her dire predicament momentarily forgotten—she was ravenous. She ate four bananas and a handful of a red berry she found, hoping—as she stuffed her face—they were not poisonous to humans. When she could not eat another bite without risking it coming back up, Velvet sat and wiped bits of banana off her fingers onto the strips of cloth, her once beautiful skirt had been reduced to.

Now that her hunger was sated, water was all she could think about. Her mouth suddenly felt dry as the sand underfoot, her tongue grinding against the gritty coating on her teeth. From what Velvet could see, her island consisted of sand and virulent forest. Among the royal palaces of France or along the rolling British countryside, Velvet could not remember seeing a land so emerald and dangerous.

"Never mind that," she said aloud, her voice only slightly scratchy, "green has to mean water—it has to. It can't be all filled with salt, can it? Oh! Who do I think I'm talking to? Do you know little bird?" she queried, directing her question to a small, bright red finch, who diligently picked at one of her discarded banana peels. The bird cocked his head at the sound of her voice, but if he knew, he did not care enough to answer. A bead of hot sweat dripped in Velvet's eye. Rather desperately, she tore a strip of cloth from the hem of her skirts, then tied it around her head, to keep the sweat from falling, and the worst of the sun from charring her burning eyes.

After that was done, she fashioned a walking stick from a broken stalk of cane, grabbed another banana for good measure, then set off.

She walked for hours, always inland, until the sun, on its own quest to scale the horizon, found itself drowning in the purple waves.

Mosquitoes the size of her eye attacked from all sides, Velvet believed they had gathered and placed bets on how many drops of her blood they could collect. The concerted effort each put forth to win was truly astonishing. They stormed at her in great number, striking true, and biting deep, leaving horrifying welts in their wake that itched enough to drive a calm soul to madness.

The air was cloying and thick, like the elements tied up all kinds of summer in a single hot wind. The way was steep at times, the foliage dense and rife with venomous critters, who all seemed to strongly object to her presence in their domain.

Despite her multiple disagreements with the unruly forest, and two bad tumbles, one, which had dumped her off the edge of a stunted ravine—a long fall eventually knocking the breath from her lungs—Velvet enjoyed the exercise, after weeks of confinement, spent first in the London Tower, then on the Bacchus. Her upper thighs burned, but it was a good burn. It was difficult to be upset at anything while in the center of such splendor—a place so vibrantly beautiful, and alive.

Alone, lost, turned about from her single myopic purpose—she felt free. Truly.

Velvet set down her stick and sat on a rocky shelf to catch her breath. Two mist-shrouded cliffs painted the distance, in Velvet's mind they seemed like giant elephants facing off for a fight. Huge, granite rocks dropped to form the slightly crooked trunks. A triangular cave lay between the rocks, the vegetation spilling through the crevasse looked lighter green than the rest. The cave was her destination, where she believed the elusive fresh water was hiding. If not, Velvet was content to make a bed among the vines, fall asleep under a sky soaked with stars—and pray to the earth goddess for rain.

Another hour, darkness fell, and the forest woke. Screams and chattering, cooing caws, throaty growls, swishing leaves, restless slithering, and whispering wind—just a square foot of this world was louder than London town on a bawdy night.

Velvet hastened her pace knowing she would be little more than a d'oeuvre for some of the creatures lurking about. Still another hour and the way to the caves was sucked up by the night —Velvet knew she was now years beyond lost—her predicament was ghastly, but such was the way with all predicaments in her life, at least in this moment, her fate was finally her own. No magic to aid her, no monsters seeking her life, just her thoughts—turbulent as they may be—wits and courage.

When she reached a pathway framed by high trails of stone stairs, the sky twinkled like a net strung with holiday candles had been thrown over the swirling darkness. Polished rocks set one atop the other, a thing which could only have been made by human hands, once upon a time, a long time ago. Humans were the only ones who made aids to help them reach all the places they should not.

Bundles of violet and magenta buds ran over the stones, bursting from the gaps between them. Tiny creatures carried by slender wings fluttered among the petals. Velvet slowly climbed the stairs. When she reached the small plateau of the pathway, that dangled like a suspension bridge, hanging over earth and sky, she saw it was strewn with clipped palm fronds, and banana leaves set out like rushes on an old castle floor.

Iridescent reels of light threaded their way across the pathway, reaching the edge of it, running on far into the distance, stretching away from her to parts unknown. The light showed shapes and shadows, colliding like oil and water with the things that moved beneath the trees.

Where she stood, there was no real way to see the exact place the light stemmed from, somewhere behind her in the in the island world of untouched rainforest. She would have followed the light down the pathway, but bone-weary exhaustion, and a mind-numbing thirst had depleted her. She knelt in a puddle of peachy rays—perhaps she should be afraid, but Velvet felt no more fear of this overgrown, abandoned place—she could not say why, yet she believed the forest had somehow accepted her. If something wanted to chew on her bones—it would have done so by now.

Velvet lay down on a bright green frond, ripped off a tree so recently that sap still flowed from the place where it had been torn away. Wadding up huge bundles of her salty hair to use as a pillow, she moved until she found a comfortable spot on her back, and settled to stare up at all the twinkling lights flickering through the night.

Velvet let her lids flutter, she placed a hand on her heart, missing her brother, wanting Henry so bad it actually ached—yet somehow feeling wonderful all at the same time. Human she may be, yet for this one night she was just another creature sleeping against the earth, wrapped in luminous threads of enchanted nature.

~

Henry woke the second time the same wave smashed his body against a sharp outcropping of jagged rock. Blood was on his tongue, hot and salty as the cruel sea currently intent on pulverizing him. His shaking hand went to his temple where pain was sparking in a particular spot. His fingers came away sticky, more blood. Henry looked up. Remnants of his sunken ship littered the water around him, long boards and beams smashed against the same bluff which had not yet managed to break him.

Ropes interlaced with kelp, bits of unrecognizable furniture, a random floating barrel. Nothing moored down besides these barnacle infested rocks. Grinding his teeth, Henry hoisted himself up—climbing the slippery rocks with care—to a wide sedimentary shelf, a plateau of temporary sanctuary, at least until the tide came in. He sat for a space, coughing water and sand from his scratched, dry throat, trying to assess his surroundings—searching them for sight of her.

The sun was dull and low, dripping reflections of its flames onto the stretch of white beach. The sand sizzled in visible, rising ripples as it burned. Bracing himself, Henry took a deep breath, dove back in the frothy surf, then fought his way to shore. Stumbling when the waves attacked his shaking muscles, and questionable balance. When Henry finally reached the shore, the imprint of tiny footprints in the sand was the first thing he saw. No one in the world but his princess and perhaps her mother could have feet that small. He glanced down at his right hand, pressed his thumb to his fingers, he could still feel the impression of her in the last place their skin had touched. The one thing in his life he had ever tried to hold onto, was the one thing always slipping through his fingers.

He had learned the hard way early in his life, that trying to hold what you treasured only made the inevitable loss all the more painful. He had held his mother and sister's hands the night they slipped away. Men in black put the two young ladies in the ground. Rain had been falling when it happened, he remembered the large drops of cold water that dripped down his face.

His father knocked him on the shoulder, made him pick up a hand full of wet dirt, and throw it on their graves—the pebbles in the mud rattled on the polished coffin lids, they sounded like falling hail—his mother and sister were the only souls in the world who he had loved absolutely. Men piled dirt in the deep holes where his family would find their rest. On that day he told his boyhood self, never to care again, totally, eternally—and he had not, not until her.

On his knees in the surf, Henry reached out to touch the first print—something deep and shouting in his heart, felt strongly, impossibly connected the unknown place where she was. From the markings she left in the sand, he knew she had run pell-mell for the unkempt grove of banana trees. There, beneath fans of palm leaves, her story extended. A small pile of discarded peels near a well-raided raspberry bush, naked in more than a few places. Henry grabbed a handful of the berries, squinted his eyes, and stared at the position of the sun while he ate them, trying to suck the water from the tiny pods of juice, knowing he may not find more for miles.

He had been marooned on an island once, eighteen years old, too green to be truly brave. Alone for nearly a fortnight, his survival had been disputed by the elements, his eventual rescue, purely a matter of chance.

Near his bare foot he found a bit of cloth, clearly torn from the skirt she had been wearing when he lost her, it was soft and still smelled a little like lavender. Beside it were a few broken twigs cluttered around the place where she had sat. Had she searched for him? Or only prayed he had met his fate under the waves? Had she begged her gods for justice and freedom? Did it really matter? He was coming for her just the same.

With a purposefulness he had hard learned in many a battle, Henry let his mind clear, around him the green brightened to a resplendent blur, all faded, there was only the clear markings of the trail which would lead him straight to her. His heart kept its own council, his mind had taken the helm, till instinct alone drove him. The cultured duke faded, as the hunter in him took control.

Time passed. Dark fell, and the path she had inadvertently left for him, grew harder to trace. Still, he followed, blindly feeling her in the electric current which had been between them from the first.

High on a moss-soaked cliff, Henry found a clump of torn leaves, and a few stripped branches that told the story of her tumble off a blunt embankment. More disturbed earth and broken roots showed him where she had clawed herself back up.

Hours passed. Henry was no less furious at the girl so determined to be free of him, but as he followed her trail a burgeoning respect for her began to grow. No woman in his acquaintance would walk through a potentially savage landscape, nothing but a broken stick of cane and her wits as protection. He started to feel her struggle for survival as if it were his own. Overall, the last thing he needed. She was deeply dangerous, her limits were flexible, as was her grasp of right and wrong. Now more than ever, he needed to remain detached, wary, watchful.

He did not need to be thinking about how brave she was, how unflinching in the face of whatever slop life threw her way. It hurt to imagine how exhausted she must be, how very painfully thirsty. His hand went to his own throat and he swallowed over the dry constriction there.

He walked on. Stars hung so close, Henry felt like he could reach up and stir them. Finally, he stopped to catch his breath, leaning hard against a smooth rock, he wiped the sweat off his brow using the back of his grit coated sleeve. He brushed the hair from his eyes, and saw his hands were shaking, he shoved them in the deep pockets of his trousers. Shoulders slumped as his eyes fell closed, he dragged air in his lungs—feeling in every joint like he had taken a beating from a boulder.

A mosquito buzzed at his ear, he slapped at it, looked up when it zipped past his eyes. He saw a pathway stretching far above his head, like a bridge running along a cliff summit, framed by twin set staircases that curled up the mountain.

Thirst always makes me hallucinate, thought Henry, comically straining his neck for a better view, then rubbing at his eyes. Blinking rapidly, like that action could somehow drive the fog from his gaze, Henry began to climb the stairs. The stones had been set in place by human hands, many years ago by the look of the vines who had made these rocks their home—which meant this island was once populated.

Was once? Or still is? Henry did not know the answer to his own mental question, all the same he felt naked without a single weapon.

Panting, Henry heard himself make a rough, annoyed sound when he reached the final stone stair set crookedly atop its fellow. The pathway was suddenly under foot, strewn in palm fronds, illuminated by a light that filtered in from the foot of the trail. A glow of apple-green and starlight.

He sat down, not meaning to. Lethargy was a wet blanket settling over his shoulders. He thought he saw the apple lights flicker, then seemed to sway, blowing like Chinese lanterns. In front of him, Henry could see the exact spot where she had stood. The ground recently disturbed, the muddy indentation where her heel had dug in was still soft. It was here where her trail disappeared. Vanished, as though some giant hand from the sky had simply reached down and lifted her off the earth.

On her journey here, Velvet had not trodden lightly, or bothered to cover her tracks in the slightest—yet the earth stretching out in front of him looked as if it had remained untouched for many a dead generation.

Bemused enough for it to morph to annoyance, Henry tried to stand. She was close—he could feel her, a breath in the air. According to the infallible nature of tracks, she should damn well be on top of his fool head.

He made it halfway up. His whole body shook, he fell back, cursed loudly, and tried again, his second effort garnered the same results as his first. When he tried to stand a third time—he realized dimly he could not. His exhausted limbs adamantly refused to cooperate with any of his brain's dizzy commands. The world spun around him like the tail end of a tornado. He tried to fight it with all his strength—again he could not.

The vague, disoriented feeling was all too familiar. It's like had engulfed him before, once on the Bacchus's deck with the witch who had cast the spell that bound him, arching like a rainbow in his arms, her lips weaving their own enchantments.

Henry struggled hard against the invisible force holding him down, but the air he sucked up his lungs seemed to work like laudanum. He felt powerless, a thing Henry had begun to realize was an unfortunate side effect of any good spell. It was safe to say he abhorred the feeling with all his soul.

The lights glittering at the end of the pathway grew closer, bobbed above his head. The position of them told Henry he lay flat on his back. Angry, immobile, afraid, Henry closed his eyes. For a man extremely assured of his own strength, it enraged him how often he found himself with none.

CHAPTER ELEVEN

Unpredictable magic
Was it you? Was it us? Was it ours?

Sparkles in the air, millions of swimming lights were all Velvet saw when her eyes opened. She blinked, her cheek resting on one of the palm fronds draping the pathway, felt sweaty, and stuck to the leaf a little when she tried to lift her head. Everything around her appeared unchanged, like time had paused while she slept. It was difficult to ascertain if the night was a touch darker because of all the flying, flickering lights. Apple green, rosy gold, and pure, burning white.

Velvet brushed her hands down the dusty bodice of her gown and stood. Her movements light and smooth, as if the short sleep had done her worlds of good. The air rippled around her like she was underwater, and the thirst which had threatened to drive her insane, was now a side thought in her mind. Both things together made Velvet wonder if she was still lying on the fronds fast asleep or trapped in a hallucination brought on by dehydration.

In the distance she could see the green soaked trees waving, hear the chattering birds. All appeared normal, save the thick mists, which had not been present when first she lay down. In the pit of her stomach sleeping butterflies woke and burned, the way they did each time she came face to face with Henry. Inexplicably, she felt him in the air, hovering around her like the broken remnants of an exquisite dream. The feeling of his nearness stayed with her as she started walking down the path. It twisted and curved, narrow in some places, wide in others.

Walking it gave her an overall feeling of disorientation, combined with the fog, and moving lights, Velvet felt like she was lost, somewhere in the Milky Way, traveling across a bridge of stars.

When she reached the end of the pathway, Velvet paused beneath a linked canopy of deep green leaves. The lights were lanterns, she realized with some shock, bright lime, and peachy pink. She could see them clearly now, set high in the branches of the tall trees, then strung between them on silver, braided ropes. From the silver rope closest to her, hung a varied collection of broken finger bones, long jagged teeth, and tiny skulls. She moved closer, reached up a hand to touch one of the skulls. It was smooth as glass. She dropped her hand and stepped back. Her eyes were slowly adjusting, she was clearly able to see the moss climbing up the stout tree-trunks, studded by little for-get-me-nots growing between the roots.

She heard a bird cry out, and over that, the distinct, wonderful sound of splashing water. Velvet started to run. Her feet seemed to fly over the ground, and the living forest closed in around her. The sound was coming from her left, without slowing down, she managed to correct her course, successfully dodging a jumble of treacherous roots—*a shocking first,* she thought, jumping a little before landing lightly on her feet. It appeared she was finally figuring out how to use them—either that, or this alone proved beyond anything that she was dreaming.

The mosquitoes were noticeably absent, the air free of the muggy threat it had carried earlier in the day. Point of fact, the faster she ran, the clearer her vision became. The fog did not so much lift as conform. It glowed now around the edges of all living things lending brilliant clarity to her world, giving her a type of night-vision. Vision she had as an owl and missed every day since.

"I wish for my wings," she said out loud, thinking for a moment that speaking the words was a fixed necessity—as if wishing for things in this place was right. The response to her quiet plea was instant and agonizing pain, stabbing each of her shoulder blades. Terrible. Familiar.

Her stomach tightened; a touch of sudden dizziness made her feet waver. Velvet tripped, then came to running stop, nearly slamming into an unsuspecting tree. A hot point of light charred the center of her forehead, in that sensitive place just between her brows. Her hands flew back to touch her shoulder blades, for a stunned second Velvet could not believe what she felt there.

Feathers, she thought, dazed, reeling. Blood burned in her cheeks, the lights from the swaying lanterns brightened.

The next stabbing pain came, and Velvet screamed behind clenched teeth. Her hands were violently knocked away from her back as wings—white feathers tipped in her blood—cracked through bone, tore her skin, burst violently from her body, and finally unfurled.

When the blaring pain faded to a pulsing throb, Velvet pealed open her eyes to see she was lying flat on her stomach. Huge wings flapped on either side of her, feathers still dripping blood. Slowly, she turned her head from side to side, and looked at them.

It was a dream after all, and she was going to fly. It was just like remembering to breathe after taking a blow to the lungs—a shuddering hesitation, a brave, careful try. Her fingers curled, her arms twitched, then her wings flapped, strongly. Velvet made a high-pitched noise, that awkward sound somewhere between a laugh and scream. The wings moved again. She took a long breath, and silently let it out. She had done that—made them move. In this dream it appeared she could do anything, and Velvet wanted to fly.

The muscles in her back flexed and strained. Her wings stroked the air, then swiped at it with huge, scooping moves that lifted her off the ground. She screamed again, laughing, rising higher and higher. She had made an impulsive wish, and by some enchanted magic present in the very bones of this place, it had come true—she was flying, really flying. The feeling was exhilarating even more so now that she was human. Velvet had wished for and envisaged this moment ever since the day Queenie poured the sizzling spell over her feathers, and that golden stone disintegrated, melted in her skin, hot as lava.

Wind combed through her hair, dragged tears from her eyes. Velvet mentally replayed times past when she had soared the sky, swung out her arms, swooped from side to side. Soon, she was above the treetops looking down on a crystal waterfall that flowed into a wide stone pool shining like the purest emerald. She dove for it, letting the feathers fold down her back so her body gained speed.

Velvet neared the water and saw her reflection in the glassy ripples. She stared in astonished wonder. With her arms outspread, the full snow-white feathers of her wings framing her waving, golden hair, the water showed her the reflection of an angel.

Blood was drying rose gold on the tips of her wings when Velvet landed beside the crystal pool, shooting fractals of light, a million shades of wild jade.

The wings did not vanish when her feet touched the ground as Velvet suspected they would—that was abnormal. Her dreams were never beautiful for long, and this one, more than any of the others, was so terribly vivid.

Her bare feet rested lightly on the stone lip of the pool, wings folded down her back, dragging on the dark green forest floor, like some exotic bridal veil. She dipped her big toe in the water, it was warm and perfect. Velvet sat down letting both her feet dangle, then gulped in a breath—just in case she could not breathe under water in this particular dream—and slid down until her head disappeared beneath the glimmering surface.

Velvet drank and swam for what felt like hours, though it could have been no more than mere minutes. None of the stars had moved, even the thin whips of violet clouds hung in the spot she had left them. This was not all that strange to Velvet, in this place where her wings were real, and the very laws of nature seemed otherwise defined.

She ignored the frozen sky, and floated on her back, kicking her feet, letting her fingers play through the water. Her mind moved in lazy, looping swirls, she let it wander, content in the magic of this hallucination, dream, or fantasy, she wanted to stay a while.

Eventually, Velvet became aware of a presence. Her back was turned, her hackles rose, senses tuned to the vibrations behind her. She spun, making waves with her wings. A woman sat at the edge of her pool, and Velvet stared wide-eyed. The woman's skin was the richest caramel, rouged in places by scattered starlight. Bone piercings cluttered her brows, and an ivory ring was looped through the middle of her straight nose. Her lips were full and smiling, her eyes the color of warm cherry. She wore a simple black slip, the strap of which hung from one of her muscled shoulders. Ink swirls pierced beneath her skin made intricate patterns that wrapped her arms from wrist to shoulder. Velvet did not think she had ever seen such a creature, so strong, the very presence she emanated was like encountering a flaming sword.

The woman had taken Velvet by surprise, but she was not yet alarmed. What was the worst that could happen? This was all a befuddling hallucination, wasn't it?

"It's about time, child. I was wondering when you would notice me. Seems like I've been waiting centuries for you to get here, though it can't have been more than a few years—time is a strange thing when you're no longer a part of it," said the woman. Her smiling lips did not move, yet Velvet heard the deeply accented voice loud as a shout in her mind.

Velvet used her arms and the balance of her wet wings to lift herself from the pool. She sat on the stone ledge across from the woman and began to wring the water from the tattered shreds of her skirt, then spread the cloth—demurely as its state would allow —over her bare legs, and the daggers somehow still strapped to her thighs.

"Waiting for me? What are you talking about? Do I know you? I'm sorry if I met you as a child, I've some spells cast on me, my memory isn't quite what it was." Velvet giggled. The color flaring around the woman's irises looked like a blood-red rose at midnight.

"Ah! I see, you do not know what you have, or what you are?"

Velvet sighed. "Seems I keep running into all sorts of things I don't know," she said honestly, looking down at her fingers, relieved to see they were pink and perfect once more, the nails appeared buffed and had a slight polish. *That is all the proof I need,* she thought. *The storm tore my hands apart, if this were real, they would both be a bloody wreck, like they were when first I closed my eyes on that blasted pathway.* The thought chased away the creeping fear making goosebumps prickle down her back.

"What do I have?" Velvet asked, her gaze still trained on her fingers. "What am I?"

"You have touched the stone of Tamora, I see it in your skin, fused to your bones, the Island has called you home."

"I left all the stones far behind me, and good riddance," said Velvet, narrowing her eyes at the turn this mysterious dream was taking.

"You cannot leave something that is a part of you," said the woman. "I am a guardian of the stones, older than the forest we stand in, I know when one of them has returned to me. Why do you think I'm here?"

"I honestly have no idea," sighed Velvet.

"You summoned me, royal girl—I gave the stones away when they became too heavy for me, I am sorry they fell to you."

"So am I," Velvet said. "I did not mean to summon you."

"When the last guardian cast the spell to change your form, she used the stone of Tamora. It melted, fused with your skin, and now you carry its power in your veins. The stones always find their way to me, such is the nature of their curse, and mine."

"This is a dream," Velvet said by way of denial.

"Reality is whatever the mind believes. Perhaps this place is merely a mirage created by the stones, or in this case, you," the woman said, her voice loud, her lips still frozen in their smile, her eyes glowing bright as fire-lit blood drops.

"The first is a rather overly simplified statement, the second is beyond conception. I am not a stone," said Velvet. She shivered slightly, and water rolled like spherical diamonds off her wings. "I would say my reality has been forced on me by the vicious beliefs of others."

The woman shook her head. Her silky black hair rippled down

her arms. "Not here, Île Sainte-Marie is the birthplace of first life. The cradle of everything—here you are in control."

Rather disconcerted, cold, and a little afraid, Velvet stood. "I suppose I should wake up now, my body is sleeping somewhere, probably dying of thirst, and I can't perish here. My brother needs me and Henry..." her voice trailed off.

The woman got to her feet, the image of her seemed to flicker in and out as she moved. She took Velvet's hands, her fingers like ice. The night around them appeared to darken, a fresh chill coursed down Velvet's spine. Velvet lowered her eyes so she would not see the woman's eternal smile.

"As you need them," said the woman. "You bring fortune and blood. Danger will follow you always."

"Well, a touch of the familiar then, danger is a constant for me," said Velvet. "What does it mean to be a guardian?"

"It means I was once a great and powerful goddess; the stones were mine, a gift—I used them, made a choice, it was the wrong one. I could not pay the price. Now I must watch others use the very magic I once coveted. They were safe here for many centuries. Capricious greed prompted their first departure from this place, their return is sporadic."

"Is it?" asked Velvet. She blinked as her mind fogged up again, and started to run sluggishly, disjointed as a wheel missing a few of its spokes.

The woman nodded. "Do you think the storm blew you to this island by chance, or the captain of the Bacchus and his destination were a strange coincidence? The stones always wish to return home. The last time they were stolen from this place was nigh on twenty years ago—I told the thief they could only be used by the worthy, I predicted her quest would end in blood—did it?"

"Yes," Velvet said, then, "can't you speak?"

"I haven't moved my lips in a thousand years," the woman said.

"Well, that makes sense," Velvet said.

The woman tilted her head to the side. "Does it?" she asked.

"No." Velvet sighed. "But not much of this does. I am glad of the company though as it was beginning to feel a bit lonely."

"You must be hungry," the woman said, and Velvet nodded.

"What's your name?" Velvet asked.

"You may call me Minerva," said the woman, and lightly squeezed Velvet's fingers.

"Am I dreaming, Minerva?"

"Do you think you are dreaming?"

Velvet laughed. "Yes, I must be, you know, due to the fact we have just decided on, that none of this makes any sense," she said, relieved to see the eerie moment retreat. They walked for a time beneath a roof of leaves and stars that remained stationary in the sky no matter which direction they went. Eventually, the dense forest opened to a flower-soaked glen. Here the stars were gone, a full, silver moon decorated the dark, surrounded by three rings red as the woman's unblinking eyes. They sat together in a mushroom patch, wrapped by little pink flowers that looked like church bells.

Minerva handed Velvet a mushroom she plucked from the ground. It had a slender, orange stem, and small yellow patches on its slouched head that looked to Velvet liked a dozen flattened daisies. Minerva lifted her mushroom to her mouth, stopped just before it reached her lips, then motioned with her head and hands for Velvet to take a bite.

Velvet did as she instructed. Her teeth sunk deep into the spongy thing. It tasted about as good as a mouthful of dirty air, but it went down easy and helped to calm the stomach acid groaning around her gut. She took another bite and did not stop until the mushroom was gone, and she was reaching for another.

Minerva watched her eat, her own mushroom never moving past the barrier of her frozen, smiling lips. "Strange," she mused, while Velvet started on her third mushroom, this one white and fluffy as wool. The dust the mushroom left on her fingers glowed violet as the moonlight.

Velvet smiled up at the woman and spoke over the bite in her mouth. "A lot about tonight is strange. I'd be interested what struck you as most odd," she said.

Minerva's smile widened so it looked like the corners of her mouth were slit with a knife. Velvet almost screamed, but another bite of mushroom choked it back.

"In times past, the stones of Avialia have always linked to souls with dark intentions. You are not like the others."

Velvet took another bite and realized she had finished. "The purity of my intentions tends to wane when people I love are in danger."

"Choices made in desperation," Minerva said.

"Reason does not alter result," Velvet returned. "I don't know anything about the stones, or their power—I only know I have to use them once more, to change my brother back to a human prince —then the stones of Avialia can go to the Devil, with my wholehearted blessing. I hate them."

Minerva nodded like Velvet had spoken some great truth. She stood then, leaving Velvet sitting in a pile of colorful mushrooms. "You—winged, royal girl, you are the proper guardian for the stones, whether you wish it or not. This night I have interfered for the first time in a thousand years, to give you one of your own."

"My own what? A guardian? Goddesses save me, I cannot take the drama of another protector. I am more than capable of taking care of myself," she said, as Henry's face flashed brightly in her mind.

"That's good," Minerva said, now flickering so violently—like flashes of lighting behind dark clouds—Velvet could scarcely make out her features. Only white teeth and red eyes.

Velvet wanted to wake up then, she even pinched her own thigh, but all it did was hurt. "I don't want a protector, I don't want to be one of those horrid stones," Velvet almost shouted, terrified now.

"What a shame, when your survival depends on both," said Minerva in that lulling mind voice, Velvet believed she would remember forever.

~

They say the man could never see what was right in front of him, he only followed her star in the sky.

When Henry woke, the pathway and stone staircase was gone. He was standing in a field of flowers looking at an angel. She knelt in a pool of her own golden hair, a bright red mushroom was clasped in her hands, and a luminous pair of pearl white wings were folded behind her, framing her in the elusive. Angelic as a prayer. Her lashes fluttered, her eyes flew up, blue as the ocean he loved.

"Velvet," he breathed, unable to say any more.

She flashed him a smile so brilliant it blinded. "No need to look alarmed, Henry. You can sit beside me as you're only visiting a dream of mine," she said.

Henry knelt. He could do nothing else. "Better than any of mine," then, "is that what's happening?"

"Why does everyone think, I'm the authority on this?" She giggled, the sound girlish and lovely, her smile enchanted. "I guess we must be, I have wings after all."

"Yes, I can see." He almost groaned. "Why do you have wings, Velvet?"

She threw up her hands, bits of mushrooms fell from her fingertips. "Who can say? I wished for them, and they were mine." She reached for him, touched his arm, stared into his eyes. "I'm glad you found me, even if only for a time."

Henry hardly comprehended her words, she was so beautiful, and the hazy fog had not left him.

"I fear we are both the victims of some magic. I was quite afraid a moment ago, and you're right, Henry, it doesn't feel good at all."

"I was wrong," he said, meaning it. "I'll take what we had over nothing at all." He brought her fingers to his lips, kissed her knuckles, her hands were clean, the nails unbroken. "What happened to your fingers?"

She tilted her head, waves of hair rushed over his thigh. "I woke up, walked, swam, and they were like this when I finally looked." She flexed her fingers and regarded them quizzically. "The state of my hands is one of the main things telling me I am actually asleep somewhere—wanting water. Are you thirsty, Henry? I'm not sure if it will make any difference when we wake up, but it feels nice to drink just the same."

"I'm very thirsty," he said, realizing that he was, though he had not thought about it for a time.

"We can swim, maybe afterwards, and if you are not too heavy for me, we can fly," she said.

"I don't think I want to fly," he said, his eyes now locked to her lips when she smiled at him again.

"You won't know until you try," she said, then stood. He moved with her, wanting to keep her hand in his. "I wonder who will visit me next," he heard her say. When he asked her what she meant the luminous girl only looked over her shoulder to flash him another blinding smile. Lust, pure and scalding scattered his thoughts as she led him to a small pool hidden amidst a tangle of trees and vines.

Since the first, they each fought a cause too righteous to be surrendered. Both assured of their own purpose, in this moment Henry had no idea what in hell he had been fighting for, if not her. What did it matter that she had bewitched him? He was her willing slave.

Hips full and lush, near spilling from her torn gown, swayed in front of him, it took stupendous effort not to close his arms around her, drag them both beneath the crystal water and make her his once and for all.

"Come," she said, stepping in the water. "It's quite warm."

Henry let go of her long enough to tug off his shirt. Saw her eyes go wide as she traced him from head to toe. Henry stopped moving and let her look. "I've never swam with an angel before," he said, listening to the seduced sounds of his husky, contralto voice.

Velvet shook her head, her eyes rushing back to his face. "You, more than any other should know, I am the furthest thing from that."

"I'm not so sure," he said, reaching out to touch a lock of her shining, golden hair. "Why are we here, darling? Can you tell me about this place?" he asked softly, trying to keep the demand out of his voice, somehow knowing this world was her doing. Her essence was in the very air as he well knew the feeling of her witchcraft.

Only this time was different, rather than being forced by it, he was sharing the magic with her.

Velvet rolled her round eyes at him, her lips pouted slightly, and in that moment, she looked too young and innocent to be any man's wife, especially a scoundrel like him. "I've been running with the assumption that this is a dream or fantasy of all my favorite things," she said.

"You expect me to believe I've fallen into that elite category?" he asked derisively.

She sighed rather dejectedly. "Yes, it appears so. I should be blushing, but this is all a conjuring of my subconscious, I suppose there is only truth here. At times I loathe you, truly, yet it would be a lie to say you are not always in my mind," she confessed.

Henry searched for a sufficient response to her words but found none. He could neither breathe or speak, for she bewitched him, her incomparable face, her eyes, her wings. "If this is a dream, then we are sharing it," he said, "besides right here, I don't know where I am."

Velvet giggled, the sound musical as the waterfall, and warm, crystal ripples washing over their feet. "Me neither, I've been lost in this place for hours, though the stars have not moved at all. The moon is over there," she pointed past his shoulder, "shining in the place you found me, but we can't see it from here. I find that quite odd, don't you?"

"Yes," he said, wanting to reach out and touch her, wanting her so desperately, Henry knew he would have agreed to anything. She stepped back from him and her velvet wings swished through the water making her dress transparent as smoke, then silently slipped beneath it. The pale pink tips of her breast jutted against the wet cloth, swaying with her small movements, taunting him till he thought he would go quite mad.

His hands were fists at his sides. Tensed in the permanent pose they adopted around her. Like it took constant, physical effort to hold back from simply attacking her each time they locked eyes. She splashed, kicked her feet like a sauced mermaid, and dove away when he lowered himself in the pool. He swam toward her, glancing briefly at the thick, living rainforest running into a sky of frozen stars, then his eyes fell on the winged girl in front of him, glowing brighter than all else.

"Odd it may be, but perhaps my mind palace can grant you a wish." She cupped her hands, scooped water over her face, then pulled it through her hair. Her eyes were blue sapphires, his gaze fell to her lips when she asked, "What do you want, Henry? Most in all the world?"

"You," he said raggedly, "only you. Always you. Since the first moment I saw you, a small girl in a forgotten place."

He watched her lips part over her sharp intake of breath. "Even though you don't trust me?" she whispered.

"Yes," he breathed.

"Why?" she asked, her eyes wide, so innocent for what he wanted.

"I've never met anyone like you, I've never—"

"I will use the stones again, touch the power you hate, perhaps take a life," she said.

"It would change nothing!" His voice was harsh, he could not help it. "No, don't look at me like that, I'm speaking truth, no matter what you do, I will always want you, frantically, madly, the devil knows why!"

A smile curved her lips then; she was sensuous as Eve in the garden. She used both hands to lift the mass of hair off her shoulders, sighed and let it fall enticingly. "If you want me, why are you all the way over there?" she enquired.

Henry felt his expression darken, in the water's reflection, he saw his eyes. They were fixed on her breasts, despite the handfuls of water he had drunk, his mouth felt terribly dry. "You've sworn I will never have you. If I come closer you will resist. I fear in my current mood I'll attack you, force you."

"I will not resist," she said. "We have decided this is a dream, a place of wishes, here there is no bad blood between us—so that leaves all the rest."

Henry's heart raced, loud and perceptible as hers. Her wings curved through the water, one stroke of her hands across the surface and she was in his arms. He knew so well the rhythm of her breath, the soft feel of her small, strong body. His fingers lightly traced the damp skin of her throat, ran over her shoulders, touched her wings. The individual feathers twitched when he brushed them, he felt more than heard her shivering sigh. Everything was fantasy now.

"Tomorrow we will both wake and the struggle to survive will start all over again," she said, her eyes tangling with his, blue and crystal bright. "People get so many things, often times whether they deserve it or not. We can have this night."

His free hand caught the nape of her neck, cupping lightly beneath her wet hair. She affected him like some exotic drug, sugary opium, or the most potent wine. They both held their breath when he reached for the lacy bow resting in the hollow of her throat, the only thing holding the shredded dress in place.

She swallowed hard, but did not stop him, just stared mutely at his face, her gaze flicking erratically to his lips. "Are you going to do it n...now?" she whispered, her shaking voice tripping over her words.

The tie fell apart under his fingers, the dress sloped over her shoulders, Velvet caught it with both hands, and held the wet cloth to her breast, her face was white, her cheeks infused with hot blush.

"I've never undressed before a man in my life," she said.

Henry leaned down to kiss her knuckles, heard her pounding heart, felt her breath rustle his hair.

"Your hands are shaking," she said, her low voice exquisite, just another shade of magic in this place.

"It's what you do to me," he told her, pressing his lips to her throat, slowly pealing her fingers away from her body, motion nearly suspended, the dress slipped to her waist. "You are breathtaking," he said reverently, aching for what he did not yet have—many a beautiful lady across three continents had sauntered through his life, never had he encountered a creature like her. "You are truly the prize, despite a religion pounded into my head since birth, regardless of what you have done, or will yet do, I can well understand my compulsion to die for you," he said, his mouth touched her cheek, her lush bottom lip, "be enchanted by you, crave you." His finger brushed a drop of water trembling on the tip of her breast, caught it before it fell. Her nipples tightened in a rush that weakened his knees. Henry felt like the world was burning down around them, singed orange light saturated everything. His hands went to the laces on his trousers, and he smiled up at her, saw a tremble in her lips as he undid the final lace. "It is a dream, right? Your dream, you can touch me in a dream," he told her, his eyes following the path down his body, that her own traveled.

Hesitantly, she placed both her hands on his chest, her touch light as air. Her fingers traced invisible lines over his stomach.

Henry closed his eyes, let his head fall back, and allowed himself to simply exist. He had always imagined it would be like this, from the moment he had first seen her, Henry intrinsically knew her touch would have the power to change the very alchemy of his soul.

Henry was all around her, his brilliant eyes heavy lidded as he traced scalding hands over her body. She opened her lips to say something. What it was, Velvet did not know. A hard hand on her neck drew her to him, his mouth fastened on hers with primal greed, his lips were open flame. Water sloshed and rippled, reflecting all the stars, making lights waltz over his bronze skin.

The reality of Henry, his blistering touch, his drugging taste, was always better than fantasy—which made this moment all the more confusing. Her arms went tentatively around his neck, resting on his tense, strong shoulders. The way she moved crushed the tips of her breast against his marble chest, and she heard him make a deep, husky sound. She saw all the fractured memories of them unfurl in her mind like spools of lace, touched by brilliance and darkness. She felt his hand fall to the curve of her hips, and sighed, lost in him.

What if this is not a dream? What if this is real? You are giving yourself to him forever, warned her treacherous mind. Velvet ignored it, her heart and sizzling nerves were wrapped up in him as he lifted her in his arms, then carried them both from the pool.

He lay her gently on the damp grass, her wings splayed around her. His lips went to her throat, burning where they touched. He dragged them down her body, kissing, biting, Velvet began to pant. "If this is real, will you forgive me?" he asked, his lips pressed against her hip, his teeth grazing over where the bone curved beneath the skin.

"Yes," she gasped, suddenly afraid of his proximity, wanting to escape the intimacy of his touch. His hands clamped down on her hips, preventing retreat. With his teeth he tore away what remained of her dress.

Her hands fell to his shoulders, shoved at his weight. "Henry, no!" she gasped as his lips trailed ever lower to find the aching center of her. She felt his chest shake against her thighs, heard his husky laugh. "I knew you would say that," he muttered.

"Please," she began to squirm in earnest.

"Let me," he breathed.

Velvet shook her head, mortified, blood boiled in her cheeks. "No," she panted, "you cannot kiss me there."

"I must." He lifted his eyes, fire bright, to hers. "I've imagined you like this so many times, let me taste you, Velvet," he rasped, "let me have this, and if it turns out we are not in fact dreaming, you will still be a virgin."

"Will I? Henry, I... I—" she stammered as his hands went to her knees, then drew them apart with aching slowness, that made Velvet want to scream. Her head fell back, she looked at the stars, they blurred out of focus. His lips, and tongue moved then, and soon the forest was full of her breathless screams.

His mouth was evil, moving over her with devastating skill, his hands stroked her thighs, reached up to cup her breasts. Velvet lost all sense of everything but him, and what he did. Under his hot lips, her body squirmed, bucked, then writhed. She trembled on the pinnacle of euphoria, reached for what she did not know, strained to touch a thing illusive and spectacular.

She screamed his name, the pleasure so acute it frightened. "Don't fight it, my love, come for me," he almost growled.

It was the deep sound of his voice, low and desperate, or it was the hot look in his heavy-lidded eyes, perhaps it was the way he called her 'my love'—yet finally, that thing she reached for, she touched. For a stunned moment, everything was pitch black, pulsing, ringing, screaming in breathless silence, then, millions of colorful lights spun through the darkness, soaked in iridescent glow, coursed like liquid sunlight through her veins, and her arching body shook in his arms. Distantly, Velvet heard her own broken scream, listened to the way her voice called his name. *If this truly were a dream,* Velvet thought, before all thought faded away, *it would follow her to the grave a legend.*

12

CLUTTERED CABINS, AND BROKEN HEARTS

To lose you once broke my heart like a song,
finding you again left patchy scars,
could I really bear losing you once more?

The first mate's cabin was small, cluttered by sparse bits of furniture. A table nailed to the ground, a chair with wicker legs, and a rope bed just big enough for one. The squat window behind the single-basin washstand was thrown open. Through it, Devon watched the crescent moon make its nightly journey across the cloudless sky.

Two days since the storm passed, two days since first he held the amethyst in his hand. Tonight, he held the amethyst...and her. Katie Miller, transparent as water—grave cold, serenely lying in his arms, head on his chest, cheek pressed to his pounding heart.

All shock, questions, and fear had left him hours ago. Now he was content to just hold her, close his eyes and listen to her soft-spoken words, in that voice which had narrated all his dreams.

Katie's slender fingers coasted over his chest; he could feel their chill through the linen of his shirt. He shivered when she reached his throat. So long as he held the amethyst clenched in his sweaty palm, he could see her, feel her.

Nearly four hours ago he had stumbled into this cabin, exhausted by his time at the helm. He had gone directly to the bag of stones and carefully removed the amethyst because he could not bear her absence a single second longer, and sometime in the last hour, with the salt wind beating at his face, Devon had convinced himself what he had seen the first time he held the stone, was in fact reality.

At first, they simply stared at each other, too many words between them to speak only a few. Katie's eyes wide and glittering with all the tears a ghost could not cry.

"Don't you dare let go of that stone," she finally said, then threw her smoky self into his waiting arms. For Devon, the feel of her, even thus altered, had been like coming home. He went to his knees, her fingers laced in his hair, they had not been able to let go.

Eventually, he lay them down on his bed, her small body cradled to his heart. Neither of them had moved for hours, both paralyzed by the sheer wonder of it.

Hand resting on his chest, Katie leaned on her elbow to look down at him, her grey eyes huge. "I wish we could stay like this forever," she said.

Devon reached up to cup her cheek, touch the arched ridge of her brow. "I'm sorry for not telling you sooner. I should've said I loved you every day you were alive," he said.

"I believe I always knew," she said, "however, I also believed I was going to a place called heaven, yet here we are. My body is bled out six feet underground, my soul is a ghost on a pirate ship, so what do I know—though, I am in your arms at long last, so maybe this is Heaven after all."

"Hardly," Devon grunted. "A battered ship and broken crew following an ancient map to the heart of no-man's-land."

"Velvet will find the spell with or without the stones, she knows her map by heart, I watched her go over it with Nora, not an hour before she danced her fateful dance. My gut tells me she's close." Katie's forlorn expression turned serene. "I never much believed in what she was about. The lot of us running after her like chickens with our heads cut off—tripping on our own shadows. I stumbled straight into my own grave—on top of it all, no one thought to tell me what was going on. Yet," she sighed, "I had a choice, Nora would have let me go—"

"But you followed her," said Devon.

"I always do," she admitted. "When I saw captain Chance's hands around her neck, I moved before I thought." She met his gaze; he saw terrible sadness drench her expression. "I watched you fall to your knees when he cut my throat."

"I wanted to die," Devon said, shifting irritably, pierced by the memory, "still do, really."

Katie settled back in the crook of his shoulder, lifted her hand, and peered through her translucent palm. "This was my greatest fear," she said, her smoky lids lowering over her rain-colored eyes. "To die unshriven, locked to the place of my death, destined to wander the in-between for eternity. Purgatory. Now?" Her hand moved to his cheek, her smile only a little forced, she lifted her eyes to find his. "Like this?" She stroked his jaw. "I think I could stay here forever with you. It is a shame though, that I had to die to hear you say you love me."

Her bright eyes searched his, awaiting a response, his heart was a stuttering thing in his chest. "I could not have told you—what would have been the point of speaking my truth? Either you loved me in return, and we battle to exist in a world hell-bent on tearing us apart—in the end we would inevitably find ourselves divided— sad, forever alone. Or, you rejected me, and I, too in love to look away, watch from a distance, sad, forever alone."

Katie walked her fingers over his bicep, and he could feel the touch in the marrow of his soul. "I've never known you to be sad or alone, even as a boy you always wore that same, irrepressible smile."

"All a dreadful façade, I'm afraid. A delightful shell of my own design, formed to mask my own external burn of unrequited love."

Katie lifted her hand to his face, pressed gently against his cheek, turned his head until their noses brushed. "I've always loved you, Devon," she breathed.

The pad of his thumb touched her bottom lip, he leaned in pulled by a force outside himself, toward the magnet of her bloodless lips.

"Land! Land ho!" The urgent call came from without. Devon flinched at the sound; Katie sighed. Together, their eyes fell to the stone in his hand.

"I suppose you have to let go of it now, Nora will need you," Katie said, her voice nearly tripping over her lady's name. Her eyes twin pools of regret.

"I need you," Devon said, locking his fingers tighter around the amethyst. Holding the thing felt like grabbing the wrong end of a red-hot branding iron. He was surprised it had not yet bored a burning hole through the center of his palm. The pain was there, but nothing. He would have endured anything to keep her forever. Katie sat up, he tried to hold on to her, but she was made of insubstantial fluff that flitted through his fingers. She floated to the opposite side of the cramped room, before turning again to face him. The shout above rang out once more. *"Land, land ho!"*

"Put down the stone, Lord Eden, I'll be waiting here next time you chose to pick it up."

Devon shook his head. He was on the verge of another denial, parting his lips in protest when Nora burst through the door, brighter than a sunspot with her autumn hair clashing wonderfully against her hot pink ensemble, slouched top hat, trousers, and sharp waistcoat.

Devon set the stone on the bed, it leaked lilac light over his serviceable, grey blanket. Katie vanished instantly. Exhausted, spent, Devon rubbed his eyes, before lifting them to meet Nora's blazing, excited stare.

"Madagascar," she panted, her face wreathed in radiant smiles. "We will make port by morning. The men say they can take me to St. Mary blindfolded, yet repairs may take a few days." She chewed thoughtfully on a chunk of her lower lip. "Henry is probably halfway back to England now, and Velvet with him—"

"If the Siren survived the storm," Devon muttered. He tried to stand, and the room spun. His hand went to his head and he sat back down.

Nora's sharp gaze tracked his odd set of actions. "Are you well?" she asked and took a step toward him.

He tried to lift a hand, wave away her concern, his head

seemed to swing on his shoulders. "Oh! Devon, your nose, it is bleeding, quite badly." She rushed the rest of the way to him and pressed the underside of her wrist to his clammy brow. "You are burning up!" she stated wrathfully, and her eyes shot to the stone, still bleeding light on the coverlet. "You used the stone? Why?"

He shook his head. "You wouldn't believe me if I told you."

Nora rocked back on her heels, folding her arms across her chest, the gesture made masculine by the hard cut of her clothes. Her right brow arched dramatically. "Try me," she taunted.

"If I hold it...I...if...if—"

"Do spit it out!" snapped Nora. "Being pregnant isn't known to give one an extra helping of patience, you know?"

Devon patted the space on the bed beside him. "You might want to sit down for this."

Nora looked at his hand, then his face, her stance remained unchanged. "Tell me what the hell is going on, Devon. I'm the girl who chats up thin air, remember?"

"If I hold it, I see Katie," he said, and wiped his nose on the back of his hand, then stared at the streak of blood painting his knuckles.

Nora made a soft, screeching sound, like shattering glass, or the clash of blades. Her hands went to her cheeks, she took a step toward him, tripped, then sat down hard on the bed in the spot previously indicated.

"Truly?" she asked.

Devon nodded. His eyes fell to the stone. "I heard it calling to me the first time I saw it, her voice in the air, in the fog—music, even in my dreams."

Nora reached for the stone, her face intent. Devon caught her wrist. "No," he said, "don't touch it, I know you want to see her, believe me I understand, but it makes you feel..." he shook his head. "Depleted, weak, like it takes something from you."

"You think I care?" Nora wailed, fighting his hold, trying to wrench free.

"The baby," he said, and she fell still, then her shoulders shook, and she began to cry, loud, hiccupping gulps that further broke his smashed heart.

Devon gathered her in his arms, shoving the stone away with his knee, he lifted her onto his lap. "No, no, darling, don't cry," he soothed, feeling hot tears smart in his own eyes. "I'm already in a great deal of pain, now why would you go and make it worse? You know how female tears maim me."

"I miss her," she sobbed, burying her teary face in her hands.

He stroked a lock of hair away from her damp fingers. "She knows, she misses you. Perhaps I should not have told you," he said.

Nora blotted at her tears with the tips of her fingers. "Perhaps I should throw you overboard and make you swim to shore," she retorted. "Don't mind the tears, it's the child. She's tampering with my constitution." Linking her arms around his neck in a brief hug, she sniffed and wiped her nose on his sleeve then stood, and let out a long, shaky breath. "Abigail knows where we can put in for repairs, our haul is in shatters, masts broken, and there is sufficient damage to the stern, she says there are many places along the coastline where such things are done."

"I know all that, Nora," Devon said, lying back on his bed, and slinging an arm over his eyes.

"I know you do. I suppose I just needed something to say. I can't ask questions about Katie or I'll cry enough tears to compete with the Atlantic."

"So, will I," said Devon honestly.

"Then let's dispense with such talk for the moment, shall we? Better speak of things we can fix, find, or change, like the state of my ship, or Velvet's map." She reached in the pocket of her waistcoat and retrieved a fold of yellow paper. "I've been studying it for hours, most of the island is populated, by pirates and brigands—"

"We are pirates and brigands," interrupted Devon, his voice muffled by his arm.

Nora snorted in dainty derision. "Don't I know it. St Mary's island—or Île Ste-Marie—apparently I've been saying it wrong."

"You have been," said Devon, and she threw him a blazing glare.

"Abigail tells me the island's true name is Nosy Mbavy, which, literally translated means 'the woman's island'. There is a legend to go with that telling name. Of an ancient goddess who took pity on a shipwrecked man, in a place where no men were allowed. She fell in love and hid him when the other women tried to kill him. In the end, she used magic to save him, and it cost the lives of her sisters—nearly took her own. The human man lived, yet the goddess would have died, had it not been for the kindness of a young girl, who took pity on a thirsty crone."

Devon pealed his arm off his eyes. "From the tone of your voice I take it this story-time has a significance?"

"Yes," said Nora as she knelt and spread the map on the floor. "It's part of the stone's story. Velvet told me a piece of it once, about a girl who brought the same crone a drink of water. The woman gave her the stones the next day in gratitude, but the girl dreamed a horrid dream of crystal pools with sand for water."

"I have a deep, healthy fear of the calculation in your eyes right now," said Devon warily.

"I think the pools have some significance," Nora said, not looking up.

"Why don't you just hold different stones, till one of them lead you to the spell?" he asked.

"I don't know. Louis said it does not work like that. He told me spells of that nature must want to be found."

"Statements like that give me chills," said Devon, turning to stare at the small, splayed map.

"I know," said Nora, sounding thrilled. Devon rolled his eyes. "I will make inquiries when we reach shore. Abigail will come with me."

"What does Louis say to all of this?"

"What he says doesn't matter, it is not only his choice, not anymore. The fault is his, he is in my mind, always. I do not think I could live without him now. He is smart and brave, wise, kind, vicious." Her hand fell to her stomach, her mouth turned down at the corners. "I'm four months pregnant. I'm running out of time." Her eyes squeezed closed; Devon knew she was fighting a fresh bout of tears. He knelt beside her, put a hand over hers. Her skin felt hot to the touch, either that or he was very cold.

"Sleep, Nora, while you can. Tomorrow is another day. We will find what we need to change him back. I swear it."

"You cannot swear such a thing," she countered, though she sounded somewhat mollified.

He kissed her brow, holding pressure there for a moment, ignoring his dizzy head. "I can, and I do."

13

ENCHANTED THINGS

*T*hunder rumbled somewhere in the lemon horizon when the Bacchus crawled, battered, and haunted into the Bay of Antongil. Aqua water and gold beaches embraced by full, vibrant rainforests. In the painted sky clouds made square towers, flocks of birds in formation flew beneath them. Lining the beach were anchored ships flying similar symbols and colors to her own.

Nora had to fight for breath as she took in the seemingly endless miles of unbridled splendor. This place was close to heaven as Nora knew she would ever get. She could pitch a tent under the leaning palms and stay here forever on this diamond slice of paradise.

Long boats made of stripped bark and sappy pitch roamed the shallow waters. The men and women rowing them were near naked and well colored by the sun. Exotic feathers decorated their long hair, and Nora felt a moment of trepidation—no matter what outfit she chose today, there would be no help for it. Here, she would be visible as a fire atop a dark mountain. With her ruby hair and pearly skin, it was no vanity to acknowledge she was merely a sparkling treasure of a different name, and she would do well to take extra care. Keep her men close and weapons ready.

"Beautiful isn't it?" asked Abigail, coming to stand beside Nora at the helm.

"Like a bloody fantasy," Nora confirmed. "A bastard girl could start a new life here."

"It is a shame prince Radama gave Captain Chance a chest of gold for you. Stories say the man is fierce as a lion even asleep. We need to have a plan in place when we run into him, as we must on an island this size," said Abigail, looking toward the frothy shore and beyond.

"I believe I will simply have to tell him my circumstances have changed," Nora replied, nonplussed.

Abigail lifted a dark brow. "It was a great deal of money."

"It wasn't spent on me, not precisely—" argued Nora.

"The prince ordered a girl with red hair and skin like cream, he even specified freckles, if I recall. It won't matter to the prince what your altered circumstances are, if Radama lays eyes on you, god himself will have no hope of convincing the man that you are not his."

Nora lifted her chin and settled her blue-satin tricorne more firmly on her head, bracing it well against the wind. "He won't be the first man I have had to instruct thusly, and I dare say he won't be the last. No matter, I will endeavor to stay clear of this princely wretch. I have no desire to run into any of our deceased Captain's old friends—is that enough?"

"I don't believe so," said Abigail thoughtfully, "if it pertains to magic of any kind, no matter how dark, prince Radama will know of it.'

"Will he indeed?" mused Nora, "not more than Alfonso, I'd wager. Besides I—" Nora's words broke off abruptly, her hands flew to her temples and she was unable to do anything, save listen to the voice in her mind.

"You've clearly abandoned your wits, my girl," shouted Louis. Nora spun to face him. His huge body was braced against the foremast, his front hooves tangled in a mess of fallen shrouds. His glow was sable and bronze, it always darkened when he was angry at her—lately, a regular occurrence. Nora knew he saw the defiant insolence in her eyes, his horns drew back while his nostrils flared. His golden eyes shimmered, mirroring the color of the polished amber stone in the bag. She wondered if it was the one that had changed him.

"Yes, it was," he snapped. "What's more, your plan is stupid, and it reeks of failure," he finished, briskly reading her mind.

"Stay out of my head," she snapped, seething.

"Who will die for me, my lady? Who?" His voice rose. "Who? Tell me!"

"I don't know!" she cried. "I don't care! Some murderers bound for the gallows, a rapist, a monster wearing human flesh! I don't care!"

"A soul is a soul no matter what they have done. It is not for you to play judge and executioner," said Louis. His hooves clicked on the deck as he moved to close the distance between them, in the diamond shape between his spiked antlers, Nora watched the rising sun.

"Why not?" she shouted. "Must I stay silent so some stodgy old judge can choose their fate? I am the daughter of the king of England, the blood of William the conqueror runs in my veins. I say the right *is* mine."

"Nora," he said, the dreaded plea in his voice, in his huge golden eyes. "Please, let me stay as I am," he finished, and she closed her eyes. There, he had finally said it, and she wanted to slap him. In the past he had hinted at such things, yet never had he come straight out and said it. Had they been a couple of youths in a glittering ballroom, Nora would have tossed the contents of her champagne glass in his face, as it was, she could only stare back at him in mute rage, while her crew observed her argument with the air in amused shock.

Many of the pirates stopped work to stare at their mad queen, who spoke to golden ghosts. On either side of them, men dropped the long boats that would take them ashore, she watched them toss weapons and food bundles over the rails. The ship fair bustled with activity, and they were in clear view of everyone—Nora simply did not care what any of them thought. She took the final step to Louis, then wrapped her arms around his neck. She rested her cheek in the warm plain between his eyes. "I won't let you disappear," she whispered. "There is nothing you can say or do that will change my mind. I'll go blind if I lose your glow."

"You know the glow will fade if you turn me human," he said softly.

Nora shook her head. "I wouldn't be so sure. Not a month ago I saw your sister shine like the north star." She stepped back, used the underside of her wrists to wipe her eyes. Against the stormy canvas of the rising sun, Louie glimmered with such vividness it was difficult for Nora to look directly at him. "I'm going ashore with my men. Will you come, or leave me to face the prince of misogyny himself? From what Abigail says, Marcus Atilius and all his women hating ways, cannot hold a candle to our prince."

A wave broke against the ship, and it rocked under their feet. "I need someone strong, and trustworthy at my back. I want it to be you," she said.

Louis turned his head, pressed his cold nose to her ear. "You are the most stubborn creation in existence," he said. The capitulation in his voice told Nora she had won.

She sighed in crushing relief. "Yes, that is the prevailing opinion."

"I won't let anything happen to her," Abigail said, tucking her dark curls beneath a bright red kerchief and tying it off at the back in a serviceable knot. "Sides, there be as much good here as bad," she said, stretching languorously, reaching her arms high above her head. "Even if the balance is at times slightly flawed, these are the shores of my homeland, and there's nothing so sweet as home. Never thought I would ever walk them again a free woman."

"You are more than free," said Nora, "you are wealthy enough to purchase a kingdom of your choosing."

"Only because you decided to divide the fallen captain's loot with the crew."

Nora lifted her chin. "That was no act of charity, simply as it should be."

"Yet, not how it is," said Abigail.

Nora shrugged. "I don't see why not? It is the only way everyone wins. Now those who remained are here by choice. There was a touch of personal gain in my actions, never fear."

Abigail gave her a blank yet speaking look. "And what was that?"

"This way there is less chance of munity," Nora said simply.

Abigail laughed, and saluted Nora. "You are a good captain, sir."

Nora smiled and returned the salute, then to Louis she said, "See, it is not the meek, but rather the stubborn who are on course to inherit the earth."

"With you at the helm, leading the charge like Joan of Arc," he said. His voice was soft, still, she could hear the threads of anger in her mind. Nora turned away from them both to stare at the stain of color on the sky left by the blazing sun. "If I must," she said finally, and meant it.

14

DISCOVERIES

When I opened my eyes and saw you,
I could make no sense of my memories—
I close my eyes and see a string of fantasies.
I wonder if they are mine.

December 1, 1800

The moment was timeless. Motes of sunlight fell on Velvet's skin, landed all around her on the palm strewn pathway, got lost in the golden strands of hair wrapped around her arms. The day was overly bright, sharp refractions of moving light burned her eyes, she blinked against the sting, disoriented. The drowsy scent of tropical gardenia was overpowering, and the pathway where she slept was no longer an abandoned land for spirts and ghosts. Now, it was a cheerful place, full of laughter and chattering children.

Velvet yawned hugely, stretching her arms above her head as she came fully awake with a start. Panic seized her chest when the events of the faded night rushed back. Her hands flew to her shoulder blades, touched the skin there—she breathed a deep sigh of relief at finding it unbroken, bowed her head and took another breath that burned as it went down.

All around her were sounds of life, splashing water, the sizzle of broiling fish and bits of charring driftwood. *It was just a dream,* her mind said, and the thought brought another rush of dizzying respite from her scalding thoughts.

Footsteps fell here and there, a soft patter on the right turned her head. A small girl, hair curling around her cupid face like a storm cloud, stood and watched her through huge hazel eyes. Tentatively, Velvet lifted her hand in some modified version of a formal wave. The child shrieked when Velvet moved. She threw up her hands and spun on her heels before darting back the way she had come. Her small sack dress blew around her chubby ankles as she ran until the thick underbrush swallowed her tiny figure. She returned seconds later with three of her bonny friends in tow. One, had a chain of violets braided into her waist length hair, her brown eyes too big for her slender face. There were flowers strewn all over the ground around them, lush lily petals that stuck to the bottoms of their bare feet. Velvet waved again, and this time, all of them exploded in reels of giggling squeals, though none ran.

Velvet stood, her knees were terribly weak, wanting to buckle. She bent to retrieve her cane, thorny bougainvillea burst through the fronds, poked her heels. Her hand closed around the stick, and she saw with some dismay that they were all wrong—the scratches and bloody wounds of yestereve still remained suspiciously absent.

The girl with the violet chain held a stout, earthenware jar in her small hands, Velvet could almost smell the water she heard swishing inside. Her parched throat suddenly screamed. She opened her lips to speak, perhaps beg, but her tongue lugged around like a wooden thing in her mouth, and no sound emerged. She swallowed hard and tried again. "Where am I?" she finally managed. "Où suis-je?"

"C'est l'île de Sainte-Marie," said the child, in flawless, gently accented French. "Avez-vous soif, madame?" she continued, raising the jar, and swirling the water inside.

"Oui!" Velvet gasped.

The little girl kicked a loose rock with her big toe, her eyes darting between Velvet's gaze and the flower struck ground, her little nose downturned, cherry red from the hot sun. "Es-tu dangereux?" asked the child.

Velvet shook her head. "I'm not dangerous at all. I'm just lost. Je m'appelle Velvet," she said, pressing her hand to her heart.

"Enchantée, Velvet," said the child. "Je m'appelle Machi. My mother says humans are flowers who will wilt without water, are you wilting?"

"Yes, I think so," said Velvet, unable to take her eyes off the water.

The child hesitated a second longer, and one of her companions shook their head in a decisive negative. Machi ignored the warning, threw her friend a look, then skipped on ahead, her wild curls bobbing.

"Merci," breathed Velvet, when Machi placed the jar in her outstretched hands.

"Drink," commanded the child. Velvet obeyed with gusto, water trickled over her lips, dripped down her chin. It was glorious.

"Slowly," cautioned Machi, lightly touching Velvet's shaking hand. "You must go slow, or you will make yourself ill."

Velvet tried, yet it felt she reached the final drop in seconds. She wiped her mouth on the back of her hand, then returned the jar to its tiny owner with a word of thanks, and a grateful smile.

"You're welcome. You will feel better now," Machi declared. "An hour ago, I thought you might be dead. I hoped you were not. My sisters' wishes went a different way. We do not like strangers on Sainte-Marie."

Velvet sighed. "Not dead, just dreaming." It felt like a fact when she said it, despite the state of her hands. A thought hit her then, and she asked, rather breathless, "Was there a man? Here with me?"

The girls giggled again, but Machi stared forward, her expression unchanged. Eventually she nodded. "Yes, a British man," she said, scrunching her nose. "He wears a red coat, and he thinks we do not see all the bloodstains."

'You are only visiting a dream of mine,' she had told him, on her

knees in the dark, staring up at a sky overrun with frozen stars, and a full, ringed moon. *What if I was wrong?* Velvet leaned hard on her cane. A rush of scalding heat flushed her cheeks as the ghosts of those very dreams stalked her.

Something moved behind her, Velvet felt the powerful disturbance fair ripple the air. She closed her eyes, heard the strong beat of a pounding heart. She knew that rhythm, and her feelings toward the realization were...complex. The girls shrieked. Even Machi cracked a smile, they held hands, jumped, and laughed, then scampered away to observe from a distance. Sounds of their laughter disappeared between the trees.

Velvet's own heart fluttered, in her stomach the glittery butterflies turned to fire breathing dragons. She knew Henry was standing directly behind her yet could in that moment muster no courage to turn and face him.

"Velvet," he said. His dark voice flowed over her shoulder, colored a million shades of honey. Her limbs felt frozen as the stars in that magical, impossible design. Fear was a shot of acid in her mouth, and she felt a low throbbing begin in her head. She could feel herself start to tremble, and something about that small thing —infuriated her. She clasped her hands against her midriff to keep them steady. Her fingers refused to flex as she tried to twist them. Giving her numb body orders seemed pointless as she could neither move nor think. He had always affected her so, even before the dark imaginings.

"Velvet," he said again. Urgency in his tenor. He would touch her soon, put those nerve destroying hands on her body. Velvet's eyes watered, her chest began to burn, it seemed forever since she breathed. She remembered those hands—goddess of wind, earth, and sky, she would never forget them. Never forget the way his fingers wrapped around her knees, how his eyes had burned as he gently drew her legs apart. His breaths ragged, rapid. Ever would she see the way his dark head moved between her thighs. Velvet's whole body shuddered. The humid breeze stung her eyes. More images of him flashed through her tripping mind, she had to bite back a groan and she was truly afraid. Perhaps the whole thing really had been some projection of her lusty thoughts, but that did not explain how she had managed to imagine such unimaginable things. Such wicked, spellbinding things so far afield of her own world.

Twisting her fingers till they ached, Velvet gulped in a warm, perfume-soaked breath then spun to face him.

His dark eyes moved over her face, neither of them said a word. Velvet had some strange suspicion that he was checking her for the presence of wings, yet if that were true, it would mean—what? *What the hell would it mean? If they had shared the same moment, did it even matter if it was only a dream?*

After a scalding perusal, he seemed relieved at what he found. His eyes fixed on hers. Per usual the man appeared entirely unruffled, as if being marooned on a storied pirate isle was a common occurrence for him. If only he had been a weak, pathetic, even an evil specimen, it would have been so much easier to hate him. He was not though, not at all.

Handsome was too weak a word for the daunting figure he cut against the crisp blue sky. His linen shirt was tied around the low waistband of trousers which had been recently hacked off at the knee. Perspiration oiled his chest, made it look impossibly huge and overly bronze. In the golden cast of netted light that fell like rain through the canopy of trees he was a pagan jungle god, a panther in human skin.

Her hands felt terribly hot, she wiped them on her bodice. His eyes traced her actions. Their gazes locked, sealed. His full lips lifted in their crooked, intoxicating smile, then he clicked his bare heels and dropped in a quick, courtly bow. "Bonjour, mon amour," he said, his voice slow, nearly romantic, and she knew he mocked her with it. Still smiling, he motioned to all that was around them. "Bienvenu sur l'île de Sainte-Marie, home to pirate, slave and king. Last true strong hold of the Brotherhood, or so I have been previously informed. I cannot tell you what it does to my heart, finding you well and alive."

"Do spare me, Henry. I am presently too worn to bear the weight of your wit."

"Careful," he said stoically, "unless you intensify the hold your front teeth have on your lower lip, I fear you are in real danger of cracking a smile." He laughed. "Poor Velvet, I bet you wish you were wearing shoes so you could throw one at me, don't you?"

Through her teeth Velvet said, "Yes!"

Henry laughed again; the sound was like stepping into a warm patch of sunlight. Breeze rustled through the trees, cooling the humid day with its spiked, rainy tips. "Come," he said, sobering slightly, and holding out his arm. "I promise I won't bite; your virtue is safe from me today—I only mean to take you on a tour of our new domain."

"You're rather cheery for a man who just lost a crew, a ship, and nearly his own life."

"My life? My lady, I have been far closer to the grave than that, let me assure you. A ship, yes. Though most of the crew managed, like us, to make it ashore. I believe the worst of it must have hit when we were about two miles out from the bay. Our casualties were minor. Rhee broke his leg. My first mate lost a peace pipe of dramatic value." He sobered then, a single step he took closed the distance between them. "We lost two men, Corbin, his head was smashed in a fall, we mourn him deeply."

"I saw him," gasped Velvet, "when I was looking for you, I saw him."

"I'm sorry," Henry said, and sounded for once like he meant it.

"I tried to help, but he was already gone."

Henry nodded. "Borag, our ship's surgeon believes he was killed on impact so there was nothing you could have done."

Velvet nodded, accepting that. "Just another life I could not save," she whispered, then, "who was the other?"

"Captain Reg, the men called him, he was seventy-three, the man sailed with his majesty's navy for over half a century. I believe he went with the waves willingly. The men will have a small service tonight, commit our fallen to the sea and their god. Come," he repeated, that irrepressible command heavy in his voice. "Today we will morn and drink to the dead, tomorrow we will find a ship— should be a simple task on an island full of them—with any luck at all, we should set sail within the week."

Velvet paused in the act of reaching for his arm. Her hand hung in the air for a few awkward seconds before she retracted it.

"I don't want to find a ship. And I'm not going anywhere, certainly not to England, or any place that boasts of numerous dark castles you could lock me in." Her eyes darted over his shoulder, searching out quick routes of escape. "This is exactly where I want to be," she said, blinking.

Minerva's face flickered into focus behind Velvet's lids. In her mind she heard the woman say, *'The stones always wish to return home. Tamora, it melted, fused with your skin, you carry its power in your veins. They always find their way to me, such is the nature of their curse, and mine',* as the words rang in her head, Velvet wondered briefly if the island would even let her leave.

Henry lowered his arm. Behind him, the passel of giggling flower chain girls had grown. They whispered to each other, staring and sighing. Velvet had a feeling the island girls found him every bit as beautiful as she.

"Very well," he said after a time, "I will take you to the men, and you may make your case—you are searching for the spell to save your brother I assume?"

Velvet said nothing, but Henry nodded as if he she had confided a great truth. "I see, so it is to be more blood, mayhem and death then?" he asked. His expression darkening like his voice.

It occurred to Velvet that it might be prudent to change the topic. She locked on a promise all men loved. "There is whisper of a treasure," she said. "Somewhere beside the spell, both on this very island."

"Yes, I know—the lost chests of Sainte-Marie, the pirates talk of little else, darling, my father even searched for them a time or two. Every soul here is a master of their legend so you will get a different tale from each person you ask," he said, speaking slowly as if to a child.

"They are not lost, I have a map," she snapped, internally wondering why his mocking smile infuriated her so. Like the flames from the dragons breathing hellfire in her gut had invaded her very bones.

Henry's eyes flashed, they were so dark, blinking like portals to another world—she had read about such things once, though she could not remember when—like with a look alone he was able to exert some force over her mind.

"Do you now?" he asked, his voice low as to be inaudible.

Velvet retreated a step, seeing danger in him—she always had. The way his eyes roved hotly over her scantily clad body made her want to pant. "Where?" he asked pointedly—so husky it cost Velvet a moment to recall her own words—when she did, her right fingers went to her temple, she rubbed softly where it ached. "It's in here," she said.

Henry opened his lips to voice a denial, yet no sound came. She could see in his eyes that he believed her. He extended his arm to her once more. "There is an old woman down the way, a weaver —I believe she may have something suitable for you, if you go prancing before the men dressed as you are, there will be bloodshed."

Velvet gave him a blank look, struggling to understand his intent. He was changeable as the sea he loved, wild and just as turbulent. He stepped close to her; she could not move away. He reached for a lock of her hair, caressed it between thumb and finger. "Stay close," he breathed, "a treasure like you would fetch a pretty price. I don't feel like killing a man today, mayhap tomorrow." There was a thing in his voice that was nearly cruel. He leaned back to regard her then, his chiseled face expressive as stone. "Now come, I'll give you three more seconds, then I'm carrying you. Your choice."

"You're a true brute! A vile, spiteful man," she spat, her eyes flicking to his extended arm, despite the annoyance radiating off him in waves, she held back—fearing his threat, weighing her options of two evils.

Henry sighed. "Must we ever play this game, princess?"

"Swear you will not try to take me from this place by force," she demanded, "swear Henry, though your word is worth little to me, it is all I have." Her brash words were a mistake, and he closed their distance in a single stride, bent in a flash, and swung her up in his arms.

"Bastard," she hissed. Knowing it would do nothing she

slapped her open palm across his bare chest. Henry flinched—his eyes snapped and his cool, mocking façade slipped a little.

"I have never broken my word, you little hellion! Against express command and my better judgement, I swore to protect you and your brother. I have done so!" he railed, staring down at her, his face twisted in what looked like utter contempt. "To keep your pretty head attached to your shoulders, I made a vow I detested, and saddled myself to a spoilt chit who thinks of nothing and no one but her own interests. A royal brat who plays with dark arts and people's lives, a witch who would cast her spell on a man sworn only to serve."

Velvet swallowed hard and said nothing, she even stopped struggling. His hands were gripping her hips, hurting her. She licked her dry lips as his voice rose. The moment could not have been more unbearable if he had struck her. "I told you, that was an accident. I did not mean to bewitch you," she breathed.

"Yet you did not stop it!" he roared. "Now that I have saved you, you will hold yourself from me, deny what is my right, what you once wanted to take from me when I was senseless. Your puppet, your slave." His voice lowered, so deep it played on her senses. In his eyes, past the enraged loathing was lust she realized, pure, thirsty lust—she knew the same desperate look was in her own.

Her eyes fell to his lips, and his breaths turned ragged. "Set me down," she pleaded. Terrified by her reaction and all the wanting.

Visibly shaken, Henry obeyed. He set her on her feet, and they came apart gasping. She would have stumbled, but he caught her around the waist, his fingers brushed the bare skin there and it was like a hurricane in her mind. He just held her like that for a few silent moments, his breaths whistling between his teeth while the sounds of life moved all around them.

The groups of watching girls were not so young now. They gazed at Henry from beneath the cover of their thick lashes, whispering hushed secrets through lips of Roman red. More flowers were threaded through plaits of beads that fell like aqua waterfalls down their unclad bodies.

Henry did not seem to notice their needy regard. His eyes

remined locked on hers, like she was all he could think or breathe, now there was a boyishness in his face, a gentle candor infused by desperation—like all he craved was a moment surcease from their battle. He had dark circles under his eyes, and she relented a little. "Very well, I will go to your men and plead my case. Perhaps one or two of them will believe in me and my map."

"I believe in you," he said, "you are a force of nature. I believe you could do anything you set your mind to, even find the lost chests of Sainte-Marie—therein lies the problem and the sum of all my fears," he finished wryly.

"You have nothing to fear from me at the moment, today I am a simple girl with basic needs." She tried to smile. "Food and clothes will set me right."

"I believe it is in my power to give you both," he said. She felt it as the last of his anger seeped away, and like she had told him in her dream, that left everything else. Neither of them moved, they stood there on the pathway where she had spent the fitful night, just staring at each other like there was no place else in the world to look—an amusing spectacle for all, she imagined.

"Last night this place felt so empty, I sat here for hours, never saw a soul—"

"Nor I," said Henry, "I slept in the spot where we stand."

"As did I," she whispered. He gave her an odd look, but Velvet had no explanation for her words, they were simply true.

"I felt you," he said, after a heavy pause. Velvet could not take the way he looked at her a second longer. She crossed her arms over her chest so he would not see her tremble. He opened his mouth to speak, but she turned away so she would not hear it. There was a telling thing in his eyes. Memories she could nearly see, share with him. *Dear goddess, what if it had not been a dream?*

❧

The Siren's survivors had found a place to hunker down on the beach. A group of hutches braced the rear of a torch-lit tavern. Rustling palm rushes for the roof, huge colorful tapestries hanging for walls. They blew in and out, hypnotic in the restless, evening wind. Henry had taken them on a direct route to the beach and the return affair had transpired in less than two hours—most of which was spent in uncomfortable silence.

Velvet struggled to keep her footing for the duration of their descent—to keep her eyes off his firm lips, and perfect face. The latter was extremely difficult. This unruly land suited him in every way, from the hard, chiseled cliffs, to the distant encroaching shrubs, dark as crouched human shapes. Varying shades of light and dark, raw, and dangerous, beautiful.

Henry spoke occasionally, regaling her with tales of the island that she found too interesting to ignore, though she diligently tried. When the shore was at last in sight, twilight had fallen, that witching hour when all the daylight sleepers stirred. The heavy perfume of some night-blooming flower saturated the air—so strong it seemed to have a life of its own. Velvet could not recall if she had ever smelt anything so wonderful. She stopped to inhale, and remove a stone lodged between the underside of her bare, scratched toes.

"Enchanting, is it not?" asked Henry, his eyes on her. "Orchids," he said. "There is a legend on this island regarding the flower." Leaning forward, he plucked a perfect blossom from a bundle of them and straightened, twirled the pretty thing between his fingers for a moment before he stepped close, then quickly tucked the long stem behind her ear.

Velvet closed her eyes when the back of his hand brushed her jaw, turned away from him nervously, lifted her face to the wind and listened to it rustle through the tall palms, heard the crackle of campfire flames, and the laughter of men crowded around them. They sang loudly and passed jugs of rum. Something about their near tangible comradery reminded Velvet of the gypsy caravans she had loved.

Two men sang louder than the rest, they swung the jars of rum above their heads. Their free arms were slung around each other's shoulders, their sea-stained bodies swaying from side to side. The sight made Velvet think of noisy tambourines and campfire nights.

Henry's fingers curled around her jaw, recapturing her attention, a strange look played in his eyes, like there was a lost thing he battled to recall, and Velvet feared she knew all the thoughts in his mind. Hot blood rose to her cheeks, and she dropped her gaze. "Why are you looking at me like that?" she half muttered.

"Because you are beautiful," he said simply, his words slow and soft. "Like a stained-glass window made by a master, you serve the island moonlight," his thumb brushed her lips, "change colors when it touches you. Your skin, your hair—" His words broke off, his fingers coasted down her bare shoulders. Velvet could not take her eyes from his beguiling lips. Looking at them gave her the mad urge to press her body against his, lock her legs around his waist and wrestle him to the ground—kiss him, see once and for all if it had been real.

"I had a dream about you last night," he breathed, scattering her thoughts. Velvet stepped out of his reach—her movements choppy. With all the words in the world, she could not think of a single one to say.

"Henry!" a voice called, saving her in ways she did not care to analyze. She felt vague for a moment, as if she were missing the sense of things. Then came the dizzying knowledge that threatened to lay her low, as his words imprinted on her mind. It had been real for him too. *Stars! What did it mean? Was it all true? Was the stone apart of her, were the wings?*

Henry stared at her for a long moment before he turned toward the heavy voice of his first mate. Ritchie, a few meters off, waved joyously. His steps were sprightly, and on his broad shoulders was none of the weight he had carried over the gangplank to the Bacchus. His whole aura had changed, as if on ship he had been in chains, but here, in this magical land, he was free. Velvet had a feeling they all were. Even with Henry's indomitable presence looming behind her like a bad choice, Velvet felt lighter than she had in days, happily she lifted her hand and waved back.

Ritchie's weathered face was a wreathe of smiles, his hair a cap of silver in the climbing moonlight that bounced off the restless waves. "Well met, my lady!" Ritchie called, offering her his hand. Velvet took it and he shook vigorously. His grey eyes made a quick pass over her ensemble, and Velvet saw him grimace slightly, before the smile returned. "In one piece you are!" he stated, "stronger than you look, and too beautiful for the sea to claim."

Velvet dipped in a small curtsey. "Thank you, kind sir, I too am glad to see you survived the tempest," she said, then glanced up to find Henry glaring at her. He untied the shirt from around his waist and shoved the linen in her hands, barking, "Put this on, before you start a war. The men are beginning to stare."

She took it from him appreciatively despite his hostile attitude, and pulled it over her head, quickly shoving her arms through the long sleeves. Beneath it, she slipped off her dress, it made a tattered puddle of dirty white at her feet. The hem of Henry's shirt hung clear past her knees, covering her drawers and daggers. She tore a long strip of cloth from the hem of her old dress, then used the ribbon as a makeshift belt, and drew it tight around her waist. The shirt was fairly clean—smelled like him. Velvet twirled full circle, craning her head to see over her shoulder. "What do you think?" she asked, genuinely wanting to know.

Henry grimaced. "Perfect, madam, with your hair falling just that way, you look like a mermaid searching for her fins."

"The most ravishing thing to ever wash ashore," Ritchie declared, then took her hand and tucked it warmly in the crook of his arm. "Come, you must be famished, my dear—I doubt this boorish lout has seen to your needs a 'tall. Rhee, caught some white fish off yonder, speared them straight through with the sharp end of a stick. Strange boy that, ate one of them raw, right in front of me, head and all." Ritchie shuddered at the memory. "Not to worry though, Zoe has broiled them with dandelion leaves, and fried bits of coconut—a veritable feast I'd wager. The men traded some tea with the locals for a few jugs of uncut, black run. The devil's own brew, I vow."

"I've never had rum," said Velvet, "once, Nora gave me wine, but I did not much like the taste."

"That one does like to drag others into sin," Ritchie said, and Velvet laughed, charmed.

"Sir, isn't that what you intend with your rum?" she asked.

Ritchie's silver brows went up, arching like cupids bow, making him resemble an amused, silver fox. "Smart and beautiful," he sighed, "it appears I must watch my heart."

"Only fish, I have no taste for hearts tonight," Velvet said.

"For such things, god, we mortals are grateful," she heard Henry mutter, and rolled her eyes unperturbed. She was busy listening to the full surf rush against the sand and watching great streaks of orange cut the indigo sky, bleeding through the seconds of remaining day like a determined drop of ink on a watery canvas and could pay his needling no heed.

"You must feel quite lost, my lady. Captive to a sinking ship, bound to a man who claims to be your husband, and beset by a crowd of rowdy men too long at sea."

"I cannot answer to the first, mainly because I have yet to resign it all in my mind, but as to the last," she said and shrugged, glancing at the largest of the fires, and the men who played with swords before it, egged on by the small crowd of men who jeered and cheered. "This all makes me feel quite at home. I grew up with the Romani. Did you know that? The first home I really remember was a caravan, all my food cooked over an open fire."

"I did know. I'm sorry, my lady, Henry speaks of little but you," said Ritchie, dropping his voice like he confessed a great secret. "He cares for you, my lady. His temper is a great and terrible thing, but I've learned his bark is far worse than his bite."

"I have my serious doubts," whispered Velvet, casting a cautious glance over her shoulder, searching, of course, for him. He was a few paces behind them, walking slowly, eyes trained on the sea.

He looked more exhausted than she had ever seen him, his hair long taken by the sandy wind had turned to a mane of deep black strung with glowing cerulean threads that shimmered when he moved, each ignited by the moonlight. There was that feeling again that he was made alive by this place, as if the magic here resonated with his own.

15

CAMPFIRE TALES

A near panic rose in him, a curious dread as he watched her walk away on the arm of his first mate. Henry tried to ignore the frightening violence he felt toward the man when Velvet flashed him a saucy smile in exchange for his appreciative wink. Henry had thought his shirt would cover what he so coveted, all it did was tantalize. Christ! She was unthinkably beautiful with her golden locks tumbling past the hem of his shirt, swaying over her hips as she skipped away. Staring at the rhythm of her walk, and the luscious way her weight shifted from side to side, flashes of last night rushed him, momentarily severing the now. Somewhere in his mind he was groping like a blind man, trying to remember where he had been, what he had done. If he blinked, he could see glimmering, blood-tipped wings, practically feel her soft skin, hear her husky cries.

Should he tell her what he had dreamed? Drag her under him and see if she tasted like fantasy? God's blood! His whole body shook with the effort it took not to confess all he remembered, then demand answers from her. Would she give them? Did she even know? Sometime in the last hours with her, the once unshakeable knowledge that he had her last night, faded to an illusion. *Had it really all been a dream?*

Confused, nearly raging, Henry ran his hands through his hair, a rain of sand poured through the strands and into his eyes, momentarily blinding him. Had she done it to him again? Cast some spell that brought him once more under her control? Was she even now laughing, plotting her next revenge? Just once he wanted to hold her as himself, no enchantments or deadly magics. Just once, when he was not under some illusionary mind warp, just once with nothing at all between them.

That possibility seemed ever distant as he watched her sashay away from him. His men greeted her warmly, taking turns hugging, and carefully passing her between them. Henry wanted to gnash his teeth and tear her away, keep her to himself forever. Velvet's face glowed brightest for Zoe. The boy grabbed both her wrists, his dark skin a stark, beautiful contrast to her pale ivory, he kissed her knuckles then pulled her down to sit beside him. He tipped his head to whisper something for her ears alone, and her laugh rang out like a bell. He handed her a flat rock laid over with a steaming cut of broiled fish, Velvet beamed up at him like the boy had given her a string of diamonds. Henry thought he might have paid all he had in the world, to have her smile at him like that, just once.

Martin, a weathered seaman with a taste for the bloody, knelt before Velvet, staring in childlike awe. He handed her a pile of dandelion leaves—Henry believed if the rabbit fair were not to her taste the besotted man would have readily offered to go slay a lion. The old jolly tar had the gall to blush, when the princess leaned forward to kiss his cheek.

"You're eyeing the chit, like she's Lilith in the garden," Ritchie mused as he stopped before the largest of the fires, bent and retrieved a jug of half-drunk rum. He took a hearty swig, then handed it to Henry.

A roar went up from the men. Someone threw a bottle in the fire, aqua and orange sparks attacked the night, Henry watched them illuminate her face. He took the jug from Ritchie, his gaze never straying from her. Rhee was telling her a story, a good one judging by Velvet's rapt, undivided attention.

"Do you fear Napoleon comes for her?" asked Ritchie, picking his front teeth with a pale fish bone. He spat on the ground, then kicked sand over the mess with his foot. "He wants to stabilize the

French economy, restore order to the nation and ultimately establish a democracy. There are many who stand with him, but still there are those with deep purses and even grander sympathies. They would support him if he had one of their precious heirs. The golden princess no less. He set could her up with some charitable causes, place her on a pedestal of his design, and tame those who would fight him. She is the perfect weapon. A dear commodity."

Henry grunted. "On top of which, the king fears her, and she is deemed by church of England to be an unrepentant and powerful witch. I fear them all."

"We could get a message to your brother. Charles always has a fair handle on Napoleon's whereabouts, he might be a little prick, but the rest is in the blood. He is a fair spy, always has been."

"I could try, though I doubt he would be in any mood to offer assistance, since he rarely is. Besides, I don't want him anywhere near Velvet, power like that—in the hands of Charles Newcastle is violently unthinkable," Henry said, his thought trailing away.

The men had stood, they formed a circle around the fire, stomped their feet, clapped their hands, one of them helped Velvet stand, Henry did not see who, then she was spinning, her arm linked with Zoe's, they jumped and pranced around the flames, twirling in circles which made Henry dizzy to watch.

A sailor, not one of his, handed her a jug of rum. She took it, smiling, and drank down a huge gulp. The face she made as the uncut rum sliced a burning path down her throat, was so adorable it almost broke him. He had to clench his fists to keep from wrapping her in his arms and carrying her deep into the phosphorous waves. He sat down beside the fire, rested an arm on his drawn-up knee, drank more rum and watched her dance till he tasted the last drop.

Backlit by the flames she glowed, soon the men stepped aside, continued to clap, sing, and stomp their feet as they let her move unmolested. They passed her their own jugs of rum, and she took them all, thanking each man by name, still dancing while she drank. She seemed a wild thing, hair running everywhere, liquid waves of the purest gold. Her legs moved beneath the hem of his shirt, and there was a chorus of collective sighs when she twirled, and it rucked up high. Henry saw a dagger strapped to each of her shapely thighs and smiled. *Vixen*, he thought, wanting her.

She twirled again and again; Ritchie let a low whistle slip between his teeth.

"Like a bleeding sea nymph," Henry heard another say. It was enough, if he did not put his hands on her soon, someone else would. He stood, swayed, steadied himself, reached out, then caught her. She glanced up at him through her fan of sooty lashes, and the hint of a smile came to play with the corners of her mouth. "Dance with me, my lord," she said, lifting her hands, twining her fingers behind his back.

"Must you dazzle them all?" he growled.

Her look turned sultry, she lifted her lips to his, stopping a breath from touching, her smile gentle, and sweet. "Do I dazzle you?" she whispered, and the desire he felt for her in that moment confounded all his senses.

"As the serpent dazzled Eve," he managed to rasp.

"Villain," she chuckled, pressing tighter against his bare chest. Up on her toes, his arm slipped to her lower back, and she arched against it, curving toward him. She cocked her head to the left and fixed him with a saucy glare. "I dreamed about you too," she breathed, staring at him. Her eyes brighter than the moon.

"What did I do to you in your dream?" he asked, feeling her shiver when his whisper touched her ear.

Her eyelids fell closed, and she said, "I can't tell you as that might make it real."

"Did you cast another spell?" he asked.

"If I did, I, too was its victim, so you can dismount from your eternal high horse."

"Another accident?" he pressed.

She swayed a little and he held her closer. "I don't know, Henry. Does it really matter?"

"No," he said, her parted lips the focus of his world.

"Then will you dance with me?" she asked again.

"Yes," he said, and did.

They danced until the moon was high, their straining bodies damp, and clinging, danced until they fell to the sand laughing, drinking more rum to quench their thirst. The men cheered them on, and sometime during the night, one of them laid a wreath of flowers on Velvet's head. Now it hung lopsided over her left eye. Chuckling, enthralled, Henry lifted the flower chain so he could kiss the pink tip of her nose. Her eyes seemed impossibly blue, reflecting the stary magnificence surrounding them. It felt like someone stuck something sharp in his chest, when she tilted her chin and touched the tip of her tongue to his nose, then tumbled back to the sand, giggling.

"You're drunk, vixen," he accused.

"I must be," she said, her lashes fluttering. "I see four of you, and I think the earth is spinning. Perhaps it is always spinning. Do you feel it?"

"Yes, I feel it," he said, and sighed. Looking at her like this, eyes and lips flushed, cheeks the color of a rose, Henry realized he was going to give up. There could be no more anger at the helplessness she had wrung from him. She was the enchantment, and he feared the spell she cast on him was eternal. He was going to want this brilliant eyed, fiend to his very last breath.

She reached for the jug of rum in his hands, and he found himself fascinated by the tiny dimples in her cheeks. He let her have it, she put the jug to her lips and drank until she hiccupped, then giggled and wiped her mouth on the corner of his shirt, momentarily showing him her pretty thighs, and lacy white drawers. "I like rum," she said, then "did you know that it makes you feel quite strange?"

"Figured that out when I was thirteen," he said, reaching out to steady her when she swayed.

"You're welcome and thank you," she said, her eyes rolling a little. "I think I might topple over and just stay there."

"Lean on me," Henry said, and drew her close, so her hip rested on his leg. She was so small, he easily settled her against the crook of his arm. She snuggled in, crossing her feet at the ankles, and smiling, contented with the jug of rum she clasped to her chest. He brushed away golden, vagrant strands of her damp hair, could not help kissing her brow, and she sighed when his lips touched her skin.

Perhaps for the first time in his life, Henry reflected, he felt a moment of true peace. Here there were no kings, or conquerors, churches and silent gods set up to tear them apart. Here, beside the waves, cast in firelight, with sailors and stars for witness, there was only Velvet and Henry, a girl and boy who had met as children— parted as strangers, and came together again through fate.

Rhee limped over, and sat down near Velvet's feet, a small snail-shaped flute in his hands. Borag—the second son of a British doctor, was a small, nervous man who served as ship surgeon and chef—sat calmly beside Rhee, fiddling with his broken spectacles, and humming soft words that went along with the lilting tune Rhee had begun to pipe.

Velvet swayed to the music for a time, then tilted her head so their eyes could meet. "It's a very sad song," she said, her golden brows pulling together in a show of displeasure.

"It's the song of Sainte-Marie—tells the tale of a woman who loved a stranger over her own blood kin," Henry said.

"How do you know it?" she asked, turning to face him fully, commanding all his attention.

He smiled down at her. "My love, I serve his majesty, but I am no saint. This isn't my first foray to these shores."

"Hum, looking for lost treasure, I'd wager," she said.

"But of course, among other things."

"Villain," she whispered again, though this time on her lips the slur sounded like an endearment, she settled back against him, and took another sip of her rum. "Tell me about this woman."

Rhee's eyes were bright at her question as he set down his flute and leaned forward. "It's wicked, a marvelous story, my lady. 'Bout a goddess who called on an ancient artifact and cast a spell so powerful that it used every ounce of magic she had."

Zoe cut in. "Some say the magic sapped her life force, turned her into a decrepit crone."

"A millennia ago, this island was a woman's place—all men knew to set foot here was death," said Rhee. "None came, not a one, not until a storm cast a sailor against those rocks yonder." He pointed to the outcropping of dark rocks which had tried to break Henry, black and white waves crashed all around them. "The youngest of all the sisters who called this island home, found the man dying. Using the magic of the land, they say she stitched the blood back inside his body and mended his broken bones with a single touch. There's a great magic here," continued Rhee, his flashing eyes a piercing grey. "Magical stones which come from a hidden shelf in a bottomless pool. The women—the sisters, you understand? They were the guardians of these artifacts, tasked to protect but never use. Anyways, used them she did. Months passed—"

"Years," Zoe interrupted again, "and it was the elder sister who found and saved the sailor."

"Are you telling the story? Or am I?" snapped Rhee.

"Actually, she asked me," grumbled Henry.

Velvet giggled. "Do go on, Rhee, months it is," she said, giving Zoe a slightly apologetic smile.

Rhee sniffed. "Doesn't matter. Point was the sister and sailor were in love. The goddess and that sailor deeply coupled as the sun and moon. Stories say that for a time even the old gods woke from their sleep to watch this great romance. Now, Poseidon loved the goddess who loved the human sailor, and when he couldn't watch their passion anymore, Poseidon went to the eldest sister, and told her what the youngest had done. In the dark of night, the sisters came to kill the man who had defiled one of their own. But the youngest sister heard whisper of the plot from the North wind. She took the stones and used one of them to change the man into an eagle, so he could fly away from the wrath of her sisters."

"The spell was grueling. It killed all her sisters, and sucked the life form the young girl who had dared to use its power."

"Personal gain," said Zoe, "it's against the witches code."

"Witches don't have codes," argued Rhee.

"Sure, they do," drawled Zoe, "why the hell else was the sister so cursed? She broke the damn code."

"Then what happened?" asked Velvet. Henry saw she was sitting forward, her eyes fixed on Rhee's fire-lit face.

"The young girl was forever locked to this island, stripped of her beauty, her riches bound up in chests and cast to the bottom of the bottomless pool. She wanders now, forever. A dead goddess who cannot die. The power of the stones has called many a privateer, pirate, king, queen, and desperate woman. The goddess walks these shores now, searching for her next victim."

"They say when the moon changes the water to diamonds, you can see in her dark, glowing the colors of all the stones, dancing atop the waves, always trying to call, to reach the man she loved, but never does the eagle return. The bird was known from then to evermore as the symbol of freedom," Zoe finished, and Henry saw that Zoe's low-voiced words had sent chills coasting over Velvet's arm.

"*Oooh*, you got her good," cawed Rhee, "I see them shivers..."

"I think our lady might know more about this legend than you, Rhee," Ritchie said, eyeing Velvet quizzically. "Maybe we should let her speak for a time."

All the men looked to Velvet expectantly, some with open admiration which Henry found rather annoying. This irritated him to infinitum. He was not a jealous man. Never once had he found enough bother in himself to care. Trust in his own brand of wretched luck to have it be this girl, above all other, who scrambled his senses and brought him to his knees.

His! She was his, by the laws of god and country, and he wanted to shout it at any man who cared to look. He wanted to grab her by the arms, shake her until she admitted it. She was staring at his first mate wide-eyed, started to shake her head, then sighed. Henry saw the exact moment when she decided to just come straight out and say it. She shifted against him, pulled away a bit, and went up on her knees, facing the men. Her hair blew wildly around her face, wrapped her waist and thighs and, in the dying light of the fires, she looked to be a statue of the finest gold.

He saw her bite at her lower lip, gulp in a shaky breath like someone preparing to launch themselves in an icy lake, then said, "The lost chests of Sainte-Marie are real, and I have a map that will take us straight to them. The stones you speak of—I have held them in my hands—been changed by them, even took their power for my own." Her voice was halting and held a slight tremble. She did not drop her gaze but looked at all of them, her bright eyes reflecting silver moonlight. The men presented her with a varied array of thunderstruck expressions, and Henry heard a few audible gasps.

"There were rumors, my lady," Rhee managed to rasp.

"Velvet," she corrected, smiling at him.

Rhee shrugged like he would never be able to fulfil such a request. "We talked about it amongst ourselves, the night our duke brought you aboard the Siren—just gibberish and fragments, you know?"

"We decided princesses' stories were for the rich," said Zoe. The rest of the crew drew nearer, crowding her close as they dared. Deterred by Henry's ever blackening scowl. Danger and the threat of piracy be dammed, he knew his crew—she already had them. Whether they believed her or not, Henry feared the lot of them would follow her to hell—and very well may. A feeling of inevitable reservation settled in. Ancient artifacts were never what they seemed; the Catholic church learned this lesion during the final catastrophe of the crusades. He wanted her safe, which meant he and her destiny would be ever at odds.

"You don't strike me as your run of the mill treasure hunter," said Ritchie, still picking at his teeth with yet another slender, white fish bone.

"I don't care about the treasure," she said, "I need the words used by the goddess to transform her lover."

"Because your brother, Louis the seventeenth, is a stag who travels with lady Hartington on a pirate ship she won by blood?" Zoe asked, expressing his question in a single, exuberant gasp.

Velvet dropped her eyes to the pearly sands. "I would never ask any of you to risk your lives for such a thing, but the map which will lead me to the spell, also leads to the lost treasure of a great goddess. The youngest sister, I presume. The Romani people call her the 'pillar of regret'. My grandmother—" she broke off and shook her head. "Queenie, the woman who used a stone to transform me, carried a few pieces of this treasure with her. Always. I would present it as proof, but I left it all in the care of Lady Hartington, and Lord Eden."

"Why?" asked Henry. There was raw misery in her eyes when they flicked up to find his.

"Whether you believe me or not, I hate those stones. I am not too fond of magic either. You were coming to take me, Nora wanted to fight—I want no more lives lost on my behalf. Perhaps I am a royal brat, but I hate being the cause of anything's death. I feared you meant to return me to an English dungeon. I gave Nora the stones, and the map, so they would have all they need to save Louis."

Henry heard the pain in her words, hurt he had caused with his own. He opened his mouth to say something, take back what had been shouted in anger—Zoe cut him off.

"If they have the map—"

"I know each line by heart," said Velvet, answering his unspoken question. "I have every line and errant marking committed to memory; it would be a simple thing for me to recreate it for you."

"Well, if you could do a thing like that it would be proof enough for me," huffed Martin, and a small ripple of assent followed his words.

"Hundreds have died searching for those chests—desperate to capture the power of the stones. There is no way to reach the bottom of a bottomless pool," said Henry, speaking to Ritchie more than the others.

Velvet lifted her pert nose and took another swig of her rum. "Very well. I shall find it on my own," she declared. Swaying a little and drinking some more.

"Then you condemn yourself to certain death," Henry growled, "it cannot be done alone."

"I believe, Captain, since it involves us all—that we should bring the matter to a vote," said Ritchie, raising his voice for the benefit of all.

"Is there really treasure?" asked Rhee. "None of you is funnin' right? Cause when I'm not sailing with the crew, I work on the docs for half-crown a week, or my mother and sisters don't eat. I'd like to get my hands on some treasure, might even be willing to die for it."

"We are gentlemen of the court, and pride of his majesty's navy," said Henry.

Martin coughed and spat on a dying bit of flame. "Well, his majesty isn't here."

"Yeah," Zoe laughed, "we'll bring him back a gift, maybe a real big one." He tugged at the tie round his throat, his redcoat tossed aside long ago. "You really think you can find the pool?" he asked.

"I know I can," Velvet declared. "Since I was a little girl, Queenie taught me the way, I think, if I really tried, I might not even need the map."

Zoe slapped his knees with a hearty thwack! "I say we vote, Gents."

"And I say it's a fool's errand," Henry said.

Ritchie smiled. "So noted," he said, then stood and raised his rum. "All those who wish to sacrifice life and limb for a treasure of dubious origin and existence—"

"It exists," muttered Velvet.

Ritchie nodded. "Very well—to sacrifice life and limb to search for a mythical treasure—which definitely does exist, say aye!"

A loud chorus of assent rocked the night.

"All those opposed, say nay!" shouted Ritchie.

"Nay," said Henry, "It's a legacy of death and blood. There is more to the history of the stones, macabre legends going back to Roman times. We would be wise to set our rudders to this island and forget."

His words fell like stones. Ritchie said nothing for a prolonged moment, then clapped his hands. "The 'ayes' have it!" he crowed.

"Yeah!" Rhee exclaimed, shooting to his feet, and punching the air. "Golly or' are we pirates now?"

"We are not," Henry stated.

"Corbin would've liked this, he always wanted to be a pirate," said Zoe, ignoring Henry completely.

"To Corbin, and Captain Reg," said Ritchie, lifting his jug aloft. "May the sea always quench their thirst, and may the waves ever carry them home."

"May the waves carry them home," Henry said. He took a drink of rum, and watched Velvet close her eyes and repeat the old sea-faring words, then she lifted her jug and poured a bit of rum on the ground. At his look of askance she whispered, "For all lost souls."

She bowed her head, kissed her fingers, then placed them on the sand. "May the angels give you wings," she said, and Henry, deadly assassin, ruthless spy, and heartless duke, feared he might be falling in love.

CHAPTER SIXTEEN

I can only ever dream—too afraid am I, to speak of all the ways I want you.

Blue water, waves full of stars, rushing up and over her bare feet. Behind her, then men cheered and sang again, drank their rum, saluted their fallen. Not wanting to bemoan her own lot in life at always being the outsider in any scene, Velvet decided to walk along the shore, right at the water's edge, and stare at the glowing, layered waves, watch their magical surge and retreat.

Taking a steadying breath to hush her noisy thoughts, Velvet closed her eyes and tried to recreate the map in her mind. Little spidery black lines crawled across her vision, squirming until each placed themselves where they belonged. Even sore eyed and sluggishly weary, she felt a great sense of satisfaction at her nearly flawless recollection. For a moment she lingered, her toes playing in a warm patch of waves. The silky water felt terribly good on her scratched, aching soles. Moonlight filled the little puddles left by her steps, she stood and watched the waves wash the slight impressions away.

Night wind, full of glowing embers touched the island with mysterious fingers. It seemed many legends were born in this place, walking now, along this strip of paradise, Velvet found it easy to believe them all. It was in the air, a living shifting thing, that said there was far more to what moved around her, then what met the eye.

Minerva had said the island called her. Though Velvet wanted to believe it had all been a dream, with the way events had played out, she was forced to acknowledge at least that much had been true. There was no way her journey from Cheapside to where she now stood, was a thing of happenstance. Too much had seamlessly fallen into place, like a play orchestrated by a master. That it was all horribly, impossibly real somehow made better sense. The thought made her shoulder blades twitch, Velvet closed her eyes—she could almost feel her wings.

She began to walk again, took three more steps. His firelit shadow crossed hers in the second before she heard his voice. "Don't stray too far, my love, Poseidon's been known to assault beautiful innocents."

Velvet turned and smiled up into his eyes. "I welcome it, I would love to have a good chat with the god of the seas."

"He'll make a meal of you," Henry said, glancing out at the waves, before his eyes roved back to her.

Velvet raised a telling brow. "And you won't?" I think there is far more to fear from current company, than some old, tired god."

"He is immortal, fierce—he forced a girl once, in the halls of Athena's temple. The goddess was incensed, and she cursed the girl since she could not touch the god." Henry fell in step beside her, and they began to walk.

"What happened to the girl?" asked Velvet, pulled in as she always was by his stories.

"Her name was Medusa. Her story is rather legendary, you've never heard it?"

"If I have, I don't remember."

Henry shrugged. "The spell Athena cast, transformed the young girl's face and form, changed her strands of beautiful hair, to hordes of poisonous snakes. She hid in the hills for almost a century, and eventually lost her head to a young warrior named Perseus. It was said that any who looked in her eyes were instantly turned to stone. Athena gave young Perseus a shield. He used the reflective face of it to find her, and he cut her head off while she slept. Many a warrior since have searched for that severed head."

"In my opinion that story casts Athena in a far worst light than Poseidon. Queenie told me something once, 'in the battle between gods, it is only ever the humans who lose'. In that story, her hypothesis holds true."

Henry stopped walking, Velvet glanced over her shoulder to see they had strayed far, the men were smoky dots in the distance clustered around the dying fires that sent up plumes of dusky, amber smoke. "I wonder if one can see Poseidon's immortality in his eyes? The skin doesn't really matter you know, but you cannot hide what is in the eyes—they never lie."

"Your eyes say you are nearly a thousand, strange in someone so young," Henry said. Reaching for the jug of rum she held, he took a long swill before returning it to her.

"Age doesn't matter. It happens the day one sees too much, after that, you can always tell."

"I'm sorry, Velvet," he said, a fierce intensity suddenly lightening his eyes. A lock of hair fell over his forehead, impatiently he shoved it away, then ran a hand through the rest.

Velvet tilted her head. "Are you? For what, Henry?"

"For giving you away, for my anger, for past horrors I laid on you, pick a reason." He caught and held her hand, brought it to his lips. Velvet swung her gaze to his, meaning to snatch her hand away, but he stepped closer, and his gorgeous face swayed in and out of focus. Wind tugged and tossed his hair, moonlight slid down the hard cut of his jaw. Oh, she truly could not think when he stared at her like that, as if he could see every inch of skin beneath her borrowed shirt.

The moon sat directly behind his head, hanging huge as a hot air balloon over the water. It hallowed him in silver—like he was the god he had warned her of, fresh risen from the black waves. He stepped closer. "What did I do to you in your dream?"

Velvet's mind went blank. "I beg your pardon?" she screeched.

"You never answered my question," he said low.

Velvet felt her blood ignite, it scalded her cheeks, and she dropped her eyes to stare at their clasped hands. "I told you I could not tell you, it—"

Henry put his fingers over her lips, stopping her words. "Might make it real, yes I know, but how could that be true?"

"I cannot say," she breathed.

"Coward," he accused.

"No, I mean I don't think I am capable of actually putting it into words," she managed.

"Did I kiss you?" he asked.

Velvet squeezed her eyes shut; her head gave a nearly imperceptible nod. "Yes," she practically squeaked. The next step he took pressed their bodies together, his lips hovered inches from her own, Velvet saw the reflection of the waves move in the black of his eyes. "Did I now?" She heard him chuckle, a soft gush of air that rushed over her lips. "Where?"

If it had been physically possible to blush any harder, Velvet suspected she would have burst into flames. "Henry," she pleaded. "I cannot speak of such things."

"Shall I guess?" he asked, his head dipped, hot lips touched the corner of mouth. "Did I kiss you here?"

Velvet nearly screamed as his fingers coasted down her arms. "No," she breathed, "no, I don't know what you are talking about."

"Has anyone ever told you what a very terrible liar you are?" he asked before his lips fell to her neck, his next words touched like fire. "Was it here?"

Velvet said nothing, she was shaking, she realized distantly. His mouth traced a maddening path across her collarbone. "Here?" he breathed, "tell me, if I guess the right spot, will you let me do it again?"

"Judas, Henry!"

"How did we share the same dream, Marie?" he asked, and Velvet started at the use of her real name.

"I don't know!" she said, "and that is the truth."

"I'd wager you have a few ideas, so don't insult me by denying it—I know how your quick mind works, today alone I bet you've gone through a dozen scenarios."

"It wasn't real, can we not forget it?"

"Not even for the price of your life," he vowed, then lowered his head slowly, gave her ample time to pull away. She did not. Could not. She wanted him and it was worth noting that she too would never forget that night as long as she lived.

"Ah, Velvet," he said, lightly touching his lips to hers. "Thoughts of you are always in my mind, I fear you are the siren of my soul. Ever am I dragged back to you—if you were not mine, I would do anything to make it so." His hands moved to her hips. She could feel him, hard and hot, his heart beat an endless drum against her breast. "I want you, Velvet. By the laws of god and man you are mine, yet I find I cannot force you. Tell me what I must do, what it will take for you to let me—" his voice broke off. Velvet trembled like a leaf in a cyclone. She could think of no good reason. That she might not trust him? What did that matter? What could he do to her, that in the end, she did not plan to do to herself?

"You could help me," she said on a desperate thought, "work with me. Together we can find the treasure and the spell to save my brother, and perhaps save me too. Swear you will not try to stop or betray me. Swear you will listen to my explanations before jumping to a host of rash conclusions and I swear I will, you can...we can —" Her hands flew to her cheeks. Velvet had no idea if it was feasible for someone to die of embarrassment, but she had a feeling she was about to find out.

Henry pealed her fingers away from her face slowly, one at a time. He gathered them between his own, and brought her knuckles to his lips, then met her eyes over the bridge of their joined hands. "Marie, you cannot be so innocent...fuck!" he hissed when in her distressed face, he saw she truly was. "You are going to be the death of me," he swore, "and I mean that statement in the literal."

Something jolted in her stomach, a sharp twisting thing that made her eyes water, a sickening liquid filled her mouth, her body went straight as an arrow.

His lips brushed her cheek, kissed a shivery place behind her ear.

"Henry," she gasped.

He made a low, rumbling sound against her throat. "Yes, love?"

"Henry...I—" Her voice fell away as she began to struggle, and he leaned back regarding her gently, raising that slashing black brow. Her hand flew up to cover her mouth, and Henry needed no further clarification. He let her go, and stepped back, grimacing.

"Goddess," Velvet gasped, the sound muffled by her fingers, "I think I'm going to be sick."

Henry burst out laughing. "Yes, I believe you are. Not to worry. Close your eyes and think of it as a rite of passage. My advice is to revel in this moment, 'tis certain you will feel a thousand times worse on the morrow."

Velvet could not stare at his smiling face a single second longer. She rolled her eyes, spun away, and dashed for deeper waters. Then arms clutched across her howling stomach, and the sound of a Duke's laughter drifting over her shoulder, the last princess of France vomited up a bottle of black rum.

~

Hot sun, sticky sand everywhere, clogged up her nose, mouth, and ears. Velvet opened her eyes; knives of blazing white light stabbed her retinas. She groaned miserably. Her head was a cacophony of disorganized pain.

Her mouth felt made of dry cotton, and the taste within was a thing of horror. The urge to vomit that had followed her into sleep, had not completely passed. Velvet tried to swallow but found herself coughing instead. The dry scratch in her throat was annoying to the point of madness. She shook her head and blinked desperately. It took her a moment to assimilate her surroundings, and when she did, her vision was full of Henry's face, wreathed by his beautiful, insufferable smile. Far too cheery for so foul a day.

"Good morning, my darling," he said, as if there were no such things as cares in the world. He settled back on his haunches, holding out a skin of water.

Squinting, Velvet glowered hotly at him. "If you say so."

"Not a morning lover, huh?" said Henry, sounding on the verge of a good laugh, his eyes were twinkling madly.

"Not when it is the worst morning in the history of mornings'," Velvet declared, lying her head back on the sand, and slinging an arm over her face. For moment, it was just dark, then it all came rushing back in a prickly, cringy wash of memories. The men, the campfires, dancing in Henry's arms, then ending the night by tossing up her accounts, less than three feet away from him. After that, everything just faded to a discordant blur. Embarrassment came then, boundless, scalding waves that swept over her body. Under the shelter of her arm, Velvet could feel her face turn bright red. "Oh! Godstars!" she moaned. Rolling onto her side, she dragged herself to her knees, and lifted her hands to bury her head in them. Henry nudged the jug against her right hand. Velvet took it and drank deep without opening her eyes.

"The men have been watching you sleep for hours. For a while, you snored a fit to wake the dead—even I was startled so powerful a noise could come out of such a tiny person."

"You're a liar," Velvet accused, drinking again.

"True, you were silent as a sunrise, however, at one point you did blow a small spit bubble, and the men placed wagers on when it would pop. Martin made five quid."

Velvet moaned into her hands as her head spun, and stomach churned. "Mercy," she whispered, tilting as she swayed, knowing she would never be able to truly show her face to any of them ever again. She dropped her hands then and struggled to open her eyes. The day was soaked in sunlight, splashing around Henry who wore a clean white shirt that clung like a second skin to his bronze chest. It was open at the throat, his hair loose, and curling around his shoulders.

"Come on now," he said, and gave her shoulder a rather hearty slap. "On your feet, duchess. You need to walk it off."

"Walk it off? My head will tumble from my shoulders if I stand. I am never drinking rum again, it's a truly evil brew," she said, and heard him make a suspicious series of strangled sounds.

"I made the same vow, once, broke it soon as the headache faded."

"You're laughing at me," she accused.

"Undoubtedly, for a good part of the morning, actually—"

Velvet took a swing at him, dropping the skin of water.

Henry captured her hand, before it made impact with his jaw, then with the other hand caught her chin, held her face still. "Enough of that, you'll hurt no one save yourself—and possibly make me laugh some more. I promise to try and behave myself, keep the rest of my smiles behind my teeth, if you get up now and come with me."

Velvet shot him a venomous look. "Go to hell, Henry."

"Already been there, and done that, twice, I have the scars to prove it," he said, his words an icy counterpoint to his scalding touch.

She shook free of his hands. "What on earth makes you think I would go anywhere with you right now?"

"I have a present for you," he said.

"I don't like presents," she stated obstinately.

Henry captured her chin again, forced to look at him, and flashed her one of those devastating smiles. "You'll like this one. I swear it."

"I..." her voice fragmented into silence. "Oh, alright, I'm in too much agony to fight you anymore." Velvet stood, holding her head tight with both hands to keep it in place. "I hate feet," she said, "they are, unequivocally the worst things on earth. How is it that crows and vultures got wings, and humans are forced to walk on two stilts which never do as they are told?"

There was no response from Henry, only more chuckles as he turned and motioned for her to follow. She did, all thought of conversation abandoned. A half hour later, Velvet's aching eyes shot fire daggers into the back of Henry's swaggering form. He brandished his sheathed sword, bashed stinging branches from their path, and used it as a walking stick for the uphill parts of their trek. He whistled as he strolled. Velvet had no idea where he was taking her and was far too miserable to open her mouth and ask. Her head pounded like it had been hit with an iron mace, and the water she had drunk sloshed uncomfortably in her empty stomach. How had she ever thought rum a magical drink of the gods? It was a monstrous poison! More than anything, Velvet wanted to burrow a hole in the forest floor, bury her head in it and simply die.

She tripped on a root just then, the rough bark clipped her smallest right toe. Velvet had to bite back a wretched groan. Just as she was struggling with a fresh onslaught of dizziness, the cadence of Henry's whistle changed, the song turned almost chipper. It was far too much. Velvet bent down and picked up a fist-sized rock, with every intention of fulfilling a personal dream by throwing it at him.

He turned around when her arm was in the air, seconds before she let the rock fly. He eyed the stone with deceptive ease. Velvet was not fooled—she had seen mountain cats preparing to pounce look less dangerous than this man, huge arms folded across his chest. "For shame my love, you'll knock out what little sense I have, and this, after I've gone out of my way to bring you to the edge of paradise? For shame," he tisked.

Velvet glanced at their surrounding dubiously, the thorned vines, and jagged shards of bark falling from the reaching pines. The day had gone stale, muggy, like an old shirt left too long in the rain. Idly, her fingers picked at a rock stuck to her heel while her eyes went back to him. "What are you preening about? You look proud as God on the seventh day."

"It's not any man who could give a woman her truest desire," he said, motioning vaguely to the wall of green surrounding them.

Velvet rolled her eyes. "How well you know me?" She sighed. Henry only smiled at her, then used the tip of his sheathed sword to move aside a curtain of green. "I thought you might enjoy a bath, or a private place to vomit, since you are looking rather green around the gills," he said, motioning to a pool that hid behind the leafy veil, glowing, tantalizing as a moonlit river.

Velvet could not help the glad cry that escaped her barrier of raw misery. She scrambled the rest of the way, tripping twice in her haste. There was no pause to her stumbling momentum, not even to remove his shirt—she dove in, gulping a big breath before her head went under. Glorious.

Slowly, she let out her captured air in a giant cloud of bubbles, and let her body sink to the shiny, rocky bottom, where ripples of light moved like visible sound waves—it was there, that she simply allowed herself to be. Floating breathless for a time in perfect silence.

The water held a crisp chill and performed instant miracles on her aching head. When her air finally ran out, she let her body rise, kicking her feet to aid her assent. Soon her head broke the glassy surface where Henry's reflection wavered. Tilting her head, Velvet swept her hair back with her hands, it fanned out around her, and floated like sea foam.

Henry's eyes darkened as he watched her swim, he leaned against the pool's edge, and twirled a single finger through the water. "How much of last night do you remember?" he asked lazily.

"Enough," Velvet said, quickly swimming to the furthest edge of the pool, far from the reach of his hands.

"Do you remember the deal you offered me?" he asked.

Velvet realized it did not matter how far she moved from his hands, she could feel his eyes, knew each place on her skin where they touched without needing to look at him at all.

"Yes," she said slowly, "help me find and save my brother. If I live through it, you have my word that I—you can—I will let you do what you want with me," she finished in a rush.

"Even if that means we are bound forever?"

Velvet nodded.

"You will not go back on your word?" he asked, then said, "Velvet look at me."

"I am not the one who stands guilty of breaking my word, but no," she breathed, unable to fully conceal her irritation. "You have a dastardly effect on the temperature of my blood, I'm dizzy and ill enough already."

"Your word, Marie," he said, and his voice was sandpaper and satin.

She spun to glare at him, water swirled around her. "Fine, you have my word. Now give me yours. Swear to help me find my brother—promise you will not stand in the way of what I must do."

"I swear it," he said.

Velvet closed her eyes. "Alright then," she breathed.

"Alright then," she heard him echo, a slow collection of words that flowed through the air and sealed their fate.

CHAPTER SEVENTEEN

It is no secret that I would die just to hold you once.

December 5, 1800

$\mathcal{D}$evon went down on his knees and lifted the amethyst. It was the third time he had held it in as many days. Katie appeared instantly, as always—like she had been standing right there all along, and some unseen force had merely lifted the shroud. Katie was two feet in front of him, arms folded across her wavering stomach.

"I'm not a genie, you know. You cannot just summon me whenever the mood takes your fancy—it's not like I'm not busy, the sea is a truly engaging place, so many ghosts, endless stories, like the racy novels Nora loved to read, I'm not so sure I wouldn't —" her voice tore, the tumbling words coming to an abrupt halt when she saw his pale, pinched expression. "What's wrong," she asked, rushing forward to run her hands over his face, tugging her fingers through his auburn curls. Her hands on him were an undiluted heaven, and Devon closed his eyes, loudly sighing in bliss.

"I'm fine, a touch of ague, nothing to concern you." Devon kissed the curve of her rounded cheek, touched the open wound on her throat. Each time he felt her, forced him to reevaluate reality. Her movements were stilted, choppy, yet bore unmistakable echoes of the girl she had once been.

"You don't seem fine." She brushed his curved autumn brow with the pad of her thumb. "Only you could be this pale on the shores of southern Africa."

"The sun hates me," Devon acknowledged. His heart struck a rapid beat, and he could feel a fine layer of perspiration heating his skin. Devon suspected for the past few days that somehow the amethyst was burning him from the inside out, still, he could not let it go. Knew in his heart he never again could. Evil had taken her from him, magic brought her back—whatever the cost it was worth it—even his own life.

Devon's arms went around her waist, and her form fluttered like moonlight on water. She sighed when he kissed her temple, silently reassuring her everything would be alright, even though he knew it very well may not be.

"I'm leaving the ship for a few days. I know I cannot take you with me, I summoned you so I could say goodbye. Nora has decreed we find residence in town while the ship's repairs are completed. Swears she will die if she does not take a real bath, and sleep in a bed properly tethered to the ground." He shrugged. "We must all do as the pirate queen commands," he said wryly. The fingers running through his hair tensed, pulling it a little. Devon's head dipped, he kissed her lips, wished to feel the wash of her breath against his mouth, and knew he would not. She tasted like smoke and ashes.

Katie kissed him back tentatively, then pulled away to watch his face with eyes the color of tears. "I'm a ghost," she said, "time moves differently for me. It's like, when the stone is not in your hand, I'm dreaming, you touch it and I wake with a jolt, then I see your face, and of a sudden I'm dreaming again, afraid to ever wake. I could leave this ship, go with you—I think, but I'm not sure where I would go. If I let the white silence take me, I fear I would never return."

"How unbearable," said Devon bleakly, filling his eyes with her pale, tight face, smoothing his hand over her tousled hair.

Katie lay her cheek against his heart. "It truly is."

"Do you want me to stop using the stone?" he asked gruffly.

There was an instant of stillness before she said, "Never, yet I am afraid you must." Her voice was both sad and tender.

The ruckus of pirates gathering above, making their way across the deck sounded like muted thunder—Devon knew it was those who had been chosen to escort Nora to shore.

Katie's transparent fingers fell to the sleeves of his redcoat, where she held onto him. "You should be with them," she said, still wavering, fading in and out.

Today, Devon did not think he could bear watching her disappear. One may strike a bargain with an angel, but one could never own them. He was alive and she was dead, eventually he would lose her. Devon let out his breath in a hissing curse. He let her go with effort, stepped back, and shoved his hands in the pockets of his trousers to keep from touching her. There was a real danger for him here, and he knew it. His current situation strongly smacked of Icarus' predicament—the deep desire to fly too close to the sun, wanting to be near what he could never truly have—not caring one wit about the deadly burn.

Katie took her hands from him, and floated away, already starting to vanish despite his frantic hold on the amethyst. "Nora's waiting for you, she needs you right now, maybe more than I do. The girl is too loud and smart for her own good. Nora, alone on an island like this is a stunning recipe for swift disaster," she said, then smiled when Devon's eyes narrowed to slits of sable. She laughed rather sadly. "You might need to work on your enthusiasm. The Devon we all know and love, once said he would do his best to make the hangman smile while the man slung his noose."

Devon scowled darkly. "That's a direct quote from a complete fool. What the hell did he know?"

Katie opened her mouth to respond, but the voice that emerged from her lips faded into static. Devon gripped the stone tighter, she flickered back in focus. He moved for her again, but she slipped from his reach. A hard knock sounded on the other side of the door. "Milord, our lady captain wants you topside," called a squeaky voice from beyond.

Devon clamped down on his temper, kept his eyes on Katie, watched that eternal blood drop drip down her throat.

"I'll be there," she said, reading his miserable expression.

"Swear it," he demanded, 'I'm afraid, truly. Afraid each time I see you will be the last. More than that, I'm afraid you're not real, terrified the wind, the ship, your death and this stone have driven me insane."

The fervent knock came again. Devon reached for the handle, flung the door open and shouted in the intruder's face. "Do you truly think I did not hear your obnoxious yowling the first time?" he nearly roared, badly startling the hapless Jerry Littleton.

Jerry reeled away, his eyes flying so wide it seemed the boy's veined eyeballs were plotting a great escape from the wan, pimpled face hosting them. His hair was a greasy black pelt, dramatically patted down on one side. He pushed it back with a shaky hand. "My apologies, yer' lordship. My lady said I was not to leave without verbal assent of your imminent arrival—her words. I wouldn't say nothin' like that, I—" Jerry's words died as if cut off with a knife.

His face went white as a bleached sheet. Shrieking then, he stumbled back, tripping on the loose laces of his boots, and slamming into the wall behind him. He cried out, his hand went to his throat, before he twitched and used the same hand to nervously cross himself. "It's a spirit," Jerry managed to rasp. "Behind you, m'lord," he pointed vigorously. "Sweet balls!" he exclaimed. "It's the girl old captain Chance cut, I watched her die—always suspected she was hauntin' us. It's cold, bad luck to kill a woman on a ship, brings the plague it does—we all knew it."

"I thought it was bad luck to bring them aboard the vessel," Devon said calmly, almost amused by the boy's near comical terror.

"That's cause if you bring them aboard, there's a better chance some man will kill them," Jerry retorted.

Devon glanced over his shoulder to find Katie's eyes. She blew him a kiss. Slowly, Devon set down the stone and watched her vanish. He stared at the spot until all of her had drifted away, like powder caught in the path of a strong breeze. "I don't see anything behind me," Devon lied, listening to the helpless catch in his voice.

Jerry straightened. "All's well, she's gone now."

Devon took a shaky breath. "Perhaps your litany of female shrieks frightened her off," he said, feeling suddenly, unreasonably tired.

"Blood, sir," said Jerry. He caught the sleeve of Devon's coat, his hand falling in exactly the last place Katie had touched.

Devon turned back to the boy. "Where?"

"Your nose, it's bleeding, spewing actually—like a busted pipe."

Devon nodded; he could taste the foul liquid. Blood lurched down his throat, and he coughed and turned his back on Jerry again. Outside the small, open window, the wind gusted. "I know," he said. "Tell Nora, I'm on my damn way." He lifted his hand to staunch the blood, hardly sparing Jerry a final glance. "Let's keep this spirit nonsense between ourselves, shall we?" he asked, trying to add sufficient nonchalance to his tone.

"No problem by me—not the first spirit I've seen, Devil knows it won't be my last," muttered Jerry, spinning to stomp his way back down the narrow hall that led to the main deck. "Ghosts and spells," he muttered. "My mama warned me of such things—Satan always finds men at sea because there are so few places to hide, that's what she said. Did I listen? *Noooo,* not me. I strapped on my boots and left that god awful missionary camp in Zimbabwe. Why the hell do they need missionaries, I'd like to know? They ken more about the world then we ever will, always talking to their ancestors, not that I ever want to see my grandpappy again, a right bastard that one…"

Jerry's choppy rumbling faded away as Devon slammed the door, then walked to his small, badly balanced washstand. He stared at his face in the gritty mirror bracing the cracked wooden bowl. His reflection gave him real pause. The eyes scared him the worst. They were framed with black and blue bags that looked like torture bruises—the whites were soaked crimson. It appeared he had stolen his skin from a poisoned corpse, and the lower half of his face was streaked in dark blood, still pouring from his nose. He closed his eyes and saw Katie's big, almond ones, sometimes brown, sometimes grey, and now—in death, all the smoky colors in between. Outside the night wind continued to howl, it set the curtains swaying. Devon stomped his way out of the room, feeling for all the world like he had left his heart behind him.

"Good God, Devon, you look like you couldn't find the floor with anything but your face," said Nora, as Devon moved to stand beside her, trying to add his usual animation to his stride—and failing badly.

"I'm well," he said, staring in her eyes and seeing marks of real concern there. Her eyes flicked over him from head to toe, her glare told him the subject was in no way closed, though she said no more on the topic, only reached for his hand. Together they walked to the rail, watched the busting port, it had come alive in the night bathed in the orange light of a thousand flickering torches. Shadow and smoke wreathed through groups of huddles slaves being led away to their own misery, it threaded between the blonde thatching of the straw rooftops that dotted the edge of the shore and wound deep inland.

"It's all so foreign," Nora breathed. "I feel like an alien lost on another planet, and the few redcoats I see loitering around seem like nothing but intruders, best leave your coat. I fear it may be hated. It is like they have no right to set foot on this land. It was raw and brave once, I think, before them, at least the people of this land were free." Nora grimaced. "I don't feel like I belong here."

"But you do, you are the captain of a feared pirate ship, in command of a fierce, legendary crew," said Ajax from his persistent place on Nora's righthand side. The giant had ordained himself her personal guardian sometime in the past weeks, and with the monstrous Cerberus ever her shadow, Devon wondered if she had need of him at all. Devon turned to share his musings with her, perhaps beg she give him leave to stay and stare at his ghostly love, saw the strain on her face and reconsidered his request.

Nora clenched her hands together to keep them from shaking. Her ensemble of trousers and fitted jacket was black silk tonight, her bright hair pulled tight, and shoved beneath a broad cap, and

Devon had to smile. Despite her fears, or maybe because of them —she looked the part.

"I sailed here once," he said, turning his attention back to the shore, "with Henry, years ago. I learned quick to keep my head down, and my voice loud."

"Not sure if that advice will work for me. Abigail told me that Prince Radama—a powerful creatin—gave Captain Chance gold to purchase a woman matching my exact description. Chance gave that gold to Alfonso," she said as she touched the brim of her cap and shrugged. "I tried to cover my hair, yet Abigail says it will be an easy thing for him to find me, no doubt word of the red-head pirate queen has already reached his ears. Still," she sighed, "I must repair my ship, and seek out information on the map. Then, we sail for St. Mary's island, pray Henry has come to his senses and taken Velvet somewhere safe."

Devon shot her a sideways glance. "I know, it's a lot to hope for," she breathed.

❦

Nora took a jagged breath and struggled to think past the unholy tangle which was her emotional state. She was hot, sweaty, and hated everything already, the muggy heat, the deadly, stinging mosquitoes, and the endless, horrid crack of the slave driver's whip. She loved it too. All of it. Loved the way the palm trees rustled, arching up from the whitest sand, the way the fronds swayed, and bobbed when color-soaked birds landed on their fanned-out leaves. Positively adored the all the varying architecture reflected in the dark water like it was some huge, upside down mirror—she would find threads of her destiny here, Nora knew it like she knew her name.

In the water, slaves sang as they were dragged to ships, tears smeared on their cheeks, dignity, and strength in their eyes. Nora had a wild notion to buy each slave in sight, crush their chains and set them free—but she was no hero, and this was the morbid way of her world. The crack of the lash sounded again, Louis hissed, and Devon said something savage beneath his breath.

"I see you hate it too—" she started.

Devon grunted. "Not much I like right now. Frankly, I could do with a strong drink, and a solid brawl. Maybe I'll go pick a fight with that lash happy lunatic yonder, use his own whip on him till I find bone," he muttered.

"All's ready, lady N," said Abigail, stomping to meet them. The buccaneer girl's boots had golden spurs to match the silk scarf wrapping her head, and they jangled like bells when she walked. Dark eyes alight with excitement she handed Nora a pearl derringer, clicked her tongue and cocked her head, looking out past the shore. "I've found lodging for us. The home of a dead British woman—suicide I think. The Merina people won't go near the place, they say it's cursed with the white lady's spirit—"

"Marvelous," sighed Devon.

"Well, it will keep us safe from the living at least," said Abigail. "Prince Radama is at his summer palace near Ambohimanga. Mayhap we pay him a visit, return his gold, and tell him you are not for sale."

"I'm sure that will go over like a kick in a sack," said Devon sardonically.

Abigail ignored him with a roll of her huge, dark eyes. "I have a plan. There is treasure at the end of lady N's map. We offer him a share and pray to the old gods that he's in a bargaining mood."

It was not nausea that was making Nora's skin feel clammy, she realized, passing a hand over her brow, at least not right now—it was the suffocating terror. The terror of the unknown. "I'm going below to speak with Alfonso," she said, then paused to come up with a rebuttal for the swift protests Devon always voiced—none came. Devon continued to stare at the golden shore, his eyes touching on the hundreds of lives being forever ripped from their homeland tonight. "Do what you must," he finally said.

Nora hid her shock. He looked like a man who was reaching the end of his endurance—fifteen years had she known him, and never had she seen him look so wretched. She would investigate it at another time, she told herself; when time was something she had.

Devon turned to face her, his eyes ghostly in the night light.

He gave her a small bow then motioned in the direction of the narrow stairs which lead down to the brig. "After you, my lady," he said. Nora released a breath she had not been aware of holding and marched past him. Louis and Cerberus followed close.

"I can feel your denial pounding in my head, Louis—this will all be for the best, trust me."

"I wish I could," Louis said in that soft mind voice, "yet those stones keep their own counsel. I could leave, I doubt you would ever find me, and the problem would disappear quickly as it came to exist."

Nora suspected he said that last part on an afterthought—lately she had a sense of things like that, as if she were getting brief glimpses into his mind—not the soul-searching way he could read hers of course, but it was better than nothing. She stopped and turned to him. "You would really leave me?" she asked, looking deep in his moving almond eyes, too shocked by his words to be coy. His glow touched all the dark places around them, spilling like luminous oil. Since that horrid night she had loped off a man's head, this enchanted prince had become the central focus of her life.

"Never," he said, moving close, radiating warmth. "Yet at times I feel it may be the only way to keep you from descending into utter madness."

"Making such threats will only serve to further my frenzy," she cried, her hands falling to her stomach. "The threat of never seeing you again already looms. I swore to Velvet I would do this thing, and even if I had not, you are the rightful king of France—your life may save a nation. Do you really think the life of some random villain is worth yours?"

"Yes, life is precious," he said.

Nora snorted. "Strongly disagree," she snapped, and began her descent down the muggy hole, taking care on the uneven steps.

18

ALFONSO'S STORY

What would you trade for all your heart's desires?

The smell was hot and monstrous. Nora put a hand to her nose, held her breath to keep the rancid scent from burning its way down her throat. Ignoring the others who sat on the ground and picked at the wood chips between their bars, she walked straight to Alfonso's cage. Nearly a month in the brig had done him no favors. He was thin and pale, his once thick, dark hair, now hung limp and faded around his shoulders. His cheeks were hollowed, black bags made the eyes look sunken.

Alfonso looked up when she came to a halt not three feet from him. He smiled, showing her a straight row of filthy gold teeth.

"Good evening, Captain," he said, inclining his head. "If I had known such beautiful company was to be mine tonight, I would have," he looked around, and began to laugh, "well I would not have done much to the place," he finished, chuckling deep in his matted beard.

"What do you want with the stones?" Nora asked.

"Straight to the point I see."

"There is no use bantering with a fool," she said sweetly. "Tell me what I want to know, and I will release you and your men."

Both Devon and Abigail spoke up at once and, with a wave of her hand, Nora hushed them. "This is my ship, and he is my prisoner, I can do with him as I will. I want to know everything you know about these stones, and if I find the information satisfactory, you may take your men and be on your way. I swear it. Lord knows I should probably just put a sword through your heart and be done with it, but tonight I want information more than satisfaction."

"And what would you like to know?" asked Alfonso, sitting up a little straighter.

"When you captured Velvet and I, you were looking for us, it was not just a chance meeting, am I right?"

"But of course. The princess of France is Queenie's protégé, and I have had my eyes on her for many years."

"You were looking for the stones, weren't you? Even though Velvet told you she would give you all the gold, that was not what you wanted," she said, this time it was not a question.

"What a bright girl you are," he said jovially.

"You knew Captain Chance was traveling to St. Mary's island. That is why you brought us to his ship?"

"Yes, by then I knew Velvet must have the stones on her person, after she used them so skillfully to conjure the snake who nearly killed one of my men."

"What do you want with the stones?" Nora asked again.

Alfonso smiled and shook his head; there was a terrible sadness in his next words. "Want with them? Darling, I want to destroy them."

Nora gave no outward reaction to his words, but inside she was reeling, at gun point she could not have guessed that response. "Why?"

"Because they are evil, they bring only death, the stones which aid transformation—most of all. I heard of the stones for the first time when I was two weeks from my sixteenth year. My family's caravan traveled alongside a grand party of Romani who made camp just a few leagues beyond the city boundaries of Paris. I only knew of Queenie then, whispers of her abounded. A young girl snatched from her homeland, an enraged freedom fighter who left those same shores with a great prize."

"The stones," said Nora, filled by a sudden dread of the story she feared was coming.

Alfonso nodded. "The stones yes, plus a map, and bits of treasure so old, they say that Zeus is among those who once searched for it. Then, Velvet's mother saved the life of Queenie's only daughter, and the woman's legend grew. "

My father moved our family so that we would be near this great woman—my mother was afraid; she cried and warned my father that the power of the stones was dark—evil. My brother, sister and I were blinded by excitement. My sister was ten years old and thought the woman to be a goddess. Growing up with fortune tellers and illusionists, I was fascinated by magic in all its form. My brother was six years old, copied everything I did, loved what I adored."

"I laid eyes on her only once, the night it all descended to hell. The moon was full, and Queenie called the leaders of the Rom from all those encamped in the surrounding areas. She spoke of her 'great plan' to liberate the people of her homeland. Give them the autonomy she had found on her own—the freedom given to her by the power of the stones. That night the French Revolution was in full swing, the streets of Paris were burning, embers from the blaze changed the color of the sky, smudged blood on the face of the moon. She spoke of the French heirs, and the blood debt she owed to their doomed mother, then she talked about what she could do with them if they lived, whispered of all we as a Romani people could take with them on our side."

"She's dead though, so her plan failed," said Nora.

Alfonso shrugged, studying her face with his unusual black eyes. "Who can say? I told you, mine are a people of illusion. Whatever her state—I do not believe she fully failed. What do you know of the stones your man now carries?"

Precious little, Nora thought, though she said nothing.

Alfonso lifted a dark brow; he waited a beat before he continued. "Each stone personifies the gifts of the goddess sisters who were their guardians. Love, illusion, wealth, war and transfiguration, the bloodiest spell of all."

Nora swallowed hard. "Love, illusion and transfiguration I know. Of those, I understand the cost better than most."

Alfonso nodded again. "Each time they are used, life is wasted. There is an old rhyme that stems from the island of Queenie's birth. One life, if that life is willingly given, two if it is forcefully taken, if no soul is given at all, death will flow, a bloody rain fall."

Nora closed her eyes as Alfonso recited the words. Against her right arm she felt Louis flinch. Her eyes rolled behind their lids, there would be no living with him now.

"Twice if blood is forcefully taken." Louis's voice echoed in her mind. "So many people have died already for me," he said sadly. "If I did not want you to take even one more life, how do you think I'll feel about two?"

Nora had to ignore him. She opened her eyes and stepped closer to the bars. "What happened," she asked Alfonso, needing to hear the rest of it.

"I wanted to be part of the council since I was almost of age and already a great warrior. My parents denied my request, tasked me instead with putting my brother and sister to bed. I did as I was bade then sat in front of the window, stared at Queenie's face, listened while my parents spoke of ancient things I could hardly comprehend. I watched Queenie make a tea with chamomile petals and some other herb I had no name for then. My parents drank it gratefully, so did all others present. I watched, my nose pressed against the handblown glass window of my family's caravan, as one by one the older members of our camp, the warriors, the maidens, all nodded off into deep sleep. When the last fell, Queenie stood and took a sheathed knife from the varied folds of her many-colored skirts. The blade was black, grim under the touch of silver moon. She glanced around for a moment, turning nearly full circle, I thought her beautiful enough to be pure fantasy."

"Then, she froze, slowly lifted her head and looked directly into my eyes through the dirty glass of my hand-blown window. I smiled at her, smiled and waved—"

Alfonso's voice broke off, he grunted and spat on the ground. "Queenie returned my smile. Drenched in that silver moonlight I was so dazzled, I almost believed she was one of the goddesses of myth. She started toward me and I forgot to breathe. I rushed to push back the beaded curtain hanging over our door, stopping only to check on my sleeping brother and sister. My sister, Dora, sucked on her thumb, smiling sweetly at her dreams. My brother was curled on his side, folded hands tucked under his chubby chin—of all the things in the world, I loved them the most. Dora and Vano. I have not spoken their names since that night. The pure filth of this cell must be wearing me down." Alfonso paused to take a breath, pass a tired hand over his eyes. "I opened the door then, Queenie stepped inside my caravan, moving aside the beads when they caught in her necklace and long, waving hair."

"I remember that I bowed, unsure of how one was meant to greet this great woman. My eyes stayed fixed on the black blade, the way it seemed to glow in the interior dark. 'Sit', she told me, motioning to a small wooden chair, covered in yellow daisies my sister had painted only two days ago. I obeyed, silent, awed. She looked at me for a long time, her dark eyes full of unutterable secrets. 'I must tell you, I am not sorry, yet I regret what I have to do', she finally said. I had no comprehension what she meant. I nodded, thinking her the wisest woman in all the world. As she stared at me, I noticed one of her eyes was larger than the other and differed slightly in color. At last, her eyes drifted over my shoulder and widened as her black gaze wandered over my sleeping brother and sister. 'It's right, they are exactly the same age, tis fate', she said. I said nothing, words abandoned me. She reached for a chain that hung around her neck. Lifted a glassy stone, lime green and glittering—" Alfonso shuddered. "I will never forget that damn color, for it is the shade of all my nightmares. She closed her fist over the limestone, spears of light shot between her fingers. Her hand hovered near my face, moved closer till it dangled directly in front of it. The light ran everywhere, over me, into me. 'Immobilize', she said, and every muscle, nerve ending and drop of blood in my veins obeyed.

I sat, paralyzed, a screaming prisoner inside my own body. Unable to move, or cry out, I watched, helpless as I have ever been, she knelt in front of my baby sister, raised the black knife, and slowly slit her throat. My sister never woke, her death was peaceful, my brother did, his was not. She stabbed him twice, he cried and begged for me to help him as he died. The paralysis faded a few hours later, my parents woke to find my hands covered in blood, and my word as the only explanation for the events."

While he spoke, Alfonso's eyes had narrowed until they were glitter slits of ink. Nora saw tears in them and wondered at the twist of pain and regret in her heart for the man, from who she had suffered much. She must have made some broken sound of encouragement in her throat because Alfonso sniffed, then continued speaking.

"The next night, Queenie transformed the prince and princess, spirited them away from France and saved their royal lives—on the same day I buried the best parts of my family under the cold ground, in holes I dug with my bare hands. I consumed great amounts of fire-whisky until night fell, then I began my search for her, with nothing but my gnawing need for revenge. My search ended the night your Velvet, jumped from some shrubs, and placed the edge of her knife against my throat."

"If you want the stones so desperately, why did you sell us?" snapped Nora, clearing her throat of some rather cloying, unshed tears.

"The stones can only be destroyed on the land they were created. I knew you had them. I left you and your companions tied to trees while I searched for them. I knew Queenie gave the stones to Velvet, practically made her into a stone herself with the final change."

Nora knelt before the bars, reached through them, and took Alfonso's hand. "You can destroy all the stones but one as I must return Louis to his natural state. He cannot remain like this."

"All save two," Devon said. "I will not release the amethyst."

Alfonso smiled; his eyes turned soft. "Ah, it gave her back to you. Very well, I too wish to use the amethyst, just once. I never got to say goodbye, never got to tell my brother and sister that I would have willingly died in their place."

"I will sail to St. Mary's island with you, after Louis is changed, I will give you the stones to do with as you will. Do we have an accord?" she asked, squeezing the hand she held.

"The prince's transformation will cost you," said Alfonso, "best to leave him as he is."

"I will not," said Nora, "and I will happily kill the next person who suggests it."

Alfonso shrugged again. "What does it matter? The worst has already happened for me." He looked into Nora's eyes a moment longer, seemed to like what he saw, smiled, and sighed. "We have an accord," he said.

Nora stood, dusted her hands on her skirt. "Lord Eden, the keys to Alfonso's cell, if you please."

～

What would you do, if today was your last day?

Nora gave Abigail the master bedroom of the old manor, the pirate girl had chosen as their temporary residence, situated to the north of Merina, two leagues outside Antananarivo. The house was huge. A monstrous stone structure that seemed to scrape the low, rain-soaked clouds. It had high, cathedral windows, and ivy-twined pillars positioned at its six corners. The stones of the building were white-washed, pearly as the surrounding sands.

Nora would hear nothing of Abigail's protests, choosing instead to take the small cottage on the southern edge of the lush grounds, covered in such flowers, the likes of which Nora had never seen. The rooms of the cottage were warm and cozy, the feeling of her feet on solid ground was some type of wonderful. She primed the pump at the back of the house, washed out a bucket she found in the outside privy, filled it with cool water then heated it over a fire she made in the hearth, so she could take a much-needed bath.

Standing in the cottage's small master bedroom, Nora dropped her chemise and stared at her changing body in the long, dusky mirror, her reflection murky beneath a thin layer of dust that covered the glass. Her hands fell to her expanding waistline. The babe was showing now, it made her want to cry; another bastard child, born into a world that hated them.

"What am I going to do with you, huh?" she asked aloud to

the unwanted child she almost loved. No answers awaited her in the mirror. Nora sighed and lowered herself in the steaming bath and mulled over all that had happened in the last two months. From ballroom doll to pregnant pirate queen. Once a girl who only read about magic, to a woman chasing the squiggly black lines of a lost treasure map, and possibly falling in love with an enchanted prince. Quickly, Nora tried to shove the glowing golden words from her mind, afraid Louis was lurking somewhere beyond the closed door, listening to what she was not yet ready to put in words, certainly none she was ready for him to hear.

When the bath water turned tepid, Nora stepped out, dragged on her chemise and all but collapsed on the small, feather-stuffed bed. She woke ten hours later, ravenous and in desperate need of the privy. This pattern repeated for three days, days that slipped through Nora's fingers like grey fog. Sleep constantly tugged at her senses, she seemed to exist in some kind of drugged state, like she had obliviously visited one of the opium dens, Charles so loved. Fighting nausea like some malicious familiar, Nora ate the food Abigail brought, thanked her through yawing lips. Devon visited her twice. He looked horrid—she begged him to take care—suspected he would not.

On the fourth day of this haze an invitation arrived at the manor, her name printed in platinum, scrawled across the face of a golden card. A masked ball would take place in two days' time, at the Rová of Antananarivo. King Andrianampoinimerina, and his son, prince Radama would be in attendance.

Nora penned a short note, gratefully accepting the invitation, then she crawled in bed and went back to sleep. She woke, she bathed, she ate endless slices of coconut baked in honey, and she waited. Every night dreaming of Velvet screaming, and little boys with curly black hair, who cried for their brother as they died. For all the time Nora stayed in that stuffy, cocoon of a cabin, Louis never came to her, Nora began to fear he had walked out of her life. Today she ran around the property screaming his name, cursing, threatening. Nothing. The night of the ball arrived, and Nora was truly afraid. If he left, she would never find him, would wander searching forever, holding the broken pieces of her heart in her hands. Then what? Quest denied, she would be adrift.

Breathless from her useless search, Nora knelt before her mirror and cried until her eyes were swollen. After, she put a cold cloth on her face, and dressed in a silver, satin gown. Trimmed in the finest threads of braided gold. Three days ago, Nora had commissioned a dress maker in Antananarivo to fashion her a silk mask, cut and sewn to look like owl feathers. Nora thought of Velvet when she put the mask on, and it seemed fitting. She left her mane of red hair brushed and wild, partly because it suited her ensemble, mainly because she could not perform a satisfactory chiffon unassisted.

Nora's escorts arrived at dusk. Abigail and Devon walked arm in arm. Ajax stood to their right, dressed as a pirate, his mask a single patch over his left eye. Abigail's gown was watered silk, a mask of the same material transformed her into a swan. Devon had garbed himself in ivory finery, a stiff mask covered the left side of his face, the right side of his face was so chalky white, the transition from mask to skin was almost seamless.

"Don't judge when your face has no more color than mine," Devon said, noting the flash of concern for him that lit up her eyes. His voice gentled. "There is nothing you can do, Nora, and I would not change my circumstances for all the world," he said, and Nora had left it at that. His life—his choice. If Devon wanted to die, so he could be with Katie, well she sympathized, and understood.

A carriage with gold trimming on the wheels carried them to The Rovä. Nora slept for the entire ride, on Devon's shoulder. He touched her cheek softly when they arrived, and she opened her sleep-stuck eyes. Hundreds of torches surrounding the imposing palace lit up the moonless night. The numerous flames danced in the tropical breeze. Everywhere people mulled about, dressed in fantastical creations, each masked. "They all look like villains in a play," Nora whispered, gazing at the elaborate spread.

Devon grunted, he opened the carriage door and stepped out, then held a hand for Nora to take, and descend. "They are, darling, lords and ladies all, the truest actors and actresses to ever grace the world stage—play your part to perfection or be devoured."

"In this game, at least, I know my footing," Nora said, stepping down on the soft grass. "At least here, in this setting, for the first time in a while, I know what is expected of me. How to act exactly right, so that I may belong."

"Corrupt monsters, and glittering fools," spat Abigail, unlocking the black fan that hung from her black-gloved wrist. She flicked it back and forth in front of her face. "It's terribly muggy," she hissed, kicking a clump of mud from the toe of her right boot. "I'm going to seek out a strong drink, and what information I can find, maybe drop a bit of gossip about the red-head British princess who deigned to honor us with her presence," Abigail finished, smiling at Nora so her words were not cruel.

"Do take Devon with you," Nora said, waving them both away. "I have Ajax here to guard me, if all goes awry."

"Is there any particular line of information I should listen for? Apart from the obvious, of course," Devon asked, offering his Arm to Abigail.

"The map offers sweet little to go on, scattered fragments of information at best. I want to know the history of the map, any stories regarding what it leads to, I want to hear them all, no matter how fantastical," Nora said, picturing all the squiggly black lines of the map in her mind.

Devon nodded, as he turned away, Nora saw an odd look in his eyes, like he knew something she did not. It was in her mind to pry —yet, if it were about Katie, Nora would have to tell herself the reasons all over again, reasons why she should not, could not, hold the amethyst stone. Heartbreaking stuff, it really was. And with Louis nowhere in sight for days, her heart was already in turmoil.

Abigail linked her fingers through the crook of Devon's arm, and the stuttering glow of banked fire bracketed them both in gold. Behind them, shadows receded into the windy dark.

"Have a wonderful night, darling," said Devon, and some pale reflection of his former smile ghosted around the corners of his mouth. Nora let him go, to quizzically stare at his retreating back.

Ajax conjured a chute of champagne from somewhere and

pressed it in her hands. "I'll keep to the shadows, Captain, I'm always only a scream away should you have need," he said.

"A solid plan, I think you may scare away an archangel. I don't intend to go inside until Devon returns as I do hate to be announced alone. Stay close and let us hope I'm approached by a person with something valuable to say." Nora sighed, glancing at the vapid, colorful crush. "In current company, it may be a lot to ask for."

Sipping her champagne, Nora dragged in a silent breath and search the crowd for a likely target. After a moment, she found a hopeful. A dark-eyed girl lost in a pack of gossiping women. A Malagasy native in a British dress. A slave? Concubine? No matter, Nora suspected the lady had a knowledge of this land and its neighboring islands. Nora started for her. She had not taken two steps when a man in black evening wear blocked her path. Startled, Nora's eyes flew up. He was tall, with broad shoulders and fly away golden hair. He wore a gold mask cropped across the bridge of his straight nose, it came to a pinnacle between his eyebrows, then swept into a pair of golden horns, arched and triple pronged like a stag, like a pair of horns she had seen so many times.

He regarded her with bright, indigo eyes. As Nora simply stared, the man bowed. "Bonsoir, madame," he said. "You are ravishing tonight." He moved closer; caught her hand, his voice dropped low. "Under the touch of firelight, you glow like the rarest amber." His thumb stroked gently over her knuckles, while she stared at him with shocked perplexity. "What a pleasure it is to simply touch you, strange how you miss the little things," he said. Nora heard a slight French accent influencing his speech—and she knew.

Nora's rush of expelled breath was his name, her free hand flew to cover her mouth, hold back a scream. "Louis?" she screeched between her fingers. "Judas! Louis, is it really you?"

He said nothing, her hand reached for his mask, he bent his head and let her take it. Let her untie the laces that kept it from falling, they unraveled in her hands. Fingers shaking terribly, Nora lifted the mask away and just looked at him. Simply stared wide-eyed at his perfect face like she had wished to do so many times.

Scintillating astonishment passed over her like a dizzy spell. He was far more beautiful than she had imagined, and her fantasies had painted him as god. "What? How?" Her voice thickened. "Louis, is this real? Am I dreaming?" His mask fell from her numb fingers, and she touched his face. "How?"

"An illusion, nothing more. We do not have much time," Louis said. He turned his face, and his lips brushed the center of her palm. "Alfonso told me his cast will end at midnight, when the clock strikes, the spell will fade, and I will be returned to what I am."

"You jest!" Nora accused, then rolled her eyes, when she realized he did not. "Insanity, like Cinderella?" she nearly shrieked, unable to fathom or assimilate the reality of him, the way he felt under her trembling hands.

Louis smiled a little at her outburst. "Cinderella, oh yes, I believe I actually remember that story. My nounou used to read it to me when I was a boy." He laughed. "I suppose our current situation has some alarming similarities, though I have no diamond slippers, and intend to end the evening without cutting off either of my feet." He grimaced. "Besides, Alfonso is not much of a fairy godmother."

"Why would he even do such a thing?" Nora asked, unable to stop looking at him. Here, tangible, breathing.

"It was Lord Eden's plan. He suggested that for his freedom, Alfonso was in your debt. He then went on to explain his plan of exactly what Alfonso should do about it." Louis's face when he said this was unreadable, his eyes looked haunted. "I rejected the idea at first, naturally—"

"Naturally," Nora breathed.

"Yet, in the end I—" Louis shrugged. "I wanted to see you, touch you, I wanted...this."

"Truly?" she breathed, loving the way his full lips moved when he talked.

"More than anything in the world," he said.

"And the price?"

His lips touched her brow, sent a shot of shivers rushing down her spine. "Already paid," he said.

Nora let out a broken breath. "I'm speechless," she said.

Louis laughed. "A speechless Nora, impossible, I assure you, like a cold flame, or burning block of ice."

"Burning ice?" Nora laughed. "You never know, such a thing might one day be possible."

"Even this," he breathed, bent his head, and kissed her mouth. A hot spark sizzled over the fibers of her gown, lifted strands of hair off her neck, and crackled between their lips, they both jumped, he laughed and drew her back to him. Nora felt the sounds of the party fade, like echoes from another, distant planet. His hands caressed her cheeks lifted her face so he could kiss her again. His lips moved softly over hers, while his fingers ran along the edges of her mask. Nora went up on her toes, and kissed him back, not caring a wit who saw them. She was finally touching her prince, and whoever thought her actions were scandalous could simply go hang.

"Where have you been?" she gasped when he finally let her take a breath.

"Trying to stay away."

"Don't you dare."

"I could not."

"You promise?"

"Yes, never again," he said, their words running together like voices in the wind.

"No matter what?" she pressed.

"No matter what," he said, and it sounded like a confession. This time it was Nora who dragged his mouth to hers. Louis lifted her off her toes. Flecks of luminous gold soaked her senses. The night wind blew through their hair, twining it together. The wind carried the strains of a slow waltz from the ballroom's gilded arches.

"Dance with me, Princess, just once. A single memory I can keep with me for always." Louis looked down at his big hands, nearly spanning her waist. "A beautiful piece of time I can inscribe on my mind, something to visit when all this is taken from me again."

"I don't understand. Devon, Alfonso, how did they...?"

Louis kissed her lips biting them softly between his words. "A story for another time, mon amour, besides, if it's all over soon, does it really matter?"

"No, it doesn't. Yes, let's dance. In there." Nora pointed toward the ballroom. "Dance the night away under the glittering lights, in front of all of them. Your mask, oh! I dropped it," she gasped, disentangling herself from his arms, spinning to begin her search for the thing. Louis caught her around the waist and hauled her back to him. "Chérie, no one for ten thousand miles would recognize me. Only a few alive have ever seen this face."

"Why can't I keep you?" she asked, touching his lips, memorizing him. His high cheekbones, and perfect lines.

"All illusions must eventually end," he said. "That does not mean we cannot make this one spectacular for as long as it lasts." He smiled at her. "Come, stop stalling, and let's see if I remember how to waltz."

Crystal chandeliers, champagne flutes, spinning lights and Louis. Nora did not know how long he held her on the dance floor. Yet it seemed hours later when she finally begged him to take her out for a breath of air, and he carried her back to the wind-washed gardens. He held her in the dappled shadows, under the umbrella of a swaying baobab tree. Nora was dizzy, intoxicated by him. She had loved having him in her mind, but this was so much more. He was real and warm, cradling her like nothing in the world could ever rip them apart.

The night had taken such a magical, wonderful turn, Nora had forgotten all the reasons she attended this masquerade in the first place. Her world was Louis alone, and all the varied feelings he invoked. Ideas of destiny and fate. She kissed him constantly, lay her head on his shoulder and for a time they talked of everything and nothing at all. Under that baobab tree, Nora told him her deepest dreams, dreams of freedom, and what she wished all women could someday be. Louis talked about his life, what it felt like to be human again, even if only for a time. The night lasted forever and flew by like a flash of lightening that ended in a sudden boom, all at once and terrifying.

Nora felt something akin to dismay, when she saw Devon and Abigail weaving their way through the crush. Nora gripped Louis's hand as if her strength could keep him locked in this form, her will alone could stave off the inevitable twang of the clock striking twelve.

As Nora watched, Devon turned to speak to a man on his left. The man moved into a slice of light and Nora saw his face. Charles. His name was a bitter taste in her mind; however, the leggy, casual stride of the newcomer was unmistakable.

"Bastards on a biscuit, in the name of all that is holy, what in tarnation is he doing here?" Nora hissed, going a little numb with horror, and a nagging vulnerability she had not felt since leaving Britain's cold shores. The moment held a dreamlike unreality, and for a time Nora was lost in it. Devon was speaking low; Charles shook his head. Nora tore her eyes away from them. A small, shattered sound escaped her; she slapped a hand over her mouth to stifle the next.

Louis's head snapped up, searching out the object of her distress. Face intent, his eyes passed over Devon, and he stiffened, Nora saw a break in his civilized exterior. "Lord Newcastle, the younger, I presume," he said rather bleakly.

"In the flesh," Nora nearly wailed, clinging to Louis like a lifeline of salvation.

"Handsome," Louis noted.

"As a viper," snapped Nora.

Devon raised a hand to hail her, a child of regret, Nora returned the half-hearted wave, smiling wanly. Go back, her eyes screamed, turn around, take him away! Devon either did not see, or was unable to comply with her silent, desperate command.

Charles's blue gaze touched Nora, when they moved to Louis, they stayed there. Somewhere deep in the sprawling castle, an old clock chimed out the first strike of twelve. Oh god! The echoing gong was a bullet shot straight through Nora's soul.

Louis stepped back, brought her hand to his lips. "That's the sound of my time running out," he said solemnly, then turned her hand, placed a burning kiss on the underside of her wrist.

"No," she whispered miserably, unable to do anything about the boiling tears that spilled over her eyes. "Please, don't go, I can't bare it."

"Nor I," he breathed. "If I had choice, I would stay forever."

"This was the best night of my life," she whispered, saw his slow, devastating smile.

"Chérie, all my best nights have been with you," he said, and they stood in trembling silence, as the clock chimed again, and again. Her hands gripped his until her nails left marks in his skin.

"I won't forget your face, not for a single second," she said, rushing her words to get them out before the clock struck its final note. Still, Nora closed her eyes when the dreaded moment came. It was a real struggle to keep from screaming. When the echoes of the final chime faded away, she opened her eyes. Louis, her beautiful prince was gone, and a glowing stag stood in his place. A piece of extraordinary magic, only she could see.

His voice in her mind was sad as she ever heard it. "I'm here. I won't go far," he said, then loped off to find a hidden spot in the surrounding jungle. Tears rolling onto her mask, ruining the fine silk, Nora turned to face the approaching men, focused her blazing gaze on the man who had promised her life and love, told her pretty lies to divest her of her clothes, and delivered only cruelty and pain. How handsome she had once thought him, how dazzled she had been. He seemed exceptionally ordinary now, he was no shining knight, just a man worn down by drink and dice.

Charles stopped before her, reached for hand, bowed over it, touched his mouth to her knuckles. When his lips brushed her glove, Nora had to suppress a visible shudder. Outside she offered him a platinum smile, shiny as a new penny, inside she was seething. Louis was right, she thought, looking into Charles's cold eyes—all illusions faded.

19

BLOODY MARVELOUS

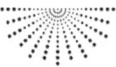

*O*range brushstrokes filled out all the lines of Velvet's thirteenth tropical sunset. The natives of Sainte-Marie were kind, overly generous with her. They gave her a dress with white flowers stitched around the low-cut shoulders, it had a tight belt and wide skirts. The material was soft, and transparent as a butterfly wing, when she moved the cloth shimmered, showed glimpses of her borrowed cotton shift beneath. The children braded dyed twine in her hair and taught her French songs that twisted her tongue. Merchants and well-armed bands of freebooters abounded, fighting, dying, sailing—Velvet preferred the villages, their soothing brick houses, and thatched roofs, to the taverns and bawdy houses.

That was all above her, now she waded in a violet pool, the material of her dress floating around her, drenched in orange, sunset light. Since the night Velvet had near poisoned herself on black rum, Henry's crew had extended her a sort of comradery, if not outright adoration, as if hurling till she cried was some glorious rite of passage. The men rushed to attend her every need, taught her sailor songs, and dirty jokes she did not fully understand.

Velvet learned from Rhee, how to spear fish in the shallow water, how to hold still so they would swim around her feet in the moments before dawn. She would fry the fish with lemon or smoke it overnight. The next day they would carry it in coconut shells, eat it as they walked, walked, and searched. Île Sainte-Marie was not a large place, and after ten days, Velvet believed they had walked the length and breadth of it a dozen times. Tonight, their search was over. In the heart of the jungle at the end of the frond strewn pathway which she had walked on a magical night, between the jagged cliffs that looked like warring elephants, they found the buried cave where sat the bottomless pool.

Henry had looked at her intently when they found the spot, his eyes prying, trying to ferret out flecks of truth in hers. *Does he recognize it?* wailed her mind. *Does he know they had lain on the grass just there? Does he remember how his mouth touched me, how he made me see black stars?* Velvet tore her eyes from his before she spoke aloud the shouting thoughts in her head.

Having no wings this time, descending the cliffs proved to be perilous. Henry tied her to his body with a length of rope and barked at her to hold him tighter the whole way down. Foolish really since Velvet was near cutting of the circulation in her fingers from clutching him with every ounce of her strength. It was the closest they had been since he danced with her ten days ago in front of a roaring campfire. He bowed when he greeted her at dawn, wished her pleasant dreams before they slept. He helped her with the search as he had sworn, but no more scalding touches, only hidden glances that burned her skin. He cast them in the moments he thought she was not looking.

His temper seemed to grow more devilish by the day. Yesterday he had nearly bitten Zoe's head off, when the boy had merely taken her hand to help her over a broken bit of ravine. Velvet told herself his artic attitude was for the best, why deepen an attachment she would soon lose? The spell they searched for demanded blood, there was no choice. Hers was the blood to pay. Perhaps Queenie had known all along this would be the way—Louis was the rightful king, and Velvet had once told the old Romani woman that she would do anything to save her brother. Since arriving on this island, childhood memories returned with frightening regularity, rushing over her at the oddest moments, interrupting her best dreams.

Velvet swam away from the rocky edge of the oblong pool,

swirling purple water rippled. According to the map, far as she remembered—another cave lurked somewhere in the dark below—reaching it was their next puzzle to solve.

A few feet from where she frolicked, Henry was attempting to build a fire using sticks he literally ripped from a tree a hundred feet above, with his bare hands. Here the vegetation was sparse, the landscape mainly comprised of short, soft grass and boulders that glittered like jewels. Zoe bit one of the boulders earlier in the day, meaning to test its validity and nearly chipped a tooth.

"Woods wet," grunted Henry, kicking the smoking pile of wood he toiled over, sending up a dusting of weak sparks.

"We don't really need a fire, it never cools here, not even at night. I have the lemons we picked yesterday; we can eat the fish raw. Borag and Martin found mangoes this morning, over there, beside your stockpile of guns which will all be rendered useless by the water. Not even sure why we carted them all the way down here. I suspect most evils we encounter from this point on will be impervious to the effects of gunpowder."

"Perhaps," was all Henry said. He took care not to meet her searching eyes, a game they had been playing for the last hour. This was the first time they had been alone in days. It seemed a magnet shivered between them, flirting, tugging.

Velvet dropped her eyes as Henry bent over the miserable fire once more. Linen shirt tossed over his shoulder, she could see the fine layer of sweat covering his bronze chest, under the sunset's ocher light, he looked cast in gold. Velvet did not wish to be his wife, certainly not in the way it had been done. Choice denied. Yet, it would be a great lie to say she did not want him. The night when she swam with him, kissed him, and last wore wings was ever in her mind. In those times she caught him staring at her, it certainly seemed to be in his.

At night when they slept, he kept her close, said it was for her protection. Never did he touch her beyond the necessary. Last night, for a heady moment, she thought he might. He caught her struggling into her shift behind a patch of trees. He had stepped close enough for her to see the indigo flecks in his eyes, feel his breath on her skin. "Cover yourself," was all he said, before turning away. He had made a point of not looking at her for the rest of the night and had been in a foul temper all the next day.

When the silence carried, he looked up, past her. "I hate raw fish," he said, and kicked the failing fire again. More sparks flew.

Velvet was forced to bite her lip so she would not laugh at his furious, crestfallen expression and smoking boots. "I know," she said cheerfully. "One of the main reasons I suggested it."

A mosquito buzzed near his cheek, automatically he slapped it away, and succeeded only in striking himself, the bug flittered off unharmed. Velvet giggled. Henry threw her a sharp look.

"Cheer up, Your Grace, raw fish probably don't like you that much either," she said.

He said nothing as he turned away, but Velvet thought she saw his shoulders shaking, then heard him make a suspiciously snort-like sound.

"You're either laughing or crying, Henry, both are equally embarrassing, so you may as well turn around. I won't disappear simply because you refuse to look at me. 'Till death do us part. Is that not what some nameless girl promised you on my behalf?"

Henry spun, face still beaming from the smile he had not been able to completely wipe away. "It is, and I mean to hold you to it."

"Do you really not hear how insane that sounds?"

He said nothing, but she could see in his face that he did. His eyes flicked to the violet water curving around her waist, finally they slid to her face. "There is no reason to look so pleased, fair or not it is your reality. The sooner you acclimate to it, the faster there can be peace between us."

"You are delusional," she said, throwing up her hands, making a waterfall of crystal drops. "Return to your fire, Your Grace and leave me to my happiness, you cannot dampen it today. I have dreamed of being here for far too long."

Henry scowled. "This is no victory. Others have made it this far, but as I said ten days ago, there is no way to reach the bottom of a bottomless pool."

Velvet sighed, spinning, making ripples twirl. "If the stones and the spells they caste are the prize, they must also be the solution. It's a puzzle, you like puzzles don't you, my lord? I remember at

French court, even as a boy you could decipher all the messages you couriered. My mother once told me you knew more gossips than the chamber maids."

"You remember that?" he asked low.

"Yes. I think it's this place." Velvet's voice dropped to match his tone. "I'm sorry I forgot you, Henry, when I was a little girl—that day I kissed your cheek—I swore I never would. You see, it's not just you, magic has taken much from me. Stole the best of all my memories." She glanced at the endless dark yawning beneath her kicking feet. "The stones and their source got us in this predicament, it seems right they should be our salvation."

"I thought you gave the stones to Nora."

Velvet frowned. "Therein lies the problem."

"No matter," said Henry, "I sent Turga with a merchant ship to the port of Toamasina, if the storm did not shatter the Bacchus, it at least forced it to dock for repairs."

"To what end?" asked Velvet.

"I gave him a missive for Nora, informing her that I did not drag you back to England in chains, rather chose to aid you in your insanity."

"Only because I made that bargain with you, in desperation promised what I did not wish to give," she snapped, meeting his eyes. It was the first time either of them had broached the topic of the infernal bargain since the day they agreed on it. Silence stretched, and the air hummed. Memories of her melting like sugar in his arms burned between them.

Finally, he said. "The girl I met two months ago could not have told a lie to save her life—now I must say, you grow quite proficient at it."

Velvet's smile felt chilly. "Just the little tricks we all must learn to survive."

"Ropes coming down," called Zoe. Velvet's head snapped up. The tall boy was a vanishing dot high atop the razor cliffs. He waved his arms wildly, then began his descent. Velvet jumped from the pool, and quickly pulled her dress on, then tied off the sash with quick strokes. She wrung water from her hair and watched Zoe, the rope held strong; after a few minutes, he made it to the ground without incident. Slung over his shoulder in a wound-up piece of cloth were a few loaves of bread and two stoppered bottles of rum. He set the sack down and went to work untying the rope from his waist.

"Rhee's coming with a few blankets, and other vittles. Ritchie says we're bedding down here for the night. Not much point hauling our asses up and down those cliffs without good reason. Ropes already fraying at the top, gonna need to finish that other one Rhee's been braiding," said Zoe. He shucked off his jerkin, unlaced his boots and kicked them. The left one flew roughly a meter and struck Henry in the back of his right knee, while the right one sailed directly toward his backside. Henry moved faster than sound, and he grabbed the boot out of the air mere moments before it hit him and seemed genuinely surprised not to find a foot attached.

Zoe caught Henry's expression and snickered. Jabbing a thumb in Henry's direction, he leaned toward Velvet then lowered his voice to a conspiratorial whisper. "Jumpier than a whore on Monday," he said.

Velvet screwed up her face. "Charming, Zoe. Why Monday?"

Zoe gave her a flabbergasted look. "You know, cause what they endured over the weekend."

"Oh," Velvet said blankly.

Zoe shook his head, still laughing. "Ah, Velvet the look on your face cannot be bought."

"I know you say such scandalous things for my benefit alone, but the joke is on you, I'm afraid. I hardly understand a word of what you say."

Zoe wriggled his brows. "But occasionally a few words slip through, don't they?"

Velvet flushed. More than a few if she was being honest. Between Martin, Ritchie, Rhee and Zoe, her ears had been figuratively burning for days, but she did not mind. It made her feel like part of the crew. It reminded her of the palace guards at Versailles who had always teased her as a girl, or the little stable boy Juan, who once soaked her saddle in honey. Even when she had been imprisoned at the Temple in Paris, the guards had tugged on her golden pigtails and loved to sit and listen to her read stories for hours.

This close to the violet, bottomless pool, almost no memory was hidden. When she swam, she could shut her eyes, and see her mother's face. Velvet sat down on the rocky ledge and dipped her toes in the water. Behind her, she heard Henry breathe a heartfelt sigh of relief as a stick of wood finally caught and held. He sat back on his haunches and tried to blow gently on the stuttering flame till it came to burgeoning life. "That was more exhausting than some battles I've fought," he said, when another stick ignited.

Velvet looked over her shoulder at him and smiled. "Your reward is cooked fish, there you go, one less thing for you to scowl about."

Henry's smile reached his eyes. "I would have bravely eaten your lemon concoction. I did yesterday, didn't I?"

"It was your first time eating raw fish, and you did not know how much you hated it then, no bravery involved."

"No honor, or bravery? 'Tis a wonder you struck a bargain with such a man."

Velvet shrugged. "You know what they say about beggars right?" she shot back; her own smile sweet as venom.

Zoe laughed, and came to help Velvet gut the fish. The three of them ate a silent dinner of fish and mango beneath the twinkling stars. The night was warm, still soaked with remnants of the day's heat. After the meal was finished, and every speck of white meat picked from the spindly bones, Zoe and Henry began to argue over the purchase of a ship from a fat merchant who was not known for his honesty. Zoe was under the firm opinion his captain was being swindled by a master.

Stepping lightly, Velvet left them to their squabbles, and walked along the cliff side, dragging her fingertips over the black rocks. The path she clung to winded like a sunning snake, running parallel to the edge of the violet pool. When she could no longer hear the bickering men, she slipped out of her dress, let it fall to the warm rocks, then dove silently beneath the moon-kissed water.

Velvet closed her eyes, let her body go weightless, the darkness thickened the deeper she swam, she would have been blind if it were not for the golden glow following her. She stared down at herself, lifted her hands for closer inspection. The tips of her fingers seemed to bleed amber light. She kicked her feet and shot downward; bubbles rushed up to tickle her cheeks. The glow augmented, grew. She could see the cliff face wavering, extending far as the eye could see. From where Velvet floated, in a swirling sphere of hair and light, she could see dozens of words carved in the rocks, scribbled inscriptions and tiny pictures, like upside-down hieroglyphs, or dizzy children's drawing. Velvet swam toward the rock, breath screamed in her lungs, then she lifted her golden hands and there was only wonder—it filled her world.

In her mind, she could hear Minerva telling her the stone of Tamora had melted, and fused with her skin, swore she carried the same power in her veins, and Velvet realized all the remnants of magic were not gone, just sleeping, waiting to be returned to their source. Slowly she passed her fingers over the carved words, when she touched them, they caught fire, aqua, sapphire flames jumped and burned, they seemed to feed on the water.

Bright light cut the darkness as above her, the surface of the water shattered. A gush of tiny bubbles engulfed her; Velvet batted them away, already knowing who disturbed her solitude. Henry, his face a drawn mask of shadows in the netted light, reached for her. Velvet kicked her feet and escaped his grasp.

"Ummm, umm, umm," she tried to say, releasing another host of bubbles, and waving her hands at his face. He rolled his eyes, shook his head, and grabbed for her again. This time she was not quick enough to escape. A startled expression had taken over his face. His arm looped around her waist, he kicked his feet once, and they shot to the surface. Henry practically tossed her out of the water, Velvet landed on her derrière hard enough to leave a bruise. While she coughed and hauled in muggy breaths, he loomed over her, his hands on either side of her head, gripped the cliff face, breathing hard, staring down at her fingertips. They looked brushed with fairy dust, shimmering brightly in the nightlight.

"Bloody hell," he said hoarsely, "bloody, everlasting hell. I'm not even sure I should ask."

"I would have no explanation if you did, I am just as shocked as you."

"Doubtful," he grunted, his eyes roving from her hands to her face. "There is something you are not telling me. If we are in this together, don't you think I should know all the pertinent details, such as your ability to glow, perhaps fly?" His voice dropped. "Do you have wings, Velvet?"

"Do you see any?" she asked tartly, starting to shiver. The wind tugged and played with the wet fibers of her shift. The burning in his eyes told Velvet he could see all of her.

"Not at the moment, no, but—"

"I don't have wings," she whispered.

"Why don't I believe you?"

"Because you are a pretentious, domineering, windbag?" she asked sweetly.

Henry laughed. The sound full of husky enchantment rather than humor. "Velvet, why are you glowing?"

"There is writing on the cave walls beneath the water. The characters burned when I touched them. Don't you think we should talk about that?" she asked, then closed her eyes so she would not see him.

It seemed all the colors around her were becoming increasingly brilliant despite the fact that her own glow was beginning to fade. Blinking, flexing her hands, Velvet pealed open her eyes, looked at Henry's shadowed face. All the lines and curves she knew well as her own. The sky loomed above him, dark and fantastically large. He touched her back, his hands coasted over her shoulder blades— Velvet knew he was looking for wings. She should struggle, move from the path of his devastating touch, but she could not. Why was it always like this with him? Her mind frozen in fear, while her body was in some kind of trance. His hands on her body were slow, soundless, a feather caress down her back that resonated through her like lightening. His fingertips skated over her ribs and her eyes flicked to his, brilliant veins of black swirled in the indigo blue.

Velvet did not dare speak for fear she would confess something ridiculous—like how much she wanted to pull his body over hers like a blanket and lose herself in him—steal a few hours from time before they found the spell to save her brother and she surrendered to inevitable death. Or she would tell him she very much suspected they had not dreamed at all, that she was afraid it had all been dreadfully, wonderfully real—she would beg him to put his mouth on her and do it again, then show her the rest. In the netted, mystical light, he seemed like a god, some king from ancient times, a creature of this land, wild, strong, timeless.

"Show me the writing on the wall," he said, his voice a thousand shades of dusk.

Velvet blinked, shocked. "You want me to use my magic?" Then beneath her breath she muttered, "Even if I can't help it."

"Is it yours?" he asked.

"I think so, yes," she said, glancing down at her hands, then back to his face. Starlight splashed around them like a sunset-soaked cloud—Velvet sincerely hoped her admission did not reveal too much.

"A part of you?" he asked, his heady voice low, his breath brushing her cheek.

"Yes...I know you hate it, but it's not the same as before. You were right in what you said. I was selfish. I used the stones, at times maliciously, to get what I wanted, what I thought must be. This time I asked for nothing. The magic seems to be a part of me, I do not even know if I call on it...it just gives me what I need. I can't...I don't know how to use it. It just happens."

"There is something you're not telling me."

Velvet tore her eyes from his; she would not look at him when she lied, because he would know. He always knew—if she looked at him, she would tell him of Minerva and the secret of her wings, and he would know what they had done was no dream. He would remember the way she had writhed in his arms, screamed his name. Then, there would be no need for her to sacrifice herself to the stones, the flames of mortification would consume her. "I've told you everything I know," she whispered.

Henry made a blunt sound. "There's a better chance I'll believe you're the Christ child reborn, then give any credence to that clanker."

"Clanker?" Velvet asked, still studying her fingers.

Henry touched her chin, lifted her eyes to his. "A clanker is a lie so big it has moving parts."

Velvet opened her mouth hoping some incensed protest would flow out. Henry brushed her lips with his, the contact so light and brief, she feared her desire had conjured hallucination.

"You're extremely pretty when flustered," he rasped, his knuckle touched her cheek. "You blush when you lie, did you know that? Ah, better not answer that, it might be another lie, then my darling, I'm afraid your poor cheeks will combust."

"Villain," she hissed, unable to hide her reluctant smile.

"Vixen," he rasped. His mouth touched her, his lips tasted, lingered. This was no trick of the mind—Velvet ignited. She locked her fingers in his hair and held onto him while he kissed her senseless. He lifted her against him, and she was falling, swimming, running in a field of black stars. When she was panting, twisting against him, struggling to get closer, he raised his head and spoke through his teeth. "Did you know this magic was a part of you?" he grated out, asking all the right questions.

"If I did, then what? Would you leave me, or would you kill me sir?"

"Nay, madam," he whispered. "Were you to send me away, build a wall against my return, all that you are would draw me back. It is the magic of you that holds me enthralled. Leave you?" He shook his head. "What madness would see me to that end? I have no want of treasures or magic stones. I only chase a single touch from you that rends the very depth of my sanity. I would follow you to the ends of the earth, do you not know that?" Sighing, he stood and lifted her in his arms. He held her close, her soaking wet shift no barrier, to his hands hot on her thighs. "Show me the writing, Marie."

"You should not handle me so," she managed.

"Recently, a scrappy princess taught me, for one to get what they want, at times that means doing what they must."

"What do you want, Henry? When all this is done, what is the one thing in the world you would wish for?"

Henry stopped in the shallows and looked at her with

unguarded eyes. "You, Marie, since the first moment that I saw you, I've always only wanted you."

"Why?" she asked.

His smile made the chiseled lines of his face into a gorgeous masterpiece, his eyes softened 'till the look in them was almost tender. "Because, I've had many women in my arms, but never have I held an angel."

"Henry," she breathed. Just that, just his name. It was all she could think to say. The way he looked at her made Velvet think she loved him—perhaps she had loved him forever. That realization hurt more than anything, since loving Henry would only make it that much harder for her to leave him when it came time to die.

~

Both of them.

Henry held her in his arms until the jeweled water rushed over their heads. Her adorable face screwed up as she tried to keep in her held breath. Reels of her hair encircled them like a halo of twisted gold —the ends glimmered like midnight fireflies. Always had she been his fascination, never more so than now. Presently, she seemed an unearthly thing—yet in the last few days he had been honored to see her other side. Gritty, unfailing kind, loyal to a fault and brave. Self-sacrificing with a smile for whoever crossed her path. A smile that never reached the darkness in her eyes. Henry knew there was more to her story, secrets she kept hidden behind her sealed lips. After a lifelong career as a British spy and mercenary, he had searched out his fair share of artifacts; he knew they always demanded a blood price—so did she. Velvet wanted no one else to die on her quest, he suspected that in her own veins was the blood she meant to pay. Henry would die before he let that happen. Hidden spells, weapons and lost gods be damned.

Velvet whirled in his arms, pressed her hands against his chest, reluctantly he released her. Legs kicking like fins, she swam away from him, toward the submerged cliff face. She moved like a siren in a dream, his mind turned her to myth. She peered over her shoulder, gave him a hesitant smile, then lifted her hands. Beams of light shot from each of her fingertips, amber and violet reels that speared through the dark water, and she was a burring flame in a pitch-black world.

Henry's eyes went wide when Velvet lifted her hands, her own gaze raked him, and the torment came knowing she must soon leave him. Villain, savior, lover. She stared full into his face seeing the wonder there. He inclined his head toward the writing on the wall and Velvet turned on the full power of her glow. The words caught flame, burning with a fire no water could quench. Fractals of light moved across his face as she watched him read the ancient Latin.

Velvet moved near him, and Henry pulled her back in his arms—he could do nothing else. Words scrawled in the handwriting of the gods burned before his eyes, still Velvet alone held his focus. She touched his face, then put a hand to her throat signaling her need for air. Henry cupped her cheek and gave her his.

He was kissing her again, and her glow was nearly blinding. His hands dropped to hers, their fingers linked like twining vines, and for a time they swam in breathless silence, and shared the light of Tamora. Velvet watched the power infuse his skin with highlights of platinum and bronze. She motioned for air, he bent his head and breathed it into her mouth, and why should he not? Since the day she had wrestled him to the ground—in a fragrant, lonely storefront—he had been her air.

Henry lifted his lips, brushed strands of hair from her face, a question in his eyes, Velvet understood, and nodded, then pointed again to the burning wall, demanding he look. He tore his eyes from hers, hand locked with his they followed the cliff down, far as they dared.

Henry felt a part of her as they swam, amber light pulsing between their clasped hands linking them to that ethereal place where spirit and flesh collide. Together they studied the rocks until breath became a necessity. She moved against him and their eyes met—in that moment Henry knew she saw all that he felt, there was no way to hide it from her—not down here wrapped in all that could not be. Reality fractured, Henry found he was speechless as he set her back on the rocky ledge, took a deep breath, and shook the water from his hair.

Velvet's chest moved as she gulped down three humid breaths. Her eyes wide as saucers, lush lips parted on her gasps.

"You can't show me all that and expect me not to demand answers," he finally said. He knelt in front of her drawn up knees, cupped her face in his hands so she could not drop her eyes. "The stone imbued you with its power," he guessed, saw the flicker of surprise in her water-burned eyes before she managed to hide it.

"Yes," she said simply and gave no more. Henry's rasping, frustrated groan triggered her own exhausted eye roll. "What does it matter how I came by the magic?"

"Trust me, it matters."

Velvet sighed. "Then, yes. Somehow during the changes, the transformation stone imprinted on me." She felt him tense. The moment between them sizzled, like she had grabbed the wrong end of a lightning rod. Goddess, how he terrified her. If he kissed her now, she would tell him all.

"Marie, do you have wings?"

Velvet lifted her chin a notch. "No," she said, when she was sure her voice would not tremble. "I only ever have them in my dreams."

Henry muttered a low curse. "I'll will find out if you're lying. Nothing remains secret forever."

Velvet's lips quivered; she was seconds from confessing. Seconds that trembled, stretched.

"Well, isn't this a touching scene." Zoe's deeply sarcastic voice cut through their fog, effectively shattering the enchantment. "Honestly, Henry, for a man known across the high seas to be ruthless as Black Beard in his prime—I must say, I expected more from you. Lovesick swain doesn't quite fit the image," he concluded, happily skipping a stone over the pool's settling surface. Velvet struggled to hide behind Henry, and her own hands. Zoe caught her eye and threw her a devilish wink.

"The Bacchus was spotted flirting with the horizon, Ritchie wants you to know she's got the wind, should make harbor by sunrise."

Henry grunted. "What of Napoleon's fleet?"

"No sign yet, but it will be any day now. You more than anyone should know how *The Eagle* flies."

Velvet looked from Zoe to Henry. "Why you more than most?"

"I was stationed as a solider in his army during a military expedition to Egypt five years ago. My years in French court and love of the language have helped me blend. The crown always needs a man on the inside, a fool who never learned not to walk through hell."

"*The little Corpal* trusted our captain like a brother, said it damn near broke him when he found out how he'd been duped. Sent some men after the captain and Lord Eden, caught up with them in Spain—then put them through the worst type of torture, they did."

"Thank you, Zoe," said Henry dryly, "your commitment to the gossips is overwhelming."

"What did they do to you?" Velvet asked.

Henry seemed to look right through her as the dark side of a memory danced through his mind. "Nothing that did not heal."

"They dunked them in freezing water," said Zoe excitedly, "held them under till their eyes bulged and their lungs were screaming like babies. They would let 'em up just enough to catch a single breath before the dunking commenced again. Went on and on. Some say our captain endured it for near on three days with no sleep or food." Zoe snickered. "I'm guessing water wasn't a problem."

"Henry used his thumb and forefinger to scrub the memories from his eyes. "Again, thank you Zoe, for your vivid recollection of my nightmares."

"Welcome," Zoe said, happily skipping another rock, lifted from the small pile he had collected.

Velvet took advantage of Zoe's brief distraction to yank her damp dress over her head. Once sufficiently covered she felt able to take a proper breath.

Zoe turned back to her, his eyes narrowing. "If Napoleon does come recruiting, will you sail with him my lady?"

"Over my dead body," Henry growled.

Zoe shrugged. "He would give you a throne—"

Velvet cut him off with a wave of her hand. "A truly uncomfortable chair, I remember how my mother hated to sit in hers. She would always say, 'how can a chair be so heavy when it's bolted to the ground?' The want...the craving of that stupid chair cost the lives of nearly every member of my family. If I run off with Napoleon and abandon the quest to save my brother—he will fade, and the Revolution will finally take the last of us."

Zoe shrugged again and skipped another rock. "He might insist."

Velvet lifted her chin. "Then he will find that I am not so easily commanded."

Henry chuckled; it was a husky, gravely sound. "Truer words have never been spoken."

Zoe abandoned his rocks; hands dug deep in his pockets. He looked at the sky, judging the position of the waning moon. "Sun will be up in a few hours, best make our way up those cliffs, and on down to the beach."

Henry shook his dark head. "You go on ahead. Velvet needs a few hours of sleep. We'll meet you topside at dawn," he said, moving to the small pile of rough blankets Velvet had stacked earlier as cushioning for his guns. He retrieved the largest of the lot, then bent to lay it on the softest part of the lush grass.

Zoe made a face of true disbelief. "Alright, Captain, but if you don't show, I'll know the two of you are down here inexplicably glowing again—you heard me, I saw it."

"Zoe," Henry called, when the chuckling boy turned to go.

"Yep?"

"Take care—that rope is desperate to snap."

"I will exercise the stealth of an elf," Zoe declared, dropping in a jaunty bow that bounced his tight black curls, then he spun on his heels and set off for the cliff, whistling as he went.

Velvet smiled. "Where did you find that one?"

"In America, at the wrong end of a knife fight."

Velvet grimaced. "Charming."

Henry shrugged. "Not much is. I made a friend the day a slave boy saved my life."

"So, you saved his in return?"

"The natives in America believe when one saves a life, a blood debt is yours. And the life you save becomes yours to protect."

Velvet snorted delicately. "That's what Queenie believed. I assume it had much to do with my dubious rescue."

Henry smiled. "And whether purchasing him saved him, remains to be seen. I have not offered him an easy life."

Velvet made a sour face, hating the very concept. "You're telling me you own that boy?"

Henry laughed outright. "Nobody, nowhere, owns Zoe. He is a prince from a great tribe, taken from his land by a people that understand nothing of ancient culture, or really anything beyond their own delusions, hubris, and greed. They brought him to America before he knew his first words. He would have been a king one day of a people who know more about the earth and its gods than the bickering Christians ever will. They may have put him in chains, but his heart runs with the wind. You may capture such a spirit, even force it to call you master, but never can you truly tame or own it."

His words made tears tickle the corners of Velvet's eyes—not the same surely, but she knew what it felt like to be in a cage, it was dastardly—but now she was afraid she loved him even more.

Henry touched her cheek, tucked a wet lock of hair behind her ear. "Sleep now, angel. I will watch over you."

"I don't think I can sleep, my mind is full of stolen princes, fire writing and chilling pictures that burn."

"How much of it did you understand?"

"Enough. My Latin tutors were nothing if not thorough," she said, then sighed. "What does Napoleon want with me, Henry? Far as I knew, he hated the monarchy."

Henry met her eyes, his own blazing. "You are a strong man's prize my love, but whether he wishes to crown or kill you I cannot say. If it helps to take that flash of fear from your eyes, I swear he will do neither. Unless it is the crown you wish for?" he let the sentence hang.

"I have told you I do not."

"Feelings change."

Velvet yawned hugely, lifted her arms above her head in a sinuous stretch. "That's true, my feelings for you have been a tornado of quandaries," she said, then lay on her side, cradled her hands beneath her cool cheek. Her eyelids fluttered and she shivered though the breeze was balmy.

Henry stretched out beside her, slung an arm beneath his head, their lips were inches apart, his face still lit by the last touches of the fading glow still resonating between them. Fully immersed in the confusing, terrifying, present—Velvet was forced to admit he felt like home.

"Sleep, Marie," he breathed, combing his fingers through the tangles of her drying hair.

"Why are you being so kind to me?" she whispered, already touched by the first dregs of sleep.

"Because my mother told me, one should always be kind to fools and fairies," he said, and Velvet fell into dreams of fire with a smile on her lips, safe in the aura of a man whose soul seemed irreparably fused to her own.

20

FOOLS AND FAIRIES

"*N*apoleon is coming for you, dear," was the first thing Nora said, when she alighted from the long boat which had carried her from the Bacchus anchored just a way offshore.

"Does he know her location?" barked Henry, extending his hand to steady Nora as she navigated a retreating wave.

"No," Nora said tartly, "though yours is suspected. Your men are closed lipped I know. My pirates gab like old biddies—there are no comrades among thieves. Word of your attack on my ship and subsequent capture of the French princess probably reached England, by teatime the next day." Nora stepped lightly on the white sand; her satin heels dug deep. "Though, I won't berate you too sorely, I'm terribly glad the stormy monsters of the deep did not carry you off to hell, for that is surely where you would go." She leaned in to place a light kiss on Henry's cheek, her bright red brows drew together in a petulant frown when she encountered his two-day growth of beard. She wrinkled her pert nose. "Saints, Henry, when was the last time you shaved? I must say you look quite barbaric."

Henry grimaced and scratched at the shadow. "I like it," Velvet said as she knelt to throw her arms around Cerberus while the monster dog treated her face like a cone of ice-cream.

Nora gave the rolling pair a fond glance. "That's because you spent your informative years in a forest, dear. Oh, your brother is with me," she added and turned to touch the air. "He's glad you're well. He felt it when you fell over the side of the ship...wait... what?" Nora spun her blazing gaze on Henry. "Really, my lord, how could you?"

"You may hate me for many things, Nora, but I have yet to brew a storm of that magnitude."

"Well, what have you done, Henry? Have you found the pool? Seen the writing on the wall? Apparently, if you hold one of the stones close to it, the writing will catch fire. A fire that burns under water. Can you imagine such a thing?"

"We've seen it," said Velvet, scratching Cerberus behind the ears and kissing his big wet nose.

The way Henry watched Velvet made Nora take a true pause. He looked at the girl with an expression that struck of deep yearning.

"By what magic are you such a font of knowledge?" asked Henry, his eyes never straying from Velvet's smile.

"I know you can't see him watching you make eyes at his sister," sighed Nora, "but her brother is right beside me."

Velvet saw Henry bow in Louis's direction—she could see his glow brighter than ever before and wondered if Henry could too. Kissing Cerberus between his huge, happy eyes, she stood and went to her brother. "I miss you, Louis," she whispered, "it's an empty world without you. I miss your laugh, the way you used to make me smile."

"He makes me smile all the time," Nora said, "and he makes me angry, he makes me—" her voice broke off, she fanned her face, suddenly flustered. "Henry, though I don't think you deserve a word from him, Louis thanks you for saving his sister." She sighed deeply. "I suppose then so must I, and my information comes from Alfonso, if you must know. I have reached an accord with the man, and he tells me all the answers we need are written on that wall. It will tell us how to reach *the cave beneath the glass*, as it is so called. There, we will find words written in an eternal flame—whatever the blazes that means—those are the words we will need to transform your brother. Now, I must eat some proper food, so please tell me where I can bathe and rest my eyes, I swear I did not sleep a wink last night."

Henry smiled. "We can offer you a pool, and a sleeping bag beneath the sky."

Nora passed a gloved hand over her glistening forehead, the sun was rising, bringing the heat. "Henry, tell me you are jesting, even if you are not, or I'm afraid I must add another strike to my growing tally of grievances already heavily stacked against you.

"It's not terrible," said Velvet, coming to link her arm around Nora's shoulders, then gently guiding the girl to the only patch of shade in sight, a skinny palm with wilting leaves. Nora paused to look over her shoulder at Henry, who stood bare chested and wild, towering against the dawn, sword and dagger unsheathed, hanging from the leather strap that belted his narrow waist. Nora sighed at the sight of him. "I leave the duke to his own devices for a month, and he turns into a sea faring savage," she muttered, then lifted her voice. "Oh, Henry, your infernal brother is aboard my ship—do bid him vacate before I return. Louis has been having violent thoughts toward him of late—as we all have at times—truth be told he's vividly imagined running him through." Nora turned back to Velvet, grimacing. "I've seen it firsthand, a nasty business to be sure."

Nora passed a hand over Velvet's cheek, concern illuminating her huge eyes. "You seemed overly sun-kissed, dear, are you sure you're quite well?"

Velvet could not help but smile. She hugged Nora until the girl squealed.

The roof of the tavern was thatched and leaking, raucous laughter rang the stout brick walls. Bad men rubbed shoulders with the truly evil, and women in colorful dresses sold a thing that should only be given. All of them sat at a round table eating a stew in which swam a few sparse vegetables, and a questionable meat. Food pushed aside, Velvet stared at each of them in turn, souls chosen or roped into her quest. Warriors all, regardless their station or state.

The situation was not ideal, but in this scene, she finally belonged. Nora's head rested on her left shoulder; Henry's hand brushed her right arm when he moved. Velvet felt safe between them, yet even more than that, she felt the need to protect, to save them from all the dark destinies that wrapped her life. She watched Henry's features, noted the intense way they moved as he spoke of his varied plans to save her, and what she loved—plans that would all end with her death. In her mind, her head was underwater, and she was screaming. How would she ever be able to do it? It was going to be the feat of her life to leave him. Velvet feared she could no more turn from him in that moment than the sea could run from the pull of the moon.

"Charles reads Latin better than any of us, we need him down there," Henry was saying, over a sip of his bubbling ale.

"What we need is speed," argued Charles, "it is imperative we reach the underwater cave Nora told me of before Napoleon arrives. Is there not one of these ancient stones that we could use against him? The man is off wreaking havoc on the modern world, yet we are sacrificing life and limb to save a single prince everyone already thought was dead. Forgive me, but have you collectively lost your minds?"

Velvet tensed. "The magic of the stones is dark and bloody—"

"Not all of the stones," Devon cut in. His usual spark was dim, his skin pale under the flickering lantern night. His eyes so silver they seemed unearthly, ageless, agonized yet strangely at peace, as if all things were as, they must be.

"That is a highly debatable topic," said Nora, over a bite of steaming bread. "They take life from whatever they touch, so," she sighed, "perhaps we should give them to Charles after all."

Abigail laughed; her painted red lips reflecting orange light. "Those stones in the hands of the wrong man could break the world. It is why they were hidden. Why they should remain untouched."

Henry set down his ale, the mug thumped hard against the roughhewn table. "Maybe a good break is what the world needs," he said, his face shadowed and grim.

Velvet closed her eyes so she would not see the tension

bracketing his. Would that this was just a chapter in a book, well read and since forgotten. A book filled with childhood dreams never realized. A story of a princess who had stepped from her tower into a harsh, visceral world. At the end of the tale, she finally understands that saving it will cost her life.

Velvet folded her hands on the table before her. They all seemed to her like fictional characters. The warriors, the gypsy, the native, and the princesses. Each fighting a battle for themselves yet joined in common purpose. Fate sat at this table too, and Velvet feared her most of all.

"It is imperative we make camp at the base of the cliffs," Henry was saying, his voice pitched low. "We are a whisper on this island, and the moment we appear divided or vulnerable, I suspect we will be set upon from all sides. My men will stand guard, while Charles and I go diving."

"I will be with you," rumbled Alfonso. Arms folded across his chest, he watched them all through his dark, hawk-like eyes.

Henry glared at the man. "Tell me again why you are here? Still breathing?"

"I have sworn to give the stones to Alfonso for destruction after we have used them to revert Louis to his natural form." Nora's bald statement drew a gasp from Velvet and loud protests from the others. Loudest of all from the Duke's brother. Blonde and chiseled like a god, superior and self-assured as Narcissus.

"You cannot destroy so ancient a thing," said Abigail.

"Not on your worthless life," Charles nearly shouted. "I would betray king and country, give the girl to Napoleon myself before I let you do to a thing like that," Charles swore, his face rapidly turning a mottled shade of red. Velvet saw Henry's fists clench as his eyes shot to his noisy, flamboyant brother.

She opened her mouth to tell Henry he needed her as well but closed it when she realized he did not. He could reach out his hand and take the stones from Devon with little more effort than the flick of his wrist, the treasure could be his with, or without her.

"I will not betray you, Marie," he said low, leaning close and reading her mind.

Velvet lifted her chin a notch. "That remains to be seen. If you take the stones, like I know you mean to, and let them fall to the wrong people..." she shrugged, "that blood will be on your hands."

Henry looked like he wanted to snarl in her face. "Will you ever trust me?" he asked roughly.

Velvet flinched at the biting lash in his voice. "I guess only time will tell, Your moods are ever changeable as your eyes."

"Henry? This is madness," roared Charles.

"Bastard," Nora hissed, her eyes shot bolts of blue ice at Charles.

Charles laughed. The sound chilled. "That's rich coming from you, sweetheart."

Henry's fist came down hard, making the table jump, and silencing their group. "Enough," he barked, looking ready to spear his miscreant brother through. "I cannot give the stones to you, Charles, nor can I destroy them—" Alfonso's hand dropped to the hilt of his massive sword. "Yet," Henry clarified. Henry's eyes flicked to Alfonso's face, whatever was in them made the Romani warlord pause.

"Ever," said Abigail. "Those stones belong in this place, like me you have simply brought them home. Here they must remain." Velvet studied her face. She seemed neither playful nor vicious now, merely contemplative—Velvet suspected the native girl considered all their fates, matching their weaving stories with the legends of her youth. Lanterns gutted and the tavern dimmed. Men packed around tables, drinking, whoring, and throwing dice added shifting shadows to the soft, interior light. Beside Abigail, Devon sat, statue still, staring in the distance, his face appeared ghastly in the low light of the lamps, pale as the ghosts that haunted him—Velvet wondered which stone had done this to him—and she was deeply sorry she had given them into his care.

"Artifacts such as these should be given over to the crown, or the church," said Charles.

Henry opened his mouth to deliver a scathing reply, but Nora cut him off. "It was the promise I made."

"My men and I will fight to see it is kept," said Alfonso, his hand hovering ever near his sword. Light played with the blue stone buried in the hilt, spinning when he moved, reflecting in hundreds of crystal tear drops.

The bench creaked as Velvet stood and extended her hand to Devon. His eyes flicked to her face, silently he read her mind, and reached in the pocket of his cloak. There was no hesitation when he withdrew the heavy black bag and placed it on her palm.

Velvet knew it was easy for him to give up the stones, the one that had bewitched him was tightly clasped in the white-knuckled grip of his left hand. She tore her gaze from the stark expression on his face, the freezing, distant stare. "The stones are mine, what I do with them is my choice," she said softly, her voice hardly audible against the tavern's din. Henry's eyes scalded her skin when they touched her face, filled with a million questions she could not answer. "I will keep them, and when it is finished, I will decide what is to be done. Perhaps there is a third option—Abigail is right, the stones belong here, to be cared for and protected by the people of this land." She closed her eyes, turning, throwing beams of light and shadow. "I will swim with you, Henry. I will read and decipher the words, if the choice is mine, the danger too must be mine."

"You have no right to make such a decision," Charles snarled.

"And I say that I do. I am the descendant of queens, from a bloodline that dates before Christ." Breath shattered in her throat as her fingers folded over the bag, and Velvet felt raw power jolt up her arm, shiver through her bones. She loathed to admit it, even to herself, but gods above and below, she missed the rush. She could hear sound in color again, see a million fractals of light hiding, gleaming in the darkest shadow. Her heart thudded in her ears, the tavern sounds went strangely dim, while all around lantern light grew brighter. A gush of air suddenly enveloped her, it lifted her hair off her neck and shoulders in soft waves. She did not need to look down at herself to know she was glowing; she could feel the racing light.

Distantly, she knew every eye in the room was fixated on the place where she stood—paralyzed by surges of dizzying power— her soul did not care. Wings tugged and pressed against the skin of her back, the slender bones there wanted to break, pierce, reform.

If she let her wings unfurl, Velvet knew—with the stones in hand —she would take to the sky like a comet, soar past the boundaries of this world, to the solar system and beyond.

Henry stood, kicked back the bench, took her hand. As it had beneath the pool, the glow passed from her to him. His stormy eyes flinched the moment he felt it. "Marie," was all he said. His husky voice flowed between them—more colorful sounds.

Henry started to pant, pressure rose in her chest, so vivid, Velvet feared it would burst out of her any second.

"Good lord above, Velvet, you are glowing like an angel and alerting every brigand for a hundred miles," sighed Nora. Velvet's dazed, unfocused gaze swung to Nora, and she fell still, movement and breath suspended. Behind Nora, pouring pale translucence over the roof's low beams, stood Louis, brilliant as her memories, strong, tall, and alive, really alive. Velvet shuddered all over. There were no words in creation to express what she felt. Never had she thought to see him again, certainly not like this. She blinked at the tears that burned her eyes. "Louis," she breathed.

"*Hi,*" said Louis, in that mind voice almost forgotten. "*A real mess we find ourselves in, eh? How very like the two of us,*" he finished, sounding cynical. Velvet was already running to throw her arms around his glittering neck. He nudged her forehead. "*I told you months ago, you must not change me. Do what Nora says, destroy the stones. All of them,*" he said.

"And I told you I would die rather than leave you like this."

His huge, slanted amber eyes flicked to Nora's face only for a moment, but Velvet saw his heart. "You want to be human for her, don't you?" she whispered.

Louis's response was instant. "*Not at cost of your life. You are my sister, you told me ghost stories in a haunted palace, read to me in a filthy dungeon. I've known and loved you every day I've been alive— how could you expect me to live, knowing I killed you?*"

"Maybe it won't come to that," she said, surprised at the frailty of her own voice. It sounded like a lie.

"*If you believed that at all, you might have a chance of convincing me. I know you; I see the plan in your eyes,*" he said, and Velvet was painfully aware of the sounds her broken breaths made. Mystery, pain, passion paved the paths of her past, yet, at last she was here. All the sounds of night died away, leaving her in a void of fear, and determination. "I will not let you die," she said, then turned away from her brother so she would hear no more.

~

Stones tucked in the bodice of her flimsy white gown, hand clutching her brother's back, Velvet made her way to the edge of the black cliffs, flanked by the others who destiny had collected. Blooming wildflowers glimmered in the night, surrounded by tall trees that cast pale shadows on their upturned faces. The wind was still in the leaves, and it seemed as if all the world held its breath.

They walked, and Velvet thought of Minerva's words, strung them together with the prose Nora had recited when they left the tavern. *One life, if that life is willingly given, two if it is forcefully taken, if no soul is given at all, death will flow, a bloody rain fall.*

Cannon blasts echoing over the wailing voices of screaming children, men and women burning, the way little Keziah's eyes had melted in her baby face—either Queenie had not known of the curse, or she had given no thought to the bloody rainfall of death, Velvet suspected it was the latter. Perhaps Queenie did not know her life would be part of the price, the way Minerva had not known that by saving one life, she would spend the lives of her sisters. Well, Velvet would not kill her family as the other women had done. Nora, Devon, Louis, Abigail, Henry, they were her family now. She would not give up a single one of them.

The rustling silence seemed to close in around them, slowly Velvet let her eyes rove over the wild foliage. A thin rain had begun to fall, warm as a hot spring. The scent of the wildflowers was in the air, both savage and poignant. Henry, sword drawn, stood to her right wearing the white rays of the moon like a cloak, it silvered the edges of his tousled hair, enhanced the fantasy of his eyes, darker, colder, than the cliffs they meant to descend. He stared at her, quietly asking for her attention. Drawing a breath to boost her nerves, she faced him, watching the rippling moonlight illuminate his bronze skin.

"Would commanding you to trust me do any good at all? There is no need for you to put yourself in anymore danger," he said. Her eyes went to his face, memorized each feature imbued with so much character and valor. His own eyes smoldered like a thousand fires blazed in his mind.

Velvet sighed deeply. "I do trust you, Henry, why do you think your betrayal hurt me so?"

"Then why the hell are you looking at me like you are trying to figure out the best way to say goodbye?" he growled.

A host of responses came to mind, not a single sufficed. His dark brows arched; she knew he judged her silence as an admission of guilt. "I am only going to ask one time, give me the stones, Marie, I swear I will return your brother to you. There is no need to further bloody your hands, mine have been soaked in the stuff since I was fifteen—there is no washing it out, if I take one more life, even two it won't make a difference. I have killed hundreds."

"In battle," she stated. "There is a difference."

"I hate to shatter your illusions, but the world has been at war since you were born. You and your brother are causalities of an endless battle that has taken many," he grated out. Hard hands closed around her arms; he shook her. "I will not let you trade your life for his, do you hear me, Marie? I will not lose you."

"It is my life to spend as I see fit," she said, glaring up at him, striving to remain calm. She knew he could feel tremors wracking her limbs. The burning fever of the stones heating the very air around her. He shook her again, his eyes brightened so the black glittered. Fear, rage, desire. He turned her, dragged her off the path, and let the others pass them.

Velvet struggled, Henry yanked her closer, a flash of sudden emotion transfigured his face—it vanished almost instantly, leaving it tense and cold as that infernal, internal wall of his dropped into place. "Why are you always fighting me?" he rasped.

"Why are you always trying to take away my right to choose?"

Henry's laugh was artic. "That's rich coming from you, darling —the woman who commandeers minds."

Velvet let out a long breath. "What are you going to do to me,

Henry? Make some more threats? I promise they will only fly into one of my ears and soar out the other."

Henry hauled her even closer—till their bodies were crushed together—and nearly roared in her face. "God's blood! You would try the patience of a saint."

"Then it's a good thing our company is not burdened by so rare a creature," she said, swallowing hard, her face working to maintain her expression of defiance, yet when she spoke, her voice frayed badly at the edges. "There is nothing you can do to me, Henry. Why can't I win with you? I try to save my brother, accidently cast a spell on you and take Katie's life—and you hate me. Now I decide to give my life instead of taking another—and you shout at me."

Henry narrowed his eyes studying her, he watched every nuance of her face for a long, silent moment. "You are changing before my eyes, each day you are a little less innocent and more cynical than the last, but none of it matters, I am terrified of losing you," he mused.

"You cannot lose what you do not have. There is an evil in me that will always make the idea of you and I an impossibility," she whispered.

The hard line of his mouth softened, his hands on her arms, gentled, caressed, a touch at war with his gaze, now challenging, almost insulting, raking her from her wooden sandals to the flowers clustered around her shoulders, the single gardenia braided in her hair. His gaze brushed the galloping pulse throbbing in her throat, lingered, then moved seductively to her lips. His mouth spoke no words, but his eyes clearly expressed his desire.

"There is evil in us all," he finally said, moving so she was forced to take one step back, then another. His bold stare fell to her breasts.

Velvet felt like mere kindling under his flaming gaze. She shivered and looked around, wildly searching the night for a savior. Louis had gone on ahead with the others, she could see him strolling casually between Nora, and Devon, Charles and the rest were shadows in the distance, only trees, and wind watched them. Henry took another step; her eyes flew to his bent head. "What can I say to convince you that this is right?" she gasped. "I promised my mother I would do anything to save my brother, it was the last thing I ever said to her. I will keep my word, Henry, I must." Velvet brought up her fists and pounded them against his chest. "Now let me go, what can I do to convince you that I want no part of you?"

"Look in my eyes, make me believe it," he breathed, his lips moving dangerously close to her own. She laughed a little wildly, fighting for breath, and wedging her arm between them so she could not feel the dizzying sensation of his body grinding against her own. Henry looked down at the arm, then wrapped his fingers around her wrist, and quickly twisted it behind her back, smothering her movements in an embrace of steel. He kissed her before she could stop him. *No matter,* her mind gasped, she had no desire to stop him. At first touch of his lips, Velvet ignited. She crushed herself to him, her free hand clutched at his iron arm, tangled in the loose linen of his white shirt. She quivered like a butterfly in a storm, arching, begging, wanting.

He drew back, panting, his eyes black all the way through. "Tell me again how little you want me," he rasped.

Velvet gave a ragged sigh. "So, my body craves you, we've already established that, but needing you will not change my mind. Mine is the blood to be sacrificed. It's not my first choice, I don't want to leave any of you, but it's the right one. You think this is easy for me, Henry? You think I don't want to drop to my knees and beg you to save me from this?" she cried, pushing her free hand in vain against his chest.

"Should I hold you to the bargain now? Since you mean to die before you make good on your promise? My crew and our resources have been at your full disposal. We have found your pool, I have made good on my word, will you?" he asked, his husky voice darker than night. "Or should I lie you down right here beneath this tree? Should I put my hands where I have imagined them so many times?" He rasped that last against her throat, her head fell back, and his kiss was hot on her skin. He clutched a hand full of her skirt, slowly he lifted it, his hand skated up her bare thigh. Velvet made a broken, desperate sound. Her free hand went to his, she meant to push him away, his fingers slid higher, and she gripped his forearm, dug her nails in his skin.

"So hot," he breathed, and kissed her lips.

She could smell remnants of the sun in his hair, see the way the night light weaved through the thick strands as they curled recklessly over his brow.

"So soft and beautiful." His hand drifted higher. "You truly mean to take all this from me?"

Velvet's head tumbled back as reality threatened to run from her. "Henry," she gasped, "you must not. Someone will see."

He released the wrist he had captured, brought up the hand to cup her cheek. "Marie," he whispered, kissing her lips between words. "I've never wanted anything in my life the way I want you. Not family or honor—" his voice broke off, his hand moved to her breast, he squeezed gently, the hand on her thigh drifted higher. Black stars imploded behind Velvet's closed eyes, she arched and swayed against him. *Let him have what he wants,* her mind begged. She was past the point of caring, he was wretched, domineering, proud, cold, and strong, and she loved him. It would be no hardship to submit, let him pull her down to the grass as he threatened, give him what she had promised, what she so desperately wanted, wanted like she wanted to fly. He stopped time with his touch.

His scalding fingers between her thighs found what they searched for. He groaned against her lips when he touched her, his teeth scored down her neck. Velvet dragged his lips again to hers, and the kiss was chaotic. He was passion and fire, his mouth wild and devastating as a storm. She held onto him as the air between them heated, exploded like dynamite. Her fingers went to his belt, tore his shirt free, she ran her hands beneath it, scored her nails down his back. He bit at her lips and caught her wandering hands in both of his, he dragged them to the small of her back, then captured her wrists in an unbreakable one-handed grip.

Velvet purred against his mouth, his lips were a drug, and she was made senseless by them. He kissed her until every bone in her body turned to liquid sparkles. Distantly, somewhere outside the haze he created with his touch, she heard a metallic clink, felt something cold brush her arm, then clamp down hard over her wrists. He let her go, the loss of his red-hot touch was like falling in icy water. Through her hair, she looked up at his face, saw the high slash of color painting his cheekbones, the harsh rise and fall of his chest. In a daze of confusion, Velvet tried to move her arms, and the clinking sound came again, the tug and cut of metal against her wrists. Henry stepped away. His stare dreadfully cold, and wary.

Velvet shook her arms, heard the chains. Her head flew to glare over her shoulder, then she stared in absolute shock at a thick pair of metal cuffs, and their strong, attaching chain. "You son of a whore!" she gasped, disbelief and bewilderment widening her eyes, making her dizzy as his touch. For a crazed second, Velvet struggled madly, uselessly. "Take these off, Henry, even the tower guards had the courtesy not to clap me in irons."

Henry folded his arms across his chest, that crooked, mocking smile—which had been absent for days—returned in full force.

She struggled again, feeling like she may yank her shoulders from their sockets. "Scélérat, monstre, fils de pute," she railed. Rage blurred her vision. Indigo eyes and laughing smile, she wanted to scratch it off his face.

He gave a little bow. "As always your love words leave me speechless. You have a mouth like a guttersnipe. Wherever did you learn such words, princess?"

"From men like you!" she spat.

"Ah, darling, there are no men like me. Now, don't hate me too much, would it burn too bad, if I said this was for your own good?"

"I shall hate you forever till I die!" she vowed, stumbling a little, tugging and yanking at her bound arms, screaming behind clenched teeth. Her low voice vibrated with fury, but Henry only laughed.

"So be it. I will set you free when it is over," he said. His eyes went to her bodice. He tugged it low, so the tips of her breast nearly burst free. Velvet felt the blood drain from her face as she realized his purpose. Lithe fingers brushed her skin while she kicked and writhed. Calmly, as if he were merely taking a sweet from a baby, he stole the stones with a smile. Velvet kicked and raved, spat every epithet that came to mind.

He let his knuckles coast over her cheek, ran his fingers down her jaw. "I will not let you die, Marie," he said, his voice dark as his deeds. "Hate me all you want, if that means you live, I will take it." He tucked a lock of hair behind her ear, kissed her brow. Velvet fell to her knees, fighting against tears, holding them back made her mouth ache, and closed her throat, when she spoke her voice was strained, threadbare.

"Henry, please, don't do this. It must be me, it's the only way. I must atone, for myself, for all the women who used the stones for personal gain, for all the lives that have been lost. One act to set everything right. If you do this now, it will break everything between us."

"Tis a risk I am more than willing to take," he said.

Velvet lifted her head, preparing to spit in his gorgeous face. Zoe stood behind Henry, his eyes like milk saucers, his mouth hanging askew as he took in the dreadful scene. His shocked gasp seemed to die on the empty air.

Henry did not turn, but Velvet saw his shoulders tense. He took a deep breath, then raised his voice so it would carry. "Zoe, if you have some words of wisdom to dispense, now would be a perfect time to keep them to yourself."

21

MORTIFICATION IN ALL ITS FAIREST FORMS

elvet seethed, mortification of what had just transpired burned over her body in hot waves. Silently she gritted her teeth until she feared they may crack. Close lipped against her curses and protests, Henry dragged her kicking and screaming to the edge of the black cliffs. There, he had left her to turbulent thoughts for a time, on her knees, hands still bound tightly against the small of her back. He had played her like a violin, and she had let him, almost begged him—memories of the way she had curled her fingers through his hair and kissed him made Velvet want to die with shame.

Minutes or hours later—Velvet was too shrouded by sickening humiliation to be sure—Henry strolled back to her, his sensual stride the soul of casual.

Velvet averted her eyes as he came to a halt less than a foot in front of her drawn up knees, but that last image of him was already imprinted on her eyes. Tall, dark, proud, and breathtaking. Black cape blowing wild from his broad shoulders, the glowing crescent moon the backdrop to his savage glory.

Velvet peered over the jagged edge of the cliffs searching for salvation below. From her vantage, the distance to the pool seemed incredible, as if the rope weaved by the men would be a pitiful tool against the stunning depth of the steep drop. Velvet closed her eyes as vertigo hit her from all sides, so her head felt like it was spinning on her shoulders. Screaming wind howled down the rocks dragging the scent of darkness through the night. She felt it when Henry reached for her, and struggled away from him, her eyes flew open. Growling behind her teeth, years past rage, she kicked at him, loath to be anywhere near him now that he had robbed her of the ability to scratch out his eyes. Eyes that blazed like a winter dawn as he grabbed hold of the rough chain binding her, then dragged her unceremoniously to her feet. Velvet snapped her teeth at him, trying to take a chunk out of his grasping hand, he wrapped his arms around her. Chains rattled and screeched. As always, the steel bands of his arms—stronger than the cuffs—made short work of her struggles. Velvet felt her body go limp against him. The loss of the stones had weakened her in numerous, indefinable ways, like some cruel thing had drawn a great draft of blood from her veins. Knowing it would do nothing—knowing she would only succeed in hurting herself—yet unable to help it, Velvet drew back her foot and kicked him in the shin with every ounce of strength she had left. She had the brief satisfaction of seeing him flinch.

"Do you feel better now?" he asked, raising that infernal brow.

"Not remotely," she said in a clipped, cold voice. "You know, for a man so obsessed with free will, you seem to suffer no guilt in removing mine by hook or by crook."

Henry's chuckle was low and carried. "You know what they say about payback, right?"

"Henry, I swear, I will make you rue this day if it takes me till my last breath."

"There," he rasped, sending wild chills running down her neck, "she is finally starting to sound like a queen—will it be off with my head then?"

"Would be a stunning change of events," she muttered beneath her breath as he yanked her closer.

Velvet felt her body go rigid under his hands as she remembered where they had been. Not loosening his hold on her, Henry bent to retrieve the end of the rope, a few quick strokes linked it around their waists, then he tied the frayed ends in a heavy knot that chaffed against her cuffs. Her breasts were crushed against his granite chest, making anything but broken, gasping breaths impossible.

Nora and Louis came upon them, then both staring at her plight with sad regret in their eyes. Flames of mortification returned, threatening to burn her alive. Blindly, she kicked and bucked again, grappling with his indomitable hold.

"Stop fighting, Marie, I will not release you, and there is no one here who would help you," he added, when he saw her desperate gaze fixed on Nora.

"It's true," whispered Nora, sounding on the verge of tears. "We can't let you sacrifice yourself. Where did you even get such a crazy notion?"

"You knew what he meant to do?" Velvet shrieked, her voice rising hysterically. Anger renewed her fight, she spit, squirming, too enraged to see anything but blooming red.

Nora dropped her eyes. "It was Louis's idea," she whispered penitently.

Tears of blistering humiliation filled Velvet's eyes; her gaze flew to Louis. Around her it seemed the air had turned to glass shards and with every breath she wrestled them down her throat. It burned terribly when she spoke. "Was it? Truly?" she cried.

Louis shook his head. Sadness dimmed his glow. "No, the plan was Henry's, but I did not stop it."

"Velvet, it's like you said, there must be another way," said Nora. The wind tossed strands of her bright hair, and she shoved a lock of it from her eyes, her fingers trembling like dry twigs in a tempest.

Nora's eyes were shining bright, but Louis's glow had further darkened the night. Henry's hand went to her chin, Velvet wrenched her head away, sending a shooting pain through her neck and down her spine. "Do not handle me so, Henry, I can't bare it."

Henry recaptured her chin and did not let her pull away. She saw her refection in his indigo eyes, noted the sparkle of her tears that would not fall.

"I will take you down to the pool, I will give you that much at least," he breathed, his hot lips brushed the corner of her mouth.

Velvet closed her eyes and willed herself to transform into the coldest ice. They were all studying her, as if each waited for the other to speak. Nora appeared the epitome of misery, her eyes pooled shimmering crystalline tears while her pursed, rosebud lips trembled. Louis's glow had dimmed to a fading haze. "Marie." Henry gave her limp bones a small shake. "Look at me, I swear to give your brother back to you, so will you at least try and trust me."

"Difficult thing to do with the chains of your latest betrayal around my wrists," she snapped, then sighed. "I want to see the cave beneath the glass. After all I have endured I deserve to read those ancient words with my own eyes."

"No," said Henry simply, his hands fell to the rope twining them. He tested the strength of his knot, tugging tight until the hemp fibers stretched.

"Then you must go alone," she said, gazing at Charles from beneath her lashes. "I do not like the look in your brother's eyes."

"Nor I," he said, his face pensive for a long moment.

Velvet softened her voice and tried a different tactic. "If I swore, I would make no attempts to sacrifice myself until we have exhausted all options, would you release me?"

Henry's smile was grim, his face solemn and unreadable. "Not a chance, my love." He brushed knotted strands of windblown hair from her eyes, tucked a tangled curl behind her ear. "I will tell you the hidden words, and you will stay on the shore, safe, as I should have kept you from the beginning. Loathe me if you must, but know this, it was more difficult to walk away from you back there than it would have been to step from my own skin. If my soul did not need yours for its very survival, I would not have been able to stop. I told you once before, you are the only treasure I am here to steal." His brows pulled together, and his smile turned wicked. "What I want from you should not be done with the dead."

"You are the vilest of men! I take back the kiss I gave you as a child. I gave it to a boy I foolishly thought was worthy."

Henry shook his head. "Impossible. The boy treasures that memory too greatly to let it go," he said, his voice the barest rasp of sound. "He has carried that kiss with him always." Hard hands went to her hips, tugged her closer against his long legs walking them to the teetering edge of the cliff. He stopped before they went over and turned to Charles. "You will stay with the others and remain guard," he commanded in that tone that brooked no refusal, though, apparent from the pinched expression on his face, Charles had many.

Henry did not see his brother's reaction, his eyes were looking past them all, to the dark mesh of jungle, baobab trees old as the earth itself. Tall giants with arms stretched high. "Zoe," he said, bringing his eyes back to the small crowd assembled to watch their descent. "Tell our first mate I want him to make camp here, if the princess and I have not returned in two days, come down and fetch us."

Devon's shadow fell over them both as he moved to stand beside Henry. Velvet watched the freezing gaze exchanged between the once brothers. Devon sighed deeply before he spoke. "Though I truly wish at some point to go a few rounds in the ring with you —my sword is yours, if you need it," he said, his hand still clutched around what they could not see. Velvet knew he held a stone, they all did, the streams of amethyst light snaking up his arm told many secrets.

Henry extended his hand. Devon took it, and the two men stood for a moment in bonded silence. "Stay with Nora, and the prince," Henry said at last.

Devon gave a curt nod. "I will guard them both with my life."

Nora stepped forward, then lightly touched Velvet's hand. "I'm sorry," she said, sniffling over the words.

"Don't be," Velvet said, gently removing her hand from the other girl's touch. "You did what you thought you must." Through her lashes she looked up at Henry, truly meeting his gaze for the first time since he seduced and chained her under a watchful star washed sky. "It is all any of us can do."

"Is that your way of saying you forgive me?" asked Henry, slowly lowering them over the edge. Muscles bulged as he held the rope with one hand, and her with the other. The sky seemed to stretch endlessly, loudly belching out the rumbling sounds of a gathering storm. A golden, crescent moon hung low, it looked dipped in blood, and dripped light on all the bad omens dancing through the air.

"Hold on to me," he commanded. Velvet lowered her head, tucked her chin against his chest. They descended into swirls of low hanging clouds. Sounds above receded, the silence between them thickened. Weaved through the screaming wind was the steady, powerful beat of Henry's heart. His deep breaths rustled the damp curls at her nape. Blankets of mists poured down the cliffs and all around them, like steaming waterfalls, wetting their skin, settling to leave diamond drops on her lashes. Blinking away blinding moisture Velvet looked past his shoulder, struggled to see through violet reels of fog. A streak of vivid lightening cracked through the black clouds above, in the brief, brilliant flash, Velvet saw a snow-white owl sweeping down the cliffside. An impossibility surly, but for a moment Velvet imagined the owl swiveled its head and stared right at her with Minerva's crimson eyes. A chill shivered her spine, colder than ice.

Halfway down, Henry passed, bracing his right foot on a jutting rock so he could adjust the rope, and flex his hands. "Breathe, Marie, I won't let you go, but if you pull back any further you may find yourself freefalling," he murmured, gently wiping a smudge of dirt from her bare shoulder. "Perhaps a pair of pearly wings will unfurl and save you, prove the worst of my suspicions."

Velvet said nothing, did not even look at him when he commenced their descent. They landed on their feet in a world of secrets, mist, and rain. The pool's reflective, amethyst light colored the night. Reels of steam lifted off the water's surface, moving sinuously, like ghosts trapped in a glass.

Henry untied the rope and stepped back. Beads of sweat rolled over Velvet's forehead, she wished she could wipe them away. Her strained shoulders were starting to ache, every move jolted the muscles in her arms, and her fingers were frozen digits abandoned by her rushing blood, the tips numb yet throbbing. Her reasons and undeniable logic waned under the over whelming hurt, and steady growing fatigue.

Henry shucked his weapons belt, then pulled off his shirt, and let it fall on the wet stones. He glared at her fiercely, though she wished to, Velvet could not break the stare. "I said two days, but we don't have that long. Napoleon is coming for you. If he reaches these shores while I am underwater, hunting one of the most dangerous spells in existence, Nora, Abigail, and the men will not be able to repel his forces for long."

Velvet snorted loudly. "And you think, your presence alone will turn the battle tide?"

Henry grimaced, ran a thumb down his jaw. "It might," he said, then, "are you speaking to me again?" His smiling lips were soft, yet there was a crackling urgency in his midnight eyes as he stepped toward her, then bent and kissed her brow, a brief burning touch insubstantial as the enveloping mists.

Velvet turned her head, refusing to react to his endless baiting. The memory of her chaotic response to his touch seared through her brain. In the depth of her heart, Velvet feared she would ever recall that single moment of crushing embarrassment when she realized what he had done. It galled bitterly to think how easily he had played her. Once, long ago, she had been reared on truth and taught to face, and embrace it—now? Her life had become a series of mirages, twisted, and warped by trickery and lies. There was no escape from it as she was, trapped between him and the bonfires of destiny. Maybe he was right, perhaps she could close her eyes, let the restless wings unfurl, and save herself from him. Yet if she did that, he would know, and virgin or not, she would belong to him, irrevocably, forever. It was only a sense, but Velvet believed if he knew the real truth, he would never let her go, and she would be again, as she always had been, a colorful bird locked in a cage. Wanted for her famous name, and pretty, useless face, not the contents of her soul.

Henry cleared his throat and straightened. "I see that you are not. Well," he sighed impatiently. "I suppose I deserve it. If it makes you feel any better, I'm about to spend the next three hours struggling to hold my breath and reflect on my actions." He shoved his hair off his forehead with both hands, and Velvet watched his mouth draw into a thin, white line. "I guess there is nothing to do, save dive in," he said.

Velvet jumped and the chains rattled. She hissed when the

metal cuff grinded over bone. She tried to stand, but with her hands locked behind her back, her equilibrium was all wrong, she swayed dangerously, righted herself, and remained kneeling. She mentally struck herself for not seeing what had been behind his eyes for so many days now. He suspected her, had from the beginning, his kindness had caused her to lower her guard, like the assassin he was, the duke had struck, deadly and true.

He drew the bag of stones from his deep, left pocket, went down on one knee and undid the drawstring. The cloth sagged when he released the knot. Multi-colored light sprayed the night. Henry stared at the bag's contents, unflinching, and unafraid, yet wary. A barely perceptible movement put his body in a defensive pose—his every sense tuned to danger. He reached for an amber gem, it had a similar shape and color to the one that transformed her that second time. Tamora.

Velvet wished she had taken the time to count each stone in the bag, wished she knew what they all did. Velvet felt the uncovered power of the stones flush her cheeks. She stared at him through the curtain of damp hair that hung over her eyes. He held up the stone, moved his hand until it rested parallel with her face. "It's the color of your glow," he said simply, then re-tied the drawstring, stuffed the bag back in his pocket, but kept the amber stone in his hand.

Velvet's eyes greedily soaked in the diminishing light, a part of her reaching, straining to touch the last residues of power. Helplessness effects everyone in different ways, she thought, wondering if in all her life, she had ever been more enraged. "Even if you do manage to interpret the burning words, you have no souls to sacrifice," she said, her own voice cold and distant as she had ever heard it.

Henry laughed, a quick, humorless bark. "We are soon to be attacked by half the armies of France, trust me, worthy candidates will emerge." He turned to face her, lifted the stone between his thumb and forefinger, then moved until the jagged edge of the gem was inches from brushing her cheek. "You shine in its presence," he said.

Velvet forcefully rolled her eyes. "Your powers of observation are astounding," she snapped, anxiously flicking her eyes for a fleeting second to the bag of wonders safe from her, in his pocket. She keenly felt their loss, the pervading sense of weakness made fresh anger rise to her already boiling surface. "This can't be all there is to you, my lord," she cried wrathfully. "More than these frequent betrayals and petty games. He is my younger brother. I loved him before I knew what love was. I am his only sister, the last family he has left in the world, his life is my responsibility. What if it was your baby sister? What if the only way—*the only way*—" she emphasized loudly, "to save her life, was to sacrifice your own? Wouldn't you do it? Do anything?"

"Of course, I would!" he snapped, dragging a hand through his beautifully mussed hair, instantly it fell back to its original place. Wet, black curls framed his face, making it perfect as a statue of some pagan god. He sighed deeply. "I am doing for you what I would have done for her," he said gently, then raised his chin and stared in her eyes. "My life for yours, if that is what it truly comes to."

"Why?" she whispered.

Henry looked up at her incredulously. "How can you even ask me that?" he said, and the intensity of his glare was breathtaking, excruciating. His pointed stare turned skeptical as he straightened and moved to the lip of the pool, his toes resting on the spot where violet liquid lapped over the rocks. The water's reflection rippled over his bare back. Vivid patches of visceral glow, cleanly edged in electric light. "The toughest choice demands the strongest will, or the deepest love," he said.

Velvet went still as a petrified rabbit. "Are you saying you love me?" she breathed, disbelief clear on her red face.

Henry violently threw up his hands. "You will have plenty of time to think on the answer to that ridiculous question while I'm below battling the monsters of the deep on your behalf. You can think about all the reasons why someone might do a thing like that for someone else. God's blood!" he growled, fisting his hands, light spilled up his arm. "These blasted stones are heavy and hot as hellfire."

Velvet sat back on her heels, her shoulders hunched, like she could invert enough to vanish. Through slitted eyes, she watched him dip a single foot in the water. He bent at the knees, preparing to spring—a shredding scream, the most wretched, tormented sound Velvet had ever heard tore through the air. The sound disturbed the mists like blast of storm wind. It was the sound of a broken heart in torment, a cry of earth-shattering sorrow. Henry swung toward the noise that seemed to emanate from everywhere. He lifted his fists, then scanned their foggy surroundings for an assailant.

Another scream shattered around them before the echo of the first had fully died. The din raked bloody furrows along her eardrums, lifted the tiny hairs on the back of her neck and arms. Henry dove in a low, forward roll, grabbing and unsheathing his sword before coming to his feet. The ground began to quake. Tiny rocks broke free of the earth and clattered against Velvet's knees. Henry's stance shifted. The world rattled and roared. He braced his feet a space apart to keep from falling. His wide gaze found hers. There was a brief second of magnificent, restoring silence instantly broken by a scream of such gutted distress, the other two paled in comparison.

Velvet shuddered hard. "Henry, release me," she begged in the scrap of time between screams.

A brief spasm of pain and indecision flashed across his face. He cursed loudly, then dropped the amber stone, and it clattered on the slick rocks. Violently he shook his now empty hand, smoke rose off his palm, she could smell the sweet, sickening scent of his burning flesh.

He took a halting step toward her, and another scream weighted the air, the earth shook again, deep fissures spit the rocks underfoot. Fountains of scalding steam shot up from between the cracks.

Velvet backed away when a particularly nasty geyser rent the earth near her toes, spraying rippling streams of blistering droplets over her face and hands. A dark thing shot at her, flying in from the right. A blast of air walloped her face like a slap, dragged at her hair, and flung it haphazardly. Even after all she had seen and done,

Velvet stared at the soaring shape in disbelief, human in aspect, but the trail it left behind was grave cold.

Henry reached her in two long strides, then lifted her in his arms. "Release me!" she shrieked against his ear; a fresh, guttural scream carried her words away. He turned his back to the sound, sheltering her as more dark shapes rushed at them. They glided down his back, running over his shoulders like inky steam. Around their feet, they rose from the geysers spraying out of the fractures in the earth, waving their ghostly arms and screaming a fit to wake the dead. Face pressed against his chest, it registered in the deepest recesses of her mind, this was the closest the stones had been to their pool of power in quite some time.

Velvet gritted her teeth hard not to growl in frustrated rage. Queenie had taught her so many things, why had she never taught her about the stones? Not once in the long eight years she spent in the sky did Queenie force her to memorize the words in the cave beneath the glass—or at least inform her the cave was so named. Was it because Queenie had known from birth there was more to it than lifting a stone and reciting some ancient prose? Like a caterpillar clawing its way through its own metamorphosis, will never fly if the cocoon is broken by another hand. Is that how Queenie had seen her? A weak creature in need of a transformation, an earthbound worm desperate to be broken in order to be sky-bound?

"What are they?" Henry rasped, his breath falling on her neck seemed to dispel the expanding chill. The darkest shape of all, a thing which seemed to be made of pure, ebony ink flew at her face, shrieking, tearing at its smoky hair. Its mouth was a gaping black hole, but the eyes were fire-lit rubies. Henry held out an arm to repel it, he touched nothing more than toxic fumes and shades. Velvet heard him shout a harsh denial, worthless, the shape flew into her chest, reached out its spiny, cold fingers and wrapped them around her heart. Wind tore at her hair as a swirling vortex opened under her feet. Velvet screamed as she fell in, fell back, deep in time. A spiral of drunken stars tugging her further and further until she landed hard on shores of where it had all begun.

They're coming for her. Tonight. Her sisters, so strong. If they found him, they would kill him, and that would kill her too. The beach is moon soaked and empty, she's running faster than the wind. Poseidon is a monster. He had wanted her for long as she remembered; she would deal with him after making sure her heart survived the night.

"They're coming, they're coming!" she screams, bashing her way into the cave they have shared for a year, a sanctuary of life, and their love.

"They will never find us here," he says, confident in the strength of the goddess he loves.

"They already have," she cries, throwing her eyes around their small, cozy space, searching for a weapon, a spell, anything? Nothing at all, save a pile of blankets making up the warmest bed she had ever known, and at the foot of it, a handful of pretty gems her sailor had collected from their cove. Amethyst, sapphire, emerald, ruby, amber, jade, four copies of each, four sisters she had.

"I will do a spell and take their power, then trap portions of it in each of these stones. Without their abilities I do not believe my sisters can hurt you, I will swear to return their powers if they promise you life. My sister Hera will never long exist without her strength, she treasures it so, she will make a bargain. Jealous and vengeful, perhaps she is the most dangerous of all."

"And if they do not promise?" he asks.

"Then I will use the power of my sister Hecate to transform you into a creature able to fly away and escape their wrath. You will be invisible to all save I, but you will live."

He takes her hand, presses her knuckles to his lips, then closes his eyes. "I do not want to exist if I am not with you," he breathes.

She pulls away from his kiss. "Nor I, but there is not much time, they already—"

Voices from without cut off her frantic predictions. "Minerva, we know what you are hiding," they say. She wants to scream with the terror of the moment. From under the feather blankets on their bed, she takes a knife, the blade black as sin. A gift to her second eldest sister from her husband Hephaestus.

The footsteps of her sisters draw closer. They are under the water now, she can hear them swimming, hear the rhythmic pounding of their ancient hearts. Minerva falls to her knees, lifts the knife, cuts deep into her palm, then pours her blood over the stones. She calls to her kindest sister the moon and begs for her help. The moon cannot bare the sight of blood and turns her face away from the deed. With no magical light to aid her spell, an ancient darkness responds.

When her sisters enter the cave carrying flaming swords, death, and fire in their eyes, Minerva is ready. She raises her voice and casts a spell of such strength even Hecate is unable to repel it.

The sisters began to scream as she chants. Soft flesh tears from bone as their powers flow into the bloody stones. The spell is all wrong, horrific, monstrous. Minerva did not know she had it in her to cast it's like. The screams continue until her sisters are nothing more than hollow wraiths. Minerva knows there is no saving them, no reversing the magic. She will snuff out their lives, she sees that now, but still, she cannot stop. Even though she wants to, with her whole soul she wants to, her sisters were her life before him, but she is weak, and the power she summoned so incredibly strong. She sways on her knees, the magic takes more than she knew she had, destroying the sisters she had loved for a thousand years.

Hecate is the last to fall, her screams have meaning. A final incantation cast by the goddess of them. Never will her sister have the man she loves, and all those who use the power of the stones must give life blood or die. With Hecate's last breath she changes the sailor into an eagle, blinding Minerva to the only thing she wants to see. He disappears before her eyes, calls her name and she cannot hear. He falls prey to a spell which can only be undone, by the sorcerous who cast it, and she is dead.

Though she knows he's still in the cave beside her, Minerva is left alone to tend the broken ghosts of her sisters, and her own, guilty, torn heart.

"Who are they?" Henry said again. "Bloody hell, I think they're speaking to me."

The harshly spoken words brought Velvet back to the turbulent present. The worst of the screams raged behind them like bad concerto in F major. And the place where the wraith had passed through her chest felt formed in ice. Blinking, she looked up at Henry's face. "They are sisters, the goddesses who died on the altar of these stones," she whispered.

Frowning deeply, Henry cradled her head in both his hands,

scraps of fear sparked in his eyes as he met her gaze, and Velvet knew they were only for her. Moving so he faced the amber stone he had foolishly let fall to the ground, now alien and engulfed in a transparent orb of alluring, amber light, Henry led them closer. Dark shapes whirled around the stone. Speeding, lucent bodies created a cyclone of vivid darkness that sucked up bits of the gem's glow.

"I see their faces," Henry said sounding shaken.

Velvet shuddered. "I know, that one there looks as if her eyes were ripped out of her head by vultures, or her own hands," she finished, catching a partial glimpse of blackened fingernails that looked like taloned claws.

"In the past I would have crossed myself, now I don't think it will do much at all. Death is its own beast, I fear, in the end, we are all nothing more than wandering, unshriven spirits," Henry said.

Velvet swallowed hard. "No," she said miserably, then shook her head. "There can be rest for some, but not for these, too cursed to live, too immortal to die."

"You sound very sure of that?" he said, an open question in his eyes and voice. "How do you know?"

Velvet felt shivers running over her whole body. "I just do," she whispered, and wondered if he heard her.

"I have to get my hands on that stone," he said flatly. "It's like the blasted thing is calling them."

Around them the earth continued to shake, the screams rose and fell like evening waves. Phantom hands—dozens of them—reached out of the stone, clawing, grasping at the thrashing spirits, while the wraiths howled like the undead houri of hell, and the off-beat boom of rapid gunfire blasted somewhere high in the distance. There was another sound, like the ringing of a tiny bell hidden under a pile of blankets, Velvet suspected it was the clash of swords coming from above.

Breathe in, she commanded herself, *breathe out, don't faint, don't scream.*

"Don't move an inch," Henry said flatly, his harsh voice cutting across her thoughts before she had time to speak; then his warm arms were gone, and he was dashing—head bowed—into the thrashing mass of discombobulated limbs weaving like wet pillowcases strung up on a line, all wearing the many, varied faces of horror.

Henry went to his knees in the center of the storm, the screaming things grabbed at him. He fought them, his fist lashed out, punched through a hollow stomach, swung blindly at a gutted face. He swore harshly when the shape caved like a cloud and swirled up his arm. Watching him wide-eyed, Velvet felt she had slipped through time to watch a bronze, half naked Titan battle the air. The water's violet light cast shadows. Over his head, Velvet saw more eyeless faces, wide, bleeding mouths, lips stitched closed by twine.

Henry growled, jabbed his right hand through the bodies, gaping black cavities that closed around his flesh. He shook and roared with effort, and it seemed an eternity before his fingers closed over the stone.

Velvet stumbled to reach him, pitched forward a few steps, then tripped on the quaking ground.

"If you die, Henry, I want you to know I probably could have saved you, if *you* had not tied me up," she shouted. His head swung in her direction, their eyes locked through the veil of thrashing heads, and limbs. A crooked smile lifted the right corner of his mouth, and he had the audacity to throw her a diabolic wink. "Noted," he said, then flexed his powerful arms and dove beneath the steaming surface. The wailing spirits followed him under, like a swath of chunky muck swept down a street drain.

The ensuing silence was immediate and deafening. Velvet let out a rage filled shriek that sounded very weak compared to what had been. "The devil take you then," she railed, kicking a stone at the last place he was. "Fine, just leave me here, tied, food for whatever creature is skulking about. You go on then, strong, brave man fighting off a host of insane dead women—I wish you fortune," she finished. Despite the sentiment, her tone implied she wished him more of the opposite. It felt good to shout, but the pointless rant had left her breathless. The world around had fallen strangely still, so silent as if sound had ever existed down here at all. The noises above became increasingly pronounced. Cannon blasts, shouting men, those endless clashing swords.

Louie, Nora, Cerberus, and the others were up there. Devon, his white face, and quick arm. Martin who laughed when he killed, Abigail—Velvet could almost hear her war cry. All of those she loved up there fighting, dying? She groaned wretchedly and shook her head; she would go mad thinking such things.

She struggled for another helpless minute, wringing, and twisting her hands, trying to contort her palms, so they would fold, and slide through the cuffs. Harsh noises from the battle raging above continued to grow until they became impossible to ignore.

Velvet moved to the softer grass, tripping on the hem of her dress. "Putain alors!" she muttered when almost on que, she stubbed her toe. Not wanting to pitch backwards or forwards, she braced her back against a rock, wincing a little when the cuff ground against her wrist bone. She looked up and peered through reels of swirling mist. Velvet realized she had not cried in a long time, not in the Tower—not after those first days—not on the walk to her death, not when a storm tossed her over the rail of ship where she had been captive, not when she woke up from a night of lying beneath an enchanted lover, in a dream that was not a dream. Did not cry when every fantasy, prayer, and desire was wrenched from her grasp, and the man she loved betrayed her again and again.

Helplessly gazing up at the people she had wanted to save, again fighting on her behalf, yet not at her behest, she wanted to lie down on the rocky, damp ground and cry for three days straight.

Dark shadows moved atop the cliffs. Women and men at war outlined by the bloody drops of crimson moonlight, as she stared, shapes began to define. Zoe was there, standing at the very tip of the rocky precipice, waving his arms and shouting words she could almost hear. After a while, Zoe seemed to realize his efforts were futile, Velvet saw him complete a flurry of movement—tying the rope off around his waist, she assumed—because he began to descend into the mists, ghostly spirals that seemed to reach out and grab at his body as he swayed with the rope.

A few feet down, his slight body jerked and bounced. For a

second the diminished silhouette of Zoe's body just hung there, trapped in suspended animation, before gravity won the battle and the boy began to plummet, fast as a speeding bullet, nothing but mere moments between the seconds they lived, and the ones where he shattered against the ground. Velvet's wide eyes tracked his death drop. No. That was the only word in her mind. Just, no. This boy who had barely tasted freedom, this boy with the sunrise in his smile—she would not let him die.

~

Drowning in immense waves of sadness and regret, Velvet watched Zoe fall. The boy hardly screaming when the fraying rope finally snapped, just the breath of a gasp, quickly swallowed by the wild night. To her it was not only Zoe falling in that moment, but it was also every single lost soul in the world cruelly snatched before their time. His deadly flight was every thread of ancient magic, which had taken more than its share.

It built up inside of her all at once, something old and powerful, stronger than the cliffs and crashing seas. It was a power that could transform reality, break, and re-shape time. Flesh rent in two jagged gashes down her back, Velvet was ready for the pain, she welcomed it. She wrenched her arms and snapped the iron cuffs like dry twigs. Each tiny sound carried by the wind was amplified. She could hear far away creatures scurrying to their homes, hear the haunting music in the moon's three crimson rings, hear the battle Henry fought with the wraiths beneath the water.

She bit her lip not to cry out, as the bones in her wings ripped through skin and muscle. Her hands started to tingle madly as she flexed her fingers and stared in wonder at streams of beautiful fire shooting from the tips. Enormous shocks of energy lifted her off her feet before her wings had fully formed, and she was flying faster than she ever had before. Flying, and burning in waves of cool, rushing flames, rising like a falling star. She flew to Zoe; his eyes were closed and limbs lax, mind at peace, confident in its present demise. She caught him gently in her arms. Slowly he opened his eyes and stared up at her, alight in all her blazing glory. He smiled.

"Always suspected you could do something like this, bet Martin ten dollars yesterday that you were an angel," he said, gazing calmly at her wings. "Gotta say, wings suit you better than chains."

"Louie, Nora, Devon?" she gasped.

"Alive, but struggling," Zoe said, as she landed lightly on her toes, and ran for a space over the wet ground. "They sent me to fetch the captain, but gosh you look like Heaven's vengeance, might scare the tiny pants off Napoleon's bowlegs."

Velvet paused at the sound of her own laugh. It was so different from the scratchy, confused noise she had grown accustomed to. It was full and enchanting and not at all like herself. She set Zoe on his feet. "Napoleon is here?"

"He's here," Zoe said grimly, "searching for the stones, and for you. Or so we were informed by a tall, thin, British man who seems to carry a blazing torch for you. You know, weird nose, body shaped like a scarecrow?"

"William Pitt," she spat out the name.

"Yep, that's what he said." Zoe took her hand. "Thanks a million for saving my life, by the way. Brilliant, really," he finished, blushing a little, and she could see her own glowing reflection in his wide, dark eyes.

"Are you terribly shocked?" she asked, her gaze flicking briefly to the broken chains lying discarded on the stones.

Zoe snorted. "Huh, more than some, less than most." He smiled hugely. "Mainly, I'm surprised you managed to keep something like a pair of angel wings a secret from us all for so long."

"As am I," said a dark voice at her back. No reason to turn and see to whom it belonged, the butterflies drowning in her sinking stomach told Velvet exactly who had spoken. She did turn though, her wings swayed, a single blood tipped feather dusted the ground.

Dripping violet light, Henry knelt with the amber stone still in his hand. Black smoke clung to him, streamed from his shoulders, wrists, and feet. Two deep cuts scored his chest, a line of ruby blood trickled between his stomach muscles in a single, hot stream.

Not trusting her ragged breaths, Velvet held them tight in her burning chest, and dared to meet the harsh accusations in his furious eyes. Henry hardly spared a glance for her shimmering face, his soul-searing stare fell on her wings, there it remained as he said, "I found the cave beneath the glass."

To be continued....

❧

Available Fall 2021
The conclusion of
The Lost Princess Trilogy
The Pirate Princess

❧

Don't miss out on your next favorite book!

Join the Satin Romance mailing list
www.satinromance.com/mail.html

THE PIRATE PRINCESS

THE LOST PRINCESS SERIES, BOOK 3

Silence drenched the night. Henry stared at her and the world stopped spinning. In Velvet's twisting heart, her guilt battled shame and crimson rage.

Henry's eyes traced the lifts and curves in her wings. Roved over the long feathers that ran atop each other like waterfalls of crystal snow.

When he spoke, his voice was low. A rasping whisper tainted with shock and his own fury. "When did you know it wasn't a dream?"

Velvet had no words. She pressed her lips in a thin line and shook her head. She owed him nothing. Nothing! So why, oh why did she want to fall to her knees and beg him to understand and forgive?

"How long, Marie?"

"I did not know for sure until I flew just now."

"Liar," he darkly accused. He straightened then, and black mists poured from his shoulders, filled the indigo pool under his feet with writhing darkness. "No matter, by your own choice you are mine."

"Nay!" she cried. "You did not take me. I am still a virgin."

"Give me a moment for this water to roll off my back and I will quickly remedy that."

"I wholeheartedly beg you not to," said Zoe, sounding deeply distressed. Mid eyeroll he turned his back on them both.

"You do not own me, Henry. Why would you believe such a thing? Because you shared a dimensional fantasy of mine? Or is it because you received a useless piece of paper from a mad king?" Velvet kicked away the remnants of the broken irons under foot. "Or perhaps you believe such foolishness because you made a silent promise with a kiss, then put me in chains?"

"Yes, to all of the above." He took a single step toward her. "After what passed between us that night, you owed me more than silence."

Velvet searched for an angry response and found none. He was right. She had owed them both far more. "I will not be owned by you, or any man," she finally said, speaking the only truth she knew.

His look seemed to sear through blood and bone, she felt his eyes ravaging her very soul. He was clearly furious, red rage was painted all over the chiseled lines of his flawless face, but there was more there too. Desperate craving, raw desire, and an emotion that sparked of awe. He moved again, reached her in two long strides. Velvet wanted to skitter away from his touch. It was the craving that held her feet locked in place. She felt it too. A desperate heat coursing over her in sizzling waves. If he put his hands on her as he clearly meant to do, Velvet feared she would either submit, or burst in visible flames.

The reels of black steam continued to pour from his skin, and it swirled up around them creating a barrier to all of the outside, cocooning them in their own hidden world.

The clashing sounds of the battle being fought above faded as the darkness encompassing them thickened. The golden light spilling off her wings tangled with shadows. He reached out to touch her cheek, and for the briefest moment his features softened. "Say what you will," he whispered, "there is no running from this, from us. I am irreparably trapped in your orbit. You are my fate as I am yours." He brushed a lock of damp hair from her eyes. "You look like an angel, Marie. A truly spellbinding shell. It is a crying shame that what is inside is bolstered by deceit and lies," he said bitterly, and the icy shroud fell again over his eyes. He stepped back a pace and took her hand. "If you still don't want me, even knowing that night was real, perhaps there truly is no hope," he finished bleakly, and Velvet knew she had hurt him in ways she did not fully understand. Again, came that odd, wrenching impulse to throw her arms around his neck, fall to her knees and beg him to look at her once more as he had before he knew her truth. But the rage on his face froze her limbs and tied her tongue. He dropped her hand, his eyes flicked once more over her wings, then he looked past her—through her—as if she had simply ceased to exist. "Come," he said, and there was a terrible chill in his voice, "let me show you the bones of your predecessors in the *cave beneath the glass.* The burning letters carved in the cliffside are a code, one which was fairly easy to decipher for a spy, assassin and villain as so oft you have called me."

"I thought you said there was no way to reach the bottom of a bottomless pool."

"Apparently I was wrong," he said, and reached in the pocket of his wet trousers to withdraw a stone of unknown color, so old it seemed to rival the very fabric of time.

Velvet could not contain her gasp. "I have never seen that gem before in my life. Where did you find it?" she asked, reaching for it before she fully comprehended her action.

Henry closed his hand around the enchanted stone. More reels of black smoke seeped through his fingers and fell around them. "I found it in the cave admidst a pile of bones, I heard words when I touched it."

"What did they say?" she breathed.

Henry's eyes found her again, black saturated the indigo in his gaze. He opened his hand and placed the gem in hers. Chills instantly rushed down her spine, prickled the tiny hairs on her arm as she heard the words for herself. They bore no resemblance to human sound, more like rushing waves crashing against jagged cliffs, or booming thunder clouds spitting white lightening, yet she understood each word just the same.

The price of life is eternal death.

The images of what she had seen when the wraiths had

attacked them only moments ago bombarded her, pictures of the heartbreaking life briefly lived, and the explosion of one witch's power which had brought so much pain and death. She thought of Minerva and her hollow crimson eyes, forever cursed to wander in some dimension of this haunted island. Velvet feared if she took Henry's hand and the final plunge with him beneath the violet water, she would never find a return to any sense of normalcy. She would be forever changed. The thought terrified her.

"And the spell to save my brother?" she whispered, trying not to visibly tremble as the power of the stone surged up her arm and into her bones, added a touch of spilt ink to her golden glow.

Henry sighed and ran a hand through his glistening hair. "The spell is right where we expected it to be. It is written in blood on the walls."

THANK YOU FOR READING

Did you enjoy this book?

We invite you to leave a review at the website of your choice, such as Goodreads, Amazon, Barnes & Noble, etc.

∼

DID YOU KNOW THAT LEAVING A REVIEW...

- Helps other readers find books they may enjoy.
- Gives you a chance to let your voice be heard.
- Gives authors recognition for their hard work.
- Doesn't have to be long. A sentence or two about why you liked the book will do.

ABOUT THE AUTHOR

JP Roth is an American Novelist, and owner of Rothic comics, founded in 2012, through which she has produced and published five of her original series. JP Roth lives in Long Beach, CA with her beautiful family, and their adorable Bichon Frise. She spends her days writing fanciful stories, walking on the beach, and attending comic conventions across the globe.

JP Roth was born overseas, and spent her life roaming the world. She still enjoys travelling to exotic locations, but admittedly prefers to say home, wrapped in a soft fluffy blanket, drinking, tea and penning her next novel.

www.rothic.com

facebook.com/jprothic

twitter.com/@iamjproth

instagram.com/jprothic